THE SURROGATE'S UNEXPECTED MIRACLE

BY
ALISON ROBERTS

CONVENIENT MARRIAGE, SURPRISE TWINS

BY
AMY RUTTAN

Alison Roberts is a New Zealander, currently lucky enough to be living in the south of France. She is also lucky enough to write for the Mills & Boon Medical Romance line. A primary school teacher in a former life, she is also a qualified paramedic. She loves to travel and dance, drink champagne and spend time with her daughter and her friends.

Born and raised just outside Toronto, Ontario, **Amy Ruttan** fled the big city to settle down with the country boy of her dreams. After the birth of her second child Amy was lucky enough to realise her lifelong dream of becoming a romance author. When she's not furiously typing away at her computer she's mum to three wonderful children who use her as a personal taxi and chef.

THE SURROGATE'S UNEXPECTED MIRACLE

BY
ALISON ROBERTS

MILLS & BOON

This is a work of fiction. Names, characters, places, locations and
incidents are purely fictional and bear no relationship to any real
life individuals, living or dead, or to any actual places, business
establishments, locations, events or incidents. Any resemblance is
entirely coincidental.

Published in Great Britain 2017
By Mills & Boon, an imprint of HarperCollins*Publishers*
1 London Bridge Street, London, SE1 9GF

ISBN: 978-0-263-92654-5

Printed and bound in Spain
by CPI, Barcelona

Dear Reader,

Have you ever been blindsided by something? Something totally unexpected that was huge enough to change your life for ever?

If you have, I really hope it wasn't something awful—like an accident or a house fire—but something amazing—like meeting the gaze of the love of your life for the first time. Sometimes, though, even a disaster can turn out to be the catalyst for something much better to take its place.

I blindsided my heroine, Ellie, in this story more than once. I gave her a baby she never expected to have to raise. And then I burned her house down!

I guess I blindsided my hero, Luke, as well—but that was a much more gradual process and it took him a long time to realise that it had happened.

And it was definitely something amazing! :)

I do hope you enjoy reading this story as much as I loved writing it.

With love,

Alison xx

For Ellie,
with thanks for letting me borrow your name. xx

Books by Alison Roberts

Mills & Boon Medical Romance

Paddington Children's Hospital

A Life-Saving Reunion

Christmas Eve Magic

Their First Family Christmas

Wildfire Island Docs

The Nurse Who Stole His Heart
The Fling That Changed Everything

A Little Christmas Magic
Always the Midwife
Daredevil, Doctor...Husband?

Mills & Boon Cherish

The Wedding Planner and the CEO
The Baby Who Saved Christmas
The Forbidden Prince

Visit the Author Profile page
at millsandboon.co.uk for more titles.

CHAPTER ONE

How COULD SO many things have gone so terribly, terribly wrong?

Ellie Thomas could feel the shape of the phone she was holding against her ear. The edges felt sharper as her grip tightened. They were tangible and real.

What she was hearing couldn't possibly be real.

Could it...?

'Ava—are you still there?'

A moment's silence and then she heard her friend's voice again. Her best friend since...since as long as she could remember. A bond that had lasted throughout childhood. Through the trauma of Ava's surgery and chemotherapy as a teenager. With happy memories like being Ava's bridesmaid two years ago and the darker memories of her best mate's despair at not being able to become a mother—a side effect of the treatment that had saved her life.

A friendship that had seemed unbreakable. Until two weeks ago...

'Yeah... I'm still here.' A stifled sob could be heard. 'And... I'm sorry. I'm so sorry, Ellie.'

Sorry? Did that somehow make this okay?

'Where are you?' Ellie could hear the sound of an announcement of some kind going on in a noisy background. Was Ava at a train station? 'Talk to me, Ave. We can sort this out. I've been trying to call you since the beginning of last week.'

Ever since she had heard that Marco, Ava's gorgeous looking but sometimes volatile husband, had packed a bag and walked out on her.

The day after that awful row... The last time she and Ava and Marco had been in the same room together.

'I was getting frantic,' Ellie added.

Terrified might be a bit closer to the truth.

The silence on the other end of the line was unnerving. Ellie could feel a tight knot of fear that was making it difficult to draw in a new breath. This couldn't be happening. A friendship like this couldn't just evaporate because of something that hadn't even been her fault. Not after all they'd been through together and especially not with what they were going through right now.

'I didn't encourage him, Ava. You *know* that, don't you? I was just as horrified as you were that he tried to kiss me.'

'It wasn't just you.' Ava had stopped crying and there was anger in her low, fierce tone. 'He's been cheating on me the whole time. He admitted it. Said I would never have been enough for a man like him. That our marriage had been a huge mistake because I couldn't accept that.' The tears were obviously flowing again and her next words were totally broken. '...that trying to have a baby was just putting a Band-Aid on a wound that was already fatal.'

Ellie could hear an odd humming and there were bright specks in front of her eyes. Oh, yeah...

Breathe...

'You're not trying to have a baby.' Her words came

out in a voice she hardly recognised as her own. 'You *are* having a baby. In about four weeks.'

'But don't you see? I can't do it now. My world's fallen apart, Ellie and I can't hang on to anything. It's not even *my* baby…'

Technically, this was true. Technically, this was Ellie's baby. Ellie and Marco's. The gift that was the one thing that could make life perfect for Ava. It had been such a huge decision, offering to be a surrogate, but Ellie hadn't really hesitated. This was something she could do for the most important person in her life—the only real family she had left.

Fear was morphing into anger, which was a relief because it made it easier to breathe again.

'I'm thirty-six weeks pregnant, Ava. With *your* baby. Yours and Marco's. A baby I would never have dreamed of having otherwise. I'm single, remember? I don't have any family to support me. I don't even have a boyfriend, as you well know. I'm supposed to go back to work in six weeks and if I don't, I won't be able to pay my rent. And you're *sorry*?'

The silence against the background noise was astonishingly loud. Time seemed to be standing still. It could have been seconds but it felt like minutes or even hours. And when it was finally broken, the words Ellie could hear were almost too strangled to understand.

'Got to go…last call…can't miss my plane…'

Fear was strong enough to feel like pain, now.

'*Plane?* Where are you going? Ava…? *Ava?*'

The beeping of a disconnected line said it all but Ellie couldn't hang up. She lowered the phone and stared at it. Any moment now, the dropped line would be abandoned and she would see the image that was on the screen of her locked phone. The picture of herself and Ava, with their arms around each other, Ava pressing a kiss to her cheek and the smile on Ellie's face making it clear that she was the happiest person in the world.

And there it was...

Ellie dropped the phone on the floor. She wrapped her arms around the huge bump that was her belly now and bent her head to try and deal with the wave of fear and pain that was threatening to wash her over the edge of an unimaginably high cliff.

A pain that was an overwhelming swirl of loss and anger and bewilderment and terror.

It wasn't going to ebb any time soon, either. It filled her chest and made it impossible to breathe again but then it seemed to move to her back as well. And then to her belly, where it gripped harder and harder...

Ellie could feel the muscles under her hands tightening with the strength of a vice. This wasn't just emotional—it was becoming very, very physical.

She was an emergency department nurse, for heaven's sake. She knew what this was but it took another five minutes and the start of another contraction to admit it. When she saw the blood trickling down her leg fast enough to be pooling on the worn linoleum of her floor, she realised just how much trouble she might be in.

Gripping the armrest of her chair, she managed to lower herself onto her knees on the floor and reach for her phone. The call was answered instantly.

'Ambulance... What is your location...?'

Lucas Gilmore was getting used to pushing through the overgrown shrubs on the front path. He'd find time to trim them soon but there had been more important things to do. Like making the house habitable.

The man walking behind him stopped beside the front

steps and brushed pollen and spider webs off the dark trousers of his dress suit. The smile was a little forced but an aspiring leader in local real estate like Mike knew how to disguise distaste.

His smile faded, however, as he turned his head to look at the rambling garden and the exterior of the huge, old wooden villa with its rusting, corrugated iron roof.

'Bit run down, isn't it, Dr Gilmore?'

'Yes. My mother's been in a rest home for several years and the house has been rented out. The agency clearly wasn't doing the job they led me to believe they were doing. The last tenants left nearly a year ago and no maintenance was done, unfortunately. And the inside of the place looked like a bunch of possums had got in through a broken window and had a party.'

'Hmm. You would have done better to use our firm. We're into rentals now.' Mike climbed the steps onto the veranda and a board creaked ominously beneath his feet. 'Hope the inside of the place is in better shape as far as maintenance goes or it's going to be a bit hard to get a good price.'

The smile reappeared. It was almost a grin. 'Having said that, Auckland prices are going completely crazy and it's the land that's going to sell this place. You've got access to an almost private beach and acres of native forest. This is an amazing property. Ripe for redevelopment.'

Lucas could feel a scowl emerging. Redevelopment was a dirty word for him right now. The house was important. Okay, it might be run down but it was a glorious example of an early nineteenth century New Zealand villa—with return verandas and even a turret, for heaven's sake.

'I'm working on fixing the house. I got commercial cleaners in as soon as I arrived back in the country three weeks ago. The garden's next on the list but I've been a bit busy.'

'Did you say you're working at North Shore General hospital?'

'Yes.' Lucas pushed open a front door in need of a new paint job. 'I took a locum position for three months. I figured that would give me plenty of time to sort things out here.'

And to decide where he wanted to go next to take his career as an emergency specialist to even greater heights.

'And you're sure you want to sell?'

Lucas covered his silence by ushering Mike into the house and walking down the wide hallway with its polished wooden floorboards towards the kitchen at the back. Beams of light made mottled red and green coloured shadows on the wall, thanks to the stained glass window over the door behind him.

Did he want to sell the only house that had ever been a home for him?

No. Of course he didn't. This had been the first place he'd felt wanted. When he was a troubled young teen on the verge of being too old to find another foster home, the Gilmores had taken him in.

And loved him.

It didn't make any difference that he'd kicked off to accelerate the abandonment process before he could get to like the place. And man, there'd been so much to like. The beach with its tempting surf, the secret silence of the beech forest. The generous home-cooked meals. Even having to take a country bus to the nearest high school had been different enough to be fun. It would have been the biggest wrench ever when the inevitable happened and he wasn't wanted any longer.

The Gilmores might have been much older than most

foster parents but they had been made of tough stuff and they'd seen something no one else had ever seen. They had decided he was worth the effort.

'You might as well stop acting up,' they'd told him. *'Kicking holes in the walls isn't going to change anything. You're not going anywhere, son. We've adopted you and that's that.'*

But, yes. He did want to sell. There was nothing here for him now. There hadn't been, ever since the death of Eric Gilmore had revealed that he'd been covering the signs of his wife's dementia for some time and the heart breaking decision that Dorothy Gilmore needed specialist care had had to be made. He'd found the best home available as close as possible to where he was living and working.

A shame it was in Sydney, Australia, because it meant taking Dorothy away from the area she'd been born and raised in but the alternative was in Auckland and the biggest city in this country had been just as foreign to Dorothy as Sydney and he certainly couldn't have made his twice-weekly visits. And it hadn't been long before she didn't know who *he* was any more so it really didn't matter what city was outside the walls of her haven.

And—after five years of being cared for so well—Dorothy had died, at the grand old age of ninety-five, just six weeks ago.

It hadn't been a surprise to find that he'd inherited this property that had been rural when he'd arrived about twenty years ago but was now within easy commuting distance of what was touted as one of the most desirable cities in the world to live in. What had been a surprise was the distant cousin, Brian Gilmore, a man in his late sixties, who'd emerged to contest the will.

'You were only a foster kid,' he'd informed Lucas.

'Aunt Dorothy and Uncle Eric never formally adopted you. You've got no right to inherit anything.'

Brian dabbled in property development. This house and its sprawling garden covered an area of land that had enough space for half a dozen properties. Or a retirement village, perhaps, with this perfect, peaceful location and amazing views of the sea and all the islands in the Gulf.

That would only happen after the house was demolished, of course. And probably more than half the native forest bulldozed.

He'd reached the kitchen. A long room with a slate floor and French doors between big windows that looked out over the garden that Dorothy had loved so much. Down to the huge vegetable garden that had been Eric's pride and joy. Amongst other outdoor jobs, his contribution to family chores had been to help Eric manage that garden.

He'd hated it, at first.

He'd actually set fire to the potting shed one evening but even that hadn't been enough to persuade his new parents that they'd made a mistake.

The wash of loss was hard enough to make Lucas pause and take in a long, slow breath. Dorothy and Eric might have been old enough to be his grandparents when they'd taken him in but they were the only real parents he'd ever had and he'd come to love them fiercely. They'd been so proud of him when they'd come to watch his graduation from medical school.

We knew you could do it, son. We knew you were special.

'This is nice...' Mike was looking up at the beamed ceiling and then his gaze ran swiftly over the old cooking range and the arched doorway into the big pantry that had once been a creamery for the original farm. He frowned at the masking tape crisscrossing one of the windows where a pane of glass was badly cracked and he was making rapid notes on a tablet device. 'Good thing you left it fully furnished. It looks like someone's living in it and these antiques look original.'

'Some of them probably are,' Lucas agreed. 'And it certainly is a lovely home. It needs to be sold to a family that will love it.' As the Gilmore family had. 'I'm not selling to anyone who wants to demolish this house.'

Brian's words still stung. Maybe Dorothy and Eric hadn't realised what was involved in a formal adoption process. They'd changed his name before enrolling him at his new school and somehow that had been enough and he'd slipped through the system. He'd been Lucas Gilmore ever since.

He'd been their son.

And he wasn't about to let cousin Brian destroy any part of the miracle that had turned his life around so completely. He had his solicitor working on the legality of the unexpected claim and he was hopeful he could have it overturned in court.

A family of his own was never going to happen—he knew too well the nightmare of things going wrong—and even if he had been planning one, it wouldn't be here— where the ghosts of what had gone so wrong in his own early life were never very far away.

But that was what this house needed.

A family. Laughter echoing through the rooms and love to be celebrated in meals taken at this old, scrubbed pine table.

Hopefully, what was left of the three months he had signed up for at Auckland General would be long enough to see that happen. As if prompted by the thought, he turned his head to where the grandfather clock in the hallway was ticking again. A slow, steady sound that had always been the heartbeat of this old house.

'How 'bout I leave you to have a look around at the rest of the place, Mike? If you pull the front door closed, it'll lock itself. I'm due to start my shift in Emergency in less than an hour and you never know what the traffic's going to be like on the motorway. I'd better get my skates on.'

If she hadn't been so frightened, Ellie would have been mortified, arriving at any emergency department like this, let alone the one she worked in herself!

She was on a narrow ambulance stretcher. On her knees, with her head on her hands and her bottom up in the air.

Knowing she was bleeding had been enough to scare her. The speed with which the paramedics checked her out, got an IV line in and fluids running and then headed for the nearest hospital using lights and sirens told her they were just as worried about the situation as she was. And, moments before they had arrived at the hospital, her waters had broken and, in the wake of the rush of fluid, she knew things had just become a whole lot worse.

'Something feels weird,' she told them. 'I think I might have a cord prolapse.'

A quick glance by the lead paramedic confirmed her fears.

'As soon as we get you out, we'll get you head down, on your knees and use gravity to take pressure off the cord. We'll support you and move slowly, okay?'

'Okay.' She felt the clunk as the wheels of the stretcher came down and locked. With help, she turned to get on her knees, putting her elbows on the mattress and lowering her head between her hands.

The warning not to start pushing even if she felt the

urge had been unnecessary. Ellie knew how dangerous this was. If the baby's head put too much pressure on the cord, it would cut off the oxygen supply and lead to a stillbirth. She couldn't let that happen. Ava and Marco would sort things out. They had really wanted this baby. They'd all gone to that first ultrasound appointment together and there had been tears of joy all round. Surely nobody would really plan to bring a new life into the world just to fix a failing relationship?

The contractions were at increasingly shorter intervals but she hadn't felt any urge to push.

Yet.

The hospital would have had advance warning of her arrival and the problem with blood loss but there hadn't been time to warn them about this new complication. Would there be a specialist obstetrician waiting for her in one of the resuscitation rooms already?

In this undignified position, Ellie couldn't see anybody's faces. Just their legs, as she was wheeled carefully past the triage desk, with the paramedics on either side of the stretcher, both with one arm over her body to support her balance.

She could recognise voices, however.

'Cord prolapse,' one of the paramedics said. 'Waters broke about two minutes ago.'

'It's okay, Ellie. We've got this…' That was Sue—one of her best friends here. 'Resus One, guys.' The hand that had given her back a quick, reassuring rub disappeared and Sue's voice faded as she turned away. 'Has anyone got an update on that obstetrics consult? Luke? Can you take this in the meantime?'

Ellie watched sets of wheels flash past. That was an ECG monitor and those were a tangle of IV stands. A drug trolley was being pushed in the opposite direction.

She could hear the sounds of a busy emergency department all around her. If she'd been on her feet, in her scrubs, with her stethoscope around her neck, this would all be perfectly normal.

She'd never been on this side of the fence before.

Or realised just how horribly vulnerable it made you feel.

'We're going to get you onto the bed,' someone told her. 'We'll lift you. Don't try and help.'

'We'll put her in an exaggerated Sims' position to start with.' Ellie didn't recognise this male voice. 'Left lateral with at least two pillows to support the pelvis. Lower the head of the bed, too. And get some oxygen on the mother.'

The *mother*? Ellie squeezed her eyes tightly shut. She wasn't supposed to be about to become the mother. This was a nightmare. Maybe she'd wake up in a minute to find Ava and Marco standing there. Smiling. Excited to be about to meet their new baby...

This was a slightly more dignified position, at least, but she still had a restricted visual field. She could see the length of the body in dark green scrubs beside her, but it wasn't until he crouched that she could see the face that belonged to that new voice. Tanned skin. Kind of wild brown hair with blond streaks. Hazel eyes. He looked like he'd just come out of some surf, on a hot summer's day, with a board casually slung under one arm.

'Hi, Ellie. I'm Luke Gilmore, one of the doctors here. I'm just going to have a look and see what's going on, okay?'

As another contraction gathered force, Ellie could only nod.

Luke Gilmore? He had to be new here. A locum? She'd stopped work three weeks ago to rest and prepare for the birth so she hadn't met him. She hadn't even heard his name.

Or had she? It did seem vaguely familiar…

With the contraction reaching its peak, the thought was obliterated by pain. She pushed her fist into her mouth but couldn't stifle a cry.

For a long moment, nothing existed except the pain but then she became aware of the voices around her.

'What was the time interval for that last contraction?'

'Two minutes.'

'Estimated blood loss?'

'Five hundred mils on scene.' The paramedics were still there. 'We put in a wide bore IV and she's had a litre of saline so far.'

'She's still bleeding. Let's get another litre going.'

That was this Dr Gilmore's voice. Did he know what he was doing? He certainly sounded confident enough. Ellie could feel that her lower body was bare now. Maybe it was a good thing that she didn't know this person but there were plenty of people she did know seeing a lot more of her than they ever had before. Not that she cared. Nothing mattered right now other than to get through this safely. There was a baby's life at stake. Maybe even her own, if she was still losing so much blood.

She could feel a hand inside her.

'Ah…' The sound was hard to interpret. Satisfaction… or concern? 'Ellie? You're going to feel me pushing. I need to take the pressure off the cord.'

He still sounded calm, this Luke. And she could feel him pushing hard against the baby's head.

'Any risk factors in the pregnancy?'

'Not that we know of.' The paramedic sounded embarrassed. It was a question they should have asked.

'Low lying placenta,' Ellie said, but her voice was muffled behind the oxygen mask.

'Sorry, what was that?' Luke was still pushing against her baby's head to ensure it was clear of the cord but he leaned sideways so that she could see his face as she turned her head. In the bustle of people and activity around her, there was something very calming in the steady gaze of those hazel eyes that were visible again.

'I've had a low-lying placenta. Only marginal but I was due for another scan this week and possible admission for observation and a C section if indicated.'

She saw the flicker of surprise in his eyes at her clinical information.

'Ellie's a nurse,' someone behind him said. Sue had come into the resus area. 'She's one of our best ED nurses, in fact.'

Luke's face disappeared from her line of sight. 'Where's our Obs consult?'

'Here.' A female voice who sounded rather nervous.

'This is Anne Duffy,' Sue said. 'O&G registrar.'

Maybe Luke had picked up on the nervousness. 'Have you got a theatre available? We've got a cord prolapse here. She's fully dilated but still in stage one. We're looking at either an emergency C section or an operative delivery.'

'No.' Anne sounded young as well as nervous. 'We're in the middle of a C section for triplets. It's got most of our staff tied up for a while but it shouldn't be too long until one of the consultants is available. Is the baby distressed?'

Maybe it was her imagination but Ellie thought she heard Luke sigh. 'Have we got that foetal monitor hooked up yet?'

'Yes. Baby's heart-rate is one-thirty. No, hang on… one-ten… It's dropping…'

Ellie could feel her own heart-rate increasing. This was suddenly getting very serious. If the baby's heart-rate was dropping, it meant that the head was finally putting too much pressure on the cord despite the interventions. The clock was ticking now…

And something else was changing.

'I need to push,' she said.

'Don't push.' The registrar definitely sounded nervous now. Terrified, even? 'Take deep breaths. Try and go limp. Relax your pelvic floor.'

If Ellie had had any spare breath right then, it might have come out as an incredulous huff. Just how much experience had this junior doctor had? She fought the urge to push, her face scrunched as tightly as possible against the pain.

'Heart-rate's down to eighty,' someone said.

'Not too long isn't good enough.' There was a different note in Luke's voice now. He had made a decision and was taking control. 'Lay out the forceps kit, please. Can someone put out an urgent page and get a paediatrician down here, stat? Anne—take over here. Two fingers on the baby's head and upward pressure, okay?'

'Got it.'

'Have you done a forceps delivery?'

'I've assisted with one.'

'Ellie? Can you hear me?'

'Y-yes.' Her voice came out sounding oddly croaky. Frightened…

Luke was crouched right beside her now, his face only a few inches from her own.

'We need to get your baby out as soon as possible. You're fully dilated and with the help of forceps we can do it. I've done a long stint in obstetrics and have experience in assisted delivery. Are you happy for me to go ahead?'

There was nothing about this that Ellie was happy about. But there was something in those eyes that gave her something to cling to.

Confidence. Hope...

She nodded, giving her consent.

'We can give you some Entonox but there's no time for any other pain relief to kick in. It's going to be a bit rough. I'm sorry...'

He was sorry. He looked as though he would take that impending pain himself rather than inflict it on her. Ellie closed her eyes to hold back tears but she nodded again. 'It's okay...'

She could feel the tension in the room around her. Hear the clatter of instrument kits being unrolled onto a stainless steel trolley. She felt her body being moved so that she was lying on her back, sterile drapes being folded around her and listened to the instructions Luke was issuing as her legs were lifted and supported.

And he talked to her all through it, too.

'I'm giving you a bit of local for the episiotomy. You'll feel it sting for a moment.'

It stung a lot but Ellie knew it was only the start. She sucked on the mouthpiece giving her the inhaled pain relief.

'I'm inserting the first blade, now. And the second. And I'm locking them. When the next contraction starts, I'm going to need you to push—as hard as you can, sweetheart.'

Sweetheart?

The word cut through the fear and pain. It was just a word that should have evaporated into the ether the moment it had been spoken but it didn't. It echoed in her head and sent ripples through her body. It was something warm and caring and lovely in the middle of something horrific. And when the instruction to push came moments after the next contraction started she pushed with every ounce of strength she could summon.

And maybe she found more strength than she knew she had because, in the wake of being abandoned by the person she cared about most, he'd called her sweetheart…

It only took two contractions, a minute apart, with her pushing as if her life depended on it and Luke pulling with the baby's head cradled between the blades of the forceps and she could feel the baby coming into the world.

'It's a boy, Ellie,' someone said.

She knew that. Marco and Ava had known that, too. They'd already picked out a name. Carlos.

Her train of thought vanished as she became aware of the silence in the room. There was no baby crying. And nobody else was saying anything, either. The silence was shocked. And shocking. Ellie jerked her head up to see a tiny, limp body that someone was rubbing briskly with a towel.

A woman she didn't know—the nervous young registrar, perhaps—saw her looking.

'It's okay, Ellie. We're doing everything we can for your baby.'

Tears that had been building for too long exploded from Ellie as she let her head drop back down.

'But he's *not* my baby,' she sobbed. 'And now *nobody* wants him…'

CHAPTER TWO

WHAT?

Surely he hadn't heard correctly?

For a split second, Lucas froze, completely distracted from what he was about to do.

Nobody wanted this baby?

One of the department's senior nurses, Sue, was right beside him.

'This was a surrogate pregnancy,' she told him quietly. 'But I have no idea what's gone wrong.'

Lucas couldn't give a damn about what might have gone wrong. There was a knot in his chest that felt like anger.

He knew what it was like to be an unwanted child. To face a world where you were not worth enough for anybody to want you.

No more than a blink of time had passed but Lucas snapped back to reality.

'Give him to me,' he snapped.

Picking up the limp bundle, he carried it to the trolley that had been hastily prepared with neonatal resuscitation gear. He gently laid the tiny body onto the sterile drapes. The miniature mask seemed to cover half the face as he delivered puffs of oxygen. He put his hands around a chest that felt alarmingly fragile, positioning both his thumbs on the sternum. Gentle but rapid compressions. Sue had followed him and picked up the mask. One puff, three compressions. One puff, three compressions.

You can do it... Come on... Fight...it's worth it, I promise...

Only Luke could hear the words in his head. Or were they coming from his heart?

Someone's going to love you...

There weren't any words that came with his next thought—it was just a flash of sensation that came from nowhere.

I love you...

He shook off the bizarre notion. Getting emotionally involved in this unexpected case wasn't going to help anyone. He needed to think ahead. Professionally. Intubation as the next step... IV access through the umbilical cord...chasing up that specialist paediatric consult...

And then the miracle happened. He felt the tiny body move between his hands. He paused the compressions and felt the push of that little ribcage against the pads of his thumbs as the baby took its own first breath.

And then another. That tiny face scrunched itself into an angry expression and the third breath was enough to provide the power for a warbling sound. The next effort was much more convincing.

This little guy was a fighter, after all.

And then Luke heard another cry from a very unexpected direction. From behind him.

From this new mother who didn't want this baby.

He could feel his face tightening as he turned. His heart hardening.

And then he saw her face.

Propped up on her elbows, Ellie must have been

watching this whole resuscitation effort and she had definitely heard those first sounds of a new life awakening.

Her hair was a tangle of blonde knots around a face that was pale enough to suggest she had lost a concerning amount of blood. And those eyes…

Huge, dark blue pools that were telling him something very different than the last words he had heard her speaking—that this wasn't her baby and that nobody wanted him.

These were the eyes of a desperate woman. A mother…

'Please,' she whispered… 'Please can I hold my baby?'

It had been that sound that had done it.

The cry from that tiny human that had been nestled within her body for so many months had taken the world as Ellie knew it and tipped it upside down. It had entered her ears but gone straight to her heart and captured it in the fiercest imaginable grip.

For a long, long moment, caught in what felt like a very disapproving stare from the doctor who'd just delivered her son, she thought that she was facing an impenetrable barrier. Someone who had no intention of letting her close to that tiny being she could just catch a glimpse of behind the solid figure of this new doctor.

But Sue was picking the baby up now.

'Apgar score is ten at five minutes,' she said, unable to keep a grin off her face. She was wrapping the baby in soft towels. 'He's looking great. I think we could let Mum have a bit of skin contact, until our paediatrician arrives, don't you think?'

Luke's response was a huff of sound that seemed indecisive but the anticipation of holding her baby against her own skin was so overwhelming that Ellie's breath escaped in something that sounded like a sob as she lay back and held her arms out.

'The placenta's delivered.' The young registrar was sounding a lot more confident now. 'Seems intact and the bleeding's almost stopped. Let's prop you up a bit so you can hold your baby.'

Ellie had barely registered the last contractions as she watched the frantic efforts to save her son. Everything was all right now, though. She wasn't about to bleed to death and the baby's perfect Apgar score meant that he had come through this crisis with flying colours. With pillows being layered behind her, she was more than ready to accept the precious bundle that Sue was bringing towards her.

But why was this new doctor in her department still staring at her as if she was asking for something she really didn't deserve?

He'd called her sweetheart only minutes ago.

Before helping her deliver her baby. Before he'd saved her life. Before he'd even properly begun to start saving the life of that baby.

And then something filtered into her brain. An echo of her own voice...

'But he's not my baby... And now nobody wants him...'

Oh, God...had she really said that?

No wonder he thought she was crazy. Or some kind of monster.

But Sue was beside her now and everybody else in this room and whatever tasks they were attending to ceased to exist as far as Ellie was concerned. Sue was unwrapping the tiny body of her baby, and another nurse was helping to remove the oversized tee shirt Ellie had been wearing. And her bra.

And there he was. In her arms and snuggled against

her bare chest, while Sue arranged some soft, fluffy blankets around them both for warmth and as much privacy as was possible, given the surroundings.

Ellie couldn't even lift her head to smile her thanks. Her baby's eyes were open and he was staring up at her and nothing could have induced her to break that astonishing eye contact.

'Hullo, you…' she whispered. 'I'm Mummy.'

The wash of emotion was like nothing Ellie had ever experienced. Something was changing in her body at a cellular level and she would never be the same person she'd been only minutes ago.

Who knew that love could be *this* powerful? So huge… and every bit of it was for this tiny little human.

Had she really believed she could have given him to someone else?

This baby was a part of herself and she would fight to the death if necessary to protect him.

It was the baby who finally broke that intense eye contact. His head bobbed against the arm it was cradled by and his tiny mouth opened and closed against the skin of Ellie's breast. Instinctively, she adjusted her position, which brought her nipple within range of the baby's mouth. And then she watched, in astonishment, as the baby found what it was seeking and latched on to her nipple as though he'd done it many times before.

Ellie's jaw dropped. 'He did that all by himself.'

'He's a genius.' Sue smiled. 'Oh…where's my phone? We've got to get a photo of this.'

But Ellie had closed her eyes by the time Sue had fished her phone from the pocket of her scrub pants and she could feel a tear escape and roll down the side of her nose. And then another.

This feeling—the silky new born skin against her

own, the shape of those tiny limbs within her arms and, most of all, the tug of that tiny mouth against her breast—was too much.

It felt like pure joy…

Luke had rather a lot of paperwork to do to document this emergency delivery that had happened on his watch. Someone had given him the forms on a clipboard and he had a pen in his hand but he hadn't written a word, yet.

He kept looking sideways. From where he was standing, beside the trolley they'd used to resuscitate this baby, he could see the back of the baby's head nestled in the crook of Ellie's arms.

And he could see Ellie's face.

She had no idea he was watching her. Luke doubted that she was aware of anything other than the baby she was holding.

They seemed to be staring at each other. Locked in a conversation that was so utterly private that Luke felt uncomfortable observing it.

So he looked away.

Eleanor Thomas, someone had filled in under the personal details on the form. Thirty-two years old. Thirty-six weeks pregnant.

He had to look back. It was none of his business that there was something weird going on. A surrogate pregnancy?

Who for?

Why?

And what had gone so wrong that she'd claimed that nobody wanted this child now?

It certainly didn't look as if nobody wanted him.

Ellie looked, for all the world, as if she was in the middle of a personal miracle. Mesmerised by the face of her child. As though this baby was being bathed in as much love as it was possible for any person to bestow.

It was weird, all right. And disturbing on a level that Luke hadn't expected. Maybe it was because this was happening so soon after he'd been standing in the home it had taken so many years for him to find.

Had his own mother looked at him like that in the minutes after he'd been born?

No. He'd always known the answer to that.

This time it was easier to look away. To try and focus on the paperwork.

Surely no mother could ever look at her child like that and then simply hand him to strangers when life got tough and never even try to see him again? Had it even occurred to his mother that the scars of being abandoned and finding himself unwanted would be there for the rest of his life?

The paediatrician arrived and Luke gave him a verbal handover. He still had the notes to write up on the baby's early resuscitation as well.

The new arrival looked at Ellie, who was now breast-feeding the infant, and he was smiling.

'I think we can get them up to the ward before we examine baby properly. He's looking pretty happy.'

Anne, the O&G registrar, had joined them. She was nodding. 'I'll leave the repair of the episiotomy until then, too. I'll see what rooms we have available and order a transfer.'

Within minutes, the transfer had been arranged. The bed, with the baby still cradled in Ellie's arms, was being wheeled out of the resuscitation room and staff members were already busy cleaning up. Luke heard the metallic clang as the forceps and other instruments he had used were dropped into a container to be sent for sterilisation. Blood stained towels and drapes were going into the contaminated linen bag and a cleaner began mopping the floor. A new bed was outside, waiting to take centre stage in a room that would have no evidence of the life and death drama that had just occurred.

Another one would probably take its place very soon but this one was over. Any odd personal connection he might have felt needed to be dismissed. He had done his job and whatever lay ahead for Ellie and her baby was none of his business.

Well, it wasn't quite over yet. With a sigh, Luke picked up the clipboard. He could finish this paperwork in the office and, if he was lucky, it would be done before he was needed elsewhere. He didn't want to be here, tying up loose ends like this, when his shift finished late in the evening.

A visitor was the last thing Ellie was expecting at this time of night.

It was after ten p.m. and she was propped up on her pillows, in the soft glow of the night light in her private room, and she was doing nothing more than being in the moment. Listening to the soft snuffles and squeaks coming from the tiny bundle in the plastic bassinet that was within touching distance of her bed. Trying to absorb this momentous change in her life.

She thought the soft tap on her door would be one of the nursing staff, coming to check that everything was okay and that she was ready to try and get some sleep. When Luke Gilmore stepped into her room, she was too astonished to even say hullo.

'Is this a bad time? They told me on the desk that you'd just finished a feed and would probably still be awake.'

Ellie was still staring at him. It was obvious she was

still awake so there didn't seem to be anything that needed to be said. She could feel a puzzled frown creasing her brow.

Why was he here? Most emergency department doctors—especially locums—didn't have the time or the interest in following up their cases. They treated them and moved them on, job done. There were always more to take their places.

But it was nice that he wanted to check up on them. Ellie's lips curved into a smile, which was taken as an invitation to come into the room, but then the smile wobbled.

Had he come to have a go at her for what had been said in a moment of both physical and emotional agony? When this whole, sorry story of her attempt to be a surrogate mother had looked as if it was about to end in disaster?

He didn't look as if he was angry about anything. Closing the door softly behind him, Luke stepped towards her bed, stopping to gaze down at the sleeping, snuffling baby.

Ellie found herself gazing at *him*. There was something about those rather craggy features and that shaggy hair that seemed very familiar. Had he worked in the same hospital as her in the past, maybe? Way back, when she was newly qualified and too focused on doing her job well to take much notice of staff members in other departments?

'I hear he passed his paediatric check with flying colours.'

'Mmm.' Ellie found both her voice and another smile. 'He's perfect. A good weight, too, even though he was four weeks early. He's almost seven pounds.'

She was still trawling through dim memory banks.

Luke Gilmore…doctor…

Or not yet a doctor?

'Oh, my God…' Ellie breathed. 'You're *Lucas* Gilmore, aren't you?'

Startled eyes met her own. 'Ah…yes. But I haven't been called Lucas in about fifteen years. By anyone other than my parents, that is…'

'You went to Kauri Valley District High School?'

His face had gone very still. He didn't say anything but he was frowning—as though he was searching his own memory banks as he stared at her face.

'I went there, too. You won't remember me—I was a couple of years behind you. But we shared the school bus every day. You lived on the coast, didn't you? Near Moana Beach?'

Uninvited, Lukc sank to balance his hip on the end of Ellie's bed, one arm over the base board, his fingers touching the clip of the board that held her observations chart.

'No way… Wait… I *do* remember you. You always sat up the front. You had really long plaits.'

The thought that he'd noticed her at all on a crowded bus made Ellie feel suddenly shy. She would have died if she'd known it at the time. Lucas Gilmore—Kauri Valley high school's bad boy—aware of *her* existence? It would have been scary. And…thrilling?

'You always sat right at the back,' she heard herself saying. 'With all the cool kids.'

'The ones who got into trouble, you mean?'

There was something intense in his glance now. Did he want to know how much Ellie knew about the kind of trouble he'd been in as a kid?

Okay, she knew quite a lot. Ellie could almost hear an echo of her mother's voice.

'Stay away from that Gilmore boy. He's bad news. Nothing but trouble…'

She wasn't about to say anything now, though. He'd clearly turned his life around. He was a doctor, for heaven's sake. A doctor who'd just saved the lives of both herself and her baby.

There was a flash of something like relief on Luke's features as she shrugged his comment away. She could sense the tension ebbing away from his body. Or maybe she could feel it, as the mattress dipped with his settling weight.

'You were always with another girl who always wore hats.'

Ellie nodded. 'Ava. My best friend. Her hair was never the same after all the chemo she had and it took her a long time to get used to it.'

'Chemo? What for?'

'Leukaemia.'

'Did she survive?'

'Oh, yeah… And her hair came back even better than ever. Turned out that she'd never be able to have kids, though.'

The sudden stillness in Luke's face told her that he'd put two and two together with remarkable speed. Almost as though he was reading her mind.

'That's who you were being a surrogate for?'

Ellie nodded. She had to bite her lip to push back the wash of loss. Ava had been such a big part of her life for ever and now she had gone and it was going to leave a gaping hole.

'Wow…' She listened to the deep breath that Luke took and then let out in a long sigh as he pushed his fingers through that mop of sun-streaked hair. The front locks immediately flopped down onto his forehead again. 'That's an incredible thing to do for a friend. *Huge*…'

There was a long silence. It had to be obvious that she

was struggling to keep herself together right now. Most strangers would have probably realised they were intruding in something very personal and made some kind of apology and then an excuse to let her have some time to herself or an offer to find someone she wanted to talk to. But Luke just sat there quietly. Absorbing her struggle. Offering his company and what felt like…empathy?

'It's all gone so terribly wrong,' she found herself whispering into the silence. 'Her husband walked out on her a couple of weeks ago. The marriage is over. And now Ava's gone, too. Just gone…' She had to stop and take a very shaky breath. 'And I can't really blame her. She's devastated and, as she told me, it's not really *her* baby. It was *my* egg. And now…now it's *my* baby and… and I have no idea what I'm going to do…'

Luke's frown had deepened but he was still listening. Nodding very slowly. 'And the father?'

'Marco? I don't think he's coming back. Apparently he said he'd never really wanted a baby in the first place.' Ellie's voice was stronger now. She was on much more solid ground. 'And I don't want him to.'

An eyebrow quirked under that shaggy fringe but Ellie saw the subtle lift of the corners of Luke's mouth. He liked what he was hearing, she realised, and that made her want to say a whole lot more.

'I thought I could do it, you know? Donate an egg and carry a baby for someone else. I thought I could hand him over the minute he was born and then just be… I don't know…a kind of auntie, I guess. We'd planned to tell him eventually. When he was old enough to understand.'

'But…?'

'It was when I heard him cry…' Again, Ellie had to stop talking to try and deal with the flood of emotion but, this time, it wasn't anything to do with loss or grief. This was joy, pure and simple. 'That was when I knew that this was *my* baby. That I could never give him away. That he's…he's the most important thing in my life now…'

Ellie had to scrub away an errant tear but it didn't matter. Luke looked as though he was blinking back some extra moisture in his own eyes. And his voice sounded a bit rusty when he spoke again.

'Have you given him a name?'

Ellie sniffed inelegantly and then smiled. 'I had the best dad in the world. He was a forestry worker and got killed in an industrial accident when I was only six but I've never forgotten how much he loved me. How much I loved him. His name was James but everyone called him Jamie.' She had to use the fingers of both hands to wipe her cheeks this time. 'So that's what I'm going to call him. Jamie.'

As if he'd heard his name, the baby stirred and started to cry. Ellie turned and leaned towards the bassinet but then froze, unable to stop her gasp of pain. It wasn't just the stitches in a very tender place. Her whole body felt bruised and battered right now.

'Let me…'

Luke got to his feet in a smooth movement that was both relaxed and confident. He picked up the swaddled bundle of baby but he didn't immediately hand him to Ellie. He stood there, holding the baby in his arms, patting him gently as he smiled down at the tiny face.

'Hi, Jamie,' he said softly. 'Welcome to the world…'

Jamie hiccupped and then stopped crying. Luke stopped patting and started rubbing the baby's back, his hand looking huge against the small bundle.

'You made a bit of a dramatic entrance,' Luke continued quietly, still smiling. 'You had us a bit worried there for a while, mate.'

Ellie was lying back on her pillows as the pain subsided. There was something about watching this big man holding her tiny baby that was doing funny things to her heart and making her want to cry all over again.

Her hormones were all over the place right now, weren't they?

And then she felt her cheeks flush. 'I haven't even said thank you,' she said. 'You saved Jamie's life…probably mine, too.'

It seemed as if Jamie had gone back to sleep but Luke didn't put him back into the bassinet. He perched on the bed again, holding the bundle as if it was the most natural thing in the world to do.

'It was my pleasure,' he said. 'The best job I've had since I came back.'

So had they been just a 'job' to him? Just another case and one that would be remembered for snatching success from imminent disaster? Oddly, the disappointment felt crushing.

'Back?' Ellie was relieved to achieve a casual tone.

'I've been working in Australia pretty much since I graduated from medical school. I've taken a three month locum here because I needed some time to sort my parents' estate. And I was ready for a change so it's a good time to take a break and reassess my future.'

So he was a locum. And he was only here for three months.

'I've heard about a couple of great positions already,' he continued. 'I'm tossing up whether I want to apply for the one in London or Boston right now. Both of them are in major trauma centres that deal with things you'd be lucky to ever see in Auckland.'

The disappointment was still there, ready to roll in on another wave. How weird was that? Was it because he represented a link to the past? They'd been to the same school. They would know a lot of the same people in the area Ellie had grown up in. She'd already lost so many links to that happy part of her early life and it had seemed as if the last one had gone with Ava's disappearance.

She swallowed hard. 'Yeah... I guess that's exactly what I have to do now. Reassess my future.'

A whimper from the baby prompted Luke to move. This time he transferred the bundle into Ellie's arms. And then he caught her gaze. He didn't have to say anything.

She was holding her future.

'Are you going to manage?' he asked quietly. 'Have you got family and friends to support you?'

'No family,' Ellie said. 'But I've got some good friends. You've met Sue, in ED? Well, she's organising an emergency baby shower. I don't have anything. Not even a nappy...'

She had to look away from that steady gaze. She didn't want him to know how terrifying it was. In a day or two, she had to take this brand new little person back to a totally inappropriate inner city apartment where there was barely enough room for herself, let alone a baby and all the gear she was going to need, like a cot and a pram and stacks of nappies.

She didn't even know how she was going to pay the rent on that apartment...

Luke was pulling a pen from the top pocket of his scrubs. He fished out a small notebook and ripped out a page.

'This is my phone number,' he told her. 'If you ever need help, ring me.'

Ellie's eyes widened.

Luke grinned. 'No, I don't usually do this for my

patients. But you're special. You're an old bus buddy so we go way back, even if my memory's a bit hazy.'

Ellie pressed her lips together. Her memory was getting less hazy by the minute. She had noticed Luke every time he'd sauntered down the bus aisle past her seat. The bad boy who'd been expelled from every school he'd been to until he got to Kauri Valley. The angry kid who'd somehow morphed into the coolest one. The one that every girl had been desperate to be with...

He put the scrap of paper on the top of her locker.

'Want me to get someone for you? Do you need help with Jamie? Or some pain relief or anything?'

'I think I'm ready to sleep,' Ellie told him. 'Jamie seems to be settled again. Could you put him back in the bassinet for me, please?'

She watched as he carefully positioned the baby on his side and then tucked the sheet securely around him. There was nothing more he needed to do but he paused for a long moment—that big, artistic looking hand cupping the baby's head so gently that the spikes of dark hair barely moved. Ellie could feel that touch herself and it felt as if it were cupping her heart.

He was quite something now, this grown up bad boy.

'Sweet dreams, little guy,' Luke murmured.

And then, with a smile, he was gone, letting himself out of Ellie's room as quietly as he'd come in. He left the door slightly ajar and she could hear the muted sounds of a maternity ward on night shift. The distant cry of another baby. Soft-soled shoes going past in the corridor.

Her baby was asleep and she needed to rest herself. It was the only opportunity she was going to get to heal and gather her strength for what lay ahead.

Adjusting her body to find a more comfortable position, Ellie could see the top of her locker where that scrap of paper lay beside her water glass.

He'd said they were 'bus buddies', she remembered.

He'd said that she was *special*...

He'd given her his phone number to use if she needed help.

Not that she would, but having it there somehow made her immediate future look a little less terrifying.

Ellie drifted into much-needed sleep unaware of the curve of her lips.

She was *special*...

CHAPTER THREE

THE BABY WAS about six weeks old.

A little girl, called Grace, but that didn't stop Luke Gilmore being instantly reminded of Jamie Thomas.

It had been more than two weeks since he'd delivered Ellie's baby in such a dramatic fashion. It felt like a long time since he'd shared what seemed like a surprisingly intimate conversation, late that night in her room.

He would never have recognised Ellie from that time in his past. What he had been prompted to remember was a girl with long blonde braids who had been too timid to interest him. The girl who wore the hats—Ava—used to stare at him but Ellie was also memorable for the way she avoided eye contact.

She hadn't been avoiding it the other night. Quite the opposite. When she had been telling him about the surrogacy arrangement that had gone so wrong and particularly when she'd explained how hearing the baby's first cry had changed her for ever, she'd held his gaze with an intensity that had made him feel as if he was glimpsing a part of her soul.

A courageous soul, he had realised. And a generous one.

She'd been prepared to do something for a friend that went way beyond the normal boundaries of friendship.

And she hadn't been planning to raise a child on her own but was facing what could be a difficult future with such determination—and such obvious love for the baby she had now claimed as purely her own.

He had to admire that.

To admire Ellie.

And, man…as he'd kept going back to that time together in his head—more often than he was comfortable with, to be honest—he realised that Ellie had matured into a very attractive young woman. Her hair was more honey than white blonde now and, thanks to her avoidance of eye contact, he'd never noticed how astonishingly blue her eyes were. There was a softness about her features, too, that he could imagine being the result of a timid, sensitive teenager gaining confidence with time.

This baby who had just come into the emergency department of North Shore General was crying miserably. So was the mother who was holding her as the nurse, Sue, helped to settle her on the bed. The young father was hovering on the other side of the bed, looking stressed and helpless.

'We thought it was just a cold,' he told Luke. 'But now she's got this horrible cough and it sounds like she can't breathe…'

'Has anyone else in the family been unwell?' Luke was looking carefully at the baby as Sue undressed her. The baby looked dehydrated but not feverish and, thankfully, there were no signs of a rash that could be meningococcal.

'I've had a bit of a cough,' the father said. 'Nothing major. Just one of those irritating dry coughs that won't go away. I heard someone call it the "Hundred Day" cough.'

Luke's heart sank as he met Sue's glance as she helped

position the baby so that he could put his stethoscope on the tiny chest. For adults or immunised people, the 'Hundred Day' cough was an irritating bug. For babies like this, it could be the life-threatening bacterial infection of whooping cough.

And, sure enough, the baby started coughing. It was too young to have the strength to produce the characteristic 'whooping' sound of gasping for air between the coughing spasms but they were severe enough to be causing a dangerous lack of oxygen and both Luke and Sue watched with deepening concern as the blue tinge to the baby's face advertised a degree of cyanosis that was going to need urgent management.

'See if we've got an oxygen hood in the department,' Luke said to Sue. 'And put out a call for an urgent paediatric consult.'

'I'm going to take a swab,' he told the mother, 'and some blood tests but it looks very likely that she has pertussis—whooping cough. We're going to need to admit her and keep her in isolation.'

'Whooping cough?' The mother looked terrified. 'But that's impossible. I had the booster vaccination that they recommend when you're pregnant. They said that would help keep her safe until she gets her first shot next week.'

'And it does help. You did exactly the right thing.' Luke nodded. 'Did everybody in your extended family get boosters, too?'

'My mother did. I told Gerry that he should get one but...' The woman glanced up at her husband, who was looking stricken. 'I guess we kind of forgot...'

'Work's been crazy,' he muttered. 'And what with Serena having to give up her job, I've had to take all the overtime I could get.' He turned away, putting his hand over his eyes. 'Oh... God...is this *my* fault?'

'The important thing is looking after little Grace, here.' Luke was pulling supplies from the containers on the bench in this resuscitation area. A tourniquet, the smallest cannula available for IV access, tape and the connecting plug that would enable him to set up a drip. 'We're going to start her on antibiotics without waiting for the test results. And we're going to try and improve her oxygen levels. You must have noticed the way she's going blue with the coughing fits? That means she's not getting enough oxygen and that can be dangerous.'

Another nurse came in with the oxygen hood that Luke had requested.

'We'll get you to put Grace on the bed by herself, now,' Luke said gently. 'This looks scary but it's just a plastic dome that will go over her head on the bed. It's an easier way to provide extra oxygen than taping prongs into her nose.'

It was clearly hard for the mother to hand her baby into the care of others and step back, out of touching range. Her husband put his arms around her as she sobbed.

'Can we stay?' he asked. 'Is that all right?'

'Of course,' Luke said. 'And I'll tell you what we're doing every step of the way. The first thing we need to do is to put a tiny needle into one of Grace's veins. Given how small she is, it might need to go into a vein in her scalp, or her foot, but don't be alarmed. It's just the same as putting one in an adult's arm.'

The new nurse was staying to help Sue hold the baby as Luke began to work on starting treatment that would, hopefully, save this baby from the potentially life-threatening complications from whooping cough that were running through his head right now. Luke had seen babies develop pneumonia and encephalitis from this disease. He'd once looked after a baby in Intensive Care who had needed extracorporeal membrane oxygenation, even, where the blood was removed from the body to do the work of the lungs in the same way a heart-lung bypass machine worked.

The sad thing was that this was a preventable disease but he could understand how the idea of having a booster vaccination had seemed unimportant to the father of this baby.

With the cannula safely secured into a scalp vein, Luke had a moment of distraction with the automatic process of attaching the IV line and setting the drip rate of the fluids.

Had Ellie had a booster vaccination while she was pregnant? How many visitors was little Jamie getting and was he in close enough contact with any of them to be in danger of having something like this passed on? A sideways glance at Sue, who was positioning the plastic dome of the oxygen hood over Grace's head, prompted Luke to make a mental note to talk to her about it. Ellie had told him that Sue was a good friend of hers. She could, at least, pass on the warning that they'd had a serious case here.

The paediatric team arrived and took over the care of Grace and her transfer to their intensive care unit but it wasn't until much later in the evening, after dealing with a man having a heart attack and a motorbike accident victim with a serious leg fracture, that Luke had the time to grab both a coffee in the staffroom and to have a word with Sue, who also happened to be in the room.

'How's Ellie?' The query was casual. 'And Jamie?'

Sue's eyes widened. Was she surprised that he had remembered the name of one patient amongst so many? Or that he knew the name she had given to her baby? He concentrated on stirring his coffee. She would be a lot more than surprised if she knew how often he'd been thinking about them both since then.

'She's amazing.' Sue's expression softened into admiration. 'I can't believe how well she's doing. She wasn't supposed to be keeping this baby so she had nothing, you know? Not even a nappy. And she's living in this tiny apartment that's not much more than a bedsit.'

The movement of Luke's spoon slowed. He could feel relief softening his muscles. If Ellie was doing well maybe he could stop worrying that Jamie wouldn't end up being put up for adoption. Or worse, going into the first of a series of foster homes...

But then he found something else to focus on. Just how tiny was the apartment she was living in? He was rattling around in a huge old house all by himself. How unfair was that?

'She hasn't got any family to help, though, has she?'

'How did you know that? Oh, yeah... I remember now. Ellie said that you'd been to visit while she was in hospital. That you knew each other from way back?'

'We didn't exactly know each other. We used to catch the same school bus, that's all.'

Sue nodded, glancing at her watch. 'I'd better get back. Break's over.'

'You don't know whether Ellie had a pertussis booster while she was pregnant, do you?'

Sue paused. He could see her make the connection with the case they'd both worked on earlier this evening and her nod told him that she knew exactly what he was concerned about. If she was surprised by that ongoing concern, she didn't show it.

'I'll check. You're right. If the bug's in the community at the moment, she needs to know.'

'Anyone else that has close contact with the baby should get a booster, too. Like her boyfriend?'

'Oh, she's safe enough on that score.' Sue was already heading for the door. 'Being single was one of the reasons it was easy for her to make the decision to be a surrogate. And she certainly hasn't had the inclination *or* opportunity to start anything since.'

Luke finally took a mouthful of his rapidly cooling coffee.

'Something up?' One of his registrars came into the staffroom.

'No…why?'

'You're looking worried.'

Luke shook his head. 'All good, mate. And it's nearly home time. What would I have to worry about?'

He abandoned the coffee and went back into the department. What would he have to worry about?

It really wasn't his problem that Ellie might be struggling to cope with limited resources and space.

That she didn't even have a partner to provide more than intermittent assistance…

It was highly unlikely that she would think of calling him if she needed help. As he'd explained to Sue, they hadn't really known each other all those years ago, so why would she?

She probably hadn't even kept his phone number.

It was right there on her fridge door, half hidden by a smiley face magnet.

Luke's phone number.

Ellie spotted it on one of her interminable circuits around the very limited space in her apartment, as she carried the unhappy bundle that was her baby. A baby who had been fed and changed and cuddled and should have been asleep more than an hour ago.

She'd glanced at the fridge because she was hungry. Hungry enough to wonder if she'd actually remembered to eat at all, today. Oh, yeah… She'd used the last of the peanut butter on the last slice of bread, hadn't she? The plan had been to walk to the nearest supermarket this afternoon to get some more supplies but it hadn't quite happened. The washing machine, tucked under her kitchen bench beside the fridge, had simply stopped working and the repairman had arrived hours later than he'd promised.

And then it was time to feed Jamie again. And give him a bath. She'd had to dip into the emergency supply of disposable nappies because none of the washing that had finally been done had had time to dry yet and Ellie could only hope that the grow suit he was wearing would last until the morning because everything else in her son's meagre wardrobe was either amongst the new load in the washing machine or hanging over the bars of the laundry rack that filled the space between one end of her couch and the television in the corner of her living area.

'Shh…shh…shh…' She rocked the baby as she turned around, stepped past the plastic baby bath that had to get propped up against the kitchen wall because there was no room for it in the bathroom, passed the end of the couch that wasn't obscured by the metal frame of the drying rack and took the ten steps available before she came to her bed.

An unmade bed that looked astonishingly inviting. She could be asleep the moment her head hit that pillow. For an hour or two, anyway, until the small person in the bassinet that had replaced her bedside table woke up again. Even the prospect of being woken was enough for her heart to sink and the threat of tears to surface. This was all so much harder than she had expected.

And so much more lonely…

Ellie hadn't spoken to anyone today, other than the washing machine repairman. Oh, she'd talked to Jamie a lot but that didn't really count as a conversation, did it? This was the longest time ever that she hadn't talked to Ava, she realised. They had always been in some form of contact—almost every day.

The total shock of the surrogacy plan going so wrong had evaporated in those first moments of falling in love with her baby. Ellie had wanted to contact her best friend, in fact, and tell her that it was just as well she didn't want the baby any more because there was no way on earth Ellie could have given him away. She'd actually tried to ring Ava a few days later. Her phone was in the pocket of her jeans right now but there would be no point trying again. Not when the number was no longer valid.

Where was her best friend now? Was she with anyone or nursing her broken heart alone? She should have stayed here and they could have worked things out. Helped each other.

Other friends were here for her but it wasn't like the bond she and Ava had always had. Despite that, Ellie would have been delighted to have a friend like Sue drop in. They could talk about all the exciting cases that had come through the emergency department recently and all the interesting things that were happening in the lives of the people they both knew. But Sue wouldn't be dropping in. Or even ringing. She was working an afternoon shift and wouldn't finish until eleven p.m.

Was Luke still working that shift, too…?

Good grief…was that unpleasant twinge due to envy

that Sue might be getting a chance she couldn't have? To work alongside Luke and get to know him a bit better?

No. It was more likely that she was simply missing her work so much. A while back, a few weeks off to prepare for and then recover from giving birth had held all the attraction of an extended holiday but, like the rest of her life, that plan felt as if it had been made by a completely different person who had been living a life that now seemed increasingly like a distant dream.

At least the raucous dinner party in the apartment directly above hers seemed to be winding down. The incessant thumping of feet on her ceiling and the shrieks of drunken laughter hadn't been helping either her mission to settle Jamie into sleep or her emotional state. Other people were having fun. She was becoming a sleep-deprived zombie who spent her nights walking round and round a mind-numbingly restricted track. There was nothing she hadn't seen on this circuit a million times. She had even memorised that phone number on the fridge without even trying.

She had to stop before she fell over from exhaustion. On the next circuit, Ellie slowed down and paused by the end of the couch. Still rocking Jamie, she eased herself onto the edge of the cushion and, when that didn't trigger an increase of misery, she inched back, tucking the baby securely into the crook of her arm, and then relaxed her neck just to let her head rest for a moment on the back of the couch.

Maybe it was her imagination but the cries were lessening in strength. Ellie knew she should get up and have another go at putting Jamie into his bassinet but the command to her legs didn't have any effect.

In a minute, she promised herself. *I'll just close my eyes for a few seconds.* They weren't exactly focusing very well right now so it was weird that she noticed that scrap of paper on the fridge again...

Her mind drifted back in time. Because she was missing the special people in her life so much right now? Ava. And her mother. How much easier would this all be if she still had her mum around to help? To give advice, or help with some of the chores or even take care of the baby and let her get some of that desperately needed sleep.

That sense of loss extended to more than simply family. Memories of growing up in a town small enough to be called a village seemed like a fantasy life now. There was sunshine and the greenery of fields and forests. A beach not that far away. People had time to really care about each other and a new mother would have been showered with help and gifts. Like all those tiny, knitted clothes that her mother's knitting circle had produced.

Had she really rolled her eyes when she got home from school every Wednesday to find that group of women in the living room with their tongues clacking along with their knitting needles? Ellie would sit in the kitchen to do her homework and dream of living in the city where people had more exciting things to do than sit around and gossip.

Jamie was a heavy weight in her arms now and she could recognise the relaxation of tiny muscles that told her he was drifting into a deep sleep. It was definitely time to put him to bed.

But what if he woke up again when she moved?

And besides...there was a new memory floating to the surface of her brain and if she moved, it would vanish.

It was thinking about that knitting circle that had triggered it. About the gossip. She had abandoned her homework that day in order to listen because they were talking about that boy. The new boy who had started catching their bus.

The conversation from so long ago came back in snatches and some of it was more like feelings than actual words but still made sense.

'Taking on a boy that age...?'

'Apparently no foster home could keep him. Too disruptive.'

'Why would the Gilmores do it, then? They're not exactly spring chickens...'

'I know the answer to that. I was talking to Dorothy only the other week...'

The silence of even the knitting needles must have been a satisfying level of attention for the speaker.

'They caught him stealing food. He'd been hiding out in that forest at the back of their place. Eric called the police because he knew someone would want to know where a lad that age was and when Stu arrived with someone from Social Services, Dorothy said she couldn't let them take him away. She said there was something about the way he looked that just broke her heart—as if he'd known all along that there was no hope in the world.'

Ellie had caught her breath at that. Really? The boy on the bus didn't look sad or pathetic. He looked...as if he could take on the world and win—every time.

'Well, he landed on his feet this time, didn't he? Shame he didn't pull his socks up a bit faster.'

'Old habits die hard, I reckon.'

'It's not as if he's breaking any laws.'

'He's a law unto himself, that one. I wouldn't let my daughter anywhere near him, that's for sure and certain.'

Ellie could actually hear that murmur of agreement amongst the women and remember how puzzled she'd been by the odd sound that followed.

Like a collective sigh that wasn't really audible.

She'd been too young to understand it then but now…

She felt the corner of her mouth lift a little. Some things had probably been the same since the dawn of time, hadn't they?

The good girls always denied it—as she had in later years—but it was a thing. That compelling attraction the bad boys often had. Or was it only the bad boys with a charisma that suggested there was something good hidden from sight?

And Luke had been that kind of bad boy. Dorothy Gilmore might have been the first person to see what was hidden but every girl at Kauri Valley District High School was aware of that attraction. Even the ones who knew they would never be chosen.

Like Ellie…

The memories faded. And Ellie's exhaustion seemed to be fading as well as she slipped into a sleep as deep as the baby she was still cradling in her arms.

He was in her dream.

Tall and gorgeous. Wearing faded jeans and a black tee shirt under a battered leather jacket that clung to those broad shoulders like a second skin. She could see the sun streaked golden stripes in that tousled mane of hair. She could feel the surprising softness of it between her fingers as she pushed them over his scalp.

He was smiling down at her—white teeth just visible between lips that were, curiously, soft and firm at exactly the same time. And as delicious as she'd always known they would be.

He was about to kiss her again. She could see it in the glint of his eyes that made the golden flecks against the tawny brown of his irises almost glow.

He was murmuring something. She could see his lips moving but couldn't hear the words but she was smiling. She didn't need to hear them because she could feel his hands on her body and she knew that he was simply telling her about all the things he was about to do to her. Things that she would never, ever be able to forget…

But then his face was changing.

Twisting.

Turning ugly.

And she could hear his words.

'*Get out*…you have to get out of my life… *Now*…'

Somebody was crying. But it didn't sound like her. It was the cry of a child waking. A baby.

And the hands on her body were rough. They were pulling at her. Shaking her hard…

'Wake up…' The voice was louder. 'You have to get out… There's a *fire*… Here… I'll take the baby…'

Ellie's eyes opened in the same instant her brain snapped back into reality.

Or tried to.

She couldn't see properly. The only light in the room was coming from streetlamps several floors below and even that was murky.

Smoky. She could smell it now. Burning and acrid in her nostrils.

She could hear shouts and thumping coming from the apartment above and more shouting from the stairwell beyond her door. Banging on other doors and people yelling for others to wake up and get out.

'*Fire*…the building's on *fire*…'

But the loudest sound of all was the baby crying in her arms as someone tried to pull him out of her grip.

'*No*…' Ellie struggled to sit up. 'Don't take him. He's…' *Mine*… The instinct to protect Jamie was stronger than her own fear but she was forced to stop speaking as she began to cough. She was moving, though. Getting herself up from the couch, grateful for the strong arm gripping her shoulders and shoving her forwards.

She had seen this man before. He lived on the same floor she did but she didn't know his name—this person who had broken through her door to come and save her.

Save *them*…

There were others in the stairwell. Someone other than Jamie was crying now and there were too many people talking at the same time. Shouting to be heard.

'Watch your step.'

'Has someone called the fire brigade?'

'Where's Carla? *Carla?* Can you hear me?'

'Why didn't the damn fire alarm work?'

And then they were outside in the dark and the shocking reality was lit up against the night sky. Flames licked the building, coming from the windows only a floor above Ellie's apartment.

Where the party had been happening.

The sound of glass shattering was accompanied by billows of smoke coming from higher windows and then more flames joined the image until there was a solid wall of flames moving upwards.

And sirens… The emergency services were arriving. A police car and then the first of many fire trucks. An ambulance. People in uniforms were herding the crowd of residents further and further away from the building until they were right at the end of the block. More ambulances were rolling up, their lights flashing against the darkness of the night. A television crew arrived, spilling out of the branded four-by-four and lifting cameras to their shoulders even as they moved towards the scene. Someone was stringing bright tape across the road so they couldn't go back. There were hoses being unravelled and ladders being raised and the noise levels were increasing steadily.

So much shouting.

Ellie was wedged into the crowd, holding Jamie as if her own life depended on keeping him safe. Horrified by the thought that she could still be in that building—unconscious now instead of simply asleep—because she would have had no warning of the deadly smoke rolling in beneath her door. She looked around at her silent neighbours, who were simply standing there, watching their homes being destroyed, trying to find the man who had saved her so that she could thank him properly.

But someone in a uniform was in the way.

'Come with us, love.' The paramedic was putting a blanket around Ellie's shoulders. 'We need to check you and your baby.'

Her baby…

It had seemed extraordinary that Jamie had gone back to sleep in her arms as she stood there rocking him. But was he really only asleep? There had been enough smoke to make her cough. What would that have done to tiny airways and lungs? The relief of being outside and safe was obliterated by fear again as Ellie let the paramedics guide her into the back of the nearest ambulance.

They checked heart-rates and blood pressure and oxygen saturation levels. They listened to Ellie's lung sounds, making her take deep breaths that made her cough. The stethoscope looked huge against Jamie's little chest and he woke up and began to cry again.

But he wasn't coughing.

'He seems fine,' the paramedic told her. 'But we can take you into Emergency for a full check if you're worried. Did you say he's only three weeks old? It might be a good idea to go to hospital.'

But Ellie knew that cry. Jamie was hungry.

'I'll just feed him, if that's okay…and then see how he is…'

'Sure. Stay in here where it's warm. We've got enough trucks to transport anybody that's urgent.' She lifted the back of the stretcher and put pillows behind Ellie so that she could sit more comfortably as she settled Jamie against her breast. 'I know you, don't I?' The paramedic was focused on Ellie's face now, instead of a detailed physical assessment. 'Do you work at North Shore General?'

'I did. I'm on maternity leave.'

'Of course…' The paramedic smiled down at Jamie. 'He's gorgeous.' She shook her head. 'I can't imagine how scary that must have been. Were you asleep when the fire started?'

Ellie nodded. Sound asleep. Dreaming about…

No…she couldn't remember. And it didn't matter. All that mattered was that they were both safe. Unharmed. Jamie was sucking steadily, his eyes drifting shut, and the snuffling sounds he was making were perfectly normal with no hint of any respiratory distress. Had being wrapped in his blanket and cuddled against her chest saved him from inhaling a significant amount of that evil smoke?

The paramedic had opened the back door of the ambulance and was leaning out. The cacophony of sound from outside sounded like a disaster movie. Something Ellie had been watching but didn't affect her. She looked down at the tiny face against her breast and the first wave of real relief washed over her. She could feel tears rolling down her face.

'Oh, my God…' The paramedic sounded awed. 'It looks like the building's collapsing in the middle…'

And then it hit Ellie.

She had nothing but the precious baby in her arms and the clothes she was wearing. Sneakers. A pair of maternity jeans and an ancient, sloppy tee shirt that had a red bird with an open beak and a cloud of tiny hearts emerging instead of musical notes for its song.

She had been frightened of how she was going to cope when she knew she had a baby to take home and she didn't have as much as a single nappy.

Now she didn't even have a home.

She needed help right now, more than she ever had.

And, of course, the first person who came to mind was Ava.

But there was no point in trying. She'd known that when she'd thought about it earlier. When she'd been aware of the lump of her phone in her back pocket as she'd been walking that track round and round her apartment.

Such a small, inadequate space to be looking after a baby but it had been home.

Their home.

She could see the last glimpses of it that she would ever have. The clothes rack with the laundry drying. The bassinet beside her unmade bed. The fridge…

The fridge with that scrap of paper half hidden by the smiley face magnet.

With the number that she knew by heart.

Was her phone still in her pocket or had it slipped out during that frantic escape of getting up from the couch and through the smoke filled corridor, down what had felt like endless flights of concrete stairs and then further and further along the road?

Trying not to disturb Jamie's sleepy, contented sucking, Ellie moved one arm, snaking her hand towards her pocket.

There'd been no traffic to speak of at this time of night but it was still a bit of a drive all the way to Kauri Valley and Luke hadn't felt ready to sleep. He'd opened a cold beer, and fired up his laptop to look up a journal article he'd thought of earlier this evening. It had been written by the person who currently led the team in the emergency department of the hospital in Boston he was about to put an application in to work with. He wanted to know how good their research program was.

A news alert popped up and, without thinking, he clicked on it to find himself watching a live feed of breaking news. An old multi-storey apartment block in one of the North Shore suburbs close to the hospital was being engulfed in fire.

Luke pushed his barely tasted beer away. Were there casualties? Would he be called in to help with an unexpected influx of patients?

Almost as the thought occurred to him, his mobile started ringing.

But it was the last person he would have expected it to be on the other end of the line.

'Luke? It's Ellie Thomas…'

Ellie…

Luke's mouth suddenly felt weirdly dry. 'Hey, Ellie…' was all he could manage.

'You…um…you gave me your number. The night Jamie was born?'

Luke nodded and then realised how stupid that was. 'Yeah. I did.' Something in Ellie's tone was making co-

herent thought difficult. She sounded…frightened? No…
more like *lost*…

He could hear a lot of background noise, too. Shouting. And a distant siren. Where on earth was she at this
time of night? And what about the baby? A sudden chill
ran up his spine. Had something happened to Jamie?

'You said if I ever needed help…' Oh, God…she was
crying. He could hear the catch of her breath that sounded
like a stifled sob. 'I think… I need help…'

CHAPTER FOUR

'ARE YOU SURE about this?'

'Of course. I wouldn't have offered, otherwise.'

Luke glanced sideways at the passenger in his car. Ellie still had the ambulance blanket around her shoulders. Her hair was a bit of a mess, with those tangled, dark blonde waves framing a pale face that was smudged with dark streaks. He was pretty sure it must have been her tears that had left cleaner patches on the layer of soot from the smoke.

He knew she was only two years younger than his own thirty-four years because he'd seen it written in her hospital notes. But right now, she looked more than ten years younger—almost like the young girl who used to share his school bus, except that he would have noticed her back then, if she'd ever looked *this* miserable. Ellie also looked exhausted and more than a little frightened and those huge, dark eyes in that pale face were so striking that Luke had to force his gaze back to the road. The expression in them made her look incredibly vulnerable and it made his heart ache in a way that he couldn't put a name to, with a strength that was oddly disturbing.

'And are you sure you don't want to get checked out at hospital? Or have Jamie checked again?'

She nodded. 'I've just got a bit of airway irritation

from the smoke.' Her cough punctuated her words with perfect timing. 'I'll be fine. Just a bit shocked, I guess. Jamie doesn't even have a cough and he's too young to have been really frightened. He's fine, too, and that's all that really matters.'

Luke might have disagreed with that but couldn't think of how he could say so without it sounding strange coming from someone who didn't even qualify as a friend. Yet...

He simply nodded and concentrated on his driving, instead. Offering Ellie a place to stay for the night had been the most obvious way he could provide the help that had been requested of him and he *had* been sure. He couldn't remember ever having wanted to help someone in trouble quite this much, in fact. Being able to do this had wiped out that unsettling knowledge that had come with that conversation with Sue tonight—the unfairness of life that had him rattling around alone in a huge old house while Ellie was caring for a baby in no more than a bedsit. It wasn't just for Ellie's, sake, of course. He still felt that odd connection with the baby he'd thought might be just as unwanted as he had once been.

He turned his head enough to glance into the back seat, now. He could see that Jamie was fast asleep in the plastic capsule with the handle. 'We were lucky that ambulance crew had a baby car seat they could lend us.'

'They know where we work. Where *you* work, anyway...' There was a note in Ellie's voice that made Luke wonder just how much she was missing her job in the ED. 'Any crew will be able to collect the seat and the blanket and return them.'

Luke flicked on his indicator. 'There's an all-night service station here. We can go shopping properly tomorrow, but what do you need most now?'

Ellie closed her eyes and Luke caught the tremble of her lips as she obviously started to itemise everything she had just lost. Again, his heart squeezed with that nameless emotion. It squeezed so hard he could feel a lump in his own throat.

Her voice, however, came out with a surprising level of determination. She wasn't beaten, yet, this young mother. With her first words, he could identify what he was feeling this time. He was proud of her. He'd already known she had guts when she'd embraced the challenge of raising a child she hadn't intended to bring into the world. Now, she was demonstrating that she wasn't going to let anything stop her. Even the trauma of watching her home get destroyed.

'Nappies,' she said. 'And baby wipes. Clothes might be a problem but a service station isn't going to stock them.' She bit her lip. 'I don't have any money with me, though. My wallet got left behind.'

'It's not a problem.'

'I'll pay you back. As soon as I can sort things. Oh, help… I don't even have any ID for going to the bank.' With a despairing groan, Ellie faltered, burying her face in her hands. 'I can't believe this has happened…'

Luke pulled into a parking space in front of the service station. He put his hand on Ellie's shoulder in what was meant to be simply a reassuring touch but when he felt how rigid she was with tension he extended his fingers and gave it a slow squeeze.

'It'll be okay,' he told her. 'We can sort everything— one step at a time. You stay here with Jamie. I reckon I can manage to find the right sort of disposable nappies and wipes.'

Ellie's face appeared and the look in her eyes made Luke feel about ten feet tall. A knight in shining armour who still had the damsel in distress on the back of his horse. And he could feel her skin, even through the layers of the blanket and her tee shirt, sending tendrils of warmth that made his arm and then his whole body tingle.

'New born size for the nappies.' She was trying to smile but it wobbled. 'And the wipes with aloe vera are really good, if they've got them.'

He came back with his arms laden with what looked like enough nappies and wipes to last for at least a week and a smile that suggested triumph.

A smile that made him look like that teenaged boy she could remember getting onto the school bus—with the kind of swagger that told everybody there wasn't anything he couldn't handle and he was going to have fun with whatever challenge got thrown at him.

A 'bad boy' kind of smile.

And it was impossible not to smile back.

Impossible not to feel as if, with this man's help, Ellie could face anything. Even when she was feeling as if she were falling into a black hole in her life that she'd never seen coming.

He'd already brought her through the worst moments of her life when she'd been afraid that she could lose the lives of both her baby and herself.

Maybe that was why she hadn't even thought to call Sue or another friend to ask for help tonight.

She'd felt so lost, sitting there in the back of that ambulance with Jamie in her arms, knowing she had lost her home and all her possessions. Even her car had been parked in the basement of the apartment block and had undoubtedly been buried under the collapsed building.

And she'd remembered that moment when Luke had

crouched beside her in the emergency department to ask for her consent to let him take charge of her assisted delivery. When she'd looked into his eyes and found hope to cling to.

And when, in that grim time of the pain and the pushing, he had called her 'sweetheart'…

So she had to smile back now. He was doing exactly what she'd hoped he would. Taking charge of an unexpected and horrible moment and giving her the confidence that she could, actually, cope with this.

'Step one sorted,' he said with satisfaction as he started the car again. 'Now let's get you home.'

Ellie had to swallow a big lump in her throat.

She didn't have a home any more.

But, weirdly, as they left the motorway and headed west, it *felt* as if she were heading home. She knew this country like the back of her hand, with its rolling hills and paddocks shaded by so many trees and the small village with its town hall and war memorial and the pub on the main street.

'I haven't been out to Kauri Valley in years,' she murmured. 'There didn't seem any point after Mum died.'

'Same.' Luke nodded. 'It was five years ago that my dad died and when it became obvious that Mum needed full time care, I moved her to Sydney so she'd be close enough for me to help take care of her.'

Ellie was struck by his choice of words. And the tone with which he used them. If you didn't know, you'd never guess that he'd been adopted so late in his childhood. He was talking about his family, here. A family he had loved very much.

And lost.

Ellie had lost her family, too.

She had lost her best friend.

She had lost her future as she'd envisioned it.

Now she had lost her home.

It was all too much. And hearing that note of such caring in Luke's voice brought tears to her eyes again. She sniffed hard as she tried to blink them away.

Luke's glance was swift.

'You okay?'

Oh, man... He still sounded as though he cared so much, but this time it was on her behalf. Ellie had to close her eyes. Just for a heartbeat, she wanted to feel as if that concern were genuinely personal. That someone really cared.

'Mmm. I just... I can tell how special your mum was to you. And... I was missing *my* mum tonight. And now, it feels like I'm heading home, even though that's crazy.'

Luke was silent for a moment. A moment of empathy for someone else who had no family?

Or maybe he understood how weird it felt to be entering such an old stamping ground again.

'It hasn't changed much,' he said. 'Kauri Valley, that is. Mr Jenkins still runs the general store.' His tone was cheerful now. Was he trying to distract her from thinking too much about her current problems? 'Do you remember him?'

'But he was ancient twenty years ago! And so grumpy. He thought that kids only came into his shop to steal lollies.'

Luke's mouth twitched. 'Maybe some of them did.'

Ellie's jaw dropped. Okay. She had been very effectively distracted.

'You *didn't*...' But then she bit her lip. 'Actually, Ava and I did, once, too. Just to see if we could... And because he was shouting at someone's dog who'd snuck in the door and the poor dog was cringing as if it was getting beaten.'

'Did you get away with it?'

'Yes…but we felt so guilty we never did it again.'

'Mmm.'

There was a world of understanding in that sound. Had it been guilt that had finally put Lucas Gilmore on a straight and narrow path? Did you only feel guilty when you were scared of being punished? Or was it because you cared about what other people thought? That only mattered when you cared about those people, didn't it?

Ellie stole a sideways glance at Luke. It wasn't the first time she had wondered about what life had been like for him as a child. How he had ended up hiding in the forest behind the Gilmores' place. Part of his charisma had come from the shroud of mystery he'd brought with him into a very ordinary New Zealand high school, but after Ellie had eavesdropped on that conversation between the group of local women, something else had captured her imagination.

How he'd come to look as if he'd believed there was no hope in the world.

Forgetting her own worries for a moment longer, Ellie felt something in her heart squeeze very tightly, as if she could see that young boy looking so desperate that he had touched Dorothy Gilmore's heart enough to make her change her life for ever. And then she had to twist her head to look at Jamie, asleep in the car seat. She would never let anything bad happen to him.

But it almost had tonight…

Maybe it was delayed shock that was making her shiver as they finally pulled into a driveway that was so overgrown, the hedges scraped the sides of the SUV. The screeching sound woke Jamie, who began to whimper as Luke unbuckled the plastic capsule. The shivering was almost shaking by the time she had followed him up some wide steps, across a veranda with creaking boards and through a front door that led into the widest, longest hallway Ellie had ever seen. Finally, having led her into a kitchen that was probably bigger than her entire apartment had been, Luke put down the pile of nappies and wipes he had under one arm, and carefully put down the baby seat containing Jamie he'd been carrying in his other hand.

One glance at Ellie and he frowned so deeply he almost looked angry.

'You're frozen… Here…' He was stripping off the woollen, ribbed jumper he was wearing. 'Put this on.'

It was massive. And still warm from his body.

It felt like a hug.

And it smelled…delicious. Ellie couldn't help crossing her arms and bringing them up to her face so that she could bury her nose in the scent for a moment. She was watching Luke at the same time, as he dropped to a crouch in front of the baby seat and rocked it a little.

'It's okay, little guy,' he said. 'Do you want to come out of this? Do you need your mummy?'

He had been wearing a black tee shirt under the jumper and, right now, it was stretched against the muscles of his back and shoulders.

And, suddenly, Ellie remembered what she had been dreaming about when she'd been shaken awake by her neighbour. Worse, she could actually feel fingers of remembered desire curling themselves into a tight fist somewhere deep in her belly as her gaze travelled down his bare arms to those large hands with long, artistic looking fingers.

Why had her subconscious chosen to give her a sex

dream about Luke Gilmore, for heaven's sake? Had it become bored with the smudged features of the purely fantasy partners that had entered her dreams on the odd occasion during more than a year of celibacy?

Oh…help…

It wasn't just the new item of clothing making her feel so much warmer. Her cheeks felt as if they had started glowing. At least Luke had his back to her so he couldn't have noticed anything and she had to make sure he never did. He would be horrified. She had been on another planet at school as far as his sexual interests were concerned and there was no reason to believe something that fundamental would have changed. How embarrassing would it be if he thought that was the reason she had called him tonight?

It wasn't.

Or was it? Trusting someone, not to mention liking how they could make you feel by simply looking at you, had to be a big part of attraction.

But feelings that were unmistakeably sexual were on a whole different—and very inappropriate—level. She was just exhausted, Ellie reminded herself. She'd been through an emotional mill tonight. And it was probably far too long since she'd had a man in her life.

With an effort, Ellie got a grip.

'I'll get him,' she told Luke. 'He probably needs feeding again.'

'Oh…of course… What do you need?' He looked around. 'Those kitchen chairs aren't very comfortable but the living room will be pretty cold—I don't use it much.'

'That couch looks perfect.' Ellie unbuckled Jamie's safety belt and picked up the baby, supporting the back of his head with one hand as she lifted him to her shoulder. It was automatic to turn her head enough to kiss the soft fluff of his hair. 'I've never seen a kitchen big enough to have a couch in it before.'

'It's always been the heart of the house.' Luke spoke quietly. 'My favourite room. I used to do my guitar practice on that couch while Mum was cooking dinner. She said she liked to have music while she worked.'

Ellie didn't say anything. Maybe because she was trying not to picture a teenaged Luke, with even longer, shaggier hair and a guitar in his arms. He would have totally owned a rock star vibe. Trying to distract herself, she focused on the room, instead.

On the old beams in the ceiling and the stone floor and the scuffed looking leather of the big couch. There were French doors to one side of the couch but it was too dark to see anything more than an area of stone paving, notable for the tall weeds filling the gaps between the big, flat stones. And one of the big windows on either side of the doors had tape criss-crossed over a large crack.

Luke noticed what had caught her attention as she was sitting down. He walked towards the window and ran his fingers over the tape.

'The place is a bit run down still. The rental firm I was using let me down and I arrived back to find a complete mess. It's clean now, though. The commercial cleaners I got in even washed all the linen and aired mattresses.'

He had his hand on the door knob now. Turning it to check that it was locked. 'It's safe, too. I had all the locks changed. Someone's coming to fix the windows and some other stuff soon. I just need to find a gardener that doesn't take one look and either say he's too busy or give me a ridiculous quote because they don't actually want the work.'

He turned just in time to see Ellie guiding Jamie's gaping little mouth to help him latch on to her nipple. She could feel the way he seemed to freeze for a heartbeat. And then another.

'I...ah... I'll put the kettle on, shall I? Would you like a cup of tea or coffee or something?'

'A cup of tea would be awesome. But don't let me keep you up. It's the middle of the night and you've got work tomorrow.'

'I've got a day off tomorrow.' He filled an electric jug and switched it on and then, without looking in Ellie's direction again, he hurried out of the kitchen, muttering something about finding linen for her bed.

Anyone would think he'd never seen a woman breast-feeding her baby before, Ellie thought. For heaven's sake...he'd told her that he'd done a long stint in obstetrics. He must be more than used to the sight of a woman's breast, not to mention every other part of their anatomy.

Or was he uncomfortable because it was *her* breast he had glimpsed?

Because he saw her as a woman and not a patient?

Maybe something had changed in the years since she had been an invisible teenager. He had, after all, told her that she was *special*...

That thought merged with remnants of desire that were still glowing deep inside and made her toes curl more than a little but Ellie was still confused.

When Luke had given up doing the kind of things that would get him expelled from school, like playing truant or smoking behind the bike sheds, he'd found a new 'bad boy' niche at Kauri Valley High—as the resident heartbreaker.

And it didn't seem to matter how many hearts got broken, there was always another girl fighting to get to the front of the queue. She and Ava used to whisper about it on the bus.

'Did you hear that Charlene got dumped?'

'Yeah...but nobody lasts more than two or three dates, do they?'

'Who's next, do you reckon?'

'Dunno...that redheaded girl, maybe. The one who gets into trouble all the time for wearing her skirt too short. What's her name... Tegan?'

She couldn't remember any more of the legendary pack of Gilmore girlfriends but it was clear that Luke would be quite familiar with breasts in both his professional and personal life.

So it was weird that he had seemed uncomfortable.

Unless he was regretting his decision to bring her home? Maybe he didn't really trust her yet, despite that curiously intimate chat they'd had on the night of Jamie's birth. She had, after all, announced that nobody wanted the baby she had just given birth to—including herself.

The memory still made her wince. And cuddle Jamie a little bit closer.

'It wasn't true,' she whispered. 'It will never be true.'

He had finished feeding. She lifted him upright and began to rub his back to burp him, tilting her head so that she could feel his hair against her cheek. Despite the weariness that was coming back in a tidal wave and the fact that life had just thrown her another rather dramatic curveball, she found herself singing softly. The old Brahms lullaby that had become a familiar part of this routine in just a few, short weeks.

Sleepyhead, close your eyes, for I'm right beside you...

Luke could hear the song well before he reached the kitchen, with a stack of clean towels in his arms. This old, isolated house was so quiet, you could just about hear a mouse scratching in the pantry at this time of night.

Ellie had a beautiful voice. He recognised the tune, of course. Who hadn't heard that old lullaby that seemed to be part of every mobile that new parents hung over a baby's bassinet? It had always struck him as being a bit mournful but maybe that was because he'd never lost the sense of yearning for something he'd probably never had.

A mother's love...

He'd learned to wall it off. So effectively it barely touched his consciousness so it had been a shock when he'd felt it so strongly only a short time ago, when he'd seen Ellie beginning to feed her baby.

And now it was happening again, as he listened to the soft sound of her song.

There was something about this particular mother and child that touched a part of him that he had considered insignificant now. Okay, he'd had an unfortunate start in life but he'd overcome it, thanks to the Gilmores. He was an adult. An extremely successful adult who had everything he could want in life—an exciting job, no financial worries and the freedom to go anywhere he chose in the world.

He didn't want to be reminded of things he had never had when he was young. Or the things that were impossible for him to have now.

Like a family...

Had it been a mistake to bring Ellie and Jamie into the only place that felt like a family home to him?

Ah well...it was only for a night. He could help them find somewhere else to go tomorrow.

Taking a deep breath, he entered the kitchen and put the towels down on the big, wooden table in the centre of the room. Ellie stopped singing as soon as she saw him come into the room and she was well covered with his old jumper again so it was easy to sound perfectly relaxed.

'Your bed's all sorted. I didn't know what to do for Jamie, though. Can he sleep in the car seat?'

'Oh… I guess so. Or I can keep him in the bed with me.'

Luke frowned. Co-sleeping with an infant was controversial. Some suggested it was less than safe but if that was what Ellie wanted to do, it was her decision. He busied himself making the tea but the urge to suggest that the plan was unwise gained momentum. As he put two mugs onto the table, inspiration struck.

'I saw a movie, once,' he said. 'Some baby got born unexpectedly in an old house and they made a bed for it in a big drawer from the bottom of a Scotch chest.'

'Oh?' Ellie was walking towards the table. She tucked Jamie securely under one arm and reached for the mug of tea with her other hand.

'I've got a Scotch chest in my room and half the drawers are empty.'

She was looking at the towels. 'They'd probably make a good mattress, wouldn't they?'

'I'll go and get the drawer.'

He was back in less than a minute. He put the old, wooden drawer on the table and covered its base—not with the towels but with the folded hospital blanket that Ellie didn't need any more. Then he put a clean towel on the top.

Ellie laid Jamie gently into the nest and tucked him in with another towel. He scrunched up his face and stretched tiny, starfish hands above his head but then relaxed back into sleep.

Ellie smiled up at Luke. 'I'm liking the Kiwi ingenuity,' she said. 'And thanks, Luke. For…' She looked as if she had a whole bunch of things she wanted to say but couldn't decide where to begin. The way her gaze slid away from his suggested embarrassment and reminded him of the shy girl she had been way back. 'For everything.'

Man...those eyes...that smile...and that little wobble in her voice that told him how much this meant to her.

What was it about Ellie Thomas that seemed so astonishingly different from any woman he had ever met?

He found himself willing her to look back and catch his gaze again. He wanted to smile back at her.

No. What he really wanted to do was gather her into his arms and just hold her. To reassure that shy Ellie enough that brave Ellie came back.

Okay. That wasn't entirely true, either.

He wanted...

He wanted...to *kiss* her.

The realisation was shocking.

He had brought this exhausted, vulnerable brand-new mother into his home in the wake of a personal disaster. Of course she was grateful. To even think of taking advantage of that in any way was appalling.

Any man would find Ellie Thomas attractive but the last thing she needed in her life at the moment was someone who was even entertaining the idea of hitting on her.

What she needed right now was a friend.

A big brother.

A very long time ago Luke had made a promise to the amazing woman who'd chosen to become his mother that he would always strive to be the best person that he could possibly be, however hard that was.

Putting Ellie Thomas completely off limits wasn't actually that hard because it was the right thing to do.

The only thing to do.

Luke turned away. 'Let me show you your room. You bring your tea. I'll bring Jamie.'

The big wooden drawer with the baby asleep inside it was a lot heavier than a bassinet would have been. And rather more awkward to hold but Luke tucked it under his arm, confident that Jamie was perfectly safe.

So was Ellie.

He'd make sure of that.

CHAPTER FIVE

HE'D GONE CRAZY.

But Ellie had been forced to stop trying to moderate Luke's behaviour thirty minutes ago.

'We'll talk about that later,' he'd said, with a hint of impatience at having to repeat himself so often. 'Stop worrying, Ellie—I've got this.' He leaned closer so that he could whisper in her ear. 'To tell you the truth, I haven't had this much fun in a very long time.'

The glint in his eyes told her that he meant what he said. The low growl of his voice so close to her ear that it tickled made Ellie feel as if something were melting deep inside her. The something that controlled the muscles in her legs, maybe? At least the need to sit down for a bit became a priority when Jamie helpfully decided that he was starving.

Which was hardly surprising. They'd been on a mission for hours now as Luke had helped her launch the sorting out process.

It had taken a bit of time for the bank to cancel the automatic debit for her rent, withdraw some of the remaining cash from her account and arrange for an emergency credit card that would be couriered to her in the next day or two. The police required a statement and she was able to tell them that yes, there had been a party going on in the apartment above her—on the floor where the fire had apparently started—and it *had* sounded a bit out of control. She was given information about emergency housing available through Social Services but it was in a part of the city that made her heart sink and Luke's face scrunch into that angry sort of scowl.

The insurance company had been sympathetic but warned that the process could be slow. And it was only her car that had been insured. Had she not been advised to take out insurance on her personal belongings?

And now, here they were, in the Baby Supermarket and the sales girls had all fallen under Luke's spell the moment he smiled at them.

'We have a little problem,' he'd told them. 'I don't know if you heard about the big fire on the North Shore last night but little Jamie here has been left with nothing but the nappies we picked up last night. We kind of need…*everything.*'

It seemed as if every staff member this huge shop employed had wanted to be part of the most exciting cause to have ever come through their doors. Even the manager had come to see what was going on.

'We'll give you the best discount we can manage,' he told Luke. 'And then take another ten per cent off on top of that. It's the least we can do to help. My word… I saw that fire on the news this morning. Wasn't there a fatality? It must have been terrifying for you both.'

If Luke had noticed the assumption that was being made, he didn't try and correct it. Maybe because he seemed to be fascinated by how much was clearly essential for looking after a tiny baby.

'A change table—so that's what this is?'

'Fully washable surface.' A girl with bright red streaks in her hair was clearly delighted to have captured Luke's attention. 'There's the shelves here to keep supplies like nappies and towels and these drawers are for creams and wipes. And look…the top is really a lid that covers where the bath clips in.'

'Do you like it?' Luke asked Ellie.

She was already a bit stunned by what was going on. 'It's amazing. But, Luke, I—'

'We'll take it,' Luke said. 'What's next?'

The bassinet, apparently. And bedding. A state-of-the-art car seat. A front pack and baby sling. They were nowhere near the numerous aisles stacked with cloth nappies and clothing and toys but Jamie's cries were getting louder.

'Let me show you our mothers' area.' A senior staff member smiled at Ellie. 'Here at the Baby Supermarket, we pride ourselves on making our mothers and babies feel right at home. Are you breastfeeding, dear?'

Ellie nodded.

'Then come with me. We have change facilities and a private feeding room. There's a rocking chair in there that is unbelievably comfortable.' Her glance slid back towards Luke as she led Ellie away. 'It's on special, too, with a twenty-five per cent discount—just for today…'

It was a good thing that Luke didn't follow her because he would probably have added one of these chairs to the scary pile of purchases being piled up near one of the check-out counters.

Even the soothing motion of the rocking chair couldn't stop Ellie's level of anxiety rising as she took the time necessary to feed Jamie. This shopping spree was going to cost hundreds, if not thousands of dollars. How on earth could she possibly pay him back when she wasn't even working again yet?

And, given the helpful advice of all those attractive

young women, just how crazy was Luke going to go in the clothing aisles?

Judging by the large bags that were being packed by the time she emerged from the mothers and babies' retreat, he hadn't held back. And when had he added that pushchair to the pile? It wasn't even an ordinary pushchair. It was one of those expensive three-wheeled mountain buggies that Ellie would never have dreamed of budgeting for.

He'd already paid for everything, too. And the manager was practically rubbing his hands together.

'We can offer free and immediate delivery.'

'That won't be necessary. I've got a Jeep out in the car park. I'm sure we can pack it all in the back.'

Jamie's return distracted the cluster of people around the check-out counter.

'He's so *cute*…' the girls cooed.

Even the most senior woman was looking misty-eyed. She looked from Jamie to Ellie and then Luke.

'He looks just like his daddy,' she said. 'You must be so proud of him.'

For just a heartbeat, Ellie let herself imagine what it would be like if Luke were actually Jamie's father and they'd been here as a family.

Pure fantasy but it was a beautiful thing…

Until Luke's mouth opened and then closed again as his gaze flicked to meet Ellie's. She could see the flash of something like horror as he finally caught on to the assumption everyone had made when they'd arrived here as a couple with their new born baby.

Was he going to tell everyone here that Jamie wasn't his child? That Ellie was nothing more than an acquaintance from long ago? A bus buddy? Maybe he didn't need to say anything. He was looking, for all the world, as if the idea of having a family of his own could possibly be his worst nightmare.

But nobody else had seen what she'd seen and he didn't say anything out loud to shatter the illusion. He seemed as stunned as Ellie had been when this mammoth spend-up had gained momentum.

'We'd better get going,' was all he said. 'Can we get some help taking this lot out to the car park, please?'

Sorting the jigsaw of fitting everything into the back of his Jeep was almost enough to distract Luke from what had just happened.

Almost…

He could understand why it had happened. He and Ellie were pretty much the same age and they were out with a brand-new baby. He hadn't been unaware of the looks he was getting from all the girls and, on some level, maybe he'd known he could enjoy the attention because they assumed he was unavailable and nobody was going to take any flirting the wrong way. To top it off, like a good, old-fashioned husband, he had handed over his credit card and paid for everything.

And then Ellie had come back, with Jamie asleep in her arms looking like an advertisement for a perfect baby and the look on her face as everybody cooed over Jamie had been…

So proud. So full of love…

He'd been watching them, caught up in the moment of admiring this recent addition to the human race, so that comment that put him into a pair of new father's shoes had blindsided him.

Just for a heartbeat, he had known what it would feel like. To have a partner as gorgeous as Ellie and a baby they had created together. A baby he *did* feel absurdly proud of for that split second. And it had felt...

Amazing.

Like the best thing that could happen to anyone. Ever.

It also felt as if one of the foundation stones he'd built his life on had just been blown up and disintegrated from beneath his feet and he was in grave danger of falling into a place that had never even been an option to visit.

Doing something practical, like loading the ridiculous amount of stuff he'd just purchased into his vehicle, was exactly what he needed to climb back into a safe emotional space. He had checked another thing off the list that was sorting out the disaster that Ellie had found herself in.

He was fixing things.

'Next stop, North Shore General,' he said, climbing into the driver's seat. 'We'll drop off that ambulance blanket and car seat.'

The silence in the car started to feel a little awkward. Was Ellie also thinking about that assumption the staff of the Baby Supermarket had made?

Had she—even for that tiny moment of time—thought about what it would be like if it *had* been true?

Something like alarm prickled in Luke's spine. He'd already overstepped a boundary or two becoming involved with someone who had actually been his patient. Okay, it was a grey area because, although Ellie was on leave, they were, theoretically, colleagues in the same department. And they had a childhood connection even though that was a bit distant. Some boundaries, however, had to be identified.

He couldn't let her imagine that he was offering anything more than the practical assistance that someone in trouble was in need of. And yeah...he was going a bit above and beyond and that was his own fault but he had saved this baby's life, after all. Even if nobody knew about his own start in life, they wouldn't be surprised that this little boy had touched his heart in a special way.

But it seemed as if something entirely different was bothering Ellie.

'I'll pay you back,' she said, finally. 'Every cent. With interest, even.'

'That's not necessary.'

She shook her head. 'Of course it is. You've already done far more than most people would for someone they barely know.'

Luke said nothing. This was good. Ellie was setting some boundaries herself and declaring them to be almost strangers. He should feel relieved.

So why did he feel kind of…disappointed?

'It might take a wee while, though. I hope that won't be a problem.'

Luke shook his head. Of course it wasn't a problem.

'I'm not sure how soon I can get back to work,' Ellie continued. 'I'll have to find good childcare.' Something like a huff of laughter broke her words. 'Good grief… I'll have to find somewhere to live, first…'

'There's no rush,' Luke heard himself saying. 'You're welcome to stay at my place for a few days if it's not too far out of town.'

A voice in the back of his head was making incredulous noises. Reminding him that he'd been relieved that he'd only have to ignore any attraction to this woman for one night. What did he think he was doing?

'Really?' Ellie sounded astonished. 'That would be *awesome*. And the insurance company said they'd approve a rental car so the distance wouldn't matter. I could still get out to view places.'

They wouldn't be spending that much time together, would they? Ellie would be out hunting for a new apartment. He'd be at work a lot of the time.

All he needed now was to firm up those boundaries—for both their sakes.

'And don't worry about paying me back for the baby stuff.' He kept his gaze firmly on the task of locating his designated space on the far side of the North Shore General's car park. 'It sounds like I'm going to get a lot more than I expected when the property sells. I don't have any dependants and I don't intend to get saddled with any, either. Consider it a gift.'

Easing the big vehicle to a stop between the designated lines, he turned his head to offer a smile that would confirm that it was no big deal. That he could afford it easily enough for it to mean virtually nothing.

To his surprise, Ellie was scowling at him. She looked…as disappointed as he'd been when she'd declared them to be no more than strangers?

'I asked for your help,' she said quietly. 'Not charity.'

It was another awkward moment, during which Luke realised how patronising he must have sounded. No wonder Ellie was on the defensive. That flash of anger in her eyes suggested that she would fight for her independence with the same kind of passion that she would use to protect her son.

He had to respect that…

And he needed to apologise.

Luke opened his mouth to do exactly that but, before he could say a word, another sound was heard.

A shriek of extreme pain.

They were still staring at each other so Luke could see the way they both dismissed any thoughts of anything personal. The professional switch had been flipped at precisely the same instant.

'Oh, my God…' Ellie breathed. 'That sounds like a child.'

Luke had his door open already. 'Where did it come from?'

Ellie was out of the car now, too. 'There…look…'

Almost opposite them, a car had stopped at an angle that cut across two parking spaces. The driver's door was open. So was one of the back doors. A woman was reaching into the car and another shriek split the air.

'*Nooo*… Don't *touch*…'

'I have to, darling… I'm *sorry*…' The woman sounded nearly as upset as the child.

'*Nooo*…' The shrieks increased in volume. This child was clearly terrified.

Jamie was still sound asleep in his flash, new car seat. Leaving the door open would mean that Ellie could hear him the moment he woke and the vehicle the screaming was coming from was only a few metres away. She didn't hesitate to follow Luke.

'What's wrong?' she heard him ask the woman. 'I'm one of the doctors from the emergency department.' A quick glance over his shoulder told him that Ellie was right behind him. 'And this is Ellie, one of our nurses.'

'It's Mia—my daughter.' The woman straightened, turning to face Luke. 'We were at the park and she fell out of a tree.' She tried, and failed, to stop her face crumpling and a sob emerging. 'There's something wrong with her arm. I think she's broken it.'

'How high was the tree? And did you see how she landed? Did she hit her head as well?'

Ellie stepped past them, as the mother was answering

Luke's questions, into the small gap by the open door. She crouched down so that her head was a little lower than the girl, who had subsided into quieter sobs now that no one was threatening to touch her.

'Hey, Mia… I'm Ellie.'

'Go away…'

'I like your shoes.' Ellie made it sound as if the sneakers were the most exciting thing she'd seen all day. 'Are they the ones that have the sparkly lights when you walk?'

Mia said nothing. She was still glaring at Ellie suspiciously.

'I want a pair of those.' Ellie sighed. 'But they don't make them for big girls like me. How old are you, Mia? Four?'

'No.' Mia was offended enough to be distracted from her fears. 'I'm *five.*'

'Wow…you're going to school already?'

Mia nodded proudly and Ellie smiled at her. She let her gaze slide down as she did so, though. The little girl had one arm cradled against her chest and she was using her other hand to hold it still. Ellie could see the unusual shape of the small elbow on the injured side. She could also see the colour of the hand below it.

'Oh…look at your nail polish… What a pretty colour. I *love* pink… It's my absolutely favourite colour.'

Mia was thoroughly distracted now. She actually smiled at Ellie. 'Me, too.'

She hadn't minded Ellie's gentle touch on the fingers of her uninjured hand as she put her own fingers beneath it to admire the nail polish. She was even more careful as she slipped her fingers beneath those on Mia's injured side.

'Can you move these fingers, darling? I want to see how pink they are.'

Mia shook her head.

'Because it hurts?'

It was a slow nod, this time.

'But it doesn't hurt so much if you keep your arm very still?'

Another nod.

Ellie nodded. And then she raised her eyebrows. 'Did you know…that if a little girl has broken her arm…when the doctors and nurses fix it, she can choose a pink cast to wear for weeks and weeks?' Then Ellie shook her head. 'But I guess you might choose a green one.'

'*Nooo*… I want *pink*…'

Ellie put her thoughtful face on. 'Hmm…but you'd have to get out of the car and come to where they make the pink casts.'

Mia's face crumpled.

'Tell you what…' Ellie was looking around the car. 'Is that your jacket? The pink one?'

Mia nodded.

'If I put it very carefully behind you, I could tie the sleeves over the front and that would keep your arm very, very still while we get you out of the car. And if Dr Luke lifts you, you won't have to move at all and it won't hurt more than a little bit.'

Mia started to shake her head but then paused for long enough for Ellie to smile at her again.

'He'll take you to the pink cast place,' she whispered, as if it were a secret.

Mia was still hesitating but Ellie knew they were running out of time. 'What say I make the jacket bandage? And, when that makes you feel better, you can tell us when you're ready to come out of the car.'

She didn't give her time to think about it, already threading one sleeve of the jacket behind the little girl's back and then pulling the puffy fabric through. She kept one sleeve at waist level and pulled the other one up to drape over the shoulder on the uninjured side. And then she made sure there was as much padding as possible around the elbow and pulled the sleeves tightly together and tied them in a firm knot. The injured arm was completely immobile and Mia had done nothing more than whimper a little bit.

It was only then that Ellie straightened, to find Mia's mother and Luke had stopped talking and had been watching her—maybe for all of the few minutes it had taken to get Mia ready to be moved.

She stepped closer to Luke and turned her head so that she could speak very quietly, right beside his ear.

'Looks like a fracture dislocation of her left elbow,' she murmured. 'Limb baselines are well down. No movement in her hand and it feels cold. I don't like the colour, either.'

His gaze met hers. A brief eye contact but, like the moment they'd both heard the child scream, she knew they were both thinking exactly the same thing. This injury needed to be sorted urgently or Mia might end up with reduced function in her hand. This wasn't the place to try and put in an IV and administer pain relieving drugs. It could be done far more efficiently and safely once she was in the emergency department.

It was Luke's turn to crouch beside the car.

He had to get this child out no matter how much she resisted but, if she struggled, it could well make her injury worse. A broken shard of bone could sever a nerve or a major blood vessel.

He had watched the way Mia had calmed a terrified little girl with a skill that had taken his breath away. Had made something in his gut feel all soft and told him that she was going to be the best mother that Jamie could ever wish for.

All he needed to do now was to follow her example.

'I need you to pretend to be a caterpillar,' he told Mia. 'And you're inside your cocoon getting ready to be a butterfly so you can't move your legs or your arms. Can you do that, sweetheart?'

Big, brown eyes flicked upwards. Was she looking for her mother? Or Mia?

'I'm here, darling,' her mother said. 'I'll be right beside you.'

'You're a pink caterpillar,' Ellie said softly. 'And you're bee-*yoo*-tiful.'

Luke used the distraction to slip one arm behind Mia and the other beneath her knees. On the middle syllable of Ellie's elongated word, he lifted Mia and stepped backwards in a smooth movement but the little girl still screamed in fright.

Luke held her close, careful to avoid any contact with the injured elbow. The splint Ellie had fashioned from the puffer jacket was remarkably good and the elbow was supported as well as it could have been with the kind of inflatable splints or other gear the ambulance service might have used. Having never worked with Ellie, he had been blown away, not only by her skill in winning the trust of a young patient, but her confidence in making an initial diagnosis and initiating the first level of treatment.

To say he had been impressed was an understatement...

Luke was confident that moving Mia hadn't significantly increased her pain level and, sure enough, the child relaxed into his firm hold and became quiet.

'Follow me,' he told the mother. 'I know the quick way into ED.'

Walking past his own car, he noted the open door beside Jamie and glanced over his shoulder at Ellie.

'I'll come too,' she said. 'I'll just get Jamie and the extra car seat and blanket.'

Knowing that Ellie would be following made it feel curiously different, heading into the hospital through the staff only door that gave rapid access to the interior of the emergency department, bypassing the waiting room and triage desks. He almost waited at the door, knowing that Ellie wouldn't have her staff swipe card she would need to open it with her, but the sense of urgency overrode the urge. This little girl had, unexpectedly, become his patient and she was his priority.

No...not just his patient.

His and Ellie's.

And that just made it all the more important to make sure Mia got the best treatment possible.

He'd only been working in this department for a little over a month but Luke was very proud of the response he got, walking in with this injured child in his arms. The treatment was all he could have wished for. A nurse applied an anaesthetic patch to Mia's arm within seconds of him putting her gently down on a bed and a fellow consultant was able to insert an IV line with minimal distress a few minutes later. X-rays were taken and an orthopaedic consultant arrived as the images became available on the computer screen.

Ellie had been correct in her diagnosis. The elbow was both fractured and displaced and the blood and nerve supply to Mia's hand was severely compromised. Thanks to the IV line, enough sedation was easily administered to make the process of relocating the joint and stabilising the fracture swift and completely satisfactory. And Ellie was there, with Jamie in her arms, as Mia blinked sleepily at the bright pink cast that covered her whole arm, keeping her elbow in the bent position it needed to heal.

'Oh…' Ellie pretended to shade her eyes from a blinding light. 'That is *so* pink. I love it.' She touched Mia's forehead, smoothing away an errant tress of red hair, as she smiled. 'Do you feel better now, hon?'

Mia's smile was all the response needed. Her mother was smiling, too.

'I can't thank you enough,' she said. 'I don't know what I would have done if you two hadn't found me.'

'It was our pleasure,' Luke said. 'Wasn't it, Ellie?'

'Sure was.'

Ellie's smile lit up her face and Luke's heart gave a curious little extra thump. He'd suspected that she was missing her job and now he realised not only how much she loved it but how good at it she was.

He could imagine what it would be like to work with her properly. To be on a difficult shift here and know that he had someone like Ellie by his side. Someone he could rely on absolutely. A second pair of hands that belonged to someone who seemed to think along exactly the same lines he did.

She wouldn't be a vulnerable young mother, would she? She would be a trusted colleague.

An equal.

How easy would it be to dismiss an attraction that seemed to be getting stronger with everything Ellie did stirring up feelings of admiration? Pride, even.

No. Luke turned away from that smile to say goodbye to Mia and her mother. It wouldn't make any difference because he wouldn't have allowed himself to act on that attraction. He wasn't even going to be in the country in a couple of months and, in the same way he knew how much Ellie loved her work as an emergency department nurse, he also instinctively knew that she wasn't the type to embark on a relationship that wasn't going anywhere.

The hints of the passion she had displayed to protect her child and keep her independence told him that Ellie Thomas was the type of woman who would fall in love and be just as passionate about being a loving and loyal partner.

The guy that won that love would be the luckiest man on earth. The image of Ellie standing there with her baby in her arms was still in his head even though she was behind him. That unknown man would not only win the love of an extraordinary woman but he would get the bonus of a beautiful baby son.

He'd better love him, Luke thought fiercely. As if he were his own. And he'd better know exactly how lucky he was and protect both Jamie and Ellie as if his own life depended on it.

He would…

In some ways, it was a damn shame he couldn't be that man but that was how it was.

And, with that reminder, Luke felt a surge of relief that that foundation stone had somehow miraculously put itself back together after the alarming moment in the Baby Supermarket.

He knew exactly what he wanted from life and a family had never been in the plan.

And never would be.

CHAPTER SIX

'THIS IS MORE like afternoon tea than lunch. You must be starving.'

'I kind of forget about eating when I'm busy. It's been quite a day so far, hasn't it? Oh, wow…that looks amazing.'

Ellie felt quietly pleased with herself. The last stop on the way home had been a quick dash through a supermarket and she'd put this lunch together. Mini baguettes stuffed with fresh slices of tomato, mozzarella cheese and basil leaves, drizzled with olive oil. She was having a tall glass of sparkling mineral water with a slice of lime but Luke had chosen an icy Mexican lager and had stuffed a wedge of lime down the neck of the bottle.

'It's my day off,' he'd said, leaning past where Ellie was busy at the kitchen bench putting lunch together to open the fridge. 'I reckon I've earned a reward.'

Even without a celebratory drink, this was a reward for Ellie, too.

They were sitting outside the kitchen on the overgrown terrace. The table beneath the canopy of a rampant grapevine was shaded from the surprising warmth of the autumn sunshine and Jamie was also in the shade, asleep inside the mountain buggy pushchair that went flat enough to be a pram as well.

For a long while, they ate in silence.

Nothing had ever tasted quite so delicious and Ellie couldn't think of anyone she would rather be sharing this food with.

Covert glances became more frequent. There was something profoundly satisfying watching a man taking such obvious enjoyment from food you had prepared. She loved the way Luke closed his eyes as he savoured his first mouthful and the way he wiped his mouth with the ball of his thumb to remove an errant crumb or drops of moisture the neck of his beer bottle had left behind.

When Luke had reached behind her to get at the fridge, his arm had brushed close enough to her back to give her a shiver that felt as if it could turn into goose bumps. Every glance she allowed herself now could bring back that little shiver that started somewhere in her spine and then sent tiny forks of lightning deep into her belly.

And they were as delicious as their meal and this perfectly peaceful, idyllic setting. The silence didn't feel at all awkward. It felt completely comfortable—as if she and Luke knew each other well enough to simply relax in each other's company.

It wasn't exactly silent at all, Ellie realised, then. She could hear the hum of bees amongst the wash of lavender flowers that were so thick and heavy, the old hedge was obscuring the stone path leading away from this courtyard. And the birds on the edges of the forest nearby… It was a long time since Ellie had heard the distinctive call and clicks of the native tui. She recognised the cheerful background song of wax eyes, and she would have known the squeak of her favourites—fantails—even if she hadn't noticed them sharing the insect life with the wax eyes amongst the bunches of grapes weighing down the vines above them.

'Do the fantails come into the house?' she asked. 'They used to do that all the time when I was a kid.'

'I haven't noticed.' Luke took a swig of his beer and gave Ellie another shiver as he brushed his lower lip with his thumb. 'But you're right. I remember them doing that, too.'

'My mother told me that there's a Maori myth that they're messengers from the spirit world and they bring death or news of death.' Ellie shook her head. 'I never believed it. They're such happy, friendly little birds.'

Luke grinned. 'So you're going to rewrite the myth to give them a positive spin?'

Oh…that smile… It made the day even brighter. And the warmth in those astonishing hazel eyes made this tiny patch of the world even more of a blissful oasis. Ellie knew she was in trouble, here.

Last night, she had been able to dismiss the pull she felt towards this man as a product of emotional overload following a traumatic experience heightened by exhaustion. But she'd had enough sleep to revive her and her immediate future was looking less worrying by the hour. Luke had even told her she didn't have to rush into finding a new place to live.

The thought of spending more time with Luke—like this—was…

A dream come true?

It wasn't just the remnants of a teenaged crush. Or that she had felt as if she was coming home in returning to Kauri Valley. Okay, both those things had probably contributed and sped the process up but there was something much bigger than that going on, here.

In that split second of holding Luke's gaze as she basked in that smile, Ellie felt something so astonishing it took her breath away.

Something that felt like a combination of liquid and light. As if it could trickle into all the gaps and cracks in her life—and her heart—and light up the fact that they had been made whole.

Oh, boy…she really was in trouble. This was way more than physical attraction. And if Luke guessed even a fraction of what was going on in her head and heart, he would think she was completely crazy and run for the hills.

Amazing how such a revelation could happen in the blink of an eye but Ellie knew she'd held his gaze long enough to give it significance, so she shrugged as she looked away, to make the eye contact as unimportant as her dismissal of a sombre myth.

'Why not? Enough bad things happen in life without looking for signs of them before they arrive.'

'True. We're both used to seeing what life can throw at people. They get carried through the doors of emergency departments every day.'

Ellie nodded. 'I had a good catch up with Sue while you were helping to sort Mia's elbow. She told me about that baby with whooping cough last night.'

Luke stopped eating. His eyes widened with what looked like dismay. 'Oh, man… I should have told you about that myself.'

'Sue said it was you who thought of it—that it wouldn't have occurred to her to worry about whether I'd had a booster or not. I have, by the way. And he's only two weeks away from getting his own vaccination.'

'And I had a booster when I was doing that obstetric stint. Just to be on the safe side.'

Satisfied, Luke turned his attention back to his meal but Ellie's attention had drifted.

It had given her an odd frisson, knowing that Luke had been thinking of her without any prompting. Sue had been just as surprised. And then her friend had been completely blown away by the knowledge that Ellie was staying with Luke.

'He's gorgeous,' she had whispered, keeping her voice down even though they were alone in the staff room. *'I certainly wouldn't have said no to an invitation like that.'*

'We're just friends,' Ellie had whispered back. *'But you should see his house. It's actually got a turret. Like something out of a fairy tale.'*

'Wow... I'd love to see it. Can I come and visit?'

'Don't see why not. Some time when Luke's at work, maybe. Text me.'

It wasn't the only thing about this situation that felt like magic. Luke had come to rescuc her like the impossibly handsome hero of the story. A prince, even, seeing as his house had a turret like a tiny castle. She had been showered with gifts. And now they were having a small feast in the most romantic of settings. What would happen next? Would Luke push his plate away and take hold of her hands and declare his undying love?

Things like that did happen in fairy tales, didn't they? Love at first sight that everyone knew would last for a lifetime...

Oh, boy...it was high time Ellie got back in touch with reality. Her gaze drifted to the path obscured by the neglected lavender hedge.

'Where does that path go?'

'Through Mum's rose garden and down to the vege table garden and then into the orchard. Or what was the vegetable garden. Judging by the state of the rest of the garden, I expect it's disappeared.'

'We had a veggie garden.' This was good. Normal, friendly conversation. Ellie could try and cover up the lingering shockwaves of that revelation. For her own sake more than Luke's, in fact. He wouldn't need to run for the hills, would he? He wasn't even going to be here for more than another couple of months. However huge this discovery felt, nothing was going to come from it.

'It used to be a chore to have to go and pick all the beans or peas for dinner.' Did Luke notice that her cheerful tone was a little forced? 'Or dig up some carrots or potatoes but when I look back, it was an amazingly healthy diet.'

'Mmm.' Luke was reaching for another bread roll seemingly as relaxed as he had been. Thank goodness telepathy didn't actually happen. 'I still have fond memories of the food Mum used to make. Wonderful casseroles that had been in the oven for hours and baked potatoes with crispy skins. I'd get home from school on a cold winter's day and the smell would hit me as soon as I walked through the door.' His smile was poignant. 'It smelt like home...'

Jamie stirred and whimpered—an oddly appropriate response to the note of sadness in Luke's voice. Ellie got up to take hold of the pushchair's handles so she could move it gently back and forth.

Her heart was being squeezed painfully from that note in his voice. This place was still his home but either he didn't realise that or he had no intention of staying here because it was too difficult for some reason. Because it meant too much? In either case, he was going to run away from it. To some huge city like London or Boston where it would take hours to fight your way through traffic and find a bit of countryside or a beach that would remind him of home.

How sad was that?

Ellie suppressed a sigh. 'I wonder how many kids get to eat food from their own gardens like that these days.'

'They probably still do around here.'

Ellie tossed a smile over her shoulder. 'It was a great place to grow up, wasn't it? Do you remember sliding down those huge sand dunes at the beach?'

'Using rubbish bags as toboggans?' The glint of remembered pleasure lit up Luke's face. 'Yeah… Surfing was even more exciting, though.'

'We never surfed. But we had a friend with a pony. She used to let us have a go down on the beach. I galloped once…bareback. Now, that was exciting…'

We. It was still automatic to include Ava in those childhood and adolescent memories. It was Ellie's turn to feel the sad whisper of loss. Maybe it wasn't so incomprehensible that Luke would want to put as much distance as possible between his current life and his childhood memories.

She searched for something positive to chase away the negative pull. What had started this trip down memory lane, anyway?

That was right…food…

'I'm going to try and find a place to rent that has enough space for a veggie garden,' she declared. 'I'd like Jamie's first food to be stuff that I've grown myself.'

'Sounds like a great idea. A house instead of an apartment, maybe.'

Ellie shook her head. 'Houses are out of my price range.'

The wheels of the pushchair caught on a particularly large weed growing in the crack between two big stones. She stooped and pulled at it, surprised to find how easily it came up. It seemed as if the stones had sand between them rather than soil. She pulled at another one and it slid out with a satisfyingly long set of roots still intact.

'Are you okay for money?' Luke asked quietly.

Ellie bristled. He'd already provided far too much and tried to wave off her offer of repayment. What was it he'd said?

Oh, yeah...

That he had no dependants and didn't intend to 'get saddled' with any...

She'd been right this morning, hadn't she, when she'd interpreted that look on his face as advertising that a family of his own would be his worst nightmare?

This oasis of peaceful countryside on a sunny afternoon suddenly seemed a lot less blissful with that cold shower of reality doing a good job of extinguishing the glow of any powerful emotions Ellie had been experiencing.

Jamie had settled again so there was no need to keep rocking the pushchair. Ellie took another step away from where Luke was still enjoying his late lunch and swooped on another patch of weeds. There was something almost soothing in ripping up these invaders and tossing them aside.

'I'll be fine,' she muttered, finally, in response to Luke's query about her finances. No way was she going to confess how tough things were. She'd had a big student loan to pay off and she hadn't hesitated to help out during the years of her mother's terminal illness.

She summoned a confident tone. 'I'm thinking that Jamie will be old enough to go in child care by the time he's three months old and that's only eight weeks or so away.'

Really? The last few weeks had gone so fast. How hard would it be to hand over the care of this precious baby to people she didn't even know?

Ellie pulled at more weeds, trying to focus on them as she blinked back the threat of tears.

'Wow...' The admiration in Luke's voice broke the new silence. 'Look at what you've done. I'd forgotten what this area even looked like.'

Ellie straightened. She had cleared a surprisingly big patch of the stone paving. And it did look great. The stone had the same grey-blue tinge of the kitchen's slate floor. If it was all cleared and swept, with the French doors wide open as they were now, it would make an almost seamless extension of the house into the garden. Indoor, outdoor flow. That was something real estate agents got excited about.

'I'll finish it,' she said. 'And I can trim that lavender hedge, too, if you've got some tools.'

'You don't have to do that. I'm going to find a landscaping firm to come in.'

'You said they were expensive. And hard to find.' Ellie looked up at the grape vine, which would need heavy pruning soon, and then at the tangle of rose bushes behind the lavender hedge. She thought about the neglected vegetable garden that she hadn't seen yet. And then she grinned at Luke.

'I could do it,' she said.

'Do what?'

'Sort your garden out. As thanks for letting me stay.'

Luke shook his head. 'It's too big a job. And you've got more important things to do—like finding a new place to live.'

But he'd said there was no rush about that. If she was doing a good job with the garden, maybe he'd be happy for her to be around a bit longer, even.

'I'd enjoy it. I'll be doing most of my flat-hunting on-line, anyway, and I'd love the chance to be doing something outside when Jamie's asleep. I've been living in a bedsit for so long. Being here...' Ellie stretched out her arms to encompass the rambling, old house and the courtyard and gardens beyond. 'This makes it seem like it was even more of a prison than it felt like sometimes.'

The idea was brilliant. She would love the challenge and the physical exercise would help her get her body back into shape. It was just a bonus that it would be a reason to stay near Luke a bit longer.

Wasn't it?

But Luke was still looking more than a little doubtful. Ellie stepped towards him.

'Please?' Suddenly this was very, very important. She didn't want to leave this place.

Not yet, anyway.

She summoned what she hoped was her best, winning smile, catching her bottom lip between her teeth when it felt a bit too much.

'You've done so much to help me. I'd really like to be able to do something for you…'

CHAPTER SEVEN

No MAN ALIVE could have resisted that smile.

Not with that kicker of vulnerability that biting her lip like that advertised.

It wasn't relief that Luke was feeling.

Okay, it *was* relief but it wasn't due to the realisation that Ellie wasn't going to disappear out of his life just yet. It was because she'd have enough time to find a perfect place to go to and then he could stop worrying about both her future and Jamie's. Expecting her to disappear in a few days was ridiculous.

She not only had to find new accommodation but probably furnish it as well.

She also had to sort out her transport issues by collecting that rental car and had she not realised how short of clothes she was? She was still wearing the same tee shirt she'd had on last night when he'd rescued them and, right now, it was getting rapidly filthier. His, albeit reluctant, agreement to her plan had apparently triggered a level of excitement that had her exploring more of the garden—pulling up the closest and biggest weeds that came to hand. What had been a largely white tee shirt with a bird and some heart-shaped spots was now streaked with green plant juice and smudges of dirt.

Swallowing the last bite of those delicious rolls Ellie

had put together, Luke wiped his mouth and had to shake his head as she pushed her way back through the rampant lavender bushes.

'I'll find you a clean tee shirt,' he offered. 'I've got plenty, as long as you don't mind black.'

Ellie looked down at herself and groaned. 'I didn't even think about that. I'd better put some clothes shopping at the top of the list after I sort out that rental car tomorrow.'

She came closer and peered into the pushchair at Jamie. Her hair had a small, leafy twig caught in it and Luke just couldn't stop himself reaching out. Ellie jumped as he touched her head.

'Keep still. You've got something caught in your hair.'

Ellie kept very, very still as he carefully disentangled it. She also kept her gaze very firmly on her baby so it was weird that this suddenly felt so…intimate?

'There you go.' He held out the twig to show her. 'You might want to wear a hat if you're really going to take on a job as a gardener. And some gloves…' He felt his gut twist as he noticed a scratch on her arm, deep enough to be oozing blood.

How ridiculous was that? He saw people bleeding all the time. Life-threatening amounts of bleeding, come to that, and he never felt anything like this. As if the damage had been done to his own skin.

'I'll add stuff like that to my list.' Ellie nodded briskly and her businesslike tone was exactly what Luke needed to make things feel normal again. And then she lifted her gaze to meet his and her smile made things even better. There was a familiarity there that only came with friendship. The kind of friendship where it was safe to relax because the people involved liked each other.

Trusted each other.

Genuine friendship was the best thing in life as far as Luke was concerned. Something to be valued enormously. Definitely not something to sabotage by letting physical attraction get out of control. To have both at the same time had proved incompatible more than once in his life because those women always wanted more.

Too much.

They wanted long term commitment. Babies…

'I could drop you in to the rental car place tomorrow, if you like. It'll be early, though—I'm switching to day shift for a while.'

'Brilliant. Thanks, Luke. And…um…' The glance she gave him was uncertain.

'What?'

'Well… Jamie looks like he's going to sleep a bit longer and I… I *really* need a shower. I could put him in the bathroom with me, but he might wake up if I move him and…'

Luke waved his hand. He could do this for a friend. 'Go. It's fine. He can stay here while I clear up lunch. It's no problem.'

Jamie wasn't the problem, he decided, as he ferried the plates and glasses back to the kitchen bench. What was a bit of a problem was that he could hear the water running in the bathroom down the hall. And his mind refused to stop picturing Ellie in there.

Naked.

Covered with soap suds.

Friends did not think about each other like that. Or, if they did, it didn't generate a fierce tingle of desire.

This wasn't going to be easy. It might even prove to be the biggest challenge Luke had ever faced.

But maybe that was a good thing? If nothing else, it could override the challenge that walking away from this place for ever was going to present. And he had to walk away because there was nothing here for him any more except ghosts from a past that could stop him embracing the future he had planned.

Jamie woke up and let out a squawk that demanded attention. Luke held the handle of the pushchair and rocked it back and forth, the way he'd seen Ellie doing earlier.

It didn't even occur to him to pick the baby up. Comforting babies was not in his skill set. He was quite happy to deliver them or to examine and treat them when they were sick or injured. He could even tickle their tummies and make them smile occasionally but to pick them up and cuddle them?

No way. He avoided that like the plague.

Okay, he had picked Jamie up once but that had been because it had been too painful for Ellie to move much on that first night. It wasn't as though he'd done it because he wanted to hold a baby himself.

It was just as well he hadn't ever wanted a family of his own, wasn't it?

He didn't actually *like* babies when they weren't presenting an interesting medical challenge.

Even Jamie? Even when he'd experienced that very odd moment of connection in the first minutes of this new life? A connection that had made holding him that first night feel different from any other infant he'd ever touched? He hadn't put him down in a hurry, had he? Even when he'd stopped crying…

Luke joggled the pushchair in addition to its horizontal movement.

Especially Jamie, he decided. That was one boundary he had no intention of being forced to break. And that was a challenge that he knew would be no problem at all to meet.

* * *

It wasn't just the change in working hours that made Luke's life so different over the next week.

He'd always chosen to live alone as an adult. Because he liked his own company and the independence of his own space.

For someone that didn't even like babies, this new arrangement should have been unbearable.

It was anything but...

He found himself looking forward to getting home at the end of the day. To grabbing a cold beer from the fridge and heading outside to admire the progress that Ellie was making. The courtyard had been cleared of weeds by the end of the first day. The lavender hedge had been clipped back the day after that and then Ellie had tackled the rose gardens, pruning bushes, pulling out weeds and uncovering an astonishing number of flowering plants that he'd had no idea were even there.

'I wanted to mow the lawns,' she told him. 'But they need something with more grunt than the lawnmower, at least for the first cut.'

'There should be a weed eater in the shed. That was one of my jobs, way back.'

'Yeah... I found that. But it's covered with cobwebs and I couldn't get it started.'

'I'll sort it on my next day off. We'll need some fresh two-stroke. The chainsaw will need that as well.'

Ellie's eyes lit up. 'You can use a chainsaw? That's awesome... There's a lot of branches that are too thick for the pruning shears. And you don't have a rotary hoe, by any chance, do you?'

'Don't think so. Why?'

'The veggie gardens are full of waist high weeds. It's going to be a big job.'

'Hmm… We'll take a look at that when there's more daylight.'

Did he really want to spend one of his precious days off working in a garden that wasn't even going to be his in the near future? It should have irritated the hell out of him.

But, strangely, it did nothing of the sort.

Watching the garden he remembered so well emerge from the neglected wilderness was a poignant kind of magic. His parents had loved this garden. It might have been a chore having to help with weed eating and mowing grass and clipping hedges when he was a teenager but it had been part of the only family life he'd ever had.

Making things good again now felt like paying homage to that part of his own story. The part that had made him the person he was now instead of what…a prison inmate?

Or dead?

Yeah…either of those outcomes had been a real possibility the way his life had been heading before the Gilmores had taken him in.

He'd fully expected that having someone else in his house would have disturbed him a lot more than it did. Maybe it was because it was helpful having someone around most of the time. He'd been able to get people in to mend the windows and those dodgy boards on the veranda and now had painters booked to come and redo the exterior of the house. And maybe it was more than acceptable because Ellie had taken it upon herself to cook dinner every evening.

He had no idea where she got the level of energy she had from. She was a new mother, for heaven's sake. Surely looking after the demands of an infant twenty-four hours a day was enough of a job? But Ellie seemed unstoppable. She had her own transport now and she'd even been out to view a couple of rental properties that had looked promising online—in between sessions in the garden, shopping for food and producing meals that meant Luke walked into a house that smelt as welcoming as this home had been to a starving teenager.

It felt…special.

Part of the paying homage thing?

Not that he was going to try and analyse those moments when something deep tugged at his heartstrings. He told himself that it was simply confirmation that this house needed a family. That he was right in having told Mike the real estate agent that this property was not going to be marketed as anything other than an idyllic family home. In telling his solicitor that he needed to do everything in his power to make sure that the distant cousin, Brian, couldn't make any claim on this land and use it as a development opportunity. Some progress was being made on the contesting of the will issue apparently but Mike was still ringing every other day to try and get the nod to start the marketing process.

'This is a property that needs to be marketed internationally. It takes time to book advertising space. Get a billboard made. Print brochures. At the very least we have to get the photo shoot done. I've got a guy with a drone who can do some spectacular aerial views. You won't even *see* any weeds in the gardens.'

That *had* been irritating. Luke had finally told him that he had to wait until the garden had been sorted before any photographs could be taken. It didn't matter that weeds wouldn't show up in aerial photographs. It was important to him that this place looked its absolute best.

If that meant rolling up his sleeves and getting his

hands dirty in the garden himself, then that was fine by him.

Like living here again, it would be a trip down memory lane. An opportunity to be thankful for the twist his life had taken all those years ago. A chance to say goodbye properly before he moved on?

Maybe the most disturbing thing about having Ellie here were the broken nights.

Not because his sleep was interrupted. He'd got more than used to that back in the days of being a junior doctor covering way too many night shifts. The cry of a hungry infant was no worse than a pager going off. A lot better, in fact, because he didn't have to get up. He could just roll over and go back to sleep.

The disturbing part was that he found himself lying there listening for the sound of Ellie's soothing voice. The sudden silence that meant she would be breastfeeding Jamie. It was easy to drift back to sleep then. What he couldn't control were the images of Ellie's breasts that haunted his dreams and meant waking, as often as not, in need of a cold shower to start his day.

But he was coping. Becoming more confident that he could meet a kind of physical challenge he'd never had to face before.

More than simply coping, in fact.

That it was Ellie Thomas he was sharing this time with was helping. They had shared memories of this area and the school they had both attended. They knew a lot of the same people. They had both stolen lollies from Mr Jenkins, for heaven's sake. And gone sliding down the same sand dunes. She was part of the past but would also be a link in the future when he no longer had a place to call home, here. She would be that link because they were developing that real friendship more convincingly every day and that friendship was making it a lot easier to resist the powerful physical attraction that he was plagued with.

He wanted to keep this friendship.

He wanted to keep in touch and hear about Jamie's milestones like his first tooth and first, wobbly steps. He wanted to see pictures of him blowing out candles on his birthday cakes and maybe a video clip of him jumping in puddles or kicking a ball. A proud smile on the first day of school...

He'd been there to feel the utter relief when this baby had taken his first breath and there would never be another child that he felt such a connection with.

Or another woman, for that matter.

Ellie had cooked a roast chicken for dinner tonight and the smell wafting through the house made Luke's mouth water. He headed straight for the kitchen. The French doors were open and Jamie's pram was positioned to catch the gentle warmth of the last sunbeams of the day. That light was also filtering through the grapevine outside, the dappled shadows shifting over the rustic table and long bench seats on either side, and dancing over the newly swept paving. Big terracotta urns had been freshly scrubbed, he noticed, and planted with bright red flowers. Geraniums?

He hadn't realised he'd spoken aloud until Ellie rewarded him with a quick grin.

'Wow...a man that can name a flower. I'm impressed. I picked them up when I went past the garden centre today. Do you like them?'

'It all looks fantastic out there. You've even started doing things out the front, haven't you? It was a lot easier to walk down the path.'

'I've started. There's some tree branches that will need your skill with the chainsaw when you finally get that day off. I've put them on the list.' The wiggle of Ellie's eyebrows suggested that the list was already quite long. 'You hungry yet?'

'Starving. Didn't have time to stop for lunch.'

'That's not good.' Ellie gave him a stern look. 'You need to build your strength up for your gardening gig.'

He found a beer and watched as Ellie took the chicken out of the oven and put it on a carving dish. Then she scooped crispy looking vegetables out of the roasting pan and put them into a big bowl. It was when she put the pan onto the stove top, clicked the gas flame into life and sprinkled flour into the pan that Luke felt another one of those tugs on his heart that was powerful enough to feel like pain.

Dorothy Gilmore used to do exactly that.

'Real gravy doesn't come out of a packet, son,' she'd say. *'It takes time. And love...'*

He had to step away from the memory. What would Ellie think if she looked up and saw tears in his eyes?

'So what else did you do today?'

'I got some more clothes. Look...*real* jeans...' Ellie left the wooden spoon against the edge of the pan as she held her arms out and did a quick pirouette.

Luke frowned. They looked like perfectly normal jeans as far as he could see. A denim casing for a pair of very nice legs and a particularly shapely bottom.

Ellie had seen his puzzled frown. 'They're not maternity jeans,' she explained. They don't have a stretchy insert to fit my enormous belly.' She patted that part of her anatomy. 'Still a bit squishy, I have to say, but it's definitely improving.'

'You've got nothing to worry about. You look amazing.'

The words came out before Luke had time to consider

any repercussions. Even if he had given it some thought, he wouldn't have expected the startled look in Ellie's eyes. Or the way time seemed to stop even as a flush of colour crept into her cheeks.

It was Ellie who broke that eye contact. So quickly he might have been able to convince himself that he hadn't seen what he thought he'd seen.

Except that wouldn't work, would it, because he recognised the intensity in that fleeting glance and he knew, beyond a shadow of doubt, that Ellie was experiencing the same level of physical attraction to him that he was grappling with in the other direction.

He was in trouble, here.

As if things hadn't been difficult enough when he thought that the attraction was one-sided.

Ellie was stirring gravy as if her life depended on making sure there were no lumps in it.

'Want to eat outside? It's not too cold yet.'

'Sure. I'll grab some plates.'

Outside would be good. Closing the doors might ramp up the sudden tension that seemed to be in the air.

What else could he do to try and defuse it?

Luke cleared his throat as Ellie put down the last platter of food on the table outside.

'Did you go and see that place in Takapuna you were telling me about last night?'

'Yeah…'

'No good?'

'No.' Ellie's sigh was heartfelt. 'The pictures didn't show that it was right on a main road and that the back garden was a junk yard. I actually *saw* a rat.'

'Good grief…'

'Not to worry. There are new places going up every day. I'll find something.'

She would. But as Luke closed his eyes in appreciation of that first mouthful of moist chicken smothered
in gravy, a sudden thought flashed in completely from
left field.

What about *this* place?

He could let her live here and care for it. It wasn't
as if he had to sell the place to survive financially. He
didn't even need the rent and the property would only
continue to grow in value, which would make it a fantastic investment.

Jamie would be safe. And he would grow up having
the kind of childhood that Luke had never had, right
from the start.

But…

Even the perfect crunch of the potatoes that gave way
to their smooth soft centres wasn't enough to slow the
out-of-control speed of Luke's train of thought. It was
inevitable that they were going to crash.

If he did that, he'd be tied. He would have a woman
and child depending on him.

He would be responsible for the safety and happiness
of others.

As if he had his own family…

'I had a call from my solicitor today.' He had told Ellie
about the problem Brian Gilmore had presented. 'The
will's been upheld and can't be contested. I'm free to put
the place on the market as soon as I'm ready.'

'Oh…' Ellie seemed to be concentrating on cutting
the food on her plate into very small pieces. She often
did that, he'd noticed, in case she ended up having to
feed Jamie and eat one-handedly. She didn't even look
up when she spoke.

'Just as well we're getting the garden in shape, then.

Not that it would make a difference. I'll bet the first person through will buy it.'

'It has to be the right person.' Luke was focusing on his plate now, too. Weird that one of his favourite meals wasn't tasting as good any more. 'A family.'

Or at least the promise of a family. Like a couple and their new born baby.

Like him and Ellie and Jamie?

Luke's fork clattered as he dropped it onto his plate.

'I'm going to get another beer. Do you want anything?'

Ellie shook her head. Her smile looked forced.

'No. I'm good.'

Luke pulled his phone from his pocket as he stood in front of the fridge. He pulled up Mike the real estate agent's number and tapped in a message.

Had the all-clear to put the property on the market. Drop over later this evening if you want to get the agency agreement signed.

He stared at the screen for a long, long moment.

And then he hit 'send'.

CHAPTER EIGHT

IT HAD ONLY taken as long as a single heartbeat but something huge had changed.

One glance…

Had Luke actually meant to give her that compliment on what he thought of her body shape?

Maybe not. Maybe he'd surprised himself and that was why, for that instant in time, he had dropped his guard and Ellie could see the blaze of desire in his eyes.

And, oh, my…she had felt it ignite an apparently endless supply of tinder-dry fuel in her own belly, the heat flooding her entire body. Even her face had probably ended up looking as if it would be possible to fry an egg on her cheeks.

Luke must have seen—and worse, understood—exactly what her response had been.

She'd thought initially that he would be horrified to know how attracted she was to him because he wouldn't be remotely interested in her in the same way. Now she knew that he was and yet he seemed to be just as appalled.

He'd put up what felt like an impenetrable barrier.

Starting the process of putting the house on the market had been the first sign of the distance being created.

A reminder that being together in the same house was a temporary situation.

On his day off, Luke had been more than willing to dust off the old tools in the garden shed and do whatever Ellie had asked. He'd cheerfully pruned back the larger branches that needed a chainsaw and spent hours attacking long grass, first with the weed-eater and then with the lawnmower. Ellie could only watch from a distance, often with Jamie in her arms, and wonder if he'd been this happy to spend his day working outside because it meant that he didn't need to be anywhere near her and conversation, for most of the day, was impossible due to the noise he was generating.

The sensation of a clock ticking to make sure she didn't forget how temporary this was increased when the team of painters arrived and put up scaffolding to work on the outside of the house. Visible changes were happening day by day as one week blended into the next.

Hidden changes were also happening as that barrier became thicker. Even eye contact seemed fraught now and best avoided. There was an elephant in the room that only seemed to be getting larger as they both avoided it so carefully. On the day that Ellie had her six-week postpartum check-up and the doctor told her cheerfully that she was fine to resume her normal sex-life, just being in the same room as Luke was enough to make her blush. She didn't dare risk eye contact. It was almost a blessing that Jamie was more grizzly than usual after his first vaccinations so he kept her fully occupied and, when he was finally settled, Ellie was too tired to do anything other than fall into bed herself.

Luke's impatience to get on with the rest of his life became clear as he spent evenings working on applications for new positions and sent them off to London and Boston. He even found one in Washington DC that piqued his interest.

Sue came out to visit one afternoon that week and, while she was watching Ellie change Jamie's nappy, she told her friend that everybody knew that Luke had also been offered a permanent position at North Shore General hospital.

'Everybody's hoping he's going to accept the offer. He's fabulous to work with.'

Ellie's heart had skipped a beat. That would mean that—in the not too distant future—she and Luke would be working together.

But then she'd shaken her head.

'He's applying for jobs that have way more to offer. Why would he choose to live here and not in London or New York?'

'Yeah…' Sue's sigh sounded envious. 'I'd be off like a shot, myself. How exciting would that be? He's so good at what he does, too. I would think that he could get any job he wants. Ooh…can I have a cuddle now?'

Ellie helped settle Jamie into Sue's arms. Her smile was automatic but her heart was sinking. Apparently, the job that Luke wanted was somewhere on the other side of the world. Anywhere that was as far away as he could get from her and Jamie?

'Oh…he's gorgeous.' Sue sounded misty as she smiled down at Jamie. 'I want one.'

'No, you don't,' Ellie told her. 'Not until you've got a baby daddy who wants to help, anyway. Being a single mother is…' It was her turn to sigh as she sat down on the couch beside Sue. 'Well…life-changing, that's for sure. Nothing will ever be the same.' She reached out to touch one of the adorable starfish hands Jamie was stretching out into space. 'Not that I'd want to be without this little one. Not now…'

'Uh-oh…' Sue chuckled as Jamie turned his head and nuzzled her chest, opening his mouth to let out a hungry whimper. 'I can't help you there, mate. Here…you'd better go back to Mum.'

She watched as Ellie adjusted her clothing and let Jamie latch on with the same ease and familiarity she'd had in offering her friend a cup of coffee on arrival.

'He's always been good at that.' Sue nodded. 'Do you remember how he got into it when you held him for the very first time?'

Ellie's smile was genuine this time. She would remember for ever just how much her life had changed in those first tugs of a tiny mouth at her breast. Breastfeeding was so much more than simply providing food for her baby, now, and she knew she would make the most of the next few months and cherish this bond that seemed capable of expanding infinitely.

'It doesn't matter how tired you are, or how difficult things have been,' she told Sue. 'When you're feeding them, you can just forget about it for a while and everything in your world is exactly how it should be.'

'Mmm…' Sue's glance was thoughtful. They both knew that Ellie's world was very different than she had intended it to be. 'Have you heard anything from Ava, yet?'

'No. Have you?' Especially in the days before her marriage to Marco, Ava had been very much a part of Ellie's circle of work friends and she and Sue had stayed in touch.

'I don't think anybody has. She hasn't even been on social media since the day Jamie was born. It's been well over a month and she used to update her status every day. It's like she's just vanished.' An angry edge coated Sue's words. 'I can't believe she hasn't at least tried to find out how *you* are.'

'Her life tipped upside down, too. She's got a lot to deal with.'

'And that's the time you need your friends the most.' Sue was frowning. 'What about her family? Do they still live out this way?'

Ellie shrugged. 'I haven't actually been into the village. I've been too busy with Jamie. And helping Luke with the garden here. When I do go out, it's usually to a viewing for an apartment. Or a mad dash through a supermarket.'

Time away from this house and garden felt like an interruption, didn't it? That was something Ellie needed to deal with. However much she loved it, this wasn't her house or her garden. She wouldn't be living here for much longer.

'She'll have to come back at some stage, surely. Will you want to even talk to her?'

'Of course…' Jamie had fallen asleep in her arms, his mouth still on her breast. Ellie eased him upright and began rubbing his back gently. 'We've been friends for ever and I'm worried about her. I want her to know that I'm okay, too. That she actually did me a favour because I know I couldn't have given Jamie away.'

'Maybe you should talk to her mother or something. If there's anybody she would have been in contact with, you'd think it would be her mum.'

Talking to Ava's mother was a good idea, Ellie decided later, but there was someone she would much rather talk to first.

Luke.

And it seemed as if that was a possibility tonight. He

hadn't sat down and fired up his laptop as soon as he arrived home from work. He was much later than usual and Ellie had already eaten her own dinner but she had the remains of the casserole and baked potatoes keeping warm in the oven. She knew he would have smelled the hot food as soon as he walked through the door and the pleasure she got from how much he appreciated her cooking for him hadn't worn off. It had become a bit of a joke to ask if he was hungry after the day he'd laughed at her query.

'You create something that smells that good and then ask me if I'm hungry? Silly question…'

But this evening, he simply shook his head in response and, instead, took a beer from the fridge and went outside, to sit down at the table on the terrace.

He was still sitting there, oddly still, when Ellie came back from feeding and changing Jamie and settling him into his bassinet for the night. For a long moment, she stared at the slump of his shoulders through the window.

Something wasn't right.

She poured herself a glass of the red wine she had opened to add to the beef bourguignon that was probably getting rather dry by now but she didn't pause to turn the oven off. She took another glass and the rest of the bottle and walked outside, before she lost her nerve. She tried to ignore the way her heart-rate picked up and seemed to be beating right in her throat.

'Want some company?'

'Sure.'

Ellie poured Luke a glass of wine, too. Asking him how his day had been would be a sillier question than asking if he was hungry when she knew perfectly well something was upsetting him, so she didn't say anything.

She remembered the way he had sat on the end of her

bed, the night Jamie had been born, when she had been struggling with the emotional trauma of the surrogacy plan going so terribly wrong. He hadn't tried to encourage her to talk. He'd simply given her the opportunity by sitting there and absorbing her struggle. Offering his company and what had felt like genuine empathy.

That was what she could give him right now. And the empathy was more than just genuine. Looking at hair that was even shaggier than usual after having fingers dragged through it and the deep crinkles around eyes that advertised distress, Ellie had never been more aware of just how much Luke had come to mean to her.

How much she loved this man.

She wanted to reach out and touch the hand that was resting on the table so near her. She wanted to lace her fingers through his and create a physical bond that would let him know that her heart was aching for him. That she would do anything she could to make whatever was hurting feel better.

When the urge became too great, she picked up the small box of matches that lay beside the collection of candles she had impulsively put out here a few days ago but had never bothered lighting because that was a romantic thing to do and that elephant in the room might have got big enough to crush them both.

Now it was just something to do. With a very different kind of tension in the atmosphere, that elephant seemed to have vanished. She took her time, holding the flame of the match to each wick, and she knew that Luke was watching each candle come to life. It took two matches, and it was while she was blowing out the second one that Luke spoke.

'Do you remember that baby with whooping cough

that Sue told you about? The one I'd seen the night of your fire?'

Ellie nodded. How could she forget? Inadvertently, maybe, Luke had let her know that he'd been thinking about her and Jamie. That, on some level, he really cared about them and was worried about their welfare. Telling him that Jamie had had his first vaccinations the other day had been one of the most relaxed conversations they'd had ever since that night the elephant had appeared.

'Her name was Grace,' Luke continued. 'She was six weeks old when she came in—not that much older than Jamie would have been, then. And she was pretty sick. The level of cyanosis with each coughing fit had me worried.'

Ellie swallowed hard. It was a parent's worst nightmare to see your baby desperately ill and even hearing the story of a baby she'd never met gave her a clutch of fear for Jamie.

'She got admitted to PICU and kept in isolation for a week. They battled what looked like the start of pneumonia a week or so later but she seemed to be improving. They still kept her in, though, because of an apnoeic episode or two and a low-grade fever that wouldn't go away. I went up to see her on the ward a few days ago.'

Ellie felt the corners of her mouth tilt as she nodded. She'd been surprised when he'd made a follow-up visit when she had been transferred to the maternity ward but it was clearly a normal part of Luke's involvement with his patients and a part of what made him such a good doctor. She was proud of him, she realised. Proud of what he did and what kind of man he was.

'She'd spiked more of a fever and had a bulging fontanelle, which bothered me. And then I heard she'd had a seizure that afternoon and been taken back to Intensive Care. They did a lumbar puncture and an MRI and made the diagnosis of encephalitis.'

'Oh, no…' Ellie whispered. She'd seen babies like that. Sedated and ventilated. Looking so tiny on a bed, with distraught parents hovering nearby. It had been hard enough to see that before she had become a mother herself. Now it was unbearable. She could feel her eyes filling with tears.

'I heard that she died today,' Luke added quietly. 'I can only imagine the agony that those poor parents are going through.'

Ellie didn't say anything. She could do more than imagine it. She could feel the edges of it touching her heart and she had to fight the urge to get up and run to her room to check on Jamie. To touch him. To stand there beside his bassinet and watch him breathing and soak in the awareness of just how precious he was.

'I couldn't do it.' Luke sounded as though he was talking to himself rather than Ellie.

'At least they have each other,' Ellie murmured. If something so terrible happened to her, she would have to face it alone and that was…unthinkable…

She took in a shaky breath. 'Is that why you never want to have kids, Luke?'

She knew she was pushing past a barrier and might very well be inviting rejection that would hurt but the question came out before she had time to think. Maybe she'd seen a tiny crack in that carefully constructed barrier and the lure of getting a little closer to what lay behind it had been irresistible.

And Luke didn't seem to be pulling away. His body language didn't freeze up. He didn't even reach for his drink. The huff of breath he released suggested surprise more than anything else. As if he hadn't really thought about it enough to put something into words.

'No. I guess it's more like the opposite scenario.'

Ellie frowned. She didn't understand. Luke glanced up in the silence and the darkness of his eyes in the flickering light of the candles made his face look haunted.

'I mean a child left bereft,' he said. 'Rather than the parents. I don't have to imagine how bad that can be because I *know*. I was that child. Left alone and nobody wanted me.'

'Oh... *Luke*...' Nothing could have stopped Ellie touching him now. She wanted to gather that child into her arms and never let him go. He was still there, wasn't he? Somewhere deep inside this amazing man. She couldn't gather Luke into her arms but she could touch his hand. Cover it with her own and give him, at the very least, the human touch of someone who cared.

And Luke accepted the touch. He turned his hand over so that their palms were together and his fingers tightened around Ellie's hand.

'That's something no child should ever have to go through,' she said, softly. She had lost her father when she was young and could remember the enormity of missing him so much but she'd still had her mother and her home—a safe place where she knew she belonged and was loved.

The silence grew. Would Luke say anything more?

Ellie wanted to hear more. She wanted to hear everything.

Finally, he spoke again. Tentatively—as if it was the first time he'd tried out this particular combination of words.

'I was too young to remember or understand, the first

time. Well, the second time if you count my mother not even taking me home from the hospital.'

'How old *were* you?'

'Two, according to the records the social services kept. I'd been taken in by a childless couple and then the woman got pregnant, after all. Apparently they didn't want me when they discovered they could have their own children.'

Two years old, Ellie thought with dismay. Just when children were starting to talk and begin to try and understand the world around them.

'The next time I was nearly five and that wasn't really the fault of my foster parents. My foster mum got very sick. She died later but I'd already been moved on by then because the family couldn't cope with looking after me as well as nursing her.'

Ellie could actually hear Luke's painful attempt to swallow. At five years of age, he would remember that abandonment.

He took a deep breath. 'Turned out that was by far the longest time anyone would keep me. I saw the list, once, and there were at least six more foster homes by the time I was ten.' He shrugged. 'I got labelled as a "difficult" child. Nothing worked, apparently—even a good hiding or not being fed. People took me on because they got paid to do it but nobody wanted *me*.'

Ellie could feel the pain in those words and it felt like a physical blow. How big was that button she had pushed when she'd said, out loud—in the first minutes of his life—that nobody wanted Jamie?

Luke must have felt her flinch beneath his hand. The pressure she felt from his fingers was gentle. A crooked smile even appeared on his face as he held her horrified gaze.

'It's okay… I understand completely what made you say that. And I know how much you love Jamie.'

'I'd die for him,' Ellie whispered. 'If it came to that.'

'I hope not.' Luke was still holding her gaze. 'I hope that nothing ever happens to Jamie. Or *you*…'

Ellie found she was holding her breath, waiting for his next words. He looked as though he was about to tell her how much he cared.

That he *loved* her?

'If something *did* happen to you,' he continued very quietly, 'I want you to know that I would do whatever I could to make sure Jamie was okay. And that's a promise. We can get it written up legally so that you'll know he'll always be safe.'

It wasn't quite what Ellie was hoping to hear but it was huge, nonetheless.

'Why?' she asked. 'Why would you do that for Jamie?'

Luke finally looked away. Down at their hands that were still joined. She could see the furrow that appeared on his brow, beneath the shaggy lock that never behaved itself well enough to stay back.

'I'm not sure what it was,' he said. 'But I felt a connection. Maybe it was because of what you said. Or maybe it was because I knew that I was fighting to save his life. I just knew he needed someone in his corner. Someone that was prepared to fight for him.' A tiny shrug rippled down Luke's arm into his fingers. 'I just knew that, in that moment, *I* was that person.'

Ellie's lips trembled. 'Thank you,' she managed. 'Thank you for being there. Thank you for being that person.'

Luke's smile was gentle. 'You're that person now. But I can be… I don't know…an insurance policy?'

Ellie found herself returning the smile without even

trying. A slow, soft smile that felt as if it were a neon sign, advertising just how much love she was feeling for Luke.

And maybe it did. Was that why Luke eased his hand away from hers? Why he picked up his glass of wine and drained it? He reached for the bottle and raised his eyebrows in a query. When Ellie shook her head, he re-filled his own glass.

'I've never told anybody about the disaster that my childhood was,' he said, then. 'And I'm not going to go horrify you with how much trouble I caused when I got older but it was when I overheard the plan to send me into the equivalent of a prison for teenagers that I ran away. I managed to live rough for nearly a week before the Gilmores caught me.' His smile was wry. 'At least you'll understand now why I'm never going to have a family of my own.'

It was Ellie's turn to frown. 'I'm not sure I do.' He knew exactly how bad it could be when a child didn't feel loved or safe. Surely he was the best person to be able to give them everything they needed. He was pre-pared to do it for Jamie, who wasn't even his own child, if something terrible happened to her.

'Things can happen,' Luke said, as if he'd overheard her last thought. 'What if I got married and had a kid and I wanted to take my wife away for a romantic weekend, say, and I could because we had hired the best nanny...'

Ellie's eyebrows rose and she smiled encouragingly but her brain had caught on his words and hit a pause button. It wanted to store that idea away, of being Luke's *wife*... Of being whisked away for a romantic weekend...

She had to make an effort to tune in properly again.

'...like a car crash or a plane going down. There's my kid still at home. No grandparents or other family to step in. Just a hired nanny who needs to get back to her own life. What can she do, except to hand over my kid to social services?'

Ellie opened her mouth to say something. To point out that his wife would have a family? But no words emerged. It wasn't a given. *She* didn't have any family. And she didn't want to think about some other woman being Luke's wife.

She wanted to be that woman.

To be with him, every day, for the rest of their lives.

To have moments like this, where he held her hand and talked to her about things that really mattered to him.

To have the support of someone who had already proven how well he could do that. When he'd delivered Jamie. When he'd rescued her after the fire.

When he'd called her *sweetheart*…

So, in the end, she didn't say anything. How could she hope to change his mind when that would mean, to some level, dismissing how terrible his early life had been?

She couldn't do that. Her heart was still breaking for that small, abandoned boy.

And Luke clearly took her silence as an affirmation of her understanding. She did understand. She might not agree with the rules that had been laid down but, yeah… it was easy to understand.

The elephant in the room had been caged and the reason for its imprisonment was valid. The breath Luke expelled sounded like a sigh of relief.

'Did you ask me if I was hungry a while back?'

She nodded. Found another smile, even, that told Luke she was still his friend. Still grateful for everything he had done for her. Still ready to fight in *his* corner for anything that he needed. And right now, he needed reassurance that she understood. That she could forgive him?

'Yeah… Silly question, huh?'

'You bet. I'm *starving…*'

CHAPTER NINE

MAYBE LUKE HADN'T been aware of how grey and dismal the world had become until the sun had finally edged out from behind a dense layer of clouds.

Ellie knew the truth.

And she understood. She was the only person, apart from Dorothy Gilmore, who had seen the scars that came from being taught that you were unwanted. Unlovable. And, as he'd seen in the eyes of the woman who had chosen to take him on as her son, he'd seen the same acceptance in Ellie's eyes.

The kind of love that came with the bond that only a real family could bestow.

Despite his determination to keep enough of a distance to keep Ellie safe, that was what they'd become over the last few weeks, wasn't it?

A family.

Oh, not the sort that he would have created if he'd chosen commit to one of those women who'd wanted him to. He hadn't set out to intentionally combine this small group of humanity into a single unit. Fate had stepped in, the way it had when the Gilmores had caught him helping himself to their food, but he could cope with this. He could be an unofficially adopted brother or cousin and offer the kind of support a loving—but separate—family member would provide. An insurance policy for Jamie's future, like the one he fully intended to get his solicitor to put down on paper.

It meant he could channel any feelings he had for Ellie into something very manageable, too. He could admire her and be proud of her.

Love her, in fact. And any sexual attraction could be instantly dismissed as being totally inappropriate. So inappropriate that it seemed as if it had been simply burnt off by the heat of that sun making its appearance from behind dense clouds he hadn't even noticed accumulating.

If he'd needed any proof of that, it had come in the aftermath of that soul-baring conversation about his childhood.

When Ellie had asked him if checking whether or not he was hungry was a silly question. He'd already been feeling as if a weight had been lifted and the mischievous smile she had offered had been...irresistible.

'You bet,' he'd said with a grin that acknowledged the welcome familiarity of what had become a joke between them. 'I'm *starving*...'

Not just for food. For *this*...this...closeness.

The feeling that someone knew more about him than anyone else on earth and could accept his limitations. Could still like him enough to joke with him.

He'd been caught up in that smile. In the first rush of the world seeming so much less complicated. So *right*...?

And yes, maybe it had something to do with the flickering candle light beside them and those gorgeous blue eyes in front of him but it had seemed like the most natural thing in the world to lean closer and kiss Ellie.

Just a soft touch of his lips on hers. An acknowledgement of a new level of friendship. A 'thank you' for being there. For listening and understanding.

And even feeling the astonishing softness of her lips

beneath his for that blink of time hadn't unleashed any fierce desire for more than that.

On either side, it seemed. Ellie hadn't even tried to kiss him back. She'd seemed surprised by the gesture but then she'd dropped her gaze and got to her feet with an easy grace that didn't suggest the kiss had been anything more than it had been intended to be—a mark of friendship.

'Let's hope that beef bourguignon hasn't evaporated completely, then,' she'd said lightly.

Being so open with Ellie also meant that Luke could relax.

He could enjoy coming home again—as he had when this had become his family home and he'd had a refuge for the first time in his life.

Everything felt brighter.

Was Jamie aware of the change in atmosphere around him? Was that why Luke had been privileged enough to witness his first smile?

A real smile that made his eyes crinkle and stretched his mouth into a grin that Luke couldn't help returning, just as he hadn't been able to help kissing Ellie the other night.

'What's funny?' Ellie asked, looking up from the pile of laundry she was folding at the kitchen table.

'He's smiling.'

'It's probably wind.'

'No. He's really smiling. Come and see.'

But the new skill wasn't in evidence by the time Ellie came to peer into the pushchair. Jamie just waved chubby fists and kicked his feet to demonstrate his pleasure in seeing his mother.

'Hey…' Luke reached in to tickle his tummy. 'Where's that smile gone, buddy?'

Jamie kicked harder, his gaze now locked on Luke's face. And then, miraculously, he did it again—his lips curling up to make him look like the happiest baby on earth.

'Oh…' Ellie sounded as if she might cry. 'He *is*…he's *really* smiling at you.'

At *him*?

Babies just smiled, didn't they? Surely Jamie didn't recognise Luke as anybody particularly important in his life? He'd never picked him up and cuddled him, or anything.

But it appeared that Jamie did recognise him and that Luke could elicit a smile far more easily than Ellie could in the next few days. He only had to make funny noises or tickle him with just one finger. Weirdly, it made this tiny human seem much more like a real person. Someone he could feel close to. Proud of—as he did of Ellie.

Those smiles were something he could take genuine pleasure in now that he felt more relaxed. Just like the pleasure he was getting in how the house had come to life again, thanks to all the work that Ellie and a small army of tradesmen had done. Damaged boards and windows had been repaired and the new paintwork looked stunning. The gardens at both the front and back of the house were a blaze of colour with the second blooming of so many roses and with the gaps that had been created by her relentless efforts of weeding and pruning now filled with new plants. The photo shoot for the house had been done and Mike the real estate agent's smile had been contagious.

'Stroke of brilliance, putting that bottle of wine and the glasses on that outside table.'

'That was Ellie's idea. She did all the jugs full of roses inside, too.'

'I just wish I'd had time to do the veggie garden,' Ellie said. 'I wanted it to be all cleared with some new rows of baby plants.'

'It didn't show up in the photos.' Mike's smile was encouraging now. 'I'm sure you can have it looking perfect by the time the first viewings happen. Speaking of which…nothing official is out there yet but word of mouth happens in the industry, you know? I've heard about someone who's very, very keen to have a sneak preview and I know they've got the right sort of money to play with. Would you mind if I set up an appointment for next week?'

For a moment, Luke hesitated. Walking away from this house—and Ellie and Jamie—suddenly seemed very, very real. Was that why Ellie seemed to have gone so still? She wasn't looking at him, though. She was looking down at the baby in her arms. Her son. Her future.

One that Luke couldn't continue to be this much a part of.

He glanced back at Mike. 'Sure. Why not?'

Some of the best things in life happened because fate just happened to line a meeting of the right people at the right time. Luke Gilmore knew that better than anyone.

Ellie's quick glance had a note of something less than happy but Luke chose to interpret it in relation to the last thing she'd said. 'I've got a day off, tomorrow. How 'bout I dig out that veggie garden?'

'It's a big job.'

'Be a good workout, then.'

'Excellent.' Mike left the advance copies of the brochures he had brought to show them and took his leave. 'I'll be in touch…'

* * *

It was really going to happen.

Someone was coming to look at the property in a matter of days and, of course, they were going to fall in love with it and offer Luke a ridiculous amount of money that he would be an idiot not to accept.

He would make a final choice from all the amazing job offers he now had to consider and sort out all the loose ends of his past life in New Zealand while he worked the final few weeks of his locum position at North Shore General.

There would be no reason for Ellie to devote all her spare time and energy to this gorgeous old house and garden so she would be able to do what she probably should have already done by now and find herself and Jamie a new place to call home.

As she tucked Jamie into his bassinet for his afternoon nap, she tried very hard to feel positive about it.

'We'll be okay,' she murmured to the sleeping baby. 'We'll find a nice place to live. Make new friends. Mummy will go back to work and you'll love being in day care with all the other babies...'

Oh, dear... The way her words got caught on the lump forming in her throat wasn't a good sign.

She hated the very idea of it, didn't she?

Every bit of it.

Finding a new place to live that had nothing to do with Luke Gilmore. Going back to work quite this soon and leaving her baby in the care of strangers.

Missing Luke with every minute of every day and worse—every night...

Unconsciously, Ellie had put her fingertips to her lips. The way she often found herself doing when she thought back to that kiss.

Just a friendly kiss. The sort you might give to a very good friend to thank them for something important. Like them being okay with knowing that they were never going to be anything more than a friend because they understood exactly why you felt like that.

Trouble was, Ellie was only pretending to understand. She was in love with Luke.

She still wanted to be with him. So much that it ached right down to her bones when she remembered that kiss because, even though the touch had been so light and so fleeting, every cell in her body had recognised that it was the first note of a song that would be a sound they had been waiting their entire existence to hear and feel.

And, yes, it was stupid to want to go there because it would only make it harder when Luke left but that didn't seem to matter right now. Would it really make a difference when things were already going to be so hard? Ellie was already having trouble imagining her life with Luke no longer in it. It was almost as hard to get her head around as the idea of Jamie not being in her life now.

With a sigh, Ellie turned away from the bassinet, checking that the old-fashioned roller blind was pulled down far enough on the window to prevent any sun shining directly onto Jamie in the next hour or so. It wasn't, so she moved to draw it further down. She would change those blinds if she owned this house, she thought, as she walked towards the window. She'd hang curtains in a romantic fabric, maybe with a flower print, to frame the tall sash windows in soft folds. No flowers if it was Jamie's room, of course, but bright colours. Gold, perhaps, so that it looked like sunshine even in the middle of winter...

Her room was on a corner of the house and this window gave her a view past the edge of the gardens around the kitchen terrace. She could see Luke working in the veggie garden, hauling out the last of the tallest weeds by hand with the garden fork and a spade jammed into the earth nearby, ready for when they were needed for stubborn roots. He'd been out there working for hours already today, with only a short break for lunch, and he had cleared and turned over the earth of more than half of the large patch of land.

It was clearly harder going now, in the burst of autumn afternoon warmth. She saw him pause to wipe sweat off his face with the hem of his tee shirt and she could see the way he pushed damp strands of hair back from his face. It made her smile because she knew how tousled and disreputable it would make him look—as he did sometimes first thing in the morning before he'd brushed his hair.

Ellie loved that look best of all.

She'd take him a cold drink, she decided, picking up the handset of the baby monitor that would let her know the instant Jamie woke up. She might even get an hour or so to help dig before that happened, which was when she was planning to take Jamie for a ride in the car to the garden centre to buy trays of vegetable plants to fill in the newly bare stretch of soil.

The cold glass of water was apparently exactly what Luke had been hanging out for but it seemed to make him feel even hotter. A few minutes later, he stripped off his tee shirt, rolling it up into a ball to mop his face before he continued digging, now wearing only his shorts and a pair of rubber boots.

Ellie was in shorts, too. And a white singlet top beneath a soft, denim shirt. She took the shirt off and hung it over the handle of the wheelbarrow to keep at least one item of clothing clean and then she took the fork and headed for a new clump of weeds, leaving Luke to pull things up by hand and use the spade to turn and chop the soil.

'I'm going to get plants rather than seeds,' Ellie told him, when she carried an armload of rubbish past Luke as she headed for the wheelbarrow. 'That way it'll give people the idea they'll be growing all their own food in no time.'

'Like we did, back in the day.'

'Yeah... I'm thinking broccoli and cauliflowers and cabbage. And beans and peas. Except we'd need frames for them to climb on, wouldn't we?'

'There's a fence buried under the weeds here. I seem to remember that was for beans. With a bit of luck, the posts won't be too rotten.'

'What else did you grow? Potatoes?'

'Of course. Not that you can get them as plants but I remember how to mound up the rows and people will know what they're for.' It was nice that Luke could feel enthusiastic about a garden when he wouldn't be here to taste its produce. 'Carrots,' he added, with a satisfied nod. 'And silverbeet. That was always here. Huge bunches of it.'

'Maybe there's still some hiding.'

'I doubt anything's lasted under this carpet of weeds.'

But Luke struck gold in the very last corner of the overgrown patch when their efforts had brought them close enough to be working together.

'Don't pull that one out,' Ellie exclaimed. 'That's rhubarb...'

Dropping her fork in her excitement, she stumbled over the rough earth to pull the veil of sticky biddi bid weeds from the huge, dark green leaves beneath. Luke reached in to help her but it didn't stop her singlet from getting covered with the tiny green seed balls. Luke even got some in his hair, which already looked the most dishevelled Ellie had ever seen it look. With those tawny streaks to the shagginess, it reminded her of a lion's mane.

And she loved it…

Just as well there was something else to focus on.

'Oh, wow…' She stood back to admire the plants they had uncovered. 'This is fabulous. It's going to make it look like something is really growing and hasn't just been planted for show.'

Luke bent down to snap off one of the long, red stalks. He bit into it but then screwed up his face as if he'd just sucked on a lemon.

'I don't remember this being so sour.'

'Don't try the leaves,' Ellie warned him. 'They're poisonous. And the stalks really need cooking,' she added. 'In a crumble, maybe. Ava and I used to eat it in the garden, though. We'd sneak out a little bowl of sugar and dip the stalks into it with each bite.'

There were so many memories of that old friendship that snuck up on her but seeing Luke's expression had given this one a peculiar poignancy. Raw rhubarb *was* sour and she and Ava had made faces just like that if they hadn't got enough sugar to stick to the stalks. Then they'd giggled and tasted it again just because it was fun.

Shifting her gaze, as if that would somehow shift her focus away from the memories, Ellie noticed all the green balls sticking to the singlet that had been white not so long ago. She'd need to get changed before she went to the garden centre and she would also need to pick off all the sticky balls before she put this garment in to the wash. She remembered this weed from childhood, too. You had to pull every one of those balls off individually, which was exactly what she started to do.

And then she realised that Luke had gone quiet and she looked up to see that he was watching her hands. Ellie had started on the nearest part of the fabric, which was the scooped neckline. Had she even realised that she was calling attention to a cleavage that was rather more impressive than it had ever been before she'd become a mother?

She could feel the warmth of a blush gaining energy. She needed to say something offhand—maybe about how annoying biddi bids were—and then turn back to her own task of forking through the clumps of soil that Luke had turned over with the spade.

Except, she couldn't move. She could feel something changing in the air around her, as if the oxygen were being sucked out by some invisible force. Luke was standing there, half naked. There were streaks on his tanned skin where the sweat had turned dirt into mud. And there were tiny green balls caught on the sprinkling of hair on his chest. A triangle of tawny, sparse hair that trailed into an arrow at the level of the waistband of his shorts.

Ellie tried to catch her breath.

She tried to make her legs work and take her away from this overwhelming temptation to touch Luke.

Neither of those things happened.

What did happen was that she reached out to gently pull a little green ball from where it was caught, just to one side of a nipple that tightened at the first whisper of touch from her fingers.

And just as instantly, Luke's hand whipped up to catch hold of hers and prevent it moving any further.

He was going to reject her, wasn't he?

Gently, of course. It would only take a look to remind her that this wasn't going to happen. That they were only friends. Gritting her teeth, Ellie lifted her gaze to accept that look, fully prepared to give him one of apology on her part.

But what she saw was something very different.

Desire, pure and simple.

A blazing desire but one that only came a little closer to what was coursing through her own veins.

For a long, long moment, they stared at each other in what felt like total amazement.

And then they moved. Ellie had no idea who moved first. It seemed to happen with the speed of light. One moment they were standing there staring and the next, Luke's mouth was on hers.

There was nothing sweet about this kiss. It had nothing to do with gratitude or friendship.

This was out-of-control need.

Pure passion.

A dance of lips and tongues and hands that slid across sweat-slicked skin. It was everything that Ellie had dreamed of except that it wasn't nearly enough...

And somehow, eventually, they both sank onto the rough earth of the garden beneath their feet. Kneeling together. Ellie had her thumbs hooked into the elastic waistband of Luke's shorts and he had his hands beneath her singlet top. Her bra was already undone and she cried out in ecstasy as she felt his hands cup her breasts.

She could hear an echo of her cry. And then another...

Only it wasn't her making that sound. It had a tinny quality that had nothing to do with passion and everything to do with a small baby waking up from his nap.

Ellie had to close her eyes against the crushing disappointment as she felt the moment slipping away, along with Luke's hands.

It was actually embarrassing to have to ease her hands away from Luke's shorts.

Their gazes snagged and held again for another long moment, but the silent communication this time was nothing like the last.

Maybe they both felt a bit horrified as the realisation of how out of control they'd been kicked in.

'I…um… I'll have to go in,' Ellie managed. She stayed on her knees for a moment longer, reaching awkwardly behind herself to find the clasp of her bra.

Luke got to his feet but he made no sound other than a grunt Ellie couldn't interpret. Maybe he was relieved at the interruption. Maybe he was disappointed. Or maybe he just had stiff muscles from all that physical work in the garden.

He offered Ellie a hand to help her up and she took it but it didn't feel anything like the hand that had been caressing her skin only moments before.

And still, Luke didn't say anything. He opened his mouth as if he wanted to, but then he closed it again, uttering nothing more than another uninterpretable sound as he bent over to pick up the garden fork.

Ellie picked up the baby monitor. She glanced over her shoulder as she went to collect her shirt.

He was turning over earth as if his life depended on making this garden look as perfect as possible.

A foot on the fork. A pile of earth turned over. Smacking it with the prongs of the fork helped it fall apart and look like soil ready to accept new plants. Again and again, Luke went through the motions, ignoring the sweat that trickled between his shoulder blades and down his forehead to reach his eyes and make them sting.

How the hell had *that* happened?

He'd had things perfectly under control. He actually managed to take those old twinges of desire for Ellie and turn them into something far more acceptable—an appreciation of all her amazing qualities.

Who knew that they'd been bubbling away under their cover like a volcano getting ready to erupt and it had only needed the provocation of seeing her fingers pulling at the fabric clinging to her breasts as she pulled off biddi bids to blow everything sky-high?

Okay, it *had* needed more than that. What had been his complete undoing had been to see his own desire reflected in Ellie's eyes. That sizzle in the air between them had completely fried his brain.

And then the astonishing *taste* of her... The sensations the touch of her hands created rippling over and then under his skin... The silky softness of her skin that he wanted to taste as much as touch...

Holy heck...if it hadn't been for Jamie waking up when he did, they would have been making love right here on this newly tilled earth. Without any conscious thought of finding protection. Without consideration that this was a woman who'd given birth not that long ago and might not be anywhere near ready for that kind of raw passion.

The kind of passion that would have had them getting even more sweaty and dirty and...

And he'd better stop even thinking about what that might have been like because it was doing his head in.

Luke smacked another solid forkful of earth and watched it splinter and separate with satisfaction. He didn't even pause before jamming the prongs into the ground again. He kept going, until he heard the sound of Ellie's car starting up and then crunching over the loose surface of the shelled driveway and he realised that she was still sticking to the plan and had gone off to buy the new vegetable plants. He could help get them in to the ground later but for now, he had done enough.

A lot more than he'd intended doing, that was for sure. He should be ashamed of himself.

But, if he was honest, he just wanted to turn back time.

And have Jamie sleep a little longer.

It was safe to go inside now, at least, and, man, did he need a shower.

It might have to be one of those cold ones, again, dammit.

The elephant was back in the room.

Somehow, they managed to get through the rest of the day, pretending that things were back to the way they'd been in recent days but, when Luke was clearing up the kitchen as Ellie settled Jamie for the night, Luke knew that something was going to have to be said to defuse the tension that even the hint of eye contact was generating.

Ellie clearly felt the same way. He had his back to her—his hands in the kitchen sink scrubbing dishes—when she came back into the room but he could sense the determination in the way she was moving. The way she pulled a tea towel from the hook beside the old coal range and then came to stand right beside him.

Close enough that he could imagine that he could actually feel heat radiating from the bare skin of her arms.

'We're both adults, Luke,' she said quietly. 'We like each other, don't we?'

Surprise sent Luke's glance skidding sideways to meet hers. *Like?* Such an insipid word to encompass everything he thought about Ellie. It didn't come anywhere near touching the respect he had for her courage and generosity, his admiration for her determination and energy or his appreciation of the way she looked and moved and spoke...

But he couldn't put any of that into words so he simply nodded, hoping his smile would convey a little more than 'like'.

Ellie picked up a plate and began to dry it, as if this were a perfectly normal kind of conversation to have while a household chore was being attended to. 'And we both know this is never going to be anything more than friendship.'

Some of the tension around him evaporated as Luke murmured his agreement but something struck an odd note. Okay, they both knew why he could never let this be more than friendship but did Ellie feel the same way?

Why?

What was wrong with him that would have excluded him as even a possibility of being a life partner?

Another part of his brain could supply the answer to that. A deeply buried part that he'd never prodded in his adult life.

There was a reason that nobody loved you when you were a kid, it reminded him. *You were unlovable. Unwanted... It's why you never stick around any relationship, isn't it? You have to end it first—before anyone else can do it...*

It took a moment to focus on what Ellie was saying now.

'...doesn't mean we're not allowed to get close. If the rules are understood and accepted, why shouldn't we just make the most of something special?'

Luke's hands slowed. He didn't even lift the plate that was now perfectly clean under those soap suds. Ellie's voice was so quiet now it was almost a whisper.

'Something we might never find again,' she said. 'Either of us…'

Luke swallowed hard. Her words resonated with a truth he couldn't escape. Of course he was never going to find anything like this again. He'd allowed Ellie closer than anyone else in his life.

He trusted her.

And she was confirming that she would never ask him for anything that he wasn't capable of giving her.

If he didn't accept this offer he would spend the rest of his life wondering what it could be like.

To be *that* close to someone you could trust *this* much…

They both wanted it. Luke could feel the sexual energy crackling around him. Burning his skin. He turned to face her, his hands dripping water as he lifted them. He caught the tea towel dangling from Ellie's hands to dry his hands and, for a moment, they were both holding it.

'Are you sure about this?' he asked softly. '*Really* sure?'

Ellie's gaze held his so he couldn't miss the way her eyes darkened. And he could also catch the way her lips tilted up at the corners as she pulled on the fabric they were still both holding. A slow, steady pressure that was firm enough to draw him closer.

Close enough to trap their hands between their bodies. For Ellie's breasts to touch his chest. Close enough for him to feel her breath on his skin as she spoke.

'I think you get the prize for asking the silly question this time…'

CHAPTER TEN

IT COULDN'T LAST, of course.

But, for a precious few days that Ellie would treasure for the rest of her life, she was inside the perfect bubble.

Living in the most gorgeous place on earth.

The mother of the most beautiful child that had ever been born.

Sharing the bed of the man she now knew to be her soul mate.

The sex was every bit as good as she'd dreamed it would be.

No, that wasn't true.

It was far better than she'd dreamed it could be.

She'd been far more nervous than she'd let on, that first time, when she'd made the first move and persuaded Luke that they could add benefits into their friendship. She knew her body had changed after pregnancy and had to hope it was still attractive enough. It was also quite possible that sex would be less than pleasant after the birth. Painful, even.

How weird was it, to feel the same kind of nerves that she remembered having when she'd lost her virginity?

Yet it was entirely appropriate, as well. Because this was her first time. Her first time to be with someone she was so totally in love with…

And Luke had been so gentle.

So caring.

So in control of a power that Ellie could sense in every touch. A passion that she desperately wanted to experience but lacked the courage to risk unleashing.

That first time, anyway...

The walls of that bubble had taken on a rainbow hue since then.

She was living a fantasy. Caring for her baby and looking after a house and garden that felt like home. Preparing meals with the extra attention to detail that was a pleasure to do when you were making that effort for someone that you loved. Watching the hands move on the old grandfather clock every time she went past, enjoying the increasing thrill of knowing that there was less and less time to wait until the person she most wanted to see would be coming through that door.

Maybe it was living the fantasy that gave rise to new stretches of imagination. Maybe letting go of the past, by leaving the place that had such a connection to it, would persuade Luke that a new future was possible.

With her...

As much as she adored this place, it wasn't what really mattered. She'd go to London with Luke. Or Boston or New York or Washington or wherever he wanted to go in the world. Home was where the heart was, after all, and her heart would always be with Luke. Jamie loved him too—why else would he smile virtually every time he saw him now?

Not that she said anything, of course. That hadn't been part of the deal and Ellie knew perfectly well that the walls of this bubble were fragile. However beautiful it was, it was a temporary thing.

Unless Luke wanted to change the rules.

Instinctively, Ellie knew that he was the only one who could do that. That, if she even hinted that something more was possible, she would break the trust between them and Luke would retreat behind the barrier he'd spent most of his life creating.

Being in this incredible bubble depended on her not breaking that trust so all she could do was to show him glimpses of what that future could be like.

Miraculously, Luke seemed just as disinclined to break that luminescent wall around them all just yet.

It had been his idea to go out, when the sneak preview house viewing had been arranged on one of his days off. Maybe he didn't want to be there to see total strangers assessing his beloved home and putting a price on it any more than Ellie did.

It had been his idea to take Jamie for a walk through the forest and go down to the beach.

And he was the one who strapped Jamie's front pack to his own chest.

'I used to know that track like the back of my hand,' he said. 'I don't want to be worried about you tripping over tree roots or something.'

Maybe that was also why he held her hand on that walk.

Not that Ellie minded being looked after as if she were fragile and feminine. She was, after all, in the middle of a real-life fantasy that was reminiscent of a house-wife and mother from many decades ago. A simple life when all that mattered was the welfare of your family and home. Her mother's generation, perhaps. Or more like her grandmother's?

Nothing like real life these days. Or certainly not hers, anyway.

She really had to do something about finding a new

place to live and making arrangements for when she went back to work. Her insurance claim was almost settled so there was no excuse not to be sorting out her life.

Except...she didn't want to.

Not yet.

She wanted to walk through a sun-dappled forest like this, feeling the warmth and strength of Luke's hand curled around hers.

She wanted to step back into childhood for a moment and slide down a steep sand dune and see the laughter in Luke's eyes and how wide his grin was.

She wanted to see him tickle her baby and make him smile and smile and smile.

In moments like this, just for a heartbeat or two, it was easy to pretend that they were a real family. That nothing would tear them apart.

In retrospect, it seemed as if it was during that idyllic time together that afternoon that things started to go wrong.

And yet it had been a sigh of pure pleasure that escaped Ellie as she stood on the amazing stretch of white sand that was Moana Beach, shading her eyes from the afternoon sun as she looked out at the offshore islands.

'I'd forgotten that this was one of my most favourite parts of the world.'

'Beautiful, isn't it?' Luke seemed to be watching the curl of the waves. 'If it was summer, I'd be tempted to dust off my old surfboard.'

You could stay, Ellie wanted to say. *You could live here again and have this beach as part of your backyard for the rest of your life.*

But he didn't want that as part of his future, did he? Luke wanted the fast-paced lifestyle of a high-octane career in a big city and maybe a low-maintenance apartment that wouldn't be a drain on his spare time or an anchor if he wanted to move on.

He wouldn't want to be 'saddled' with a property that needed so much maintenance, any more than he wanted that from 'dependants' like a wife or child.

But looking at him now, with a sleeping baby nestled against his chest, and a poignant smile on his face as he remembered the joy of surfing, made Ellie more sure than ever that he was taking his life in the wrong direction. She knew how much the property meant to him—that it was the only real home he'd known in his life—but he was prepared to let it go so that he could be free.

How could he not see that that freedom would deprive him of the best things that life could offer?

The things that she was sharing with him inside this bubble?

'I'll bring Jamie back,' she said, finally, making an effort to keep her tone light. 'When he's old enough to build a sandcastle and go paddling. I'll tell him about what it was like when we were kids and we came here to swim and have picnics and build driftwood tee pees.'

'Don't forget to take him to the General Store.' Luke grinned. 'Mr Jenkins might have been a grumpy old man, but he made the best ice creams.'

'Oh, yes…in a cone. And you could get them chocolate-dipped.'

'And the ice cream would start melting underneath the chocolate and then drip down your arm.'

Ellie laughed. 'That's right… I'd forgotten about that, too. Messy…'

By tacit consent, they headed home. Mike had probably finished showing the potential buyers around the property some time ago.

'I'm not sure that Mr Jenkins still does chocolate dip

ice creams,' Luke said sadly. 'I didn't notice them when I went in for milk that time.'

'What about the pick and mix lollies?'

'Yep. They were still there. But they didn't look the same. They all seemed to be things like sour worms and gummy bears. Couldn't see my favourites.'

'Which were?'

Luke gave the question due consideration. 'Milk bottles,' he decided. 'Or maybe jet planes.'

'I was a pineapple lump girl,' Ellie confessed. 'Good grief… I haven't eaten them for so many years.'

'And I've almost forgotten what a jet plane tastes like. Hey…' Luke stopped so suddenly Ellie bumped into him. 'Let's go and get some.'

The glint of mischief in his eyes that accompanied the cheeky grin took Ellie straight back to the time when Luke Gilmore had been the bad boy of Kauri Valley High School. When Ellie had been invisible…

But she wasn't any more. The warmth in Luke's gaze was purely for her. She was so much more than a 'bus buddy' now.

She was his friend.

No. She was much more than that, too. Whether Luke realised it or not, that was a look that could only be shared between lovers.

It was almost too much to bear.

Ellie shook her head as she smiled. 'You wouldn't…'

Luke laughed. 'I didn't mean steal them. I'm talking about a legitimate purchase, here.' He shrugged. 'It will probably be the last time I ever see Mr Jenkins so it would be… I don't know…a fitting farewell?'

There was something in Luke's gaze that made it feel as if he was offering an apology.

To Mr Jenkins?

Or to her?

Ellie could actually feel the crack appearing in her heart and it hurt. She had to force herself to pull in a breath. To keep smiling.

'Sure,' she managed. 'Why not?'

The house and garden were deserted by the time they got back but Ellie could feel that others had been there.

That something had changed.

It was a relief to buckle Jamie into his car seat for the short drive to the village. To see if things hadn't changed there, as Luke had told her that night when he'd been driving her back to her first visit to Kauri Valley in such a long time.

To outward appearances, it did look just the same, with the war memorial in front of the hall and the old pub and the peeling paint on the sign above Mr Jenkins's shop. 'General Store' was an apt description for the random collection of things sold here that ranged from a selection of fresh fruit and vegetables to garden tools, kitchen equipment and haberdashery.

At first glance, the row of plastic containers in front of the main desk where Mr Jenkins ruled over the cash desk looked exactly the same—full of the bright colours of pure sugar confectionery. The pile of tiny, white paper bags was still there, too, waiting for customers to fill by using the miniature shovels in their own container.

Ellie chose pineapple lumps, of course. Luke looked delighted to find the chewy, white lollies in the shape of tiny milk bottles. It was slightly awkward to fill her little bag as she reached around the obstacle Jamie presented in the front pack but she wasn't in the way of anyone wanting to pay for anything. They were alone at the front counter, in fact, because Mr Jenkins was busy with a woman who seemed to need information about a cleaning product. They both had their backs to Ellie and Luke, who both knew that Mr Jenkins was watching them like a hawk.

Expecting them to steal the lollies?

Ellie's lips twitched as her gaze met Luke's and the smile they shared was their own secret.

A moment when the connection between them had never been quite this powerful.

They put their bags on the counter to wait for the opportunity to pay for them, which wouldn't be long because the woman had made her choice. She turned to follow Mr Jenkins to the counter.

And then she stopped in her tracks.

'Oh, my goodness,' she said. 'Ellie…'

It wasn't the tone of someone delighted to see her. Mrs Collins looked horrified, in fact.

Frightened, almost?

Ellie could feel herself stiffen. She could feel Luke edge closer, as if he could sense her need for protection?

'Luke, this is Mrs Collins… Ava's mother…'

Jill Collins was staring at Luke now. 'Luke Gilmore?' She blinked hard. 'I did hear that you were back.'

'I am. Not for long, though.' He smiled at her. 'I didn't realise the news had spread.'

The flicker in the older woman's face told them both that Luke Gilmore would always be remembered around here and Ellie's heart sank. No wonder he didn't want to stay, when so much of the past could be resurrected by nothing more than the twitch of someone's mouth.

Strangely, her head turned sharply, then, as if she expected someone else to be with them but, finally, Jill

Collins's gaze dropped to the baby that Ellie had instinctively wrapped into her arms even though he was perfectly safe cocooned in the padded front pack.

'This is Jamie,' Ellie told her. 'I named him after my dad.'

There was a hint of a smile on Jill's face as she nodded once. People around here would approve of that choice. Ellie's father had been a well-liked resident of Kauri Valley. Even Mr Jenkins gave a grunt that sounded satisfied.

''Bout time we saw a new generation around here,' he muttered. 'Place feels like it's dying out.'

But the sense of approval—and Mrs Collins's smile—faded as quickly as it had appeared.

Of course she would have known all about the surrogacy agreement her daughter had arranged. She had probably been thrilled at the prospect of becoming a grandmother. Ellie felt a wash of sympathy and, in its wake, a renewed urge to see her closest friend. To get past the barrier that broken dreams had created.

If anybody knew where Ava was right now, surely it was—as Sue had suggested it would be—her mother.

'Mrs Collins?' Ellie stepped closer. Mr Jenkins had gone behind the counter and Luke was pulling some cash out of his pocket to pay for their sweets. She lowered her voice, anyway. 'I really need to get hold of Ava,' she said. 'Do you know where she is at the moment?'

Jill Collins shook her head sharply. 'I have no idea,' she muttered.

But her gaze slid away from Ellie.

She knew. She just didn't want Ellie to know.

Because she thought she might end up being responsible for a baby who was in no way related to herself?

Or was it because Ava had told her she wanted nothing more to do with Ellie?

Either way, it seemed that there was little Ellie could do. Except wait until fleeting eye contact was restored.

'If you talk to her,' Ellie said quietly, blinking back sudden moisture in her eyes, 'please tell her how much I'd like to hear from her. How much I'm missing my best friend.'

Luke had finished paying for their purchase but Ellie didn't feel remotely like tasting one of the chewy, chocolate covered little rectangles in her bag. Being brushed off by a woman who'd been like a second mother to her in her childhood hurt far more than she could have anticipated. It felt as if she wasn't wanted here.

To make matters worse, they arrived back at the house to find Mike the real estate agent pacing the veranda.

'Thank goodness,' he said, as soon as he saw them. 'I've got an offer written up here that's so hot it's burning my hands. You're not going to believe this...'

Ellie's heart sank to a new, low level.

Was this it?

The beginning of the end?

But Luke didn't follow Mike into the house, having opened the front door. He had turned to stare down the garden path towards the road.

'Who's that? Anyone you know, Ellie?'

She turned to see the male figure approaching and, this time, her heart dropped so hard and fast, she could feel it breaking.

'It's...it's Marco,' she whispered through dry lips that barely moved.

'Hey, Ellie.' Marco glanced at Luke but then ignored him as he moved closer. His smile was horribly reminiscent of the last one she'd seen on his face—just before his shocking attempt to kiss her—as if nothing could dent his confidence that he was about to get exactly what he wanted.

'It's about time I collected my son, don't you think?'

CHAPTER ELEVEN

LUKE STILL HAD one hand holding open the front door that was inclined to swing shut on its own. He still had his head turned, having heard the crunch of heavy footsteps on the shell path, so his body was twisted into a slightly awkward position but, for the life of him, he couldn't move.

It had been enough of a shock to find Mike on the veranda a minute ago and to realise he was about to face the final decision about walking away from the house and garden that were his last links to the people who'd made him the man he was today. He hadn't expected an outcome like this from the viewing. The house wasn't even officially on the market yet.

And this aftershock had been even less expected. Ellie had been confident that the man who'd fathered Jamie would not be returning. After she'd told him that Marco hadn't even wanted a baby in the first place, Luke had never given him another thought.

The shock was visceral. He didn't need to see the way the blood had drained from Ellie's face to know that life had just blindsided her yet again and her world felt as if it were crumbling around her.

Did he actually think he could swan in here and take Jamie?

His reaction was instant. And icy. *Over my dead body...*

'How did you...?' Ellie's voice was barely more than a whisper. Then she gave her head a tiny, disbelieving shake. 'Why are you here, Marco?'

'I told you. I've come for my son.'

'You didn't even want a baby. Ava told me.'

Marco's shrug was dismissive. 'A lot of things get said in the heat of a disagreement. I didn't mean it.'

But he hadn't even looked properly at Jamie, Luke noted. He was staring at Ellie, his gaze travelling up and down her body in a way that gave him a very unpleasant frisson.

Jealousy?

No. It was more the need to protect a woman from someone whose shallow intentions were all too clear.

'As for how I found you...' The hand gesture suggested it had been no problem. 'Once I discovered that your apartment had been burned to the ground, it was obvious where I needed to go for information about a missing person. Two missing people... The police were remarkably helpful when I explained that one of those missing people was my own son.'

Ellie took a step backwards. 'He's not your son, Marco. He's mine.'

Luke wanted to leap in and defend Ellie but he was still frozen, his brain throwing all sorts of unexpected things at him.

He'd never known his own father. Maybe that unknown man had never been aware that he'd become a father. Or had he tried to claim him and been sent away? Would his own life have been very different if his father had had some part in it?

Okay, that history was totally different because Ellie hadn't abandoned Jamie. She adored him. He could hear her whisper in the back of his mind as clearly as if she'd just spoken again.

'I'd die for him,' she'd said that night. *'If it came to that.'*

The same night she'd listened to the sad story of his early life and had made him feel as though the bond between Ellie and Jamie and himself was powerful enough to last a lifetime.

When he'd promised that he would take care of Jamie if anything *did* happen to her.

And something was happening right now. Something that felt dangerous.

But…a biological father had rights, didn't he?

Luke had to fight the urge to launch himself off the veranda and forcibly remove this threat from Ellie's life.

My God…the way he was *looking* at her.

As if…

A truly horrible thought occurred to Luke then.

Had this baby been conceived naturally? It had been a private arrangement between friends, hadn't it? Maybe they hadn't even bothered using the services of a fertility clinic and an impersonal insemination.

But why did the notion seem unbearably painful?

He didn't have any claim on Ellie—past, present or future. He'd been the one to put the rules so firmly into place and Ellie hadn't seemed to mind that they could only ever be friends so maybe that was all she wanted as well—a few benefits because they were both consenting adults and happened to find each other more than a little attractive.

They were his rules. He'd lived with them for his entire adult life without them ever becoming such a problem.

Without them feeling so very wrong.

The pain morphed into anger. Anger at Mike, who

was waiting inside the house for him to sign away one of the most precious things he'd ever had. At this stranger for turning up and making Ellie frightened. At himself for allowing something to happen that made him question the foundations of his life that had worked so well up until now.

And maybe he was even angry at Ellie, for being the common factor making all of these things suddenly become problems. For the sensation that he'd walked so far past any safe barriers that he was toppling over the edge of an unforeseen cliff.

He cleared his throat, which made both Ellie and Marco look in his direction.

'I think you'd all better come inside,' he snapped.

Mike looked surprised to see an extra person entering the house but he wasn't going to let it interfere with him doing his job.

'I don't mind waiting,' he assured Luke. 'I'll have a bit of a wander and admire the gardens again. I love what you guys have done out there in the vegetable patch. Could almost get inspired myself...'

'I'll have a coffee if there's one going,' Marco drawled. 'Unless you've got a cold beer in the fridge, mate.' He nodded in satisfaction when he stopped letting his gaze roam everywhere around the kitchen to stare through the French doors to the courtyard. 'Looks like the perfect spot to have a little chat out there.'

Luke looked as grim as Ellie had ever seen him. Furious, even.

Maybe he was fed up with having to rescue her from the disasters that her life seemed to be attracting? He had, after all, saved her life the day Jamie was born and then come to the rescue all over again on the night of the fire.

Or was it because he thought she'd lied to him when she'd said that Marco wasn't a problem? That she never expected to see him again and that it wouldn't matter if he did come back because she would never let him take Jamie away from her?

How naïve had she been?

He was her son's biological father. Of course he had rights in the eyes of the law.

And, if he genuinely wanted to be part of his child's life, Ellie would be perfectly happy to make that happen.

Well, perfectly happy was a stretch, but she would have been open to the prospect, but she just knew that Marco wasn't interested in Jamie. He hadn't even looked at him. Even now, when Jamie had woken to discover that he was hungry and wet and make his presence very obvious with his cries.

No. There was another reason that Marco had come here and Ellie felt a chill run down her spine as she realised that this vulnerable, precious baby she was holding was a means to an end as far as Marco was concerned.

Did he want to win Ava back, perhaps?

That might explain Jill Collins's oddly nervous reaction to meeting Ellie in Mr Jenkins' store. Had Marco also been trying to find Ava? Had she been worried about being able to protect her daughter from a man who'd already caused so much harm and would undoubtedly continue to do so if he got another chance?

Ava had been so much in love with Marco and Ellie knew there would be a danger that she could forgive him and try again—especially if there was the lure of a ready-made family. It was all too easy to allow fantasies to encroach on reality—look at the dreams she'd allowed herself to have of being the perfect family with Luke and Jamie?

Oh… God…

Would Marco fight to get full custody of Jamie? If he could persuade Ava to take him back, they'd present an option of a full family that the courts might decide was a better option than a single mother who had to work full-time and would still be struggling financially.

The thought was terrifying. The need to escape was fortunately easy to act on—at least temporarily—by excusing herself to change and feed Jamie. There was no way she was going to do that in front of Marco. He wouldn't look disconcerted at catching a glimpse of her breasts, the way Luke had that first time. He would probably revel in it.

Panic nipped at her heels as she dealt with Jamie's nappy. It wasn't until she had settled against the pillows of her bed and the hungry cries had been replaced with the contented sounds of sucking that she was able to let go of some of the horrible tension in her own body.

She stroked Jamie's cheek with a gentle finger and felt her determination take root and grow.

There was no way she would let Marco take Jamie away from her. She would fight with everything she could muster.

Luke would help.

Or would he?

Maybe he was looking so furious because he had to wait to go through that offer on his property with Mike. Was he impatient to sign away any links with his past so he could move straight onto his exciting—unencumbered—future?

It suddenly became harder to hold onto the shreds of confidence that she could win the new battle that had appeared in her life. She didn't want to face this without the support that Luke could provide.

He hadn't even left the country yet but, already, she was feeling more alone than she ever had before.

Alone…and frightened.

The fear became strong enough to make her gasp a moment later, when Marco stepped into her room.

She didn't want to disturb Jamie or give him a fright by moving suddenly. She could only try and protect herself from the appreciative leer she was receiving by tugging her shirt to cover more of her breast.

'Just thought I'd pop in and see if you're ready to start talking,' he said.

'You need to leave,' Ellie told him. 'If you want any access to Jamie, you're going to have to go through the courts.'

'Ah… Ellie…' Marco lifted his hands. 'Don't be like that. We used to be so close. You and Ava and me… We were such good friends.'

'Ava was my friend,' Ellie said. 'I never liked you that much, to be honest, Marco. Maybe I knew you couldn't be trusted.'

'Maybe I couldn't be trusted because I was with the wrong woman.' Marco stepped closer to her bed and that was too much for Ellie. Jamie had to be close to the end of his feed now but even if he wasn't, she couldn't sit here feeling so exposed and vulnerable.

She wanted to call for Luke. Where was he?

Marco saw the way her gaze slid towards the door.

'I told him I was going to the loo.' Marco smiled. 'He's finding us a beer. Nice chap…'

Ellie was on her feet now. Putting Jamie on her shoulder, she tried to adjust her clothing before Marco could see anything more but the way he ran his tongue over his lips suggested that he'd already seen enough.

'We could make this work, Ellie,' he said. 'I've always fancied you—you know that. And now we've got a kid together…'

'Get out,' Ellie snapped as fear morphed into anger. 'Leave us alone.' She pushed past Marco as he reached out to touch her. She could hear his chuckle as she raced back towards the kitchen.

He'd never seen Ellie look like this before.

But Luke couldn't ask what had just happened to make her look so angry because he had Mike standing right beside him, reaching for one of the bottles of beer he had put on the outside table.

'Don't mind if I do.' Mike grinned. 'Although you might want to find some champagne soon, mate. You're going to want to celebrate, believe me.'

Mate?

He wasn't Mike's mate.

And he most certainly wasn't Marco's mate. He scowled at the man sauntering in Ellie's wake. The sooner he was gone, the better, but he needed to find out just how much of a threat he posed to Ellie. And it wouldn't do any of them any good to antagonise him.

Yet.

'Nice house,' Marco said. 'Not sure where you fit into the picture here, mate, but I'm sure Ellie will fill me in. Won't you, sweetheart?'

Luke's gaze clashed with Ellie's.

Sweetheart?

'Hey…' Marco seemed oblivious to the tension around him. 'Maybe I could stay for a while? You know…to get to know my son?'

'No.'

Luke and Mike and Ellie all spoke at precisely the same time. There was a moment's surprised silence then.

Marco just grinned and shrugged. Then he stepped forwards and helped himself to a beer.

Ellie sank down on the bench seat at the far end of the table. Jamie seemed to be asleep but she clearly didn't want to put him into his bassinet or pushchair.

Mike seemed to feel obliged to fill the awkward silence. Or maybe he just couldn't wait any longer.

'You've got to have a look at this offer, Luke. The buyers are heading to Europe in a few hours and they want this signed and sealed before they take off, which is why they've put their best offer on the table. And it's a doozy... I've never seen anything like it.'

'You're selling up?' Marco took a swig of his beer. 'Hey, maybe I'd be interested. Looks like a great place to raise a kid and—bonus—the mother of my child is already living here.'

'It's not for sale,' Luke snapped. He caught the look of horror on Mike's face. 'Yet,' he amended. And it never would be to this person, he added silently—even if he could afford it. The thought of Marco being here, with Ellie and Jamie, was...well, it was disgusting, that was what it was.

An image came to mind of bringing Ellie here that night. Of her standing in his kitchen, the overlong arms of his jumper dangling as she hugged herself.

And another one, of how they'd made that first bed for Jamie in the old drawer.

They came thick and fast after that, as if a cork had been pulled from a bottle. Images that came with embedded emotions. Sensations, even...

That night that Jamie had been born and he'd sat on the end of her bed and realised how courageous Ellie was. That chin tilt that was so revealing about her determination to face a future when she had nothing more than her own courage to rely on. He'd seen it again, the night of the fire, when she'd been knocked back to square one all over again.

It didn't matter how big whatever she was facing was. Now he could see her pulling that very first weed out from between the paving stones of this courtyard, her eyes shining with the prospect of taking on the impossibly big task of taming this whole garden.

The way that white tee shirt with the bird and the hearts had been streaked with dirt. Nothing on how grubby she'd become out in the vegetable garden that day, mind you…and how incredibly delicious and sexy had that made her look?

Luke reached for a beer himself, to try and distract himself from this flood of memories but it didn't help. The taste of the beer only brought flashbacks of the pleasure it had given him, coming home to the food Ellie had so generously prepared so often.

That joke about how silly it was to ask whether he was hungry or not.

A joke that she'd used to let him know how much she wanted to go to bed with him but he'd seen through the bravado. He'd known how much she wanted it, but he'd also known how nervous she was.

Stop, he told his brain.

Just stop…

But how could it, when that memory rolled inexorably into the next? The sheer bliss of making love to this woman…

It hit him with such a jolt that he almost choked on his mouthful of beer.

He might have convinced himself that the kind of love he felt for Ellie Thomas was the kind that came with family or friendship but he'd been in denial, hadn't he?

He was in love with her. Totally and absolutely in love with her.

The one thing he'd never intended to happen—to have someone in his life that could potentially be left hurt or abandoned. And it wasn't just Ellie. There was Jamie as well. The baby with the most heart crunching smile ever. A baby he couldn't bear the thought of being another man's child.

Marco's child…

Luke tried to tune into the conversation that was going on between Mike and Marco but it was only a blur of sound.

It wasn't just Ellie or Jamie or Marco, Luke realised.

This was actually about himself. About the small boy inside the man who had learned not to get attached to anything or anyone because it was inevitable that whatever was important in his life would get torn away from him.

The Gilmores had changed that because they were so determined.

He had learned to trust them.

But he'd learned to trust Ellie, too, hadn't he? Enough so that he had opened his heart to her and shared the sad story of his childhood and the fears he had of ever having a family of his own.

And hadn't he just reminded himself of how determined a person Ellie was?

Facing a future as a single mother.

Picking herself up after the disaster of the fire.

Tackling this huge garden bit by bit until she'd triumphed to the point of those rows of baby vegetable plants that she would never see turn into food that could grace platters on this old table.

Ellie wasn't joining in the conversation here, he noted.

She was sitting silently, rubbing Jamie's back gently. Her head turned towards the pushchair nearby and Luke knew she was thinking of putting him down to sleep. Tucking him in with that cute little blanket with the ducks on it?

The blanket that had been one of the purchases on that crazy spending spree in the Baby Supermarket, where all those staff members had assumed that Luke was Ellie's partner and Jamie's father.

And, finally, Luke was swamped with the memory of how that had felt.

How *amazing* it had felt.

As if it would be the best thing that could happen to anyone. Ever.

Ellie's head was turning back towards the table now. Her gaze caught Luke's and locked onto it as securely as if a key had just been turned.

The connection was absolute.

Luke could feel her sadness and fear.

He could also feel her love. Not just for the tiny person she still held in her arms.

For *him*…

He could fight for this. To keep all of this. Okay, maybe they couldn't wave a magic wand and have Jamie's biological father disappear from their lives but they could manage it.

Together.

If that was what Ellie wanted as much as Luke did. He couldn't run away from this because, if he did, he would be running away from life, wouldn't he? The most important part of life, anyway…

He tried to tell her that, silently, in that long, intense gaze and something must have been communicated because he could see the lines of tension in her face soften.

And then he noticed the silence around them.

Were Mike and Marco intruding on what felt like the most private moment of his life?

No. They had both turned towards the kitchen. Towards a woman who was standing there, framed by the open French doors.

'Hope you don't mind,' the woman said. 'But the front door was open. I let myself in.'

Marco's jaw had gone slack. He looked nothing like the cocky young man who'd walked into their lives such a short time ago. Luke had no idea who this woman was but he liked her already because she had made Marco look so much less than happy.

Ellie, on the other hand, was looking thrilled. She was on her feet and moving towards the newcomer. Amazement had become the kind of pleasure that made anything else irrelevant. The wobble in her voice revealed how much this meant to her.

'Ava...'

CHAPTER TWELVE

THE HUG WAS kind of one-sided so that Jamie didn't get squashed between them but that didn't seem to affect its fierceness.

'I've been so worried about you,' Ellie growled.

'I know. I'm sorry, El. Mum told me how upset you looked.'

'Is that where you've been all this time? At your mum's? I thought you were flying somewhere.'

'I was. I did. I went to my aunt's place in the far north of Australia. But Mum kept calling and she finally persuaded me to come home a few days ago. She said I'd be safe in Kauri Valley...' Ava pulled back from the hug, far enough to look down at the tiny head nestled against Ellie's shoulder. 'Oh...' she breathed. 'He's gorgeous...'

Ellie nodded, tears misting her eyes. 'He's the best thing that's ever happened to me, Ava. I love him so much...'

Blinking hard, Ellie glanced up.

Seeking Luke's gaze again?

Of course she was. The way he had been looking at her just before Ava's dramatic entrance to the scene. As if he'd suddenly realised just how much he loved her. As much as she loved him...

And it hadn't been her imagination running away with

her this time. He was still looking as if he never wanted
to take his eyes off her ever again.

Okay… Jamie wasn't the only most amazing thing
that had ever happened to her. Luke—and what they had
found together—was a close second. Not even second,
really. For Ellie, at least, it felt as if the three of them
were bound together so closely it was hard to tell where
the love for one separated from the love for the other.

They were family.

And maybe Luke felt the same way but was it enough
to make him change his mind about those rules that had
guided his life virtually for ever?

Ava straightened from bestowing a soft kiss to the top
of Jamie's head. She turned from Ellie now and her body
stiffened as she glared at Marco.

'You're the last person I expected to find here,' she
said coldly.

Marco's gaze shifted. He looked as if he suddenly
didn't want to be there at all but Ellie and Ava were standing in front of the doors into the house. If he wanted to
escape, he'd have to head for the garden and he obviously didn't know that there were paths leading back to
the road. He looked trapped.

Mike was looking uncomfortable, too. He knew where
those paths were and he was staring at the side of the
house as if weighing up his options of whether he should
stay or not. Ellie saw him glance at Luke. Of course he
was going to stay. There was a deal to be done, wasn't
there?

'But why wouldn't you be?' Ava continued. 'You've
been obsessed with Ellie, haven't you? What happened?
Did the girl you ran off with realise what a bastard you
really are and dump you?'

'Aww, don't be like that, babe.' Marco was attempting a winning smile. 'I came back to put things right. I still love you.'

Ava snorted. Ellie moved closer so that her shoulder was pressed against her friend's. Ava had her total support in escaping from her marriage once and for all.

'We can still be the family you dreamed of having.' But Marco didn't sound so sure of himself.

And Ava's tone was scathing. 'Not in this lifetime. I never want to see you again. Stay away from me. And stay away from my best friend.' Her glance at Ellie was a little uncertain. 'If that's what she wants.'

'Of course it is,' Ellie said. 'But…'

'But?' Ava's eyes widened.

'But he's Jamie's father,' Luke put in. 'However despicable the man might be, he's got some rights.'

Ava actually laughed. 'Is that what he told you? That he fathered this baby?'

Marco was on his feet now. Mike's jaw looked as if it were about to hit the floor.

Luke was looking bewildered and no wonder—Ellie was just as confused.

'But he is. It was his sperm that the clinic used.'

Ava's mouth twisted into a wry smile. 'Yeah…that's what we let everybody believe but it's not the real story, is it, Marco?'

Marco wasn't looking anywhere now. He had his head bent and his eyes shut.

'Marco's got a little problem,' Ava said. 'Well, more than one, let's be honest, but the one that's relevant is that his sperm mobility is abysmal. His swimmers weren't up to the job, apparently, and the only way to have any real chance of you getting pregnant, Ellie, was to use sperm from an anonymous donor. We all kept the secret to stop Marco's pride getting dented any further but I can't believe he thinks he can keep it up. To try and use a lie for whatever sneaky plan he's got in mind.'

'Oh, man…' Mike made a disgusted sound. 'You're a piece of work, aren't you, mate?'

Ava shook her head. 'He's crazy, that's for sure. For heaven's sake, the only person here who's actually got a claim on little Jamie is you, Ellie.'

Luke was getting to his feet.

'No,' he said. 'That's not true.'

He walked towards Ellie and reached out to gather Jamie from her arms. The look he gave her asked her to trust him and she didn't hesitate because there was something else in his gaze.

A promise that everything was going to be okay?

'I have a claim, too,' he said quietly. 'I gave Ellie a promise that I'd always be here to protect him if anything happened to her.'

He turned his head and smiled at her and Ellie's heart melted completely in the sheer warmth of it. The *love*…

'And things do happen to you, don't they, Ellie? Big things like becoming a mother and having your house burn down and having stupid people think they can scare you by threatening to take your son away.' Luke paused to take in a slow breath. 'I think you need me around on a permanent basis, don't you?'

Ellie's heart felt as if it were about to burst. If this was a proposal, it was the craziest ever.

And the best…

'I do,' she whispered. 'I *do*…'

Ava was looking from Luke's face to Ellie's and back again.

'That sounded like a wedding vow.' She grinned.

'It will be,' Luke murmured. 'I hope.'

Ellie couldn't say anything. She was drowning in love,

here, unable to tear her gaze from Luke's. But she could nod. And she could move closer so that Luke could put his arm around her and hold her up because her knees had gone distinctly shaky.

Mike cleared his throat. He sounded more tentative than he ever had. 'That doesn't mean that you're going to take the property off the market, does it?'

'If that's what Ellie wants,' Luke said.

Ellie couldn't stop tears gathering at the enormity of what Luke was offering. His love would have been more than enough. This house and garden would be an astonishing bonus but it was more than that.

He was offering to share his past with her.

And his present.

And his future. Their future.

'It's exactly what I want,' she whispered. 'It's home… I think it was the moment I walked in here.'

Luke glanced at Mike. 'Well, that's that. Sorry. The house is definitely off the market.'

Mike's nod was resigned. 'Should have seen that coming, I guess. You two belong together. And you belong here.' He glared at Marco. 'You don't belong here, mate. Come on—I'll show you the way out.'

Ava watched them leave and then she took a deep breath and smiled at Ellie. 'We've got a lot to catch up on, haven't we?'

'We do.'

'Another time, maybe. I've never crashed someone's proposal before and I'm suddenly feeling like I'm more than a bit in the way.'

But Luke was smiling, too. 'Please stay,' he said. 'I'll put Jamie to bed and then I'll find a bottle of wine for you girls so you can catch up properly.' He bent his head to place a tender kiss on Ellie's lips. 'We've got the rest of our lives together.'

Ava's breath came out in a sigh as soon as they were alone.

'Wow...'

'I know...'

'That's *Luke Gilmore*.'

'I know.' Ellie could feel her smile stretching to rival one of Jamie's best efforts. He wasn't Kauri Valley High School's bad boy Luke Gilmore any more.

He was *hers*... Her best friend. Her lover. Her soul mate...

And the real miracle was that he felt the same way and the power of that love had been enough to make him realise that his rules had created a prison.

He was free.

Free to be with anyone he chose.

And he had chosen her...

'Sit down,' Ava ordered. 'And start talking. Unless you would rather I made myself scarce? I won't be offended or anything.'

But Ellie was smiling because she could still hear Luke's last words—the most beautiful words she had ever heard.

We've got the rest of our lives together.

* * * * *

*If you enjoyed this story, check out these
other great reads from Alison Roberts*

*A LIFE-SAVING REUNION
THEIR FIRST FAMILY CHRISTMAS
THE FORBIDDEN PRINCE
THE FLING THAT CHANGED EVERYTHING*

All available now!

CONVENIENT MARRIAGE, SURPRISE TWINS

BY
AMY RUTTAN

Published in Great Britain 2017
By Mills & Boon, an imprint of HarperCollins*Publishers*
1 London Bridge Street, London, SE1 9GF

© 2017 Amy Ruttan

ISBN: 978-0-263-92654-5

Printed and bound in Spain
by CPI, Barcelona

Dear Reader,

Thank you for picking up a copy of *Convenient Marriage, Surprise Twins*—my 15th Mills and Boon Medical Romance! I can't believe it's been fifteen books. It still feels as if I sold my first one yesterday.

This book was so much fun to write because of the characters—I have a soft spot for Canadian heroes—and because of the setting. I've never been to Hawaii, but it's on my bucket list. I had a lot of fun researching Oahu and Waikiki, as well as surfing.

Surfing is fascinating to me. I would never try it, because I'm not the most brilliant swimmer and I'm terrified of sharks, but it was enjoyable living vicariously through my characters.

Dr Lana Haole and I have a lot in common—except the surfing thing—but I share a lot of similarities with Dr Andrew Tremblay as well. These characters are meant for each other, but they're too stubborn to see it, and sometimes I can be too stubborn to see things too. Just ask my husband...or maybe not!

This book is also special because it was the last book I worked on with my former editor Laura, so it's a little bittersweet for me. She's been there for fourteen of my books and has made me a better writer in every way.

I hope you enjoy Lana and Andrew's story.

I love hearing from readers, so please drop by my website amyruttan.com or give me a shout on Twitter @ruttanamy.

With warmest wishes,

Amy Ruttan

This book is dedicated to all my readers.
Thank you for reading my books
and making 15 books possible.

And to Laura, for our last book together.
I'll miss you!

Books by Amy Ruttan

Mills & Boon Medical Romance

Royal Spring Babies

His Pregnant Royal Bride

Hot Latin Docs

Alejandro's Sexy Secret

The Hollywood Hills Clinic

Perfect Rivals...

Sealed by a Valentine's Kiss

His Shock Valentine's Proposal
Craving Her Ex-Army Doc

Visit the Author Profile page
at millsandboon.co.uk for more titles.

CHAPTER ONE

"HE'S AN IDIOT. I dislike him. There's no way in heck I'm going to work with him, let alone marry him!"

What Iolana failed to say was, *Dr. Andrew Tremblay may be an ass, but he's sexy as hell and all I want to do is throw him down and either kiss him or strangle him repeatedly.*

Her little brother didn't need to know that part.

No one did.

Or she'd lose her reputation. The one that she'd painstakingly rebuilt since David had left her heart in tatters two years ago. She needed to keep that reputation intact. It was bad enough that she was the daughter of the Chief of Surgery.

Being the daughter of the Chief of Surgery meant that she had to work even harder to prove herself. That she didn't get handouts.

"Come on, Lana, he's the best trainer and sports medicine guy that knows about surfing. He's going to get me into the championships in a couple of months. I need him."

"No way, Keaka. There is no way." Iolana smiled to herself, using her brother Jack's Hawaiian name, which drove him nuts. Even though he used it when he was surfing.

Jack frowned and crossed his arms as he glared at her.

"There is no point in giving me the death stare, Keaka. I invented that death stare." Iolana pushed past him. And she had taught him that death stare. She'd practically raised Jack after their mother left.

"Dad would've applied for his green card as his employer."

"No, Dad didn't want to do that. He sees it as favoritism." Jack rolled his eyes. Lana didn't find it hard to believe that her father hadn't applied for Dr. Tremblay's green card. That sounded like something her father would do.

Never take responsibility, unless it was his patient or his hospital. Which was why Jack was here, begging her to fix his problem. Like she'd done before. Many times. Lana shouldered a lot of responsibility for her little brother.

"Why didn't Andrew take care of it? He has time."

"He got busy. Now it's too late for him."

Lana rolled her eyes.

Not surprising.

The moment Andrew had walked through the doors of Kahu Kai Hospital he'd had entitled, irresponsible playboy written all over him. Not irresponsible with his patients, but with everything else in his life.

"Keaka, I love you but I don't think so."

"Come on, Lana," Jack begged. "Andrew Tremblay was the best surfer for years. He dominated the world championships. I need this favor from you."

Iolana snorted. "A Canadian who was a world champion surfer. Seems highly unlikely."

"Don't judge a book by its cover, Lana!" There was a glint in Jack's eye and Iolana couldn't help but smile, just a bit, as she sat down on the edge of her desk, crossing her arms the way her little brother had done to give *him* the death stare.

Jack was younger than her by ten years and he always got what he wanted, being the only son. Lana had shouldered a lot of responsibility since their mother left. Their father was a prominent surgeon in Oahu, claiming that he was a distant descendant from an ancient king who ruled Oahu and didn't have time to raise little kids. So Lana had raised Keaka "Jack" Jr.

Iolana knew their father, Dr. Keaka Haole Sr., wanted Jack to follow in his footsteps and be a surgeon. Except Jack didn't want any of that. He wanted to be a world champion surfer. That was Jack's passion, and it had been Iolana's too, but there'd been such a gulf between Jack and her father since their mother left that Iolana felt as if she had to constantly work to repair the rift between them.

Which was why she was an orthopedic surgeon at her father's hospital. Or surfing alongside her brother.

"Why should I marry him?"

"Because he's my friend, a lot of Hawaiian entrants are counting on him, I'm your brother and..." Jack rubbed the back of his neck. "He'll be kicked out, Lana. There is no surfing in Canada."

Iolana cocked an eyebrow. "I believe there is."

"It's not the same, which is why he came here and became a legend." Jack ran his hand through his hair. "Lana, athletes come from all over North America to train with Dr. Andrew Tremblay, which is why Dad let him have hospital privileges here."

"Don't remind me," Iolana griped.

She was all too aware that Dr. Andrew Tremblay was given privileges at her hospital, in her department, no less. The way he strutted around the halls, when he was actually here, drove her bonkers.

So smug. So sure of himself.

She'd always thought Canadians were supposed to be nice.

Jack was right. Andrew brought in a lot of money to their hospital and it would make a significant dent in their hospital profits if he left. And Jack might lose his chance at becoming a champion surfer.

Her dreams had been crushed to keep the peace; she couldn't let that happen to Jack.

"I think this is fraud," she said. "I don't relish jail time."

"You've known Andrew for some time. I think we can pull it off. Besides, isn't Dad always on your case about settling down?"

Iolana frowned. She hated it when her brother was right and their father had been on at her lately about settling down. And her father respected Andrew and knew what he brought into their hospital.

Her father would approve of her choice.

Would he?

Her father had approved of David and look how that turned out. She'd become the laughingstock of the hospital, falling for a womanizer like David.

Her father had been disappointed instead of consoling when it had ended.

People pitied her.

Poor Dr. Lana Haole.

She hated the pity. Hated that her reputation had been destroyed.

It would just be for a year or two. It wouldn't be all that horrible to marry him for convenience sake.

Jack was grinning at her, probably because he knew that he was wearing her down and she was going to say yes.

"He has to ask me," Iolana said. "That's my condition. If he wants the world to believe that we're an item and that this marriage is legitimate to protect his keister, he's going to have to get on one knee with a ring and ask me."

Jack winced. "A ring?"

"A ring." Iolana got up and walked to the door of her office, giving her little brother a subtle hint that she wanted him to leave. "And a nice, big, expensive…"

The words died in her throat when she saw that Andrew was on the other side of the door, a hand raised as if he was about to knock. He grinned in that boyish way that simultaneously made her melt and grated on her nerves. How many times had they butted heads on the ER floor? And he always ended arguments with that smile which infuriated her.

"I see Jack's spoken to you."

Iolana crossed her arms and glared at him. All he did was grin. "Dr. Tremblay," she acknowledged.

He slipped his hands into the pockets of his white lab coat and grinned, leaning forward. "You know, if you glare at me like that no one is going to believe that we're supposed to be getting married."

Iolana growled as he moved past her and into her office. She shut the door and stood in front of it, glaring both at her brother and Andrew.

Andrew cocked his eyebrow. "You don't look too happy about this arrangement."

"And what about this arrangement should I be happy about?" she demanded.

"I get to stay here and work. I get to continue on your brother's training."

"And why should that make me happy?" she asked.

"Oh, come now, Dr. Haole. You treasure me and my experience."

"Well, I'll leave you two to figure out the details of this arrangement," Jack said nervously as he walked toward the door. Iolana fixed him with an icy glare as he moved past her and slipped out into the hallway.

"Hey, Keaka, not a word to Dad!" she called out after her brother, before slamming the door again and facing her intended.

"Keaka, eh? You must be ticked off at him." Andrew didn't look at her. Instead he wandered around, looking at everything but avoiding eye contact with her. Which was safer for him because she was sure her look would grill him on the spot.

"I'm not happy about this, Dr. Tremblay." She marched to her desk and took a seat in her chair. She wanted to put something solid between the two of them. She folded her hands on her desk. "There are stipulations to this arrangement."

He cocked one of those blond eyebrows of his and adjusted his glasses. "Stipulations?"

"You want this to be believable, don't you? I mean, if Immigration were to find out, our careers and the reputation of this hospital would be at stake. Jail time as well. Besides, I'm not irresponsible. *I* would've dealt with this long ago, so as not to resort to this."

He nodded, but she could tell by the way his lips were firmly pressed together he didn't enjoy her lecture. He just tolerated it. "Fair enough. What did you have in mind, Dr. Haole?"

"I want a public proposal," she said. "And I want a ring."

"You want a ring?" he asked in disbelief that wiped the haughtiness off his face.

"We have to make this as real as possible." Iolana couldn't help but grin. "I'm risking a lot."

"Is that so?" He leaned over her desk, those blue eyes of his boring into her. "Any particular cut?"

She held out her hand, wiggling her fingers in front of him and grinning, knowing that she was bugging him immensely. "I'm partial to an emerald cut, but I'll leave that up to you. There has to be some romance in this arrangement."

Andrew made a face. "Is there anything else?"

"Well, we're going to have to suss out living arrangements, I suppose. I guess it would make the most sense if you move in with me, and we'll have to sign a prenuptial agreement."

"It's not a real marriage," he said and then looked highly insulted. "What's wrong with my place?"

"Don't you live in an apartment? I have a house. And it is a real marriage—we're really getting married. It's not a make-believe marriage. I have to protect my assets."

"Fine." He straightened and crossed his arms. "So when am I supposed to make this public announcement of our engagement?"

"I'm not sure. Perhaps at the fund-raiser at the end of the week? That would be a good place for you to get down on one knee and give me a ring."

"You have this all figured out, and so fast." Andrew grinned then. "You're secretly pleased by this, aren't you? I think there's more to you than meets the eye."

Heat bloomed in her cheeks. "I think fast on my feet. That's all."

"No, I think you secretly want this. You want me."

She was seeing red. "I could turn you in."

"You won't, though."

"Won't I?"

"No, because you're attracted to me. You just don't want to admit it."

She glared at him. "Now I remember why I didn't want to do this. You're an arrogant jerk."

"So why are you doing this if you detest me so?"

"Business. You bring revenue into this hospital."

"That I can't deny." He grinned. "Is that all?"

No.

He was her ticket to have people stop pitying her. Including David.

"I love my brother and he thinks you'll bring him to the surfing championships."

Andrew nodded. "Jack is talented and he will get to the finals. He will be a champion."

Iolana smiled then. "That's why I'm doing it. Nothing more."

"It is a lot for you to take on. You must love your brother."

"I do."

"Well, I appreciate it." And she knew that he meant it; just the change in his attitude made her think that he was sincere.

"Are you actually thanking me, Dr. Tremblay? I'm shocked."

"Don't get too used to it, Dr. Haole. And I think, because we're supposed to be intimate, we can drop the formalities and use our first names. I mean, people won't believe that we're madly in love if we refer to each other as Dr. Tremblay and Dr. Haole."

"Fine," Iolana said. Though the thought of being intimate, of letting her guard down made her stomach twist. David had hurt her so badly that the thought of letting someone else in, no matter how lonely she was, was terrifying indeed. Even if it was fake. It was risky.

Andrew grinned again. That charming smile. "So Lana, would you like to accompany me to the staff meeting?"

"Of course… Andrew."

She'd forgotten about the staff meeting with her father. She was in charge of Ortho and sports medicine, but her father was in charge of all the surgeons at Kahu Kai Hospital in Honolulu. Which was why she couldn't let another scandal rock her. It was bad enough people thought she was where she was because of who her father was.

Her father would be pleased with her choice of fiancé, but she doubted very much he would be pleased with the fact that Keaka, Andrew and her were all pulling a fast one on him. They were doing something illegal to keep Andrew in the country.

And it made her nervous to know that she'd be lying to her father.

That her father had a hold on her.

All because she wanted to keep the peace between him and Keaka.

They were late to the staff meeting. The other surgeons were waiting for them. She could feel her father's icy-cold stare boring into her as they stumbled in.

"Ah, Iolana and Andrew, thank you for joining us. You're fifteen minutes late," her father said, tapping his watch. "We all have schedules to keep."

Iolana opened her mouth to say something, but Andrew stepped in front of her, taking her hand in his.

"I'm sorry, Dr. Haole, you can lay the blame solely on me." Then he grinned at her and she had a sinking feeling about what he was going to say next.

No. Don't you dare.

Only he didn't seem to get her telepathic message.

"You see, Dr. Haole, I've been dating your daughter for some time and we were delayed because I just got down on one knee and asked her to marry me."

Iolana plastered a fake smile on her face as the rest of

the surgeons in the room, including her father, stared at them with their mouths hanging open. Even David was surprised, but then he smirked in disbelief. Which infuriated her.

"Iolana, is this true?" her father asked skeptically. And she knew he was thinking about David as well.

"Yes," she managed to say without breaking her very wide smile. "Yes. It is. I'm in love with Andrew, but we've kept our relationship a secret because of past experiences." She glared at David, making him uncomfortable because he pulled at his collar.

Good.

Andrew slipped his arm around her and pulled her close. "I don't have to tell you what her answer is. It's obvious she said yes, and I know there's no ring yet, Dr. Haole, but there is one coming. I wanted to ask her to marry me at the fund-raising gala at the end of the week, but I just couldn't wait. I love your daughter so much."

"Yes," Iolana said. "Yes. We're so in love."

"You sound like a robot," Andrew whispered in her ear, but she ignored him.

"Well, let me be the first to congratulate you both," her father said and Iolana watched him cross the room to shake Andrew's hand, slapping him on the back before turning to her and hugging her. "You two will be Kahu Kai's power surgical team. This is fantastic news. I'm so happy. Shocked, but very happy."

Iolana was still in shock as her other colleagues got up to congratulate them. All she could do was smile as she tried not to telepathically explode Andrew's head for announcing their farce of a marriage at a staff meeting.

In one fell swoop her reputation for being a bit of an ice queen had come crashing down.

And she wasn't sure how she was going to survive

being Andrew's wife, let alone his fiancée, because she was pretty sure, given the way she felt now, she was going to kill him.

Andrew winked at her as her father shook his hand again.

Yep. She was going to kill him.

CHAPTER TWO

ANDREW KNEW THAT he had poked the beast, but he wasn't in the least bit sorry about it. Lana had been testing him from the moment he'd walked into her office and she'd started making demands. When Jack had suggested that he ask his sister to participate in this marriage of convenience so he could get a green card he'd told Jack that he was nuts. One, because he was pretty sure Lana hated him. Two, they constantly butted heads. Three, he didn't know what was in it for her to agree to this; no one liked their brother that much. Four, her father was Chief of Surgery and he'd told Dr. Haole that he would take care of this green card issue himself and five, he was attracted to Lana.

So attracted to her.

In his eyes, Lana was not the right choice.

Only Jack had been damn insistent.

And Andrew was never one to look a gift horse in the mouth.

You're setting yourself up for a fall again.

He ignored that niggling thought. Whatever came of it came. He deserved whatever he had, good or bad. Even if it meant tempting his willpower in marrying, in name only, an attractive, fiery and passionate woman. Lana was tempting, but Andrew had willpower.

Are you sure?

From the moment he'd met her two years ago he had been enraptured by her. Her long black hair, dark eyes that sparkled in the waning sunlight and luscious lips that he desperately wanted to kiss. She had been standing on the beach at sunset in a wetsuit, holding a board and staring out over the ocean intensely. The way he used to stare at the waves after he surfed.

The way he longingly looked at the big waves because, since his accident, he had been unable to conquer the big waves. The groundswell waves that were generated by storms. The powerful waves that he wanted to conquer again.

Only he couldn't. And he had no one to blame but himself.

Now he was fake engaged to Lana and he was slightly concerned that she would conquer him in the end.

This is not real. You're not tying yourself down.

A real marriage and kids was not something he ever wanted. Not after his disaster of a childhood. He was selfish like his father and it was that selfishness which had caused the accident that injured his shoulder and killed his little sister.

He didn't deserve happiness.

In a year he'd have his green card and this marriage would be over. He'd be free again.

And lonely.

"You're engaged?" Dr. Keaka Haole asked, interrupting Andrew's thoughts as he shut the door to the now empty conference room. "After what happened with David, I have to say I'm surprised, Iolana."

Lana's expression changed from one of daggers to slight anxiety as she bit her full, pink bottom lip.

"I know, but this isn't like David. This is real. Which is why I've kept it quiet."

Dr. Haole looked at him shrewdly. "You love my daughter?"

"Yes, sir," Andrew said confidently. "My apologies for not asking for your blessing, but things kind of happened fast. We fell in love and..."

Dr. Haole put up his hand to silence him and Andrew knew better than to tick off Dr. Keaka Haole Sr. Keaka Haole Jr. might be somewhat of a jovial fellow, but Keaka Sr. was not a man you wanted to trifle with.

Andrew wasn't terrified of him; he admired him.

The man was one of the best orthopedic surgeons in America. Andrew only wished when his shoulder had shattered that it was Dr. Keaka Haole who had operated on him and not that hack in northern Ontario who had botched his shoulder and ended his career as a surfer. Of course he deserved what he'd got that night.

"I'm not upset. Far from it," Dr. Haole said, smiling, which was rare for him.

"You're not?" Lana asked. Andrew couldn't help but hear the shock in her voice and it was the same sense of shock that he was experiencing.

"Of course not. Dr. Tremblay is an excellent physician and an asset to this hospital. You couldn't do any better, Iolana. As long as it's real. I won't have a repeat of what happened before."

"Why, thank you, Dr. Haole. Coming from you that means so much." Andrew tried to turn the conversation. He knew what had happened with David and Lana. Even if it was before his time. Everyone knew about it.

David didn't deserve her.

And you do?

Only Lana knew this marriage was fake. According to the hospital drums, she'd been in love with David.

Lana glared at him quickly. "Dad, but…"

"Now, Iolana, it's okay. Usually I don't like it when you act impulsively, but this is really fantastic news. I've been telling you for years to settle down and get married."

Andrew put his arm around Lana and pulled her closer, beaming. "Well, Dr. Haole, we wanted to keep our relationship private while we were dating. We are professionals, after all."

Lana shrugged out of his embrace when her father's back was turned and he winked at her. He hadn't been expecting such easy acceptance from Dr. Haole. Andrew was not the kind of guy who got easy acceptance and approval from parental figures.

And then it hit him. He was deceiving a man he really admired for selfish reasons.

"So when will the wedding be?" Dr. Haole asked.

"As soon as possible," Lana said. "Just something simple, probably at the city hall or the court house in front of a judge. We just…"

"We just want to get married," Andrew said, finishing off Lana's sentence.

"We can do a proper wedding in a week."

"Father, you don't have to spend the money," Lana protested.

"Nonsense. You're my only daughter and we're going to do this right. I'll have your stepmother arrange everything so that it won't interrupt your surgical schedule." Dr. Haole stood up. "I'll call her up now and give her the news."

"Thank you," Lana said, but Andrew could tell she was unhappy. Even as her father took her in his arms and hugged her.

"I am so happy you have finally decided to settle down, Iolana. It means so much to me." Then Dr. Haole shook his hand.

"Thank you, Dr. Haole," Andrew managed to say, but he felt uneasy about the idea of a big wedding. Even though a big wedding would convince Immigration that it wasn't a fake wedding.

Only it is.

"Well, I have rounds to make," Lana said. "I'll talk to you later, Dad."

Andrew nodded and followed Lana out of the conference room. She didn't say anything as she walked quickly back to her office, but she didn't slam the door in his face either. She allowed him to come into her office and he shut the door.

"Well, you wanted a public proposal. Sorry I didn't get down on one knee." It was a halfhearted apology.

"That's not how I wanted it to happen." She was flustered. He'd never seen her like this and he felt bad because it was his fault it had been announced like that.

"I know, you mentioned one knee and a ring…"

She glared at him. "I would've preferred anything over that!"

"Why? It went well. You were nervous about telling your father. Jack was nervous over the idea of your father finding out. Now he knows and he seems quite thrilled with it."

She sighed. "Surprisingly. That actually caught me off guard, but then he's been harping on at me for the last five years to get married."

"Did you want to plan it?" Andrew asked.

"No," she snapped. "My stepmother will do a fine job. I really didn't want this in the first place!"

"I know."

"If you wanted to stay here you should've contacted an Immigration lawyer and done the right thing from the beginning, then we wouldn't be in this mess."

"I know," Andrew agreed. "Time slipped away from me. I was training the team and your brother. I kept putting it off…"

"Excuses," she raged. Then she sat down in her office chair. "You're a good doctor, but you are so disorganized."

"Office work is not my forte." His shoulder started to burn and he winced.

"I'll say," she groused and then looked at him as he rolled his shoulder. "What's wrong?"

"Just a twinge. Nothing more."

"Your shoulder hurts?"

"Nothing," he snapped as the pain hit him. "Look, I'd better go."

Lana got up and stepped in front of him. "I'm an orthopedic surgeon. I can take a look at your shoulder."

"I'm a surgeon too," he said. Although he didn't practice any more. He kept to the physical therapy side of sports medicine. Since his right shoulder repair had been botched the strength in his arm and hand came and went.

He wouldn't risk a patient's life on uncertainty.

"Let me look."

He sighed. "Anything to get my shirt off, eh?"

"Fine," she said through gritted teeth. "Be in pain."

"It's just a pulled muscle."

Liar.

He could've had Dr. Haole fix it, but again, he hadn't got around to it. Training Jack to make the World Surfing Championship was all that mattered. He didn't have the time to go under the knife, recover and then go through physical therapy.

He didn't have a year or more to waste.

What was done was done. It was a good reminder.

Besides, he didn't want Lana touching him. If she touched him he knew it would test his control. Since he'd first laid eyes on her he'd thought about her in a way he shouldn't.

This had to be an uncomplicated marriage.

He had to keep his hands to himself, as much as he didn't want to.

"Fine," she snapped.

"I have rounds to make."

She nodded, avoiding eye contact. "Me too."

"I guess I'll see you at this farce of a wedding in a week."

"I think before then. You want people to believe we're in love and you just announced it to the whole hospital that we're getting married."

"Not the whole hospital."

"You blabbed it to all the heads and chief residents that were in that meeting. You might as well have told everyone." Then she smiled a sad smile. "Word gets around fast here."

He chuckled. "You may be right on that one. So, would you like to go on a date tonight?"

"A date?"

"Yeah, we might as well have one, seeing how we're getting married and everything."

"Okay. That sounds..." She was cut off when her phone started ringing. "Dr. Haole speaking. Yes? How far out? Okay, I'll be down there in five."

"What was that?" Andrew asked.

"The emergency room. Incoming trauma; they need an orthopedic surgeon and I'm on call. I forgot. We'll have to do that date another night."

"I'll meet you down in the ER. I'll lend you a hand."

"You've never done an ER rotation since you got here," she said, astounded. "What about training?"

"The training can wait tonight. Jack will understand." Jack probably wouldn't, but Andrew didn't care. He wanted to be in that ER tonight. Show a united front to their upcoming wedding so it was believable.

He might not have surgical privileges, but he was still a doctor.

He could still help when it came to trauma.

CHAPTER THREE

LANA RETREATED TO the quiet calm of the operating room to repair a broken femur. She stood by, waiting as the trauma surgeon worked on stopping the blood flow in the major artery. She was just glad it wasn't David because he'd ply her with questions about Andrew.

Poor, pathetic, heartbroken Lana couldn't move on from him.

And she remembered how many times David and she had worked in the OR together. He'd been a fellow when she was a fourth year resident. She should've known— that was a red flag when he'd paid attention to her—but she'd craved the attention. The love and affection she'd never had.

Yeah, and look where that got you.

She shook her head and focused on the surgery. Once the rate of blood loss was managed she could go in and repair the femur. Piecing one of the strongest bones in the body back together.

As she waited she glanced up into the gallery, where residents were waiting to observe the surgery, and she noticed Andrew standing, watching. His arms were crossed and he looked pensive as he stared down into the OR.

Their eyes met and a small smile played across his face and she felt warmth flood her cheeks, but she was thankful that the surgical mask covered her face. She was still in shock and slightly angry that her father was so happy about the marriage.

Of course he didn't know it was a marriage of convenience, but after David she'd thought he wouldn't be so happy. And she was annoyed that her father was elated that she was finally taking his advice to settle down, implying that her life was worthless because she wasn't married or involved with anyone.

It wasn't that she repelled love. She'd been blinded by it. Hurt by it. So now her career was her first love. It never let her down.

After David she'd sworn to herself that she was going to get married for only the truest, deepest love. Her parents had married because they'd had to and they'd never been happy, which was why they were divorced.

And the moment her mother had been free from her father, she'd left.

Lana hadn't seen her mother since the day she'd graduated from medical school. And she doubted that she would see her at her wedding.

No doubt her mother wouldn't approve of her marriage to Andrew.

It's not real and you're not pregnant.

"Dr. Haole, we're ready for you now," the scrub nurse said.

"Thank you, Vickie." Lana took her place next to the trauma surgeon, Dr. Aeolia, who had been working on controlling the blood loss from the shattered femur.

"I hear congratulations are in order," Dr. Aeolia said as she began to formulate her game plan for repairing the femur in her head.

"Pardon?" Lana asked, not really listening to what Dr. Aeolia had to say.

"Your engagement. I was in the conference room when Dr. Tremblay announced it."

Oh, God.

This was exactly the kind of thing she wished she could avoid. She didn't like to be singled out, to have the attention drawn to her and as the words slipped out of Dr. Aeolia's mouth she could feel the gaze from all of those in the operating room fixed on her. Just like when David had dumped her. Humiliating her.

"How can you possibly think I love you? You have no spine. No fire and you're not as brilliant as your father thinks you are. This was purely a business move. I thought you knew that. I thought you knew that it would benefit us both!"

Lana shook David's cruel words from her head.

"Right," Lana said. "Thank you. Vickie, can you bring me my surgical tray?"

Vickie had been an orthopedic scrub nurse for years. She was her father's scrub nurse and knew exactly what surgical screws and plates would be needed to fix a broken femur.

"You don't sound happy about it," Dr. Aeolia said and Lana could sense the censure in her voice. Or maybe it wasn't censure, but jealousy.

She knew Dr. Aeolia lusted after Andrew, like most women did. Andrew was a playboy. A love 'em and leave 'em reputation that probably would hurt their story if they didn't play their cards right.

"I am, but right now I'm focused on fixing this patient's femur. Perhaps later we can discuss wedding arrangements, but not now." Lana's voice rose and as she glanced up into the gallery she could see Andrew grinning at her, giving her a subtle nod.

"Fine," Dr. Aeolia said with annoyance. "Since my

job is making sure the patient is stabilized and will survive, I guess I can let you continue on with picking up
the pieces. You're quite good at that, if I recall."

It was a jab that was laced with sarcasm, which Lana
didn't care much for, but was used to. As the daughter
of the Chief of Surgery she was used to people treating
her like this. She knew very well that they all thought
she was a spoiled princess. That she was Daddy's girl
and got preferential treatment because of it.

When that was far from the truth.

She was not a princess. Everything she'd earned she'd
worked hard for.

"You're right, Dr. Aeolia, your job here is done. Thank
you; kindly leave my OR. I have it from here."

Dr. Acolia glared at her over the surgical mask and
Lana shook her head in annoyance as she continued to
work on stabilizing and preparing the femur.

She didn't have many friends in this hospital and she
tried to tell herself she didn't care, but she did. She was
alone.

It was why she was known as a bit of an ice queen.

And she was fine with letting them think that. It was
easier on her heart.

Lana knew who she really was.

Do you?

And as she glanced back up at the gallery she saw that
Andrew had left. She breathed an inward sigh of relief
and continued on her repair of the femur. She was glad
he was gone because he was a distraction and that was
the last thing she needed in her life.

Just go home. You don't need to wait for her.

Only Andrew was waiting for her in the main lobby.
Just like a dutiful fiancé would. He had been so im-

pressed with the way Lana had handled herself in the operating room under the scrutiny of Dr. Aeolia, who was a big gossip and who had been hitting on him since he'd first arrived, but he had no interest in her.

Now, he wanted to show the rest of them this was for real.

Except it's not.

He rolled his stiff shoulder and then got up from where he'd been sitting in an uncomfortable lobby chair and began to pace as he waited for Lana. Her surgery on the femur had been done hours ago and it was the middle of the night, but there was a diner where a twenty-four-hour breakfast was served. He could at least treat her to some kind of meal and then maybe they could talk.

Get their stories straight so they could present a united front.

As he rolled his stiff shoulder he saw her on the breezeway, in her street clothes, walking down he steps to the main lobby. She looked tired, but that still didn't detract from her grace and beauty. The Ice Queen of Oahu.

Which was an unfair name, because even though she tried to put up an appearance of being frosty he knew there was a warmth about her when she dealt with patients and her younger brother Jack. A caring side, even if she didn't want to admit to it.

She looked up at him, her dark eyes widening in shock. "Dr....Andrew, what're you doing here still? It's three in the morning!"

"I went home and had a sleep, but thought I would come back and take you out for a bite to eat."

"It's three in the morning," she repeated.

"I know, but the Kahuna Café on the north shore is open twenty-four hours and their specialty is breakfast."

She wrinkled her nose. "That place looks like a dive."

"It's not a dive. Are you telling me that you've never been to the Kahuna Café?"

"No, it was never somewhere my parents took us."

"Jack likes it," Andrew teased.

Lana smirked. "Jack would eat his own hat if it was deep fried."

Andrew chuckled. "True. Come on, what do you say? Come have some early breakfast with me and then I'll take you home."

"Fine."

"Hey, it's not a punishment, you know," he teased.

"What?" she asked as she fell into step beside him.

"Going out to eat breakfast with me. I'm not a monster."

A smile played on her lips. "I never said you were. Perhaps I'm the monster. I am considered a bit of a…"

"You don't have to say it. I've heard it," he teased. "What I'm saying is that appearances can be deceiving and you, of all people, should understand that."

"Sorry," she said.

"No problem, sweetie."

Lana wrinkled her nose. "Ugh, don't call me sweetie."

"Pookie?"

"Nope."

"Polkaroo?"

"What?" she asked, confused.

He chuckled at his subtle Canadian joke that he knew that she would never get. "Never mind. You don't want an endearment nickname?"

"No, thank you. Just Lana is fine by me."

"Okay." Then he picked up her hand and she snatched it back as if he were on fire.

"What're you doing?" she said under her breath.

"There are people watching," he whispered.

Lana took his hand grudgingly. He'd never really held a woman's hand before. He wasn't a touchy-feely guy— well, he was never one for public displays of affection, because public displays of affection meant something more. It meant permanence, romance and he wasn't a permanent sort of guy. But holding Lana's hand felt right.

And that made him nervous.

It's because people are watching. It doesn't mean anything.

And then tension settled between them. It was completely awkward and no one in their right mind would believe that they were in love and the marriage was for real unless he eased this tension.

"How did surgery go?" He winced because it was a dumb question. He knew how it had gone. Lana was a brilliant surgeon and he knew the patient had pulled through.

There were good odds he was going to make it, although there would be a long road to recovery. Andrew knew firsthand the pain of physical therapy.

"It went well," Lana said and he could tell by her tone she thought it was a weird question too.

He let go of her hand and opened the passenger side door to his car. When he shut the door he rolled his eyes. Annoyed with himself.

Why had he thought this was going to be easy?

When had anything in life been simple?

Never.

Lana and Jack might be siblings but they were complete opposites. Jack was so warm and open. Lana was closed off and cold. He had heard the term *ice queen* bounced around about Lana and he got it. There was a social awkwardness there at the very least.

Yet, in her office, talking about the terms of their engagement she'd been warm and funny. Feisty even. And he was sure that was the real her, but she was suppressing it and he didn't know why.

The drive to the Kahuna Café was laced with quiet tension, but when they pulled into the parking lot a smile crept across her face.

"That's a lot of Tiki masks," she teased.

Andrew chuckled. The place was a bit kitschy and totally catered to tourists, but he loved it. The food was simple and good. It reminded him of the small diner outside the east gate of Algonquin Park in the town he'd grown up in.

He hadn't been back to north-eastern Ontario in several years. There was nothing for him there, but there were moments when he missed things and the Kahuna Café, a world away from Whitney, Ontario, brought back just a piece of home.

And when he thought about home, he thought about his sister, Meghan, which made his heart hurt. God, he missed her. And it had been a while since he'd really thought about her.

"You killed her! It's all your fault, Andrew! You killed your sister. How could you be so reckless?"

"This is why I've never been here," Lana teased, interrupting the memory of that horrible night from his mind.

"Why? Because of the Tiki masks?"

"My dad would never come here."

"Well, your dad isn't here, so what do you think?" he asked.

She bit her lip in concentration as she slid out of the car. "I'll let you know after I taste the food."

Andrew grinned and opened the door to the café and they walked in to an almost empty diner. There were a few people, farmers and tourists alike, but the diner was mostly empty. Another reason he liked this place so much.

They slid into a booth and the waitress brought them coffee.

"Mahalo." Lana thanked the waitress, who nodded. "So what would you like to talk about?"

"Well, our wedding for starters," he said.

"I don't think we really have to discuss much with respect to plans."

"Oh?" Andrew asked.

"My stepmother loves to plan parties. She'll take care of everything. She is the top wedding planner in Waikiki."

"How over-the-top is this thing going to be?" he asked suddenly, dreading a crazy fiasco.

Lana grinned. "Over. Way over."

Andrew groaned. "Well, at least it will be convincing."

"They don't know that…" Lana trailed off. "It's real as far as they're concerned."

"True. Okay, but what about after?" It was hard for him to talk about after. He never had relationships, just flings. There was never an after. It was weird to talk about after when this wasn't a real marriage.

"After?" she asked.

"Living arrangements. I remember that you suggested my moving in with you, but we didn't actually decide, did we?"

Lana tried not to choke on her coffee.

Living arrangements?

The waitress came over. "Are you ready to order?"

"Just some toast," Lana said because she didn't really feel like eating all of a sudden.

"Nothing for me," Andrew said. "Coffee is fine."

The waitress left and Lana found the words that were struggling to come out. The reality of 'married' life was becoming all too clear.

"To sell our marriage to Immigration, we will have to live under the same roof. For at least a year."

He sounded just as freaked out as she was.

Andrew was right, but the thought of sharing her home with him, a man who simultaneously drove her bonkers and who she was wildly attracted to, was scary.

How could she live under the same roof as him?

"It does make sense if you move in with me." She looked reluctant, though. "I mean, I don't even know exactly where your apartment is."

He grinned, that sly mischievous grin which caused a dimple to appear in his cheek.

Dang, his teeth were so white and perfect.

"That's pretty bad that you don't even know where your husband lives."

Heat bloomed in her cheeks. "You're not my husband yet."

Andrew laughed, and she liked it when he laughed. She wasn't used to this. Usually he was so serious around her. She'd watched him be charming to others from afar.

But he was never this way with her.

She liked this.

Don't get carried away. This isn't real.

"So, your place, then?" he asked.

"Well, my house is near the hospital and the beach. I have three bedrooms and a pool."

Andrew raised his eyebrows in surprise. "Really?"

"Now who doesn't know where the other lives?" she teased.

"Since I'm in a bachelor apartment I guess I'll move in with you."

"Don't be so dramatic," she said. "I'm sure it's not a hardship."

"Oh, but it is."

"Yeah, well, I'm not moving in with you." The waitress set down the toast and poured more coffee.

"My bachelor pad is nice. Sparse but nice."

"Sparse but nice?" she teased. "I don't do sparse. I like neat and organized, but sparse? That's just sad."

They laughed together and she couldn't remember the last time she'd laughed like this. She'd never laughed like this with David. Not even with her father.

"Don't be so silly, Iolana. Act your age. Be respectable."

"I like this," he said.

"What, toast and coffee at three in the morning?" she asked.

"Yeah, but also this side of you. Why do you keep this side of you locked away?"

Lana felt her cheeks heat again and she cleared her throat to regain composure. She couldn't let him in. "I don't know what you're talking about."

He frowned. "Fine."

She felt bad for throwing up a wall, but it was her best form of defense. And now the toast was like gravel in her mouth; she could barely choke it down.

"So when do you want to move in?" she asked, changing the subject.

"How about after we're married? I think your dad is a traditional sort of guy."

"That's true. He is." She sighed. "I'm exhausted. I really should get home and get some rest."

Andrew nodded. "I'll take you home."

"Just back to the hospital is fine. I have to get my car."

"Right."

They both threw down some money for breakfast and then walked out to his car. Lana was nervous, as if she were on a date—one that ended badly.

Only she wasn't on a date. This wasn't real. They had just been formulating an intricate ruse.

And she had to keep telling herself that.

CHAPTER FOUR

LANA MANAGED TO avoid Andrew for the rest of the week. Even though the wedding was creeping up fast, she was actively avoiding him. He'd made her feel things at the Kahuna Café that she wasn't comfortable with. Things that she'd hidden for so long because it was expected of her. Her father had certain expectations, but there was a part of her deep down that was like her mother.

And it was that side she hid because it was too painful for her father.

When her mother had left, shortly after Jack was born, she'd assumed the mantle of mother.

And since she wanted Jack and her father happy, she'd buried the feelings of grief, anger and loss well. Only one other person had got through her icy shell and that had been David.

David had made her feel things she'd never thought possible and look how well that had turned out.

Then there was the constant butting of heads between her brother and father. So Lana had learned to adapt to smooth things over between the two of them. She was the mediator and the peacekeeper. So, to make sure everyone was happy she'd do almost anything.

Even wear a wedding dress that slightly horrified her.

"It's so dreamy," Sophie, her stepmother, gushed, running her manicured hand over the fabric as if it were one of the fluffy poodles she showed. "Isn't it, Lana?"

You expect me to wear that?

Only she didn't say that.

Keep the peace. Keep the peace.

"Sure."

There wasn't anything inherently wrong with the dress. It was just...she wasn't used to dresses. They weren't something she was used to wearing. Especially one that was lace-covered, form-fitting, backless, ivory-colored and scattered with pearls.

That wasn't her idea of nice clothing.

She'd missed her prom because her father had been at a medical conference and someone had to watch Jack. Maybe she was the only girl who didn't dream of being Cinderella.

Give her scrubs, slacks or a wetsuit any day.

Oh, come on. You dreamt of wedding dresses when you were with David.

And she hated herself for letting that thought in.

Sophie frowned. "You hate it, don't you?"

"No, no," Lana apologized quickly. "It's just overwhelming. I hadn't planned on..."

Getting married after David had crushed her heart. Having a wedding. Getting married to Andrew ever.

"I hadn't planned on a wedding." Which wasn't a lie. "We just wanted to go down to City Hall. Do it quietly."

Sophie smiled. "Which is why I'm planning it. I am the best wedding planner on the island."

"I know." Lana smiled. Sophie wasn't her mother, but she was the closest she'd had to one for the last fifteen years. Sophie had stepped in when Lana had gone to school in California. And she sometimes couldn't help but wonder if her father had remarried just so there was someone to take care of Jack when she was away. But then that made her wonder: had he only let her go because she was following in his footsteps?

Don't think like that. Dad loves Sophie and so do you. It killed Lana to be lying to her on so many levels. "I do love it. Truly."

"I knew it." Sophie clapped her hands and put the dress back in its garment bag before swinging around with another garment bag. "I have your gala dress ready too."

Lana groaned inwardly. Right. The gala fund-raiser was the night before her wedding. Two fancy dresses in the span of twenty-four hours. This would be brutal.

Lana braced herself, but as Sophie pulled out a royal blue, long ball gown, also backless and covered in lace, she relaxed because it was completely stunning. This dress she really did love. Royal blue was one of her favorite colors.

"I can see by the way your eyes lit up you like this one more," Sophie teased.

"I do." Lana touched the dress. "Can't I get married in this?"

"No, no. It's ivory for a sunset wedding on the beach. It's traditional and your father wants traditional." Sophie took the gala dress and zipped it back up in its garment bag before handing it over to Lana. "I'll keep the wedding gown at the house, but since the gala is tomorrow night I'll leave this dress with you."

"Thanks, Sophie." And she truly did mean it. She would be lost without her stepmother. This whole thing was so out of her league.

Sophie kissed her cheek. "Any time."

Lana walked her out and then once the door was shut she sank down in her office chair, trying not to let this farce of a marriage overwhelm her.

Too late.

There was a knock and, before she could say *Don't come in*, Andrew came barging in. She startled at seeing him. In the past week she'd seen him in the halls when he wasn't training Jack, but she'd kept her nose down in whatever she was doing to ignore him and avoid him. In her office there was no escaping him. She was trapped. He took one look at her and he frowned.

"What's wrong?" he asked as he shut the door.

"Nothing."

"You looked like you were about explode." He crossed his arms, his eyes narrowing as he assessed her.

Because I am.

"I'm fine. Just busy. What can I do for you?"

"I have a patient I need a consult on."

She was taken aback. Andrew always went to her father when it came to consults. Never her. Which was a slap in the face. Her father might be Chief of Surgery but she was Head of Ortho. Her father was so busy with administration he didn't clock as many hours in the operating room any more. She was clocking more hours, but other surgeons rarely sought her opinion. "Is my father unavailable?"

"No, but I'd like your opinion."

"Why?" she asked cautiously.

"Why not?" He gave her a questioning look. "Why are you so uncomfortable about this?"

"I'm not uncomfortable."

His eyes narrowed. "You totally are."

"You've never wanted my opinion on your patients before… You always went to my father."

"I never saw you operate before and when I observed you for that femur repair and how you did that surgery I was impressed."

"How gracious of you to notice."

Andrew rolled his eyes. "Fine. I want your opinion because it would look good. You've been distant this past week; people are noticing. Is that what you wanted to hear?"

"Fine." She grinned sweetly at him. "I just wanted the truth."

"You're so infuriating! I told you the truth. You're an impressive surgeon."

"If I'm so impressive why don't you let me look at your shoulder? You seem to roll it or wince a lot. Does it bother you?"

That caught him off guard. Instead of annoyance, a cold firmness set in his jaw. The twinkle went out of his eyes. "I'm fine. A little tension, nothing a good massage won't fix."

"I think..."

"I said I'm fine," he snapped and she knew that she was pushing him too far.

"Let's go see your patient," she said, exasperated.

Andrew nodded, but wouldn't look her in the eye. She felt bad for pushing him, but she couldn't help but wonder why he was so sensitive about his shoulder. It could be a simple fix if it was injured. That was if it was more than a little tension. It might not even require surgery but physiotherapy, but it was as if he'd given up on it.

Can't you relate?

Hadn't she given up on a lot of things? Things that she really didn't want to discuss because they too were a sore spot. It wasn't any of her business, because she didn't want people prying into her life. After David she was tired of being under the microscope and it was apparent by the way Andrew threw up a wall so fast that he didn't want her to pry into his life either.

"So what seems to be the problem?" Lana asked as they walked side by side down the hall. She wanted to change the subject. "What do you need me to look at?"

"The patient came in with what appeared to be a simple shoulder dislocation, but the X-rays are unclear. I think he'll need surgery because if I try to pop that shoulder back into the socket I think it's just going to pop right back out or it'll puncture his lung if I try to put it back into place manually."

"Did he say how he did it?"

"Golfing," Andrew remarked. "He's a tourist. He's also French."

"Does he speak English?"

Andrew grinned and waggled his eyebrows playfully. "Well, he did until we gave him sedation. He's been saying a bunch of interesting things now."

Lana groaned. No wonder he hadn't asked her father to do this.

Andrew wanted to torture her. As soon as they entered the room the patient grinned at her.

"Monsieur, Je vous presenté mon collègue, le Dr Haole, voir votre bras."

The patient just grinned. *"Ah, quelle belle femme!"*

"What did he say?" Lana asked under her breath.

"He said what a beautiful woman."

"Clearly he's drugged up," she muttered as she pulled on a trauma gown and gloves so she could inspect the patient more closely.

"Why would you imply that?" Andrew asked, puzzled.

"Imply what?" she said, distracted.

"That the compliment really isn't a compliment because the patient is drugged up. You're very attractive, Lana, and, sedated or not, I believe he's speaking the truth. You are very beautiful."

Andrew's declaration made her heart skip a beat. Warmth flooded her cheeks.

"Lana, you're beautiful. Sexy. And we look good together. We'll be a power couple. Why do we need love? Isn't that enough?"

Hollow compliments. That's all David ever paid her.

Andrew was just a playboy. It was just probably part of the act of seduction.

She cleared her throat. "Get him to lift his arm, would you?"

Andrew didn't know why she'd brushed off their patient's compliment, as if only a sedated man would find her attractive. The notion was preposterous.

Lana was attractive.

Which was why the proposition of entering into this marriage of convenience with her was a scary thought indeed.

Only because he wasn't so sure being alone with her outside this hospital was a good idea. He wasn't sure he would be able to keep his hands off her.

And he respected her as a colleague too much to ruin her life, but he was too deep into this charade to change course now.

She was the most beautiful woman he'd ever seen, which was why being around her was so dangerous for him. When he was around her it was an internal struggle not to pull her into his arms and kiss her, but she was completely off limits.

Of course that complicated matters, as they were getting married in a couple of days.

He just wasn't a relationship kind of guy and he wouldn't hurt Lana. She deserved more than he could offer her.

Which was nothing. He could offer her nothing.

What she was doing for him—there was no way that he could ever make up for that. Except keep his distance, no matter how much he wanted to bridge the gap between the two of them. His blood heated just thinking about taking her in his arms, running his fingers through her long, silky black hair and kissing those soft pink lips.

A scream shook him out of his dangerous thoughts.

"Zut, zut, zut..." the patient slurred through sedation.

"Donc désolé, monsieur. Il sera bientôt fini," he quickly apologized as the man writhed in pain.

Lana winced as she held the man down to stop him from injuring himself more. "I take it that's not a pleasant word."

"See, you understand French perfectly," Andrew teased as he tried to calm their patient down with a shot of morphine.

"The examination's all done," Lana said.

Andrew translated and the patient visibly relaxed. "Well, what's the verdict?"

Although he knew. The way the man had screamed. This wasn't just a simple run-of-the-mill dislocated shoulder. This was something more.

"He's going to need surgery," she said as she peeled off her gloves. "I'll go prep the OR and if you could run all the pre-operative labs and make sure his next of kin is notified that would be helpful."

"Can do," Andrew said quickly. "Is there anything else I can do to assist you, Lana?"

"You could come into the OR with me. You have surgical training. You could advise me."

It wasn't an unreasonable request. This man was his patient, he did have a surgical license, but he didn't practice here for a very good reason. He didn't trust himself to hold a scalpel. And he didn't trust his reaction walking into that OR. The memories of what had happened to him, his crushed hopes and dreams, all because of a foolish mistake which had cost him his dreams of becoming a world champion surfer. Cost his sister her life.

And the OR, a place that he used to love, was now a place he loathed.

"I don't have surgical privileges at this hospital," he said and he hoped that would be enough to deter her. It was usually enough to deter other surgeons who asked him questions that he wasn't comfortable answering.

"I'm not asking you to assist, but this is your patient too."

She was right, but he just couldn't go in there. Even though he missed it. Even though he had been a damn good surgeon before his shoulder had been destroyed. When his hands could grip properly.

When his back wasn't so marred with scars from a surgery that had been botched.

The OR had been a place he loved. A chance to do the work he loved. It was exciting and challenging yet it grounded him. Almost as much as surfing. There was a thrill in the operating room, just like when he was on a board and shredding the nar.

And now he couldn't do either.

At least he could coach Jack in surfing. At least he could be there as Jack's sports medicine physician and get him to the world championships. Provided Lana and he were able to pull off this farce of a marriage.

"I'm sorry, Lana, but I can't. I have other patients to see. I am the orthopedic doctor on call tonight. I diagnose them, you operate on them."

She looked as if she was going to say more, but instead she nodded. "Okay, well, just make sure his labs get done and his family is notified. I'll send a resident to come fetch him when it's time to go to the OR. Start him on some antibiotics as well."

I know.

"Will do."

Lana nodded and left him. Andrew gripped the clipboard, his one good arm holding it tightly but his other arm shaking because it was weak and for that he hated himself a bit.

The surgery was almost textbook. Several times Lana looked up in the gallery to see if Andrew was up there, like he had been before, but he wasn't. He was so afraid of the operating room.

What had happened?

She knew he had been a surgeon up in Canada. And she knew that he'd been a successful one. A sought-after surgeon who was innovative and ground-breaking. So why had he given it up?

Her father would grant Andrew surgical privileges in a heartbeat if Andrew gave any indication that he wanted to get back into the operating room. It actually made her a bit nervous when he did watch her.

Andrew had developed a bone flap method known as the Tremblay that was being used widely in Canada and across most states. Yet he had never offered to show anyone that technique. She'd always thought he just wanted to keep it to himself for job security, but now that he kept refusing to go into the operating room, and didn't ask for surgical privileges, she couldn't help but wonder more.

And she wondered if it had something to do with the shoulder and arm that seemed to grieve him the most.

Muscle tension, my ass!

Once she'd made sure their tourist patient was comfortable, out of the recovery room and in the care of a nurse that spoke French fluently she was able to finally go home for the night.

As she was gathering up her stuff, including the garment bag which held the dress for the gala tomorrow night, she passed by the Attending lounge. Drawn by the flicker of the television screen, she peered in the door.

Andrew was in there; he was leaned over, staring intently at the screen. He was watching a surfing semifinal, but she didn't know from what year and it was too far away to make out who the surfer was.

When the surfer, riding on an enormous wave, fell off the board she winced.

That had to be a hard fall.

Andrew flicked off the television and then leaned over, his face buried in his hands, but only for a moment as he dragged his hands through his hair. She could see him mouthing curse words through the window.

She backed away from the Attending lounge because she didn't want him to see her standing there, staring at him.

It was bad enough that when he was around she had a hard time focusing. He made her hot under the collar. He was dangerous to be around.

She'd had her heart broken by a cad before. Ever since then she'd learned not to allow herself near men like Andrew Tremblay.

Except you're marrying him in forty-eight hours.

Lana shook her head. She had to get out of here.

Tomorrow was her day off, thankfully. All she wanted to do was get home, shower and get a good night's sleep. And tomorrow morning she'd hit the beach with her board and just forget everything for a while.

It had been a long time since she'd surfed. Usually she

was too busy, but tomorrow was a good time to burn off some steam. Some frustration and some sexual tension that she was experiencing lately since she had to deal with Andrew Tremblay on a regular basis.

She only hoped the weather cooperated or she might do something she'd regret the next morning.

And the thing was, she was going to have to stay married to her possible regret for a year.

There would be no escape. No easy out if she decided to walk down that uneasy path. She was too far down the rabbit hole now; there were too many people she'd disappoint if she backed out of the marriage of convenience now.

She was just going to do everything in her power not to fall prey to Andrew Tremblay's charms.

Easier said than done.

CHAPTER FIVE

TODAY WAS A perfect day to surf. The sea, the sun and the breeze. The water was dappled like diamonds in the brilliant sun.

The only shadow on the day and his plans was his bum shoulder and the fact tonight he had to attend a gala with Lana.

Andrew cursed himself inwardly for giving Jack the day off from training when he saw how ripe the waves were. He'd thought he was doing himself a favor by giving Jack the day off so he could just spend the day collecting his thoughts.

Last night, after he'd walked away from yet another surgery, he'd gone and watched surfing on television. Something he hadn't done well since his accident. It was a video of his days before the accident. When he had been carefree and Meghan had been alive. From the days when he was still a surgeon and not the half man he'd become. When the whole world had been his for the taking. Now he deserved none of it.

He didn't know what had compelled him to watch it. *You're sick and twisted. That's why.*

Now, he was torturing himself further by walking on the beach in the early morning and watching choice waves roll in from the Pacific. This was not going to calm him down in time to escort Lana to the gala tonight. In fact it made him more agitated and he wanted to call it all off, but he couldn't. He was in too deep.

The gala would be their first real test since announcing their engagement, proving to the world that they were a real couple.

He didn't know what he was thinking, coming to the beach. As he longingly watched the waves, his hands jammed into his pockets, he spotted a surfer paddling to the shore and then hefting her bright turquoise board out of the water.

Oh, holy heck.

He'd come down here to collect his thoughts and prepare himself for the charade tonight. To steel himself against doing something crazy impulsive with Lana. And now here she was, coming out of the waves, just like the first time he'd seen her.

The short sleeve wetsuit clinging to her curves, her black hair slicked back from the water. The ocean glistening off her exposed skin like diamonds. It took him back to that day a couple of years ago when he'd first seen her. When he was first enticed by her and then realized she was Jack's sister and therefore off limits.

Pull yourself together.

As if she knew that he was staring at her, Lana looked up, her dark eyes widening in surprise when she saw him.

"Andrew?"

There was no backing out and running the opposite way. He waved and walked over toward her, but keeping a safe distance so he wouldn't act impulsively.

"Good morning, Lana. A very nice day, isn't it?"

A very nice day, isn't it? You idiot.

What, was he in junior high again? At least his voice didn't crack this time.

"It is," she said and looked a bit surprised to see him. "I didn't expect to see you here. Jack said he had the morning off and was lounging around in my pool."

"That's what he does on his day off? I thought he'd at least go to the gym."

Lana snorted. "With my brother you have to take him there yourself. He's easily distracted."

So am I at the moment. Only he didn't say that out loud. "I didn't expect to see you here, Lana."

"I have the day off too. I thought I would clear my head before tonight." She bent down and undid the strap around her ankle. With her quick movement, he swore he could smell the scent of coconut mixed in with the salt water.

It was intoxicating. It reminded him of summer, sand and surf and all the things he loved.

Get a hold of yourself.

"How were the waves?" he asked, feeling like a complete fool for the asinine conversation. He knew how the waves were. He could see them for himself.

"They were great," she sighed. "I wish I could spend all day out here, but I have to do some stuff to get ready for the gala tonight."

"Right, the gala."

"What time are you picking me up?" she asked.

"I'm picking you up?" he asked, confused.

She smirked at him. "Don't you think it would be a bit odd if my date and fiancé didn't pick me up and take me to the gala?"

"I assumed you were going with your father," he said.

"Usually, but this time wouldn't it make more sense to go with my fiancé?"

"Right." He scrubbed his hand over his face. "I'm not used to this."

"I can see that."

"I guess I'm just used to you accompanying your father."

"I told him that I would forgo the big limousine and ride with you. My fiancé. He seemed on board with it." There was a teasing glint in her eyes. He liked this Iolana. He liked her feisty, just like she had been when they'd first agreed to this marriage of convenience.

The subdued version made him want to shake her. Tell her that she was made of stronger stuff, but that was not his place. This was just a hint of the real Iolana and he didn't want to scare her away.

"I suppose you have a valid point," he conceded. "What time would you like me to pick you up?"

"I have to be there early." She bit that lip, that luscious full lip that he so wanted to bite too. "Seven? Is that good?"

"Seven is perfect, but I still don't know where you live. I guess I should know since I'm going to be moving into your place after we're married."

"Come on, I'll take you there." She picked up her board under one arm and headed off the beach. Andrew didn't see any cars nearby and then he realized she was heading for a set of wooden steps that wound their way through some foliage and up into a house that always reminded him of a treehouse.

He loved this house, but he'd never known who it belonged to. Until now.

"This is your place?" he asked, thrilled and shocked all at once. He'd pictured her living in some quaint little cottage. Neat and tidy. A treehouse was so unexpected. He'd never seen Lana as the free spirit type. The adventurer. He'd seen her as safe and reliable. Sensible. A treehouse was not sensible.

"Yes. My father comes from one of the richest families on the island. This was my grandmother's place until she died and she left it to me."

"I've always admired this place."

"It's a great place." Lana set her board down on a landing. She unlocked a rack that held many other boards.

"You want me to wipe it down?" Andrew asked; he wanted a closer look at some of her boards.

"I'll wipe it down later."

After she locked it up he followed her up the steps again, almost to the treetops as they headed out onto a wooden balcony that had a view of the sea, but was shaded from the hot sun by the thick growth of palms and ferns. Almost like a natural lanai.

"You have a pool up here?" Andrew asked, confused. They were off the ground, in the treetops almost, so he couldn't figure out where there would be a pool.

"Out front there's a small lap pool and a hot tub. The kitchen and living room are upstairs, the bedrooms are downstairs, where the pool and the main road is. It's sort of a bi-level house."

"I hope Jack is doing laps. He needs to build up his shoulder strength."

Lana snorted as she put a clip in her wet hair. "I highly doubt that Jack is doing laps. He's probably in the hot tub."

Before he could say anything else he realized she was unzipping her spring suit. His blood heated and he tried to avert his eyes as she peeled away the neoprene body suit to reveal a bikini underneath.

Lithe, bronze and curves in all the right places.

Don't look. Don't look.

So he started to stare up at the foliage and soon came

to the realization the foliage sucked and he'd rather be looking at something more intoxicating.

"Are you okay?" she asked.

"I'm good, just checking out the view. Love the canopy you have here. Very natural."

Andrew heard her chuckle as if she knew he wasn't checking out the foliage.

"Come on, let's go see if Jack is doing what he's supposed to be doing and I can give you a quick tour of your new place."

He braved a look and saw that she'd thrown on a sundress over her bikini, but still he couldn't get that image out of his mind.

Why did he have to be so attracted to her? This was just supposed to be a sort of business arrangement.

"There's an extra bedroom up here. It's small, but I think it will work for you." Lana opened the door to a medium-sized bedroom that was off the living room. "It has its own bathroom and faces the ocean."

Andrew peered around the room. There was a bed and dresser. The bathroom was small, but had a shower and as he wandered over to the window he was impressed by the view. It would do perfectly.

"This is great," he said. "Thanks."

"It's no big deal. We have to live together. I'm not going to make you bunk out in the shed. As much as I'm tempted to." Her dark eyes were sparkling at the dig.

Andrew chuckled at that. "I've lived in worse places. I'm sure your shed is fine."

"It has spiders."

"They don't bug me."

"That's a pathetic pun," she said drily.

"Do you hate insect puns?"

"Yes."

"Do they bug you?"

"You're crazy." She rolled her eyes. "Come on, I'll take you out to the pool."

Andrew followed her and spied the kitchen and sunken living room that was open concept. It was well organized, modern, but definitely feminine. There was a vase full of flowers and other little touches that were not in his home.

He housed the few books he had in a set of plastic milk crates and his futon mattress was raised off the floor by some wooden skids he'd found.

Andrew had the money to buy a nice place, to have nice things, but he preferred living that way. He liked to be able to pack up in a rucksack and leave. He liked that most of his life could fit in the trunk of his car.

Things just tied people down.

They were anchors and burdens. He didn't want any of it, but as he walked around Lana's place he felt a twinge of something that he hadn't felt in a long time. A sense of belonging and it frightened him.

He didn't deserve it. He didn't deserve happiness or a sense of security. Andrew often wondered why he'd gone on living when Meghan died. It might've been better in the long run if he'd died in that accident and she'd lived.

Their parents wouldn't have disowned her. She had so much potential.

The steps down from the main level led to the front door. There was another small living area that overlooked the front patio that was fenced by a cement wall and more greenery. Behind him were a couple of doors that he assumed led to where Lana slept.

She slid open the patio door to head out to the pool area. The lap pool was empty. "See, he's not doing laps. He's in the hot tub."

As Andrew's eyes adjusted to the light he saw at the

far end, under another lanai, was Jack, head back, eyes closed and in the hot tub.

"You better be wearing shorts!" Lana called out.

Jack startled and Andrew waved at him. "Hey, Jack. I thought you'd be training, building up your arm strength?"

"You brought Andrew, Iolana?" Jack whined. "And I am wearing shorts. I've learned my lesson."

Andrew turned to Lana. "What did you do to him?"

She grinned. "Had a few girlfriends over. He had his headphones in, listening to music, so I hid his clothes. Made him streak across my yard. Gave everyone a good laugh."

He chuckled. "That's evil. Remind me not to get on your bad side."

"Too late." Then she laughed and he couldn't help but laugh with her. "Though you're safe for now. As long as you don't annoy me too much."

"I can't promise that." He winked and she laughed again.

Jack wrapped a towel around himself and walked over. "I thought you were out surfing, Lana?"

"I was. I was gone for two hours." She shook her head. "You know, once I'm married you can't come here and mooch off me anymore."

Jack rolled his eyes. "Where else am I going to go?"

"You could use my place," Andrew offered. "Since I'll be moving in here."

"No, thanks, your place should be condemned. No offense, Doc."

Andrew grinned smugly. "Why don't you do some laps for me? And I'm going to sit here and watch."

Jack groaned. "Fine."

"I'll leave you two to that. I'm going to take a shower

and wash the salt water off." Lana went back inside and disappeared into the far room, shutting the door. Andrew tried not to think of her in that room, naked and having a shower. Or the fact he wanted to join her.

"You looking forward to the gala tonight?" Jack asked, interrupting his thoughts.

"No. I don't have a tuxedo."

"You can borrow mine. After I do my laps I'll go get it at Dad's place. It should fit you."

"Thanks."

"No problem." Jack dropped his towel and slipped into the pool. "How many?"

"Fifty," Andrew said, taking a seat on one of the deck-chairs. He turned back and looked toward the house. He didn't really want to go to this gala; he usually avoided them, but he wanted to look good for Lana, who was the Chief of Surgery's daughter.

He wanted the world to think he deserved her, when that was the furthest thing from the truth.

Lana loved the dress, but she was so uncomfortable. Usu-ally for the big hospital gala she wore a little black num-ber with pearls and flats—very understated—and she went with her father and stepmother.

Even when she was with David it hadn't felt like any-thing romantic. It had been more like a business dinner rather than a date.

"Really, that's what you're wearing?"

"What? I like it."

"Don't you even want to try? You can be such an em-barrassment sometimes. Thank goodness you're pretty."

Lana shook away that thought. Angry that she'd let David into her life and let him walk over her, blind to his lack of emotion. Everyone else had seen it but her, which made her all the more pathetic.

Stop thinking like that.

She shook those thoughts out of her head. She had to clear her mind because Andrew was coming over soon to take her to the gala.

It was the first time in a long time she'd been on a date. Period. After David it was hard to trust men and hard to date when she had an orthopedic practice to run.

Men were interested in her looks, her money, but once they discovered she had a brain and that her first love was her career then they realized that money and good looks weren't enough. She'd been referred to as frigid and cold.

That suited her just fine.

Lana had always lived by the mantra that she didn't need a man to make her happy. Which was why it disappointed her that her father was so happy about this marriage. He'd never viewed her career with as much enthusiasm as he was showing in her marriage to Andrew. He'd told her that he was proud of her for growing up and settling down.

Why did that have to include marriage?

It frustrated her and also upset her that her father thought so little of her. That he pinned a happy future for her on getting married. He'd done the same when she'd been with David and now he was doing it again.

It's not real. It's not real.

And Lana had to keep reminding herself of that fact. This was temporary. It was only for a year. She knew it would crush her father when she came to him this time next year and told him the marriage was over.

Just the thought of his reaction made her dread it, because he would be looking on her with sympathy and she didn't need that. She would just have to take it in her stride. It would cause a bigger scandal for her father and the hospital if she backed out of it now and Andrew was deported back to Canada.

Her doorbell chimed and she took a deep breath. With one final check in the mirror, she ran her hands down over the form-fitting royal blue dress and headed to the door.

Andrew was late to pick her up, which meant they would be late to the gala and everyone would be looking at them when they walked in.

Her father wouldn't be impressed with that.

"It's about time…" The words died in her throat when she saw Andrew standing there, in a tuxedo. His blond hair was neat and combed back. He'd shaved and had put in his contacts. She wasn't used to seeing him without his black horn-rimmed glasses.

The tuxedo suited him. It was as if it was made for him, even though she knew that it was Keaka's tuxedo from the gala last year. Only it suited Andrew a lot more than it did her kid brother. And she knew she was gawking at him because she'd totally forgotten what she was going to scold him about.

"Wow," he said with a tone of awe. "You look amazing."

A blush crept up her cheeks. "Thanks. So do you."

He grinned and bowed slightly. "Thank you."

"So, you ready for this?" she asked, her voice trembling. "I'm nervous."

"I'm not nervous. I know how to work a crowd." He held out his arm. "Can I escort you to the limo?"

"You got a limo?" Now it was her turn to be surprised.

"I did," he said. "Seemed only fitting. Doesn't seem right for the Chief of Surgery's daughter to be arriving in my car. And the way you're dressed, it seems only fitting."

Lana took his arm and he escorted her down the drive to where a limo was waiting. The chauffeur opened the door and Andrew helped her down inside. She scooted over so he could climb in beside her.

Once the door was shut he pulled out of bottle of champagne and poured her a glass.

"I feel like I'm back in high school and going to prom."

He cocked an eyebrow. "You had a limo and a glass of champagne for your prom?"

"Well, my girlfriends did. I didn't go to prom, but I snuck the champagne in out of my dad's wine cellar. My only real act of defiance."

"Your only act of defiance?"

"I'm afraid so."

He winked and grinned, holding up his glass to hers. "Well, then, cheers."

"Cheers," she said and took a sip. "What about your prom?"

Andrew chuckled. "I didn't have a limo. A few buddies and I had a bonfire in the woods with our girlfriends after the dance. Our town was small, there really wasn't much to do except a bonfire in the woods. We scared the girls into thinking there were bears...got them to snuggle up closer."

She laughed as he winked. "And were there bears?"

"Probably. I grew up in northern Ontario, but black bears keep their distance for the most part."

"A bonfire sounds fun."

"We'll have to have one after we're married."

"You're making plans?" she asked, surprised again.

"You're the one that said a bonfire sounds fun and you have the perfect location for one."

"True." She took another sip of champagne. "Tomorrow will be a long day that I'm dreading."

"Me too," he said quietly and then he set down his champagne flute and pulled out a box. "This is for you."

Lana took the box from him. "What is it?"

"Your engagement ring," he said matter-of-factly.

Lana almost dropped it. She set down her champagne flute and stared at that black velvet box. Something that was just fake was becoming too real right now.

As if sensing that she was nervous, Andrew took the box out of her hand, opened it and pulled out a beautiful square-cut diamond. He slipped it on her left hand. His hands were so strong and steady, while hers trembled.

"You're shaking," he whispered. He ran his thumb in a circle over her knuckles.

"I wasn't expecting this." She wasn't expecting the rush of feeling tied to a piece of jewelry in a fake moment.

"Expecting what?" he asked gently, still holding her hand.

"The ring, of course."

"Well, we are engaged. And you demanded one, if I remember rightly."

"I suppose." She glanced up at him and looked into his eyes. Those blue eyes that seemed to melt right into her very soul. His touch was nice. Just the simple touch made her feel alive.

"It's a beautiful ring," she whispered.

Andrew leaned over and whispered in her ear, "Not as beautiful as the owner of the hand it graces."

She didn't know what to say to that. No one had ever paid a compliment to her like that before. It caught her off guard and she felt as if she was frozen to the spot. She was still in the moment, her pulse racing, trembling and yearning for his touch.

Lana realized she was holding her breath, waiting for

a kiss, but it never came because the limo came to a stop in front of the resort where the gala was being held.

"I guess we're here," Andrew said, breaking their connection and letting go of her hand. "You ready for this?"

No.

"Yes. I think so."

The chauffeur opened the door and Andrew slid out. The chauffeur helped her get out of the limo and when she was standing next to Andrew he took her hand, which was heavy with a diamond on it.

It was all fake.

Not the ring, but the promise that it spoke to the rest of the world.

There was nothing sincere about this and it made her stomach twist with guilt. She didn't want to go inside and pretend, but she'd made a promise to Jack and Andrew. This was for the good of the hospital, for her younger brother.

It would make Jack happy.

It made her father happy.

It made everyone but her happy. Which was usual. So why was this so hard for her? What made it so different from anything else she did to appease her brother and father?

Lana didn't know. All she needed to remember tonight was to keep her wits about her so she didn't do something foolish which would ruin everything because, like it or not, tomorrow she was getting married.

For better or for worse.

CHAPTER SIX

ANDREW COULDN'T STOP watching Lana all night. She was so graceful and poised, it made him proud in a weird way, because really she wasn't anything to him. Perhaps a friend, but that was all.

Liar.

There was more—he wanted her. He wanted her like he hadn't wanted a woman in a long time. He'd always been attracted to her, but she'd never, ever showed interest in him. Then they'd had a moment in the limo when she'd trembled under his touch.

It sent a rush of heat through him.

Fired his blood.

Just watching her move through the different circles of people made him want her all the more.

I don't deserve her. Yet she would be his, under false pretenses.

Andrew took a sip of wine, his gaze focused on her as he watched her from the edge of the room. When Lana had opened the door and he'd seen her in that dress, it made the bikini look like a drab piece of cloth. There was more fabric to her dress, but it aroused him more than a two-piece bikini, because this dress accentuated all the right spots.

All of her curves. The color suited her. It brought out

the richness in her dark eyes, but it was drab in comparison to her. Dr. Iolana Haole was the most gorgeous creature he'd ever laid eyes on and tomorrow she'd be his.

She's not yours. This marriage is fake, remember? And you don't deserve her.

Andrew shook that thought away, because it angered him.

"That is a beautiful ring you bought my daughter," Dr. Keaka Haole said as he came up beside him.

"Thank you, sir." Andrew turned to face the man he admired more than his own father. "Your daughter deserves the very best." And that wasn't a lie.

"I agree," Keaka said, grinning. "You'll make a fine husband and hopefully father one day."

Andrew choked on the wine he was taking a drink from, while Keaka chuckled softly.

"I'm sorry I caught you by surprise, Andrew, but I do hope to see grandchildren one day. To see my legacy continue."

"I can tell you, sir, that there is no plan in the immediate future for children." Andrew never wanted to be a father. That was not on his radar and never would be. His father was a terrible man and Andrew was never, ever going to bring a child into the world when he didn't know what a good father should be.

He wasn't going to screw up his kids' life the way his father had messed up his and his sister's life.

Didn't you screw up your sister's life?

"There may be no plan," Keaka said, interrupting his thoughts. "But surprises do happen. I didn't plan on either Iolana or Keaka Jr., but life has a way of throwing curveballs if you're not paying attention."

"So true." At least Andrew knew that the decision to have kids was something he could control. Even though he desperately wanted to take Lana into his bed, he wasn't going to, so that solved the kid issue. At least from his end.

"I'm looking forward to having you join our family, Andrew." Then Keaka looked uncomfortable. "I believe that you do care for her deeply. Unlike what happened a few years ago with David."

"Right," Andrew said, feeling awkward. He knew about Dr. David Preston and what had happened. He knew that Lana was painted as the pitiful creature and David a bit of a hero. David had used Lana as a way to further his career and wounded her pride—and broken her heart?

Aren't you doing the same?

The thought made guilt gnaw at him. Lana had believed that David loved her. There was no pretense of love between her and him, but still it wasn't real either.

"Thank you, sir." Andrew hoped Lana's father didn't notice the awkward tension.

"You can call me Keaka." Keaka grinned and took a drink from his wine glass. "You're an asset to the hospital, Andrew. I do wish you'd reconsider your surgical position. I know you performed surgery in Canada."

"Dr. Haole, you've seen my file; my shoulder was damaged and I had a botched surgery. There is no way I can competently hold a scalpel again."

Keaka narrowed his eyes, but the smile never left his lips. "You know who could fix that botched shoulder?"

"You. I know. You're the best," Andrew said.

"I am good, but Lana could fix it. It's too bad you two fell in love and are getting married so now she'll never be able to operate on you."

"Yes, that's a shame." He was lying through his teeth, but it was a good excuse to get people to back off about his shoulder and his surgical privileges. He was a good physician. He didn't need operating room privileges.

Yes, you do. You miss it.

"Well, I would like you to teach our residents the famous Tremblay flap procedure. At least in the simulation lab," Keaka said.

"I'll think about it, sir." Andrew set down his glass of wine as the music started playing a nice jazzy slow song. "If you'll excuse me, Keaka, I think I'm going to grab your daughter and take her for a dance."

Keaka grinned and held up his wine glass as Andrew made his way through the crowd. He was glad to put some distance between him and his boss. Or rather his future father-in-law. Who was asking way too many questions he was not comfortable with.

It was bad enough Keaka Sr. knew about his shoulder. At least no one beyond human resources and Keaka Sr. knew. Patient confidentiality was a blessing. He didn't want Lana to pity him the way he pitied himself.

Lana turned the moment he came up to the group.

Her dark eyes twinkling, she was still smiling. "Andrew?"

"Would you care to dance?" He held out his hand, his pulse thundering in his ears. He wanted to kiss her and he didn't know why that compulsion came over him.

"I don't dance," she said quickly.

"Tonight you do." And, without taking no for an answer, he took her hand and pulled her out onto the dance floor, spinning her around and then pulling her close as they danced together. "Whoa, I didn't realize how tall you are in those heels."

"Well, I think we're the same height, so yes, the heels do give me a bit of an advantage. I usually wear flats."

"We're not the same height, or else you'd be really towering over me."

"Would it make you feel better if I took my shoes off?" she teased.

"Perhaps, but I don't think that's proper decorum."

She cocked a finely arched brow. "Oh? And what's proper decorum, plastic milk crate man?"

Andrew laughed at her dig. "I'm totally bringing those to your house. Correction, our house."

"You are not!" Then she laughed. "I'm totally wigging out about tomorrow."

"It'll be fine." He ran his hand over her bare back, revelling in the silky-soft feel of her skin. Goose pimples rose under his light touch.

Where else would he bring out this reaction in her?

He was glad he was having such an effect on her.

"Don't," she whispered, her voice hitching slightly.

"Why?" He stopped anyways, though he didn't want to.

"Because…just…"

"I'm sorry, I can't help it. You're a beautiful woman." He wanted to lean in and kiss her, but he was holding back. This wasn't real. He couldn't have her. He had to respect the boundaries.

"Excuse me, Dr. Haole?"

Andrew inwardly thanked the hotel event captain for interrupting this moment. Andrew let go of Lana.

"Yes?" she asked.

"There's a phone call for you from the hospital. They said it was urgent."

"Okay."

"I'll wait right here," Andrew said.

She nodded, but wouldn't look him in the eye. He hoped he hadn't made her angry. He hoped that she wouldn't change her mind about helping him. He hoped that he hadn't ruined it all.

* * *

"This is Dr. Haole speaking." Lana tried to focus on the call that was coming through and tried to ignore the sensation that still was burned into her skin from Andrew's light touch. It had felt good. She wanted more. She wanted him to kiss her. Her heart was still racing and she had to get control of herself or she might do something impulsive.

She listened to the resident explain that the patient's collarbone was badly fractured, and the broken bone had punctured a lung. The lung was repaired, but the collarbone needed to be addressed. The collarbone would have to be repaired with screws and plates, because the fracture was so bad.

"Tell Dr. Young I'll be right there to fix the collarbone."

"The other lung is damaged and we may have to cut the other side of the clavicle to remove a sharp object embedded into the patient's shoulder."

Lana growled into the receiver, "You do not cut that man's clavicle without me there. Do you understand, Doctor? Cutting the clavicle is not the answer."

"Yes, Dr. Haole."

"I'll be there in ten minutes. Keep him stable." Lana ended the call.

"Is everything okay?" Andrew asked, coming up behind her.

"No," she said. "I have to get back to the hospital or Dr. Young is going to break the other side of a patient's clavicle because Dr. Young may be a fantastic general surgeon, but she's not an orthopedic one."

Andrew winced and then nodded. "Okay, let's get you to the hospital. You tell your dad why we're leaving and I'll get us a ride there."

"Sounds good." Lana made her way through the crowd. Her father had had a few too many drinks with a few other orthopedic surgeons who were attending the gala; she was probably the only one, besides her resident, in the vicinity who'd had barely anything to drink. Even David, across the room, was teetering and his new conquest looked none too pleased. Although he wasn't an orthopedic surgeon. He was a neurologist.

Good.

At least she was responsible.

As always.

The last thing she drank was that sip of champagne before Andrew had slipped this ring on her finger over three hours ago. A cup of coffee before she scrubbed in would chase away any remnants, but really there was nothing in her system. She was the only one who could do this surgery.

Her father wished her well and she was headed straight for the entrance they'd come in. Andrew was pacing by the door.

"A cab is waiting."

"Good, let's get out of here."

Andrew helped her into the cab and gave instructions to the driver while Lana pulled off her expensive necklace and earrings and put them in her evening bag. In her bag she carried a hair elastic, so while the cab negotiated the streets from the resort to the hospital she quickly braided her hair and put it up. All she had to do now was slip out of her dress and shoes in her office, throw on some scrubs and scrub in.

Then she remembered the ring on her left hand, glinting in the street lamps that they raced past. She didn't want to take it off and lose it.

"Pin it to your scrubs," Andrew said.

"What?" she asked.

"I saw you staring at the ring. The way you were frowning at it, you seemed confused about what to do with it, like you forgot it was there when you took off your other jewelry."

"I did forget," she said sheepishly.

"It's okay, Lana." He nodded. "Pin it to your scrubs; that's what I see the nurses do all the time. They pin it over their heart."

She tried not to roll her eyes. "I'll do just that."

He grinned. "That's my girl."

"Don't call me that!"

"Snookums?"

"Didn't we already have this conversation, Tremblay?"

He chuckled. "I suppose we did."

The cab pulled up in front of the hospital. Andrew took care of the fare while Lana got out and raced toward her office. Andrew ran after her. As she tried to undo her dress she realized she couldn't reach the zipper but, before she could curse in annoyance, she felt Andrew's hand on her back.

"Let me help," he whispered.

Her body shivered in delight as he undid the hook that was just a bit above her waist and then pulled the zipper down. It was such an intimate thing to do and it heated her blood just with the thought of him touching her.

Of Andrew doing something so intimate. Something only a lover or husband might do.

Well, he's almost your husband.

"Thank you," she managed to squeak out.

"No problem." He undid his bow tie, slipping it off, and then took off his jacket. Her pulse began to race and a bunch of naughty thoughts crept across her mind.

It had been so long since she'd had any sort of physical contact with a man. She'd never really missed it before. Didn't care for it much when she had been intimate with a man, but being close to Andrew, getting to know him and being so attracted to him was giving her pause.

Maybe it wouldn't be so bad with him? Just once.

Don't think like that. You can't think like that. He's off-limits.

She had been expecting him to leave, but he was still standing there. "Are you going to get into a set of scrubs too?"

"Yeah... I think I would like to watch, if you don't mind, and not from the galley." He was pale when he managed to get the words out. "Do you have an extra set of scrubs in here?"

"Only women's, but I'm sure there's some larger ones in the residents' lounge."

He nodded. "I'll see you down on the OR floor."

Once he left, Lana was able to take a deep breath and calm her erratic pulse. She had to get everything under control because she had to focus on the surgery at hand. A clavicle that was broken and protruding, lung damage and the other clavicle that might need to be broken surgically to remove something that was imbedded into the patient's other shoulder? This was going to be a long, tricky surgery.

Lana hoped that the other side of the clavicle didn't need to be broken. That the object could be removed and then she could just repair the side of the clavicle that was broken. Right now she had to get her game face on.

This was what she lived for.

This was what she'd dedicated her whole life to. It was her passion. But a hospital setting had never been her passion. Lana had wanted to travel the world, work in third world countries doing orthopedic repairs.

Actually, she'd wanted to live out of the back of a rucksack, much like Andrew had been doing. Only that wasn't what her father had wanted for her. If he was going to spend money to send her to prestigious schools like Princeton, then she was going to become a world class surgeon. He was going to groom her to take over the hospital one day.

It just wasn't what she wanted, but it was what she was fated for.

Lana had given up hoping for anything different. This was her life now and, as much as she felt trapped by the way her father had planned out her life, at least she could still practice surgery. At least she was still helping people.

She took a calming breath. First she pinned her engagement ring to her scrubs like Andrew had suggested. It was heavy over her heart and she was very aware of it.

Focus.

As she stepped into the scrub room she watched the trauma surgeons work on the patient. The man had been impaled by a metal pole. And she winced when she saw it.

"It's nasty," Andrew said, coming up beside her, scrubbing in. He had to be sterile too, even if he was only observing.

"It doesn't look pleasant." She shook off her hands then grabbed a paper towel to dry them.

"I'm glad you took my advice about the ring."

"Now everyone will see it," she muttered.

"The surgical gown will cover it." Then he leaned over, grinning in that charming sexy way that always made her weak in the knees. "Besides, everyone knows we're engaged. Unless, of course, you're afraid that a token, such as a ring, makes you appear weak."

Lana rolled her eyes. "You ready to come in there?" she asked.

He frowned. "Why wouldn't I be?"

"This is the first time I've seen you in the operating room since you came here. You've always avoided it since I've known you. Though I've noticed you in the gallery, I was surprised when you suggested you'd come in and observe."

The frown intensified. His eyes narrowed and she knew she'd pushed him again. She'd pushed those invisible buttons that he was so sensitive about.

"Do you not want me in there?" He spun it around, trying to change the focus.

"I want you in there. I would love if you assisted me."

"No surgical privileges, except observation, remember?"

"I haven't forgotten." She headed into the operating room, shuddering at the change in temperature. The OR was chilly and she'd been in a packed gala for most of the night. Not to mention that it had been muggy outside as well. Even though she knew the operating room was kept at a lower temperature, her body still was shocked and she couldn't help but shiver as a scrub nurse helped her on with her surgical gown and gloves.

"Sorry to tear you away from your gala, Dr. Haole, but I figured that you might be the only orthopedic surgeon in a five mile radius who would be sober enough to help me." Dr. Young was giving her a dig.

Lana bit her tongue. Figuratively. "I am the orthopedic surgeon on call, so your assumption would be correct, Dr. Young."

Dr. Young snorted in response but continued working on the punctured lung. "I'll soon be done here and then you can go about repairing the clavicle."

"What about the object in his other shoulder? Will you remove that?"

"I would like to, but I think that I will have to break the other clavicle to remove it and you gave strict instructions for us not to touch it." The tone was sanctimonious. Dr. Young was older than her and had been a trauma surgeon overseas while she'd been serving the country. She'd probably done this on her own, but when it came to orthopedic procedures at this hospital Lana oversaw them all.

No one was touching the unbroken part of the clavicle until she'd gotten a good look at it.

"Do we have any recent imaging?" Lana asked.

"Here, Dr. Haole," a resident said, lighting up the screen to show X-rays.

Andrew walked into the operating room.

"It looks like the object has lodged next to the acromioclavicular joint and the clavicle."

Lana nodded. "It's lucky it wasn't dislocated, but it's jammed in there."

"The main concern Dr. Young had was whether dislodging it would damage the lung," the resident, Dr. Page, said.

"If I manage the dislocation I don't need to break the clavicle. If I dislocate it from the joint in a controlled manner we can remove the object without damaging the lung and repair the joint with this side of the clavicle intact."

"I agree," Andrew said. "I've done this before."

"Are you certain?" Dr. Young called from the table, where she was finishing up her part of the job. "I don't want to have to come back and clean up your mess when you damage the lung."

"Then you don't have to. I've repaired a lung before or Dr. Page can help me. I'm sure he's capable of it as well."

Dr. Young shook her head. Lana knew she was overstepping some boundaries, but she didn't know why Dr. Young had her knickers in a knot over her. Of course, when didn't Dr. Young have her knickers in a knot?

"Since you're so confident in Dr. Page's ability, I am finished here." Dr. Young handed over her surgical tools and walked away.

Lana gritted her teeth but didn't say anything. Dr. Young was so passive-aggressive and didn't trust anyone unless they'd been doing surgery for at least fifteen years. And it wasn't as if her father had instilled a lot of confidence. He'd overseen most of her surgeries like this in the past and Dr. Young was digging at her for being the daughter of the chief.

"What a diva," Andrew whispered under his breath.

Lana snorted as she took the lead surgeon's spot. "Dr. Page, would you assist me?"

"Yes, Dr. Haole!"

"Get a surgical gown on and gloves."

Dr. Page nodded and headed over to a scrub nurse to get gowned up. He was eager and Lana couldn't begrudge the resident that, though Lana would rather have Andrew, who had done this before. She'd rather he'd assist her, but Andrew made no move to assist. He stood where the X-rays were, watching her as she went to work.

It was a delicate procedure, but it would be the only way to dislodge the object from the patient's shoulder without damaging the joint, breaking the clavicle again or damaging the lungs. Lana took a deep breath and glanced over at Andrew again. She had a moment of uncertainty. She hadn't done this procedure a lot of times. Especially without her father here. Whenever she came into the operating room with something like this, her father insisted on assisting.

If she screwed this up…

Don't think about it.

Andrew nodded. "You got this."

Just like that, his belief in her entered her and it shocked her how much he calmed her in that moment. No one had ever been able to calm her down so fast. It was scary, but she also liked it. And she was surprised by how much she liked it.

Lana took a deep breath and waited for Dr. Page to join her at the table. The X-rays were wheeled over so that she could get a closer look at the object. Then the fluoroscope was turned on, so she could see the joints in the shoulder. After the object which had impaled the patient was removed, then she would repair the dislocation and then fix the broken side of the clavicle. The patient would be in the long haul for physiotherapy and would be in a lot of pain.

Tonight would be a long night. She just hoped that she got a bit of sleep so she didn't have dark circles under her eyes for tomorrow night's wedding.

"Are you ready, Dr. Haole?" Dr. Page asked.

"Yes. Let's get this patient on the road to recovery." She took a deep breath and held out her hand to the scrub nurse. "Scalpel."

CHAPTER SEVEN

RUN.

That was his first thought, but he couldn't do that to Lana. Instead he pulled at his collar, which felt too tight. Stifling, almost.

Andrew had worn this tuxedo last night at the gala. It hadn't bothered him then, but now, standing on the beach with the ocean behind him and a bunch of strangers sitting on either side of the torch-strewn aisle with a minister and Jack, it suddenly felt that the collar on the tuxedo was shrinking.

Run. Just run.

Jack leaned over. "Stop pulling at it, Andrew."

"It's bothering me," Andrew whispered, but he continued to fiddle with it.

"Yeah, 'cos you're pulling at it." Jack shook his head. "Why are you so nervous?"

Andrew didn't answer Jack's question and stopped fidgeting. He was still tired from watching Lana perform that surgery last night—a surgery he was all too familiar with—and his arm twinged, reminding him of his accident.

"Meghan, you should buckle up."

"I'm fine. I just have to take off my coat... Oh, my God. Andrew! The moose!"

Andrew winced as the sound of screaming filled his head.

If only his surgeon had done to him what Lana had pulled off so beautifully. Instead they had cut the metal out, tearing his joints and muscles around his shoulders. His shoulder blade had been shattered and pieced together incorrectly. He was lucky to have his arm still.

Yeah, lucky.

"You should've been the one to die!"

"There was a moose, Dad. I couldn't..."

"I don't care. You should've died. Not her. You killed her."

He'd watched Lana throughout that surgery with absolute awe and admiration. In the moment before the surgery started she'd looked at him for reassurance. In that moment she'd trusted him. It had been so long since he'd felt that kind of connection with someone.

It was unnerving.

As soon as the surgery was over he'd left, because he'd had to put some distance between them. She stirred something in him. Something that scared him. The problem was he was marrying her. There was no place to hide.

There were so many emotions running through him right now.

When he'd first thought of marrying to stay in the country he'd had no real emotional attachment or feeling about Lana other than attraction. She'd always been icy to him. She annoyed him and he knew that he annoyed her.

They were civil, polite, but they hadn't had much interaction. So he'd never really worried about the ramifications of any emotional attachment to her. He'd figured that he'd be able to walk away after the year and go on with his life.

Until recently. Now, he was enjoying her company,

He wasn't so indifferent to her. He was setting himself up for something dangerous.

This is not real. It's platonic.

Though right now, standing here, this wedding felt real. It was legal and real in that sense, but there was something more.

Sophie Haole, Lana's stepmother, had made this wedding as real as any he'd seen. Torches were arranged in the sand, forming an aisle, and amongst the guests there was no one he recognized. Andrew wasn't surprised by that really, since the only friends he had were Jack and a couple of other guys he trained.

He had no family here. His family didn't care much about him.

The sun was setting, slipping into the ocean, and the wind picked up, causing the flames on the torches to flicker.

Deep breath.

Then he thought again about turning and running, except it would humiliate Lana. She was in this as deep as he was. He had to stick it out. There was no going back now.

The music started. Even though everything about him was telling him to run, he stood his ground. Then he saw Lana and everything that told him to flee was silenced in one quick moment.

In fact, he forgot to breathe.

Oh, my God.

She was beautiful.

Breathtaking.

And he knew then and there that he was in big trouble.

Dr. Haole was beaming as he walked Lana down the aisle toward him. Lana, under the veil, seemed a bit shell-shocked. It looked as if he wasn't the only one who was unsure and terrified. A smile crept across his face and then he just couldn't stop smiling as she came closer.

Suddenly he was ridiculously happy and he didn't know why and couldn't remember the last time he'd been this happy.

"You're an idiot!" Meghan had screeched happily as they'd walked out of the movie theater.

"Oh, come on, you're happy to have me home, admit it!" He'd slung his arm around his sister.

"I am. I've missed you. It's been terrible here."

"Well, that will all change. You'll come back to Vancouver now that you're going to school there. You can live with me. I'll take care of you, Meghan."

"Promise?"

"I promise."

Only he'd broken that promise that night.

He wouldn't break his promise to Jack.

When Dr. Haole placed Lana's hand in his, hers was trembling.

"You okay?" Andrew whispered as her father stepped away.

"Perhaps." Then she smiled. "What happened to our simple wedding at City Hall?"

"Nothing about us is simple, it seems," he teased.

They both laughed at that, melting away all the tension and uncertainty about what they were about to do. The officiant stepped up and began the ceremony. Andrew was only half listening. All he could think about was how beautiful Lana was.

She glowed.

He wasn't sure if it was the waning sunlight or the dress, but all Andrew could think about was that she was going to be his wife.

Mine.

Only she wasn't his. There would be no honeymoon. No night of passion between them. Even if he wanted it. Lana would only be his on paper. He would never be able to take her in his arms and make love to her. This deal wasn't forever. There was an end date.

An expiry.

"Do you, Andrew Francis Tremblay, take Iolana Sarah Haole as your lawfully wedded wife?"

"I do." It shocked him how easily the words came out. He had been worried he wouldn't be able to say it so smoothly when it was all a lie.

"Do you, Iolana Sarah Haole, take Andrew Francis Tremblay as your lawfully wedded husband?"

"I do," she whispered. She squeezed his hand after she said the words, as if she too had been worried about the vows. It was nice not to feel alone.

"Do you have the rings?" the officiant asked.

Jack handed him her wedding ring, while her stepmother handed her a gold band that would be his. He slipped the band on her finger and she slipped the thick gold band on his hand. It was heavy. It felt awkward. Like a shackle.

"Then, by the power invested in me by the State of Hawaii, I now pronounce you man and wife. You may kiss your bride."

His pulse roared in his ears as he lifted the veil.

Just one kiss to seal it. That's all.

Her dark eyes were twinkling in the twilight. They were wide as she looked at him. He'd wanted to do this. He wanted this, badly. So he cupped her face and bent his head down to kiss her. Electric heat, like a burn, moved through him. And he knew as the kiss ended and everyone clapped that one kiss would never be enough.

* * *

Lana was still in a daze as Andrew took her hand and they moved down the aisle. People were tossing flower petals at them. The memory of Andrew's kiss was still burned into the flesh of her lips. The thing was, she wanted more.

Every time she got closer to Andrew, the more she wanted. She glanced down at her hand to see the wedding band and it shocked her. She'd only got her engagement ring last night at the gala and now she had a wedding band on her hand. It felt foreign, but she liked the look of it as well—and she'd thought she would never wear a wedding band, because she had no interest in the idea of matrimony.

Or at least didn't think that it would happen.

"You're still shaking," he said as they headed down the path to the tent on the golf course overlooking the ocean where their reception was waiting.

"I think I'm in a bit of shock. Did that really just happen?" she asked.

"I'm afraid so." He kissed her hand as they walked the path. "Thank you, by the way."

"For what?"

"For marrying me." And he was serious. This wasn't a tease or a light-hearted moment. This was a moment of sincerity, which made her stomach flip flop with anticipation. She didn't know what to say, but could feel blood rushing to her cheeks and she looked away.

"No problem."

"You're stuck with me now," he teased, which eased the tension.

"I could say the same. Thank you for the ring, by the way. Both the rings."

"You deserve it." They waited outside as the rest of the guests filtered in from a different direction. "Your stepmother went all-out."

"I told you that she would. It's her profession and I guess I'm her showpiece."

"A luau, though? I thought your father didn't like the gimmicky touristy things people expect about Hawaii."

"Usually, but he likes luaus. What my father wants he gets," Lana sighed. She'd really had no say in it all. Ever since Andrew had announced their engagement in the staff meeting, it had felt as if she didn't have much say in a whole lot of things. Her father had taken over—as usual. Her whole life, she had been dictated to.

All she'd wanted was a simple wedding. She hadn't even picked out her dress.

You didn't even want this, though.

Which was true, so she shouldn't be saddened by her father planning it. It wasn't real after all.

"What did you want?" Andrew asked and it surprised her he asked. No one ever asked her what she wanted. She didn't know what to say.

"City Hall."

He chuckled. "No, I mean what did you really want? What did you dream about as a young girl?"

That was something she hadn't thought about or even entertained since she was about ten years old. She'd forgotten about those dreams. That was when her mother was around still and she could just be a kid.

Since her mother left she'd really let go of all her childhood memories. All those hopes and dreams and the make-believe. When her mother left was when she grew more pragmatic. That was when she'd started playing peacekeeper and parent. It was when she'd had to grow up.

"Actually, I wanted to be married on the beach, but there were a lot more unicorns involved."

Andrew laughed. "No luau?"

She wrinkled her nose. "No, pizza dinner would've been nice. And root beer floats."

"That sounds like fun," he said.

"A lot of fun. Then honeymoon in a castle, but I suppose this resort is good enough."

"It would be nice to have a couple of nights here," he agreed.

Then her cheeks heated as she thought of a couple nights here alone. "You know we're spending our wedding night here."

A strange look passed across his face. One of restraint and fear.

Before he could respond, Sophie opened the flap to their private tent. "We're ready to announce you two now."

"Okay." Andrew cleared his throat and took Lana's hand. "You ready for this?"

"As ready as I'll ever be." She squeezed his hand as they were led into the reception area, where they were announced as Dr. and Mrs. Tremblay, which made her grit her teeth just a bit. She was a doctor too, but her dad was old-fashioned. Then the Polynesian dancers that her father hired gave them a traditional welcome.

After the dance they were led to the head table, where her father welcomed everyone. Lana just sat there like a centerpiece. She hated the attention. The reception was a blur because it felt a bit unreal and she felt guilty for tricking her loved ones.

Everyone was enjoying the food, including Andrew, but it tasted like sawdust in her mouth. She just wanted this whole farce to be over and done with. This wasn't real and she was tired of acting. After dinner and some more entertainment, a band started playing and Andrew turned to her.

"It's time for our dance," Andrew stated.

"Our what?"

"As man and wife—our first dance." Andrew stood and held out his hand. "What do you say, Mrs. Tremblay?"

"Seriously? It's Dr. Tremblay," she teased. At least the wedding reception would soon be over. Then they could get back to normal.

You mean being lonely normal?

Andrew chuckled and she took his hand as she stood. He led her out onto the dance floor and pulled her close as they moved across it.

"I do enjoy dancing with you, Lana."

"We've been dancing a lot lately. I don't think I've danced this much in my life," she admitted.

"Are you complaining?" he asked.

"No, I'm not." She gazed into his blue eyes because she did like dancing, especially with him. "For someone who spent a lot of time at bonfires drinking beer and seducing women you're a very good dancer."

"Well, the girls did like to dance around the fire as well. And I didn't mind holding them close, but I like holding you close better."

She blushed and then wondered how much was true. They were out in public and had to put on a show. Andrew was a known flirt.

It's all pretend.

For once, though, she didn't care. She craved the human touch and she just wanted to have a stolen moment with a man she found attractive. Just one moment where she wasn't responsible, sensible, boring Iolana.

"You okay?" he asked.

"Why?"

"You seem sad all of a sudden."

"No. I'm not sad, I'm just tired. The surgery from yesterday was so long and late into the night. I'm still not rested enough."

"Want to slip out of here early?"

"People will know we're missing. It's our wedding." Though she desperately wanted to. She was done pretending for all these friends of her father.

"Exactly, it's our wedding. People are partying. Let's go and we'll get you some peace and quiet."

Lana saw her family and friends were enjoying the party. They could escape. She already had the key card to the room. She just needed to get away from all of this.

"Let's go," Lana said. She wanted out of here. This was all too overwhelming.

Andrew nodded and they snuck out of the reception. She'd never snuck out of one of her father's parties before.

It was kind of thrilling to rebel this way.

She never rebelled.

They took a back stairwell in the resort to the honeymoon suite, which was ready and waiting for them. The terrace doors had been opened and faced the ocean, where a full moon was reflected on the water. The palms were swaying and their gentle sound was mixed with the faint strains of the band from the reception.

There was champagne and chocolate-covered strawberries. The large king-sized bed was strewn with rose petals. It oozed romance.

Her pulse began to race. This room was supposed to be for two people in love.

Not for two fakers.

"Wow, your stepmother likes to go all-out." Andrew whistled. "This is something."

"Yeah, that's Sophie."

Andrew undid his bow tie and unbuttoned his shirt. Her heart hammered as she thought about him getting undressed. It had been so long since she'd been intimate with a man. Completely out of character, she was longing for his touch. Being in his arms on the dance floor had been nice. So nice. Comforting.

"You're getting undressed?" she teased.

"The collar was too tight." He then slipped off the jacket and rolled up the sleeves of the shirt, but still kept the vest on. She was disappointed, but it was probably for the best. He wandered out on the terrace and Lana poured champagne, kicked off her shoes and followed him outside. She handed him a flute.

"Thanks," he said and then took a sip, leaning against the balcony.

"Sorry it's not beer." Then she nodded toward their reception on the green. "There's a bonfire where they were cooking the pig down on the beach."

"Nice." Andrew held up his champagne flute to clink with hers. "Sorry there're no unicorns."

And he winked at her, his blue eyes sparkling in the dim light.

"It's quite all right." She drank down her champagne and then leaned over the terrace. "At least we have a nice view." The ocean was like glass with a full moon rising over the water, the palm trees swaying and the flicker of flames against the night sky made her sigh.

"That's not the view I'm enjoying."

She glanced over at him and he was staring at her. It sent a delicious shiver down her spine. She wanted him. Rarely did she take what she wanted. She was too shy about men she was attracted to. And David had completely shattered her self-esteem and heart. Andrew was a playboy like David.

Yet they were married. They were adults. Why couldn't she just indulge this one time?

She set down her flute and walked over to him. He watched her as she stood in front of him.

Lana kissed him then, swept away in the fairy tale fantasy of it all. The kiss was gentle at first, but then it deepened into something more dangerous. His mouth opening and his tongue entwining with hers. One hand went into her hair and the other around her waist as he pulled her tight against him. She knew then he was feeling what she was feeling. He wanted her just as much as she wanted him.

Why couldn't they indulge this once? Why did she always have to play by the rules?

People had casual sex all the time. They were consenting adults and she wanted this. She didn't have to give him her heart. Just her body and just for this night.

Heck, she'd wanted this the first day she'd met him. Even when he annoyed her. Even though she knew he was bad for her.

The kiss ended but Andrew didn't let her go.

"Andrew, I want this."

"Are you sure?"

"Yes."

"I don't want…" He trailed off. "I want you too, Lana but…"

"It doesn't have to mean anything, Andrew. I know this isn't forever and I'm fine with that. I'm not expecting more. If I was, I wouldn't have done this."

"Okay." He sounded a bit off.

"I won't get hurt, Andrew. Why can't we just have this one moment together?"

"Lana, I…"

She kissed him again. "I want you, Andrew. I'm sure about this. Make love to me."

"I can't. I want… I can't." Andrew pushed past her and left the terrace.

Lana stood there, stunned, until she heard the door slam. Then she just felt stupid and tears stung her eyes. She didn't know what she'd been thinking.

All she'd been thinking about was her need.

How lonely she was.

She shouldn't have taken the chance.

Every time she took a chance she was burned.

CHAPTER EIGHT

LANA'S REQUEST HAD caught him off guard, but he wasn't displeased by it. Not at all. It was just that he couldn't. He'd just never expected it from her. She was always was so careful, guarded, but the more time he was spending with her, the more he realized a hot fiery passion burned beneath the surface.

And that was something he wanted to explore, but he had a sneaking suspicion that if he tasted this once, he was going to want more and more. So, even though it killed him, he left the room. Walked the beach, far away from the wedding, to calm his senses, but it didn't work because all he could think about was Lana's lips pressed against his.

The feeling of her in his arms.

And her begging him to make love to her.

You can't.

Although he wanted to.

After what seemed like an eternity he returned to the room. Hoping that everything had blown over, that she might be already asleep even, but instead he saw her sitting on the couch, a flute of champagne in her hand. She turned to look at him when he shut the door and he could see the tearstains on her cheeks.

Pain hit him hard.

He'd hurt her.

"Oh, I didn't expect you to come back," she said quietly and she wiped the tears from her face.

"I just needed a moment to myself."

"I see," she said quietly. Then she sighed. "Well, I think I'm going to turn in."

"Lana, I think we need to talk," he said.

"What is there to talk about?" She frowned. "You didn't want me and you have nothing to apologize about. I'm the one that wanted to step out of the boundaries we set. Not you."

"No, that's not it."

"What do you mean?" she asked, confused.

"I want you too, Lana. It's not for lack of desiring you. I want you. More than anything." And, though he knew that he shouldn't, he closed the distance between them and kissed her, fully expecting her to pull back from him the way that he had pulled from her, but she didn't. Instead she melted into his arms and he knew that he was a lost man.

There would be no walking away from her again tonight.

He was so weak.

Without asking any more questions, he scooped her up in his arms and carried her back into the room. He laid her down on the bed and kissed her again, pressing his weight against her, but he hated the fact there were so many layers of clothes that were separating them.

He wanted nothing between them.

All he wanted was just skin on skin. No words, just raw need driving their passion. Lana seemed to be feeling the same thing as he was because her fingers began to undo the buttons of his vest and then his shirt, but he didn't want to be the only one completely naked—he wanted to undress her.

And he didn't want to get her dress ruined.

"Let's get that dress off you and then we can work on my tuxedo."

She grinned at him and stood up. He spun her around, but let his hands linger on her bare back, just reveling in the silky softness of it. Lana sighed and where he touched there was a trail of goose pimples. He loved the way her body responded to his.

It made him want her even more.

He undid the clasp and unzipped the dress. It was similar to the dress she'd worn last night, only this one was ivory and of a heavier material.

Lana shrugged her shoulders out and the dress fell to the floor, pooling at her feet. Andrew was not prepared for the visual onslaught of her standing there in bridal lingerie. The slip, the garter belt and stockings, the bustier.

She turned around to face him, those dark eyes sparkling with that fire he knew was buried underneath. He could see the blush that he so adored creep up from her slender neck and blossom in her cheeks.

"Now it's your turn." And she undid the rest of the buttons on his shirt. She pulled it down off his arms and then ran her fingers over his chest. The mere light touch of her fingers on him sent a jolt of heat from where she touched straight to his groin.

He was so aroused by her.

And he couldn't remember ever having wanted a woman so much that a groan slipped past his lips. Her hands slid in the waistband of his trousers and she undid the button and then the fly. He shimmied out of his pants and then pushed her back on the bed before removing his socks. All that was left between them now was their undergarments, but those would soon be gone.

He kissed her again. Hungrily.

"I hate to break this up, but do you have protection?" she asked.

Crap.

Usually he carried one in his wallet and he couldn't remember if he'd put it in his pocket or not. Even though sex was the last thing he had been expecting with Lana, because he didn't want to push something he knew could be so dangerous for both of them.

As luck would have it, he did have his wallet and there was one.

He pulled it out. "Yep."

"Thank goodness."

"No one is more thankful than me." He joined her back on the bed. "Now, where were we?"

She cupped his face. "I think we were here."

The kiss fired his blood, but he sensed that there was no nervousness that was there before. The uncertainty that seemed to sometimes plague Lana when dealing with things that were beyond the scope of medicine and only dealt with emotion.

There was no uncertainty now. She seemed to know exactly what she wanted and that made him burn for her.

This was the confident Lana that he knew in the hospital.

The one who knew exactly what she wanted. Although he liked the one that was vulnerable, he liked this version of her as well. As they were kissing she ran his hands over his back and her hands paused on the scar, touching it gently as if she was trying to figure out what it was, but she didn't linger long.

She didn't stop and question him. Which was a relief. He didn't want to talk about that right now. All he wanted to do was focus on this moment. He wanted to feel with her. He wanted to forget everything.

He wanted to bury himself inside her.

Not soon enough all that remained between them was gone. And it was just the two of them, heart to heart. She was completely bared to him.

When he ran his hands over her body, she responded, arching her back. He wanted to take her now, but he wanted her to give him a sign, he wanted her to be ready. He wanted her to want him as much as burned for her.

Lana didn't need to say a word to let him know that she was ready, with a slight arch of her hips and her legs wrapped around him. He didn't kiss her in that moment, instead he gazed deep into her eyes, his fingers entwined with hers as he entered her.

It was almost too much for him to hold back. And he couldn't recall any time before this moment. It had never been like this with anyone else.

It scared him, but thrilled him. He hadn't had such a rush, such a thrill since he was surfing. That had been when he was truly free.

Lana made him feel truly free.

She came around him and it wasn't long until he was joining her. He rolled over on his back, trying to catch his breath, and she snuggled in beside him. Her hand on his chest. The way that Lana had made him feel things terrified him.

Things that he never wanted to feel with anyone.

He liked living his life alone. And he wondered why he'd even agreed to this marriage. Right now, holding her in his arms in their bridal suite, he was scared about how he was feeling. How in one moment Lana had got to him when no one else had been able to.

Except his sister, but when she'd died and his family shut him out, he'd felt that he didn't deserve this. He felt guilty.

"Are you okay?" Lana asked, propping herself up on one elbow, her black hair cascading over her shoulders, making it impossible to shut her out.

"I'm fine." He grinned at her.

"That was great. Thank you."

He grinned. "I've never been thanked before."

"Well, I was taught to have manners," she teased.

Andrew laughed and then kissed her. "You're welcome then."

"So, the scar?"

Andrew stiffened under her. "What about it?"

"Now you're definitely not okay," she said.

"I don't like to talk about it."

"What happened?"

"An accident."

"Is that why you won't operate?"

Andrew sighed and pushed her away. He got up out of bed and pulled on his pants. He didn't look back at Lana because he didn't want to be tempted to be drawn back into bed.

She was so tempting, but she was delving into a conversation that he wasn't comfortable having. His accident happened, it ended his surfing career and it ended his surgical career. It was done. There was no need to discuss.

He was all too aware of the consequences of accidents. And the last time he'd tried to talk about it, about his sister's death, he'd been shot down by his parents. Not that they'd always had the best relationship, but they blamed him for her death.

They said he'd killed her.

His best friend. The only person who had been there for him, his beloved baby sister. He'd lost his family back then and learned a valuable lesson—hide your emotions. Don't talk about painful things.

It was better this way.

Yet Lana was prying into something that he wasn't willing to talk about.

"Andrew, I didn't mean to upset you."

"You didn't upset me." He was lying through his teeth.

"I just know that it pains you and it's a significant scar. I just want to help."

"There's nothing you can do."

"But..."

"I don't want to talk about it, Lana," he snapped. "It's done. There's no use in talking about something you can't change."

She frowned and then hugged her knees. "You're right. Talking never really solves anything, does it?"

It was sarcasm.

And, just like that, the magic of their moment was shattered.

There was a wall between them again, but the wall needed to be there. It would keep them both safe.

You mean it will keep you safe.

He shook that thought from his mind as he slipped on his shoes and buttoned up his shirt.

"Where are you going?" she asked.

"For another walk."

Lana nodded, but she wasn't looking at him. "Okay. I think I'll have a rest. I'm still tired from that surgery yesterday."

"Sounds good." Andrew sighed inwardly and left the room. "I'll see you later."

He hated himself right now. He hated hurting her, but she was treading on dangerous ground.

You mean you are.

Lana knew that she had been treading on dangerous ground. Any time she'd mentioned his shoulder pain in the past he'd thrown up a wall. Why had she thought that this time would be different? She was beating herself up that she'd asked him about his scar.

He'd mentioned an accident, but she couldn't help but wonder what had happened. The first thing that came to mind as she thought about the way the scar was that his shoulder had been shattered and the repair hadn't gone well.

Or at least he didn't think so.

And maybe it hadn't, given the pain he was in, but really, unless she examined it, she was just speculating. Lana seriously doubted that Andrew would let her look at it.

She needed to just let it go.

He didn't want to talk about it so she wasn't going to push. To keep the peace, she would keep quiet about it, although she didn't want to.

Lana got up and had a shower. She found her overnight suitcase in the luxurious dressing room and changed into some comfortable clothes. Instead of heading back to the bed, which she was trying to ignore, she went to the sitting area of the suite and settled down on the couch to watch some television.

She didn't want to think about what had happened in that bed.

She was glad that it had happened, but now it was going to be awkward between the two of them. Which she didn't want, so she was going to make sure that there wouldn't be too much awkwardness between them as they had to live together and work together.

To the rest of the world they had to appear the loving and happy couple.

The door opened and he walked in, his hands in his pockets, and he looked as if he'd calmed down.

"Lana, I want to apologize," he said. "I didn't mean to storm out again. I just had to get my head together. I'm not used to people being a part of my life. I'm used to being alone."

"It's fine." Even though her father and Jack were always around, Lana understood where he was coming from. She spent a lot of her life alone. She didn't share much with anyone. She liked to keep parts of her life private. "There's no need to apologize. We're both adults."

As long as it was just her then she wouldn't get hurt or disappointed. She could just live her life.

No, you can't. When have you ever done that?

"Right." He sounded shocked.

"Yes. Some things are just better kept to ourselves and I'm sorry for prying."

He nodded and then took a seat on the chair in the sitting room. "I'm not sorry for what happened between us. I hope you don't regret it."

"No, I don't. And I stand by what I said. There doesn't have to be anything else between us. We'll just go on as originally planned until you get your green card. That's it."

Only she wanted to ask him why he was keeping her out, but then if she started prying again then he would start prying into her hang-ups. And she didn't want that.

All she wanted to do was keep the peace for the next year.

"Thanks, that's what I was hoping for." He looked as

if he was going to say something more; instead he just said, "Thank you for being so understanding."

"Well, I want the same thing. I just want this year to be as peaceful as possible. We'll figure out a routine to work and live together. One that will let outsiders think we're having a happy marriage."

"We never really did talk about the end, did we?"

The question caught her off guard. "Other than divorce, I suppose we didn't."

"What're we going to say? And when, like right after I get the green card?"

"I don't think it should be right after you get the green card. That would be suspicious."

He nodded. "Good point."

"I'm not sure of timings but we'll have to come up with a plausible reason for us to end the marriage. My father stayed with my mother despite their unhappiness and I think if my mother hadn't have left he would still be with her now."

Andrew frowned. "That sounds miserable."

"Marriage is for life," Lana mimicked her father, making them both laugh and breaking the tension of the subject. "So, what do you think it should be?"

"Well, I want your father to still respect me. I do like my job, but then again he may not if we divorce."

The word *if* caught her off guard. "You mean *when,* right?"

"What?"

"You said *if* we divorce, but you meant *when,* right?"

A funny expression crossed his face. "Right. When."

"How about if you don't want kids and I do? If I tried to flip that he would try to convince me to have children."

"You don't want kids?" Andrew asked.

"Not really."

It was a lie, but it was a lie she'd always told herself because after David she'd never thought that she'd ever get married and have a chance to have them. She was also sure that she wouldn't make a good mother. She loved her career too much, just like her own mother had, and there was no way that she could ever walk away from a child, so she didn't want to risk it.

She didn't want to have a child, to protect both her heart and the child she'd never have. It was just easier to say it out loud that she didn't want them.

"I'm fine if you want to tell him that I don't want kids, because I don't. I've never been the paternal type."

Lana nodded. "Okay, so it all comes down to when you get the green card; the timing of our divorce will be determined by that. Until that moment we'll just live in the same house, work at the same hospital and just try to live a civilized life."

Andrew nodded. "It sounds like a plan."

"Good." Only Lana didn't feel too good about that plan. Something gnawed at the back of her mind. Something unsettling. And she was exhausted. "I think I'll get some sleep."

"You take the bed and I'll just hang out here in the sitting room."

"Are you sure?"

"Positive. I'm not the one that did an extra-long surgery the night before our wedding. Go and have a good night."

"'Night." Lana left the sitting room and headed off to bed alone. Even though she'd been planning to go to bed alone since he'd walked away and even before they'd decided to sleep together, she really didn't want to be alone in the bed tonight.

She wanted to be with him, but after the talk they'd just had she knew that was next to impossible.

It would never happen. This marriage was just one of convenience.

There was an expiration date.

She'd spent her whole life alone and nothing was going to change now.

CHAPTER NINE

One month later

IT'S JUST A *stomach bug. Or stress.*

Stress was believable. Since her one stolen night of passion with Andrew, things had been awkward between them. He was rarely at her house, which was good, but when they did pass in the halls it was weird.

He'd seen her at her most vulnerable. It unnerved her that he'd seen her like that. Yet that night of passion had been incredible and, even though things were awkward between them, she couldn't get that night out of her head.

All she could think of was his hands on her body. His lips against hers and the pleasure she'd felt. It had been intoxicating.

Her stomach turned again as she crossed the ER floor and she knew then she couldn't hold it in any longer.

Lana ran to the bathroom, her hand over her mouth, as fast as she could. People got out of her way in the emergency room, because all day Lana had been running to the bathroom, where she was sick. She just couldn't keep anything down. Smells that had never bothered her before, she could no longer stand.

The thing was, she had no fever but she was hot and sweaty. She had a feeling she knew exactly what it was, but she hadn't had the time yet to confirm it. And, frankly, she was too terrified by the prospect.

"Dr. Haole, I think you should go home," Clarissa, the charge nurse, said as she knelt down next to her, holding back her hair and then passing her a cool wet towel.

"I'm not sick," Lana tried to explain, but she sighed when she held the towel on her forehead. "I'm under the weather, but not sick."

Clarissa grinned at her. "I know."

Lana grabbed some toilet paper and wiped her mouth, the feeling of nausea subsiding. She leaned her head against her hand and sighed. "Thanks for holding my hair."

"You're welcome," Clarissa said. "I think you need to page your husband and do a test."

Lana closed her eyes and took a deep breath and then looked at Clarissa, who had been a charge nurse for as long as Lana could remember. She was one of the only nurses who didn't think she was cold-hearted, who looked at her as a skilled surgeon and not the chief's daughter. "I can't be."

Clarissa just shook her head. "Doctors can be so stubborn and obtuse sometimes."

Lana took another deep breath, because she'd suspected it a couple of days ago when her cycle didn't start—and it was never late.

He wore a condom.

Of course, those were not infallible.

Great. Now how am I going to get an easy divorce?

"You might not be," Clarissa said, interrupting her thoughts. "It could be stress or a stomach bug. Still, it's better to be tested. You were married last month."

"Right, can you page Andrew for me?" Lana asked. "I have to clean up."

Clarissa nodded. "Sure. Should I page him to the ER or to your office?"

"The ER is fine. Send him to exam room five. I'll be waiting with a lab kit. He can draw my blood."

Clarissa nodded and got up, shutting the bathroom door behind her.

Oh, God.

There was no way they would be able to convince her father that divorce would be the right thing if she was pregnant. And terminating this pregnancy was something Lana didn't want to do either. This was her mistake and she stood by her mistakes.

Something her father had taught her to do.

I can't be pregnant.

A baby was not in the plans and she didn't know how Andrew was going to take it. Ever since their one night together, things had been awkward.

No, I can't be pregnant.

Of course it all made sense. Karma was such a pain in the butt. She got up from where she'd been kneeling over the toilet bowl. She flushed and then cleaned herself up. When she finally made her way down to exam room five she was thankful that she didn't get another wave of nausea. It had been the strong smells that wafted out of the emergency room, mixed with the disinfectant that had set her off. Now, as she navigated the hallway through the ER toward the exam room, she breathed through her mouth so that she could hold it together.

When she opened the door she saw that Andrew was in there, waiting for her. When he looked at her he wrinkled his nose.

"Whoa, are you okay?"

Andrew had been pretty scarce since their wedding

night. Work kept her busy and when Andrew wasn't at the hospital he was out at the beach with Jack and his other clients, training them for the World Surfing Championship that was coming up.

Andrew had been oblivious to the last several mornings where she'd run to the bathroom to be sick.

Which was probably a good thing. Things between them were strained enough.

"I don't know," she said as she took a seat, because she was dizzy and the room was spinning. "I need you to run a test for me."

"Sure. What kind of test?"

"A blood test that's looking for levels of human chorionic gonadotropin in my blood."

"Human chorionic..." Then his eyes widened, the blood draining from his face, and he had to push his glasses back up. "Are you asking me to give you a pregnancy test?"

The words came out like a shout and Lana had to hush him and then hissed, "I don't think the patients in the next pod heard you."

Andrew ran his hand through his blond hair, his eyes wide behind his black-rimmed glasses. "Sorry, it's just... I thought we used protection."

"It's not infallible. You know that. You're a doctor."

"So, you're late?"

"No, I'm right on time," she snapped. Then she scrubbed a hand over her face. "I'm sorry. I just haven't been feeling well the last few mornings. It could be a stomach bug."

Andrew's mouth still hung open in disbelief. "Right, okay. Well, I'll draw the blood and get it off to the lab."

"Thank you. If word gets out to my father that I am,

he's going to make me stay at home barefoot and pregnant to raise his grandchild," she muttered.

Andrew frowned. "Well, fathers can take paternity leave."

Her heart swelled at the thought of him taking time off for their baby, which she wasn't even sure existed at this point, but then she recalled the conversation that they'd had on their wedding night. He didn't want kids. He didn't want to be tied down.

That was what he'd told her.

And now she was probably pregnant. Only he didn't look too thrilled at the prospect of paternity leave and she felt guilty.

"If I am pregnant you don't… I can raise the baby." She was used to shouldering the burden of responsibility.

Andrew didn't say anything. "Let's not jump the gun."

"You said you didn't want kids."

"I don't." He pulled on surgical gloves as Lana peeled off her white lab coat. She was wearing scrubs so she didn't have to roll up her sleeves. He put a cuff around her arm and then swabbed her arm. "You'll feel a small pinch."

Lana rolled her eyes and he took a blood sample. Once he was done he pressed a cotton ball to her arm and then labelled the test tube.

"We'll figure it out," Andrew said, but she could hear the worry in his voice and the fear. "It could still be something else. Like rotavirus or something."

"Fingers crossed for food poisoning then?" she teased.

He smiled, but it was forced. She could see that he was just as worried as she was. And he wasn't making eye contact with her. Still as awkward since the night they'd slept together.

"I'll take this to the lab. Just sit tight. I don't think

you should be out on duty right now, especially if you're vomiting everywhere."

"Agreed."

"I'll be back as soon as I can." Andrew left the exam room.

Lana lay back against the exam table and stared up at the ceiling. It was the first time she'd ever hoped that it was nothing more than a virus because it would make the separation from Andrew so much easier in a year, but deep down she really did want a baby.

It would cramp her career and it would make it more complicated for Andrew to leave cleanly, but she wasn't going to force him to stay if he didn't want to be a father. However, she was going to be the best mother she possibly knew how to be.

At least this child would love her unconditionally. She didn't have to be anything other than a loving parent with this baby.

She could do this.

Maybe.

There were things she'd do differently—and she'd never leave.

You don't know that. Your mother left.

And that thought scared her to her core.

Andrew was pacing outside the lab. He was waiting for the results. He didn't say who the test was for. He just called the patient Jane Doe and made up an elaborate tale about how a patient needed an X-ray for a broken shin but wasn't sure if she was pregnant or not. So he needed a rush on the result.

The lab assistant bought it and now all Andrew could do was wait.

He'd never wanted to be a father. That was what he always told himself. How could he be a good father when he didn't have a good example to emulate?

Meghan liked you well enough.

The memory of his baby sister punched him hard in the gut. He hadn't thought about her in so long. She was always in the back of his mind, but since he'd married Lana memories of her came bubbling up everywhere. Good times and the night where he'd lost her.

And he didn't like it much, because it was a loss of control for him. Control he'd worked so hard for. It got him through the days, months and years. It was how he lived with himself.

"You're worthless! You've always been selfish, Andrew. Always!"

His father's words still echoed in his mind. It played on repeat, which was why he deserved everything he got. The loss of his career, both as a surgeon and a surfer, being alone—that was what he deserved. If only he had seen that moose before it was too late. Or reacted differently, faster...

"Dr. Tremblay, your patient's results are in."

Andrew spun around and thanked the lab technician. He didn't want to open the results without Lana present, but then if it was the news he wasn't looking for, if she was pregnant, he would have to be prepared.

Then she'd know you looked before her and she'd kick your butt.

He stared down at the report but he couldn't bring himself to look at it without her. So he headed back to the exam room where Lana was still waiting. She was staring up at the ceiling and when he entered the room she sat up slowly.

He could tell the simple action made her dizzy.

That's not a good sign.

"Well?" she asked.

"I thought we'd look at it together." He handed her the paper. "You open it and we'll both read it." He girded himself for the prospect.

She nodded and took the paper from him. She unfolded it and he was hit with the whammy the same moment that she was.

Iolana was pregnant.

"Oh, my God," she whispered. "We were so careful."

"Yeah, well, as you said, condoms are not without fault." He raked a hand through his hair.

What am I going to do now?

This was all his fault. He'd ruined another life.

"I'm sorry, Lana. I know you didn't want kids either."

"Well, we have one." She bit her lip. "I'm not going to get rid of it, so that's not a suggestion I would even entertain, unless something medically came up."

"I can respect that. So what do we do?" Deep down he wanted her to tell him to leave. To be angry at him so he could walk away. It would be better for the kid. He couldn't be a father. He didn't know how to be. His own father was terrible, he wouldn't do that to a kid, but then another part of him didn't want to leave her. He had to stay with Lana. It was the right thing to do.

"I can raise this baby on my own. Nothing has to change."

"Like hell nothing has to change," Andrew snapped. "That's my kid in there too."

"I am aware," she said. "We don't have to stay married to raise a kid. You're trying to get your green card to stay in the States, yes?"

"Yes."

Or he wouldn't have gone through all of this to try and stay.

"So we can co-parent this kid and not be married. People do it all the time."

"Yeah, but what about the reasons for our divorce? That I didn't want kids but you did? Your father is going to be none too happy."

"I know," Lana sighed. "Well, he'll be happy about the grandchild and that I'm becoming a mother."

That was said with contention and Andrew couldn't help but chuckle. "Your dad is a bit of a dinosaur that way, isn't he?"

"He's old-fashioned."

"Lana, there's old-fashioned and then there's prehistoric!" They both laughed at that and then he took her hand and squeezed it to give her a sense of reassurance he wasn't feeling. "We'll figure it out."

"I know, but I just wanted you to know that I can handle this on my own. I don't want you to feel pressured, especially with the World Championships coming up." She was throwing up a wall. She was obviously just as scared as him.

Or she doesn't want you because you're worthless.

Andrew nodded. "Thanks. So what happens next?"

"I'll make an appointment with my OB/GYN. I just hope my dad doesn't get wind of this yet."

"Do you want me to come to that appointment?"

"If you want, but again, training Jack is your first priority. I mean, this is why we did this whole thing." She slid off the exam table. "I'm going to make my appointment and then finish my rounds, but preferably away from the emergency room so I don't have to continue breathing out of my mouth."

"What?" Andrew asked, confused.

She grinned. "The smells down here are getting to me."

"Ah, gotcha."

There was so much he didn't know about pregnancy. He knew the biology of it. He'd delivered a baby, but obstetrics hadn't been one of his best or favorite subjects during residency. He'd done his rotation and left it behind to study orthopedics. So he didn't know all the quirks, what set women off for morning sickness, but he had a feeling he was going to learn it fast enough. And it scared the hell out of him.

"I'm done for the day so I'm going to head down to the beach. Jack is waiting," he said. "When you get off you should come. The fresh air will help."

She nodded. "Yeah, that would be nice."

An awkward silence fell between them.

"Good. I'll see you later." And then, without thinking, he kissed her on the top of the head, catching them both off guard.

He had to put some distance between him and Lana, but he also was going to do right by his baby. Even if that meant leaving in the end.

When Lana got home the first thing she did was shower, because she needed to wash the hospital off herself. Once she'd showered, she tied back her hair and put on a comfortable sundress and her sandals and made her way down to the beach, where she knew that Jack and Andrew were training.

Andrew was standing in a long sleeve wetsuit. It was unbuttoned and off his shoulders and as she came up behind him she got a good look at his scar. The one she had felt under her hands as they'd made love, when she'd held him tight through her pleasure.

Definitely his shoulder had been fractured. The scar ran over his right shoulder and down his arm and she knew she'd felt the rough skin in the front of the shoulder and she couldn't help but wonder if his accident had something to do with an impaling, only it had gone right through the bone, muscle and tore the joints.

He was lucky he still had his arm.

When she came closer, he turned and saw her there. So he set down his board and pulled on his board suit to hide his scar. "Hey, I didn't think you were going to come."

"I said I would," she said.

"I saw your car pull up and you went straight into the house so I thought you were tired."

"I am, but really I just wanted a shower first." She turned and looked at the waves, where she could see Jack shredding the nar. He was just a small figure riding a large wave and then Andrew handed her binoculars.

"Take a look. Your brother has good form."

"Thanks." She held the binoculars up and could see Jack, so focused as he maneuvered the board with precision. Their father might have wanted Jack to go into surgery like him, but Jack was born to do this.

Weren't you? You liked doing this.

Only she didn't get a chance to do this very often, but she did like surfing. When their mother had left, Lana became responsible and tried her best to make her father happy. Even if it meant giving up her dreams of being a sports medicine doctor and her dreams of surfing on an international stage, like Jack was doing now.

"You have a dreamy expression on your face," Andrew said. "What're you thinking about?"

"Surfing, but I'm not sure if I'll be doing much of that in the coming months." She handed him back the binoculars.

"Well, then, you'd better get it in while you can," he suggested.

"What?"

"You can surf still. Come on, you can still do it. You were doing it a month ago."

"I'm pregnant," she argued.

"Yeah, but it's not like you're taking up a new sport that your body is not used to. Your body is used to riding the waves. Go get changed, grab your board and get out there."

"Only if you'll come with me."

Andrew frowned. "I can't ride the big waves."

"I'm not talking about the big waves, but we can body surf some of these small ones. Come on, I know you do that. I've seen you out here too."

He narrowed his eyes and then a smile broke across his face. "Fine. Go get changed and we'll hit the surf."

"Good." Lana hurried back to the house and quickly got changed into her two-piece and then her board suit. She tied her long hair up into a bun and then grabbed two small body boards. When she got back, Andrew was down at the shore.

She handed him a board. "Race you?"

"Race?"

"Go!" She didn't wait as she ran out into the surf, the cold water soothing her hot skin. She was still sweating, so the water and the surf crashing over her was welcome. When the water was waist deep she lay down on her board and paddled out, angling herself to catch a small wave. Andrew was behind her; he was grinning as the wave crested behind them and they rode it together back to shore.

Andrew was tossed before they hit the shore. When he popped up out of the water, still clutching the board, he shouted, "You cheated."

"No way. I won. That wave didn't toss me."

"I think your gods probably shine favor on their *wahinis* who are pregnant."

"Well, then, if that's the case I'll take full advantage." She waded over to him and pulled him up, where he was sulking in the shallows. "Come on, that attempt was pathetic. You need to try harder."

"Fine." Then he turned and raced through the water, not waiting for her this time. Lana laughed as he paddled out to the next wave. "You're falling behind, Haole. You need to keep up."

Lana just shook her head and waded out in the water.

For one brief moment she forgot she was pregnant, that this marriage wasn't going to last and that she was probably going to have to raise this child alone.

For one moment she was just Iolana, enjoying her time in the water like she always did. It just made it all the more sweet to share it with someone.

Even if that someone was only temporary.

CHAPTER TEN

THEY WERE LYING out on the sand, letting the late afternoon sun dry them. Lana's eyes were closed and Andrew was mesmerized by her. She was fantastic in the water... that he knew.

And the thing that amazed and terrified him the most was that she was carrying his child.

The panic sunk in again.

How can I be a father?

He'd never wanted kids. All his life, even before Meghan died, his father had told him how becoming a father had ruined his life. Andrew didn't have a normal childhood. He didn't know how he could be a good father when he'd had no role model at all.

So he was terrified at the prospect of being a father. Of trapping Lana, who didn't even want to marry him in the first place.

And he decided to change the subject so that he wouldn't have a mild panic attack on the beach.

"Have you ever thought about surfing professionally, like Jack?" he asked.

"Once, but my father is a formidable force. He told me there's no future in it."

"There's a women's league and there would be a definite spot for you. I would've trained you."

"*Would* being the operative word," she teased. "In about nine months I don't think I'll be able to stand on a board. Heck, in three months, when the championships are happening, I don't think my center of gravity will comply."

"Still, Jack was pressured into becoming a surgeon but he didn't. He went after his passion."

She shot him a strange look. "Surgery *is* my passion. I've always wanted to be a surgeon."

"Really?" he asked; he wasn't so sure he believed her. He believed she loved surgery, but he didn't really get the feeling that she wanted to be Chief of Surgery or Head of Orthopedics.

"Why is that so hard to believe?" she demanded.

"You just seem to come to surfing naturally. So many don't."

"Well, once I entertained being a sports medicine doctor for the American surfing team, but my father vetoed that. It was a silly idea. I mean, they weren't going to hire me straight out of my residency."

"It's not a silly idea; you could've done it. You seem to belong out there. And you'd know how to care for an injured surfer."

"I like surfing, but it's a hobby."

Andrew's father had always thought it was a waste too. The only one who had supported him was Meghan, so Lana's words were like a slap to the face. The sport had been his whole world, as had surgery, and both had been snatched away from him in an instant. It was hard to hear Lana being so dismissive of something he thought they shared a passion for.

That's what happens when you assume, Andrew.

"So your plan is to work at your father's hospital until what? When he retires and you become Chief?"

Her lips pursed together and her eyes flashed with annoyance; he'd pushed her a bit hard. "And what's wrong with that?"

"Nothing. I guess it's safe."

"There's nothing wrong with being safe."

"That's where we differ."

She cocked an eyebrow. "Do we now? You don't seem the type. You're not a risk-taker."

Another slap to the face.

Before he could say anything else, Jack came jogging up the beach with his board under his arm. He was panting, but he had been out there for some time.

"I think that's it for me tonight, Coach." Then Jack saw his sister. "Hey, Lana, what's got your bees in a bonnet?"

"Oh, nothing, just that your coach here knocked me up."

Jack's eyes flew open in rage and Andrew jumped to his feet as Jack threw a punch that missed.

"You got my sister pregnant?" Jack shouted.

"Jack, I can explain."

"No, I don't think you can!"

"We need to take this somewhere private." Andrew turned to Lana. "This is your fault. If he blows it…"

"Come on, Keaka. He's my husband. I'll make you some dinner and we can talk about this in a calm, rational manner." Lana grabbed her brother's arm and started pushing him up the beach.

Andrew was relieved, but he had a feeling this wasn't over. He picked up the discarded boards and followed his wife and brother-in-law up to the house. And laughed at the absurdity of it all.

After he'd got the boards wiped down and locked away, Lana had changed and had Jack sitting on the couch. He had changed as well, but he was obviously really annoyed as he glared at Andrew when he walked into the living room.

"Andrew," Jack said in a haughty tone. Lana just rolled her eyes and handed Jack a bottle of water, before taking a seat at the opposite end of the couch, tucking her long shapely legs under her.

"Listen, Jack, I didn't mean this to happen. Your sister is a beautiful…"

"Don't say it," Jack groaned and pinched the bridge of his nose. "This wasn't supposed to be a real marriage. You weren't supposed to touch my sister."

"Your sister had some say in it too, Keaka," Lana said, but it wasn't helping.

Jack glared at Lana. "Don't call me that."

"I'll call you Junior if you don't ease up on Andrew," Lana growled at Jack, just like a mother to a son rather than a sister to a brother.

"So now what?" Jack asked. "Are you telling me this marriage is for real now?"

A blush crept up into Lana's cheeks as their eyes met.

"No," Andrew said, guilt eating at him. "But I'll be there for your sister and help raise the baby."

"Oh, man. Dad is going to be pissed when you two call it quits after you have his grandchild."

"I know," Lana mumbled. "Accidents do happen."

"I don't want to know," Jack moaned again. "I feel like this is my fault, Lana."

"It's not your fault, Jack. Although the debt you owe me will be astronomical."

Jack groaned. "Lana, you're making me feel bad."

"Good," she said firmly.

Andrew chuckled as he saw that feisty spark of humor bubble back up in Lana. "Jack, I plan to do right by your sister and our baby."

Jack scrubbed his hand over his face. "Okay. I believe you. I'm sorry for taking a swing at you, Andrew."

"Hey, I would've done the same if it was my sister." He regretted the words the moment they tumbled past his lips. They both looked at him with curiosity and he didn't want to talk about Meghan. He quickly blurted out, "If I had a sister, that is."

Pathetic save.

It seemed to work. Which was good, because he didn't want to talk about his sister. That was private. No one needed to know that.

That's no way to honor your sister's memory. Burying her in your mind. Not remembering the life she led.

"Jack, you can't tell Dad that I'm pregnant," Lana said, breaking Andrew from his guilt-ridden thoughts. "You have to swear that you'll keep it secret. I'm not that far along and I'm not ready to tell him yet."

Jack rolled his eyes. "He'll find out, you know. He has spies everywhere."

"He's right," Andrew agreed. "I'm sure we'll get a call tonight when he gets home from the hospital, congratulating us."

"On that note, I have to go." Jack bent over and kissed the top of Lana's head. "See you, sis."

Andrew felt a pang of longing. The last time that he'd seen his sister alive, he'd kissed the top of Meghan's head just like that, before they'd got into the car to head for home after a late night movie. He'd promised to look after her, because they were both united against their anxiety-ridden mother and angry, abusive father. The movie had been an escape. He'd been away working as a surgeon in Vancouver for three years. He'd come home because Meghan had begged him to.

Meghan was all he had.

Then she was killed in a head-on collision with a moose.

There was nothing he could do to save her because he'd almost died that night too, but that didn't stop his father from blaming him for Meghan's death.

You're not responsible.

"Are you okay?" Lana asked.

"What?" Andrew asked, shaking the thoughts of his sister from his head again.

"Jack said he'd see you tomorrow and you didn't even acknowledge him. You just stared out into space. I thought you went into shock."

"Nah—" he rubbed the back of his neck "—I just zoned out, but I wasn't thinking of anything in particular."

"So why don't you tell me about your family?"

Andrew stared at her. Her dark eyes penetrated into his soul and, though he should walk away, he felt like talking to her about his family. For once, in a long time, he didn't want to keep it all to himself.

He wanted to talk to someone about it.

"What is there to tell?"

She cocked her head to one side. "Come on, Andrew. We're going to have a baby together. I know our marriage isn't exactly real, but shouldn't I at least know about my baby's family? I know you're Canadian, but I don't know where you're from. I don't know your parents' names. I really know nothing about you."

"I like to be a man of mystery." He raked his hands through his hair and then saw that stubborn expression of hers set in. "Fine. What do you want to know?"

He didn't know where to start with it all, but he had a feeling that once the gates were opened everything would come pouring out of him and he had to regain some control.

"Where were you born?"

"Actually, I was born in Algonquin Provincial Park."

"You were born in a park?" she asked in disbelief.

"My mother was driving home from Huntsville to my hometown of Whitney. The park is this huge nature reserve and the road that connects Huntsville to Whitney is about sixty kilometers. Or thirty-seven miles for you Americans." He winked and grinned.

She chuckled. "Thanks, but converting something into metric doesn't explain the birth in the park thing."

"She went into labor right smack dab in the middle of that road. I came pretty fast and all she could do was pull off at the parking lot to a hiking trail and give birth. Thankfully, there were lots of tourists up from Toronto to see the fall colors and there was a doctor on one of those tour buses."

"So you were born in the fall?"

He nodded. "And you were born when?"

"Winter. Though I've never seen snow. After high school I went to Stanford in California."

"I've seen lots of snow. Too much, really."

She smiled. A sweet smile which made his heart skip a beat. "I'm sure. So you have a mother. Any siblings?"

"I lied before. I did have a sister, but she died." He was surprised at himself for telling her that. No one knew that outside of Ontario.

Her expression softened. "I'm sorry."

Andrew braced himself, expecting her to ask why or how, but she didn't. And he was relieved. Inevitably, everyone that found out he had a sister always asked those questions and he just didn't want to discuss it.

"How about your father?"

"There's not much to say." He shrugged. "He wasn't

very supportive. My parents are still alive, but I haven't been home in quite some time."

"So, surfing? Why surfing? If you grew up in northern Ontario there really aren't many places to surf there."

He laughed. "I went to medical school in Vancouver and picked it up there."

"Ah, well, that does explain it." Her stomach grumbled and she winced. "I suppose I should try and eat something, though I don't feel very hungry."

"How about some chicken soup?" Andrew got up and went into the kitchen, poking around her bare cupboards. "Uh, when was the last time you went shopping?"

"Me? Why do I have to always go shopping? Don't be sexist!" She was teasing him. "Honestly, I forgot."

"Let's go out to dinner." He scooped up his keys from the kitchen counter. "Whatever you think you can stomach and we'll go there."

"That sounds great." She stood up, but teetered a bit. He raced over and steadied her. He'd been avoiding her for a month and just touching her again, being near her, reminded him how she felt in his arms.

A longing set in. He missed her.

"Are you okay?"

"Just dizzy," she sighed. "I hate this. I have a knee replacement tomorrow afternoon. If I'm wobbling around like this, how am I going to stand for all those hours?"

"I'll go with you," he offered. It was the least he could do.

"You will?"

He nodded. "Yeah. I'll make sure you don't throw up into the patient's incision."

Lana was going to laugh, but instead her eyes widened, her complexion turned green and she pushed him away, running to the bathroom, where he was privy to some not so attractive sounds on the other side of that closed door.

Good job, Andrew. You had to mention vomiting and incisions.

After Lana got over her spate of nausea the only thing she wanted more than anything was an ice cream cone. So Andrew drove to the nearest ice cream truck, which was parked beside a beach not far from her home, and now she was sitting on a bench, enjoying the sunset and her chocolate-dipped soft ice cream cone.

She said it was heaven.

He was chalking this up to the first of many pregnancy cravings. He'd complained that ice cream wasn't a good dinner choice. There was no sense in complaining; she was growing his kid after all. It was the least he could do.

"I think after you go to sleep I'm going to order in a pizza. Ice cream is not a very filling dinner," Andrew complained again.

"Yes, but please wait until I go to bed. You order some weird stuff on your pizza and no, I don't want to talk about pizza right now unless you want to see this ice cream come back up."

He chuckled. "I thought that your perfect wedding had something to do with pizza?"

"And unicorns, but you don't see me talking about those," she warned.

"Okay, message received. Enjoy the dairy goodness." He didn't particularly like the cones, so his ice cream was in a tiny paper bowl. It was cookie dough, something he'd always liked as a kid. The ice cream was okay, but the company was better. Lana looked so relaxed, her long bronze legs stretched out but crossed at the ankles. Her hair was braided back and she seemed to be glowing in the waning sunlight.

"You're glowing, you know," he said in awe.

"What?" she asked in disbelief.

"Isn't that a pregnancy thing?"

She snorted. "Maybe because of the sweat."

Andrew chuckled. "You know, you're quite funny when you're not trying to be so serious all the time."

"So you've said." She grinned at him. "It's been a busy month."

He knew she'd been avoiding him too.

"It was a fast month since our wedding." And the moment he mentioned the wedding all he could think about was the wedding night. The wedding night that he'd never meant to let happen, but he was powerless when it came to her.

He wanted her. Even now. He tried not to think of her, but memories of when he'd taken her in his arms plagued him constantly. He could still taste her on his lips, feel the softness of her skin on his fingertips and he wanted those long legs he'd just been admiring wrapped around his hips.

They finished their ice cream in silence.

There was a bit of ice cream on her cheek; he reached out and wiped it away with his thumb. Her eyes widened as he touched her and, before he knew what he was doing, his hand was cupping her cheek and then slipped behind her head, pulling her close to kiss her.

Lana melted into him and she tasted like chocolate and vanilla. The familiar scent of coconut and the beach wrapping him in a heady memory of the first time he'd kissed her. He'd known then that once was never going to be enough. And dammit, he was right.

She touched his face as the kiss ended. "What was that for?"

He wanted to tell her—because he couldn't resist her, because he was falling for her, but he couldn't formulate the words because he didn't want to believe it. There really was no future, because once his green card was in he could move to California and pursue a job that was made for him. The one with the International Surfing Committee, where he'd be the lead sports medicine doctor. It had been the dream all along.

Lana belonged to Oahu. She would never leave.

And, even though she was carrying his baby, he knew that eventually he would have to leave them behind. It would be the best for both of them. He wasn't father material. He wasn't going to screw up a kid like his father did to him. Besides, he didn't deserve the happiness of a family.

Then you shouldn't be kissing her.

And he hated himself for doing that.

"I don't know what came over me. I'm sorry. It won't happen again." Then he put distance between them, but as he tried to slide away she held tight to him.

"Andrew, I think we should talk about it."

"There's nothing to talk about, Lana."

"Isn't there?" she asked, confused. "We can't keep falling into this trap."

"I know. I'm sorry it happened. I truly am."

She nodded, but her eyes filled with moisture, as if she was about to cry. "Damn, I don't know why I'm crying. I totally agree with you. Freaking hormones."

"Another pregnancy thing?"

She nodded. "I'm really sorry, Andrew. I do think you're right. We have separate lives to lead, after this is all said and done. We can co-parent this baby and not be together."

"Right." He hated himself for thinking that he would one day leave Oahu and that he'd be leaving her with this responsibility, but it was for the best.

Wasn't it?

"Come on, let's get you home." He stood and then helped her to her feet. "You have to get your rest if you're doing a knee replacement tomorrow afternoon."

"That sounds great. I'm exhausted." As they walked back to the car Lana's phone began to buzz. She pulled it out of her pocket and frowned.

"Who is it?" Andrew asked, but he had an idea.

"It's my dad."

Andrew sighed. "Sounds like he found out."

"Clarissa was the one holding my hair and suggested I get a test." She accepted the call. "Hi, Dad, what's up? What rumors? Oh, those. Yes, it's true. I'm pregnant."

The cat was out of the bag.

Lana continued to talk to her father and for a brief moment Andrew entertained the notion of calling his parents and letting them know that they were going to be grandparents, but what was the use? They wouldn't care. They would just tell him how Meghan was never going to have children and it was all his fault.

His parents wouldn't care that Lana was carrying his child. That he was going to be a father. Calling his parents wouldn't put to rest the ghosts of his past; it would just remind him why he'd always said he never wanted to be a father.

How could he be a good father when his only example had been his own father?

CHAPTER ELEVEN

LANA COULD FEEL the beads of sweat pooling on her forehead. Once her father had found out that she was carrying his grandchild and that she was suffering from extreme morning sickness his first suggestion was that she go on maternity leave.

Right away.

When Lana kicked that suggestion to the curb in a very delicate manner, which stressed her out, standing up to him, to her relief her father acquiesced but stipulated that she see Dr. Peters right away. He prescribed her Diclectin, a safe medicine to ease her morning sickness so she could continue as a surgeon. And it seemed to be working.

It didn't take away the exhaustion and standing in an orthopedic hazmat suit while she did the knee replacement surgery didn't help. It was stifling in the suit. And even though there was filtered air cycling through she felt as if she couldn't breathe.

Focus.

She wished someone could wipe the sweat from her brow, but at least she was almost done with the surgery. Then she could shower and rest.

Andrew stood across from her and was actually holding a retractor. She had never seen him hold a retractor since he'd been here. She had seen him operate once on a surgical video. Maybe he would come to miss the surgery and start to perform here. If she had him doing surgeries on her service then she could ease off just a bit.

The other surgeons on the orthopedic surgical rotation were her father when time allowed and Dr. Sims and Dr. Kay. Dr. Sims and Dr. Kay both had a full practice.

There was room for the world-renowned Dr. Tremblay who had disappeared from surgery to aid with hers.

No one knew why Andrew had stopped performing surgery, but she had inkling it had to do with the surgery done on his shoulder.

He glanced up at her through the visor of his own hazmat suit. "You okay, Lana?"

"Fine. Just tired." She turned back to her work and tried to ignore the fact he was standing there. It was hard, but she didn't want him to give anything away. Though she was pretty positive that most people in this room knew that she was pregnant, given the way that gossip moved through this hospital, but she didn't want to blurt it out in case her surgical team didn't know.

She didn't want anyone to think that she was weak.

It was bad enough that her facade had been cracked when she'd married Andrew so quickly during a sunset ceremony on the beach. And the speculation that Dr. Iolana Haole maybe wasn't quite the Ice Queen was starting to spread around the hospital. There were also rumors of Andrew using her to secure a green card and she knew those rumors were initiated by David. The problem was they were true.

And she didn't like it.

How the heck was she going to eventually take over the hospital if people didn't respect her the way they used to? The respect she'd worked so hard to regain after David used her before publicly humiliating her. The thing that scared her was she didn't care at the moment. She was enjoying herself at work. She wasn't so tense, wasn't so lonely.

Maybe because you don't want to run the hospital when your father retires. Maybe because you want to leave Hawaii. See the world.

Of course, those dreams were dashed now that she was pregnant. She couldn't go traipsing all over the world with a baby in tow. She had to give their child stability. She needed a steady job to provide for their child. That was what her father had said when he'd constantly worked after her mother had left. He needed to provide for her and Jack by working. That was the right thing to do and she'd do the same.

Any thoughts she'd had of having an adventure were dashed and she really had no one else to blame but herself, because she hadn't taken the chance.

She'd let her father rule over her. Let her fears of the unknown do the same.

Others made the decisions about her life. Not her.

You made the decision to sleep with Andrew. You made the decision to keep this baby.

She snuck another glance at Andrew and his gaze met hers and the way his eyes crinkled behind the surgical mask and visor let her know that he was smiling at her. Then he nodded slightly, giving her that boost of confidence she liked.

Lana went back to work. She was almost done with the knee replacement. A couple more solid taps to put the new joint into place and the replacement knee was in position.

"Good work, Dr. Haole," Andrew said.

"Thanks." She continued her work, closing the small

incisions of the minimally invasive procedure. Her father still preferred the larger incision, but she'd trained
to do the less invasive surgery.

She finished closing and gave her instructions about
antibiotics in the IV and blood thinners and decompres-
sion stockings to the residents so they could monitor the
patient in Recovery. Once that was done she headed to
the scrub room as quickly as she could to get out of the
stifling hazmat suit.

As soon as the scrub room doors shut she pulled off
the helmet and took a deep breath of antiseptic scrub
room air. Her hair was plastered to the top of her head
under her scrub cap. Andrew followed her into the room
and pulled off his helmet.

"You're drenched in sweat."

"I know," Lana said. "These pregnancy symptoms
are magnified. Surely I shouldn't be feeling this bad?"

"Maybe it's twins." It was meant as a joke, but then
he spun around, his eyes wide, as the realization hit the
both of them. "Oh, my God, do you think it's twins?"

"I don't know," Lana said, dumbfounded. "It could
be. Twins run in my family. My mother was a twin. Oh,
Lord. Two babies." A wave of nausea hit her.

"Don't jump to conclusions. It might not be; you just
might not handle pregnancy well."

"Then why did you suggest twins in the first place?"
she shrieked.

"I was reading that pregnancy book you had on the
coffee table last night while I was eating pizza."

"Are you seriously trying to make me hurl?"

"Sorry." He winced.

"So what did you read?"

"That sometimes pregnancy symptoms in the first
trimester are amplified if there's more than one fetus."

Oh, my God.

The thought of two babies just sent her head spinning.

"Your mother was a twin, you say. That's what you said, right?" Andrew asked.

And, just like that, the mention of her mother sent a douse of cold water over her. It reminded her that her own mother couldn't handle her or Jack. That she'd hated being trapped with Lana's father. She'd hated Oahu. She'd hated it all and felt that Dr. Keaka Haole had ruined her life.

So she'd left. And Lana had become head of the household and tried to keep it all together afterwards. "Yes. I think so anyways. I'm pretty sure, but I could be wrong."

"Can you call and ask her?"

"Did Jack not tell you about our mother?" Lana asked in disbelief.

"No, well, other than she left your father, but that was it."

Lana sighed and she could feel tears stinging her eyes. "She left when I was a kid and Jack was a baby. I haven't seen her since. She didn't want anything to do with us. So no, I can't call my mother."

A strange look crossed his face for a brief moment, as if he understood what she was saying, but how could he? His parents had never abandoned him. He wouldn't understand.

"I'm sorry. Why don't we go up to Obstetrics? I'm sure, seeing how you're Dr. Haole's daughter, that they'd be more than willing to do a sonogram on you. It'll put your mind at ease."

"Yours too," she said sarcastically.

"Yes, twins would be…complicated."

She almost wondered if he was going to say *the worst*, but didn't.

"They won't see much."

"They'll see enough to tell whether there're two in there."

"Okay." Andrew was right. She wanted to know. It would drive her crazy not to know. She needed to plan and prepare herself. Lana had already mentally prepared herself for one baby, but the thought of two was a bit mind-boggling.

They finished scrubbing out and then headed straight from the operating room floor up to Obstetrics.

Dr. Green wasn't busy and took them right in. Which was rare.

Lana climbed up on the exam table, the paper crinkling and sticking to her sweat-stained butt. Andrew was chuckling to himself.

"Are you still having nausea, Iolana?" Dr. Green asked.

"Not as much, at least not since I've been taking the medication, but…twins run in my family."

Dr. Green didn't blink an eye. "I'm aware. Your father told me when he first told me you were pregnant."

"Why would he tell you that?" Lana asked.

"He was covering all his bases," Dr. Green said nonchalantly. "You know how he is."

"Can you just ease our minds and tell us if there're two in there?" Andrew asked, interrupting. "Lana's been having more pronounced symptoms. Isn't that an indicator for the possibility of twins?"

Dr. Green didn't bat an eye. They called her the bulldog of the obstetrics floor because she didn't put up with any nonsense. Which was why Lana liked her so much.

"It can be, but usually measuring larger than your dates and the presence of two heartbeats is how we determine twins, but it's too early to catch a heartbeat with my sonogram. You're only five weeks in."

"Can you measure me or give me a transvaginal ultrasound and see what's going on?"

"Lie back and I'll measure you first. Then I'll do the ultrasound and we'll hopefully relieve some of your anxiety. Anxiety won't help with the symptoms."

Lana lay back and lifted up her scrub top. Andrew took a seat at her head while Dr. Green pulled out her measuring tape and measured Lana.

"Well… I'll be…" Dr. Green whispered.

Lana's heart did a flip flop. "I'm measuring larger, aren't I?"

"Yes, slightly. It could be just a large baby. How much did you weigh at birth, Iolana?" Dr. Green asked as she recorded the measurement in Lana's file.

"I was five pounds seven ounces, but I was early."

"And you, Dr. Tremblay?" Dr. Green asked.

"Ten pounds."

Lana bolted upright. "You were ten pounds and your mother gave birth to you in the middle of a park on the side of the road?"

Andrew grinned and winked at her. "Yep. We're hardy stock up in the north."

Dr. Green was chuckling. "It could be a larger baby, but we'll check if we can see how many are in there. I'll be back in a moment, so if you could put on a gown and remove your pants and undergarments in prep that would be great."

When Dr. Green left Lana groaned. She got up and grabbed a hospital gown out of the cupboard in the exam room.

"Should I stay and watch?" Andrew asked, looking uncomfortable.

"Yes, because if our kid is ten pounds I'm going to kill

you," she hissed half-jokingly, but also terrified of the thought of giving birth to a toddler-sized infant.

He laughed. "Promises, promises."

Lana removed her clothes while his back was turned and put on the gown. She got up on the table and Dr. Green rolled in the machine. She got the wand ready and Andrew continued to look away while she placed it and then covered Lana up with a sheet.

"You can look now," Lana said.

Andrew turned around and took a seat back by her head. Dr. Green fiddled with some dials and stared at the screen.

Lana held her breath as the doctor recorded measurements and studied the monitor. What was she going to do with twins? It couldn't be twins.

"Well, your hunch was right, doctors." Dr. Green turned the monitor around. Lana stared at the grainy picture and, though they looked nothing more than a couple of peanuts in a sack, she saw what was just about to be confirmed.

"Twins," Lana whispered in disbelief.

"Yes, you're expecting twins, Dr. Haole. Congratulations."

"Oh, my God," Andrew whispered and now he was the one that was looking a bit pale as he covered his mouth with his hand and stared at the screen. "Oh, my God."

Lana lay back down as reality sunk in. Now she really was trapped. Two babies. She'd told Andrew that she could do this on her own, but now she wasn't so sure.

How the heck was she going to raise two kids on her own?

They hadn't said much to each other when they left Dr. Green's office. Or during the ride home. Now they were just sitting on the couch side by side, not saying a word. Lana felt as if at this moment she should probably buy a state lottery ticket or something.

First the condom broke.

Then twins?

"What're we going to do?" Andrew asked finally, breaking the silence that had descended upon them ever since they'd found out that there were two babies in there.

"I know," she whispered. "You know I still stand by what I said before. I can raise these babies on my own."

"Lana, see sense. This is going to be more difficult." Andrew cursed under his breath.

"I can handle a challenge," she snapped, annoyed with his swearing. It was obvious he was unhappy about it.

Aren't you?

She got up and walked into the kitchen. Grabbing a glass, she poured herself some ice-cold water.

She was used to challenges. Her whole life had been a challenge. She'd had to teach herself a lot of things when she was a kid because her mother hadn't been around. She was the one who negotiated peace between her father and Jack. And because of who her father was she always had to prove herself more in her professional field.

There were a lot of times people thought she was given more opportunities because of who her father was and that was not true. She'd constantly sacrificed and worked hard for everything.

Now, two babies. It was a challenge, but she could do it.

Couldn't she?

"I know you can handle a challenge, Lana, and I know that you could handle this on your own, but I'm not going to let you." He touched her face and she backed away from his touch. She couldn't let herself get attached to Andrew, not when he kept putting up walls between them.

Not when this marriage was just one of convenience and would be over as soon as he got his green card. And not when he obviously saw her and the babies as a burden.

She couldn't let herself fall for him. She couldn't risk her heart. When her mother left, she'd seen how crushed her father was. Lana had taken it upon herself to try and comfort her dad, to make him happy again, but she'd been naive.

Her father's heart was broken and as she got older and understood that she knew that she would never, ever put her heart on the line like that.

Except she did and then David crushed it. She'd sworn she never would again and then she'd slept with Andrew. She was so weak. Her heart was totally on the line and now she was carrying his children. She'd have double the reminder of him when he left and she knew he was going to leave. Once he got what he wanted he'd leave.

She set the glass down on the counter. "I'm going for a swim."

"A swim? Where, in the ocean? It's night."

"No, the pool." She strode past him and down the stairs to her bedroom.

Andrew followed behind her. "Don't you think we should talk about this? I mean, this changes everything."

"I know that it does, but I can't think straight right now, Andrew. I need to swim." She turned around. "This is a lot to take in."

"I know."

"I'm going to have to leave work sooner than I'd like. You know that twins often deliver early."

He nodded. "Yeah, that's going to be hard on the department."

"Well, if you had surgical privileges you could take over for me."

Andrew frowned. "Don't start this again."

"Why not? You want me to talk about this pregnancy? Well, I want to talk about why you gave up your surgical privileges when you came here."

"I can't operate." There was deadly calm to his tone and she knew that she was pushing him to the brink again. "You need to stop pestering me about this, Lana. I just can't operate."

"I know, because you don't have privileges," she said a bit too sarcastically, but she was tired of not knowing why. He still had his surgical license and if he would just do surgeries again he could take her place while she had their babies.

She knew that he'd be good at it. He was a brilliant surgeon and she didn't know why he was giving it up. She didn't get it. He was willingly giving up surgery and in a few months she'd have no choice but to go on bed rest and walk away, but she'd come back. She wouldn't give up the only thing in her life that brought her joy.

There were a lot of dreams that she had given up over the years, but surgery was not and would never be one of them.

"No, it's because my arm was damaged in an accident four years ago. My surgery was botched and I can't hold a scalpel. I lost everything that day, Lana. I regained what I could, but I can't operate. I can't. My hand shakes, my arm is in constant pain. I don't react anymore because I've learned to filter it out or maybe my nerves are dying. I'm not sure. I was impaled after the car I was driving collided with a moose. Impaled by a metal signpost. It smashed right through the windshield and into my shoulder. My shoulder was damaged and the surgery was done by an old school doctor up in northern Ontario. So, that's why I don't operate. It's not safe for anyone. I can't do it. I won't."

And before she could apologize for pushing him too hard he stormed away to his room and slammed the door.

Lana felt bad for pushing him.

She knew the shoulder pained him. She'd seen and felt the scars and knew that his shoulder had been damaged, but she couldn't believe that he couldn't operate any more. He was terrified because of what had happened.

Some scars ran deeper than the surface.

She knew that all too well.

CHAPTER TWELVE

ANDREW GAVE UP on tossing and turning for the night. He got dressed and then checked on Lana, who was sleeping soundly. It was four o'clock in the morning and, even though his shift didn't start for another four hours, he just couldn't sit here stewing about it.

He grabbed his wallet and keys and headed out to his car.

At first he didn't know where he was going to go, but after driving around aimlessly for about fifteen minutes he made his way to the hospital. He changed into his scrubs and lab coat, but the hospital was quiet for now and he wasn't on call.

Not many people knew that he was here.

Which was fine, because he didn't really want people to see him standing in front of the skills lab, staring at it with contempt and a bit of fear.

He glanced down at his arm and his shoulder pained him. He flexed his arm and it trembled. It had been four years since the accident, since the botched surgery. Since Meghan died, he'd been alone after that. His parents blamed him and had left him to recuperate alone.

You're not alone now.

Except that he was. He wasn't in a real marriage.

Still, he couldn't face this fear. The couple of times

he'd been in the operating room with Lana had been terrifying, but he missed being there. He missed surgery. He might not be able to compete on an international scale with surfing again, but he could reclaim surgery. He could help Lana by being a surgeon again. It would take some of the burden off her.

You don't deserve this. Your arm was penance for your sister's death.

He swiped his identification and entered the skills lab. It was dark and quiet. Later it would be filled with interns and residents as they tried to hone their art, just like he'd done when he'd been in their shoes.

Andrew took a seat and pulled out a surgical tray. He stared at the instruments and pulled on his rubber gloves. His hands shook as he picked up the scalpel. He took a deep calming breath and held it over the prosthetic abdomen.

You got this.

And then it came flooding back to him. Even though it had been four years, he knew exactly what to do. What kind of pressure to apply and the incision came so easily. Then pins and needles shot down his arm and he cursed, slamming the scalpel down.

What am I doing? I can't do this.

"Who did your surgery?"

Andrew's head jerked up and he saw his father-in-law standing in the doorway, his arms crossed.

"Sir, what're you doing here so early?"

Keaka shut the skills lab door and took a seat across from Andrew. "I couldn't sleep. I was thinking about Lana's news. About how I'm going to be a grandfather to twins no less. And you couldn't sleep either, I see."

Andrew sighed. "Yeah, I thought… I don't know what I thought."

"When I first hired you on here I knew that in time you would try and return to surgery, but I didn't want to rush you. You're a brilliant sports medicine doctor and you've helped many of our patients. You're a valuable asset, Andrew, but you were an impressive surgeon."

"My arm is useless. It's like a dead weight. There's nerve damage."

Keaka nodded. "Who did your surgery?" he repeated.

"Dr. Wilbert Guzman in a small backwater hospital up in Canada."

"I don't know of him, or that hospital. I don't know the severity, but a simple laparoscopic arthroscopy might release the scar tissues, ease the inflammation of the nerves and help with that shaking. I could do the procedure later today if an arthroscopy is called for."

One voice inside him said, *Do it*. The other said it would never work. He was too damaged.

"And what about my rounds, my patients?"

"I can handle that for you and I'm sure Lana could pick up some slack. If a simple procedure is needed you'll only be off for a week at tops."

Andrew looked down at his shaking arm. He was tired of being afraid. Tired of living in the periphery of his life. If he could regain control of his arm and practice surgery again he would have something.

Maybe then his kids would look on him with a sense of pride, because he wasn't giving up any longer. He'd run for so long, hiding his shoulder damage like a shameful secret. He might not know how to be a father, but at least his kids wouldn't be ashamed of him the way he'd always been ashamed of his father.

"Okay. Let's do it," Andrew said.

Keaka grinned. "Good. Now, let's get you down for a CT scan and we'll get some imaging done of that shoulder. I would do an MRI but I assume there's hardware in that shoulder?"

Andrew nodded. "You're correct."

"Well, let's go then. Let's see what we have to work with, shall we?"

Keaka opened the door but Andrew stopped him. "I just want to say…whatever happens, thank you. I will take care of Lana and the babies. Whatever happens, they're my first priority."

Keaka smiled and clapped Andrew on the shoulder. "I know, son. If they weren't your first priority then I wouldn't have found you sitting here in the skills lab. You would still be hiding from the damage that was done."

"I suppose you're right."

"I know that I am. And I know there are rumors that you only married Lana for a green card, but now, with the babies and your agreeing to surgery, I know those rumors are unfounded. Now, let's get down to the CT scan before it's flooded with patients from the emergency room and residents."

Andrew nodded but his stomach was knotted, guilt eating at him as he shut the lab skills door.

Keaka was reaching out to him, willing to help him like a father, and Andrew was lying to him. And he was terrified about the outcome, but he had to try. There were thoughts replaying in his mind that this surgery wouldn't work. That his arm would be worse off, but if he didn't take this risk then he couldn't take the biggest risk of all—trying to prove to Lana that he was a worthy man.

That he would be a good father.

Though he seriously doubted he would be. He didn't deserve happiness. He was responsible for Meghan's death. Still, he wanted to try with her, even if it didn't work out in the end. He wanted to try.

* * *

When Lana woke up at six in the morning she was surprised to see that Andrew had left already. So she got ready and headed over to the hospital. When she walked into her office her secretary informed her that her father and Andrew were down at CT. Andrew was waiting for his CT and her father had booked an OR for Andrew for three in the afternoon; her father wanted her to bring in an overnight bag for her husband.

"What?" Lana asked in confusion.

"Just what I said. Dr. Haole wants you to bring an overnight bag for Andrew because he's scheduled to have an arthroscopy late this afternoon."

"They're in CT right now?" Lana asked.

Kelley, her administrative assistant, nodded. "Right now."

"Thanks, Kelley."

Lana made her way down to CT and found what room they were in. She could see her father and the technician discussing images that were coming on the screen and when she glanced into the room she saw Andrew with an IV attached, his damaged arm raised above his head and lying on a bed as he passed through the CT.

"Dad, what is going on?" Lana asked.

Her father and the technician turned around at the same time.

"Iolana, come see for yourself." Her father stepped aside so that Lana could get a good look at the screen.

And there she saw the details of Andrew's shoulder injury. What should've been a simple dislocation and repair to remove whatever had impaled him had been cut away instead, causing adhesions which pinched the nerves and were probably responsible for all his symptoms.

"I was worried that it might be a bit more complex and

I would have to completely open up the shoulder, but I think a simple arthroscopy will take care of all his issues." Her father was grinning and Lana was dumbfounded.

"Did Andrew agree to this or did you coerce him?" she asked. Although she seriously doubted her father could coerce Andrew.

"Iolana, I don't coerce anyone."

Yeah, right.

She rolled her eyes, but her father didn't see that. "So, he's actually going to go through with it?"

"If it is minimally invasive, yes. Come on, let's go tell him." Her father headed into the room where Andrew was now out of the CT machine and sitting upright again, rolling his shoulder and a pained expression on his face.

When he saw her he didn't really make eye contact with her. And it stung. He was still mad at her.

"Well?" Andrew asked her father instead. "What's the verdict?"

"Adhesions," her father said. "A simple arthroscopy will take care of it."

Andrew nodded and then looked at her. "Will you be okay if I do this?"

"Why would it affect me?" Lana asked, trying to be nonchalant instead of telling him *I told you so*.

"Iolana!" her father said in shock.

Andrew grinned. "No, she's right. It's my decision."

"Exactly," Lana said. "It's your decision, but I think you should let my father do the surgery. The adhesions are impinging on a nerve and the surgery will allow a release and improvement of the arm."

"After extensive physiotherapy to build up my strength again," Andrew added, not breaking the connection with her.

"Not so extensive, as an arthroscopy is minimally

invasive," her father interjected. "Well, if you're giving approval, Andrew, I will get the operating room ready for this afternoon. We'll get you into a room to wait until your procedure."

When her father left she turned back to Andrew. "Are you sure?"

"Yes…no. Actually, I'm not sure this will work." Andrew then shrugged. "What do I have to lose?"

"I will help you any way that I can," she said.

"You don't have to. You have enough to worry about; I don't want to add any more stress to your plate. You don't need that."

"What would've been more stressful is you not telling me that you were having surgery and I found out after the fact." She sighed. "I'm sorry for pushing you."

Andrew chuckled and she knew she was forgiven. "You know that you can't be in the operating room, right?"

"Seriously, you're letting me know this? Am I not a surgeon here? I know the protocols."

"Yeah, you are, but sometimes surgeons and doctors can overstep their bounds when it comes to…" He trailed off and Lana couldn't help but wonder if he was going to say *loved one* or imply that they were family. Instead he rubbed the back of his neck. "They sometimes need a reminder."

"I understand," she said quietly. They might be having babies together, but there was no love; they weren't family. They were in a business arrangement.

The orderlies came in with a gurney. "Dr. Tremblay, we're here to take you to your room now."

"I can walk," Andrew said.

"Uh, what was that about doctors needing a reminder,

Dr. Tremblay?" Lana teased. "Hospital policy. Get on that gurney and I'll come by and see you before your surgery."

"Yes, Doctor." Andrew winked and climbed onto the gurney while the orderlies got his IV bag. He waved as they wheeled him from the room.

Lana couldn't believe he was doing this. She was happy that he was doing it, but also a sense of terror hit her hard. The thought of Andrew in surgery, where something could happen to him, made her worry all of a sudden.

Don't think about it. He's in good hands with Dad.

Her father had done multiple arthroscopies for the same issue and they had all been successful. Next to her father, she was highly adept at them, but she couldn't perform the surgery on Andrew since they were married.

What she had to do today was bury herself in her work and not think about Andrew going under the knife. If she kept busy, the time would just fly by.

After she left the CT floor she headed straight for her rounds, making sure that all her surgical patients on her floor were comfortable and were healing well. And when that was finished she grabbed a quick bite to eat and then did a skills lab on arthroscopy with the residents with her father, who was looking for a keen resident who was interested in orthopedics to assist him in Andrew's surgery later today.

It didn't take long to pick the resident. Once that was decided she went back to her office to grab a few things before she headed up to the surgical floor. She might not be able to be in the operating room while Andrew was undergoing his surgery, but she was going to be in the gallery watching and she would be there when he woke up.

And she told herself over and over she was doing this

because people would expect this from her as his wife, but she wasn't convinced, because it felt right to do that.

When did she go from pretending to be a wife to feeling like a wife?

You're not a real wife. Don't think like that.

"Ah, well, if it isn't the beautiful bride."

Lana groaned and turned around to see David standing behind her, smirking.

"Dr. Preston," she said through gritted teeth.

"Oh, come now, you're the blushing bride who is head over heels in love." He snorted in derision. "You couldn't marry me for a business arrangement, but you marry Dr. Tremblay for a green card."

"What're you talking about?" she snapped, though inside the butterflies in her stomach were having a field day.

"Oh, come on. You honestly expect me to believe it was love when I saw him chasing skirt around this hospital from day one."

Heat bloomed in her cheeks, but from rage. Not embarrassment. "No, you have the wrong person. That was you, David."

"He's using you, Lana."

"What does it matter to you?" she asked.

"I'm at least a surgeon still."

"I'm in love with Andrew, Dr. Preston."

He snorted and rolled his eyes. "Right."

"Andrew has never once cheated on me. Andrew is in love with me and if you're not up to date on hospital gossip, then I'll let you in on a little secret—Andrew and I are expecting twins."

David's mouth dropped open. It was apparent he hadn't heard and she was pleased for making his head spin. She had nothing left to say to him, so she turned on her heel and left him standing there, gawking.

Even though the only thing true in that statement was the fact she was carrying Andrew's babies, it felt good to give David a bit of a comeuppance. To stand up to him finally.

She headed back to her office and as she rounded the corner she saw Kelley was not at her desk, because she'd put her sign up that she'd be back in ten minutes, but there was a woman standing there waiting. She had her back to Lana. She was well dressed in a business suit and heels, her grey hair tied back in a neat bun, and the first thing that popped into Lana's mind was that she must be a drug rep and that she probably had a meeting she'd forgotten about.

Yet there was something about this woman which tugged at the corners of her mind. A nagging sensation which was telling her that she should know this woman.

"Can I help you?" Lana asked cautiously.

The woman's spine stiffened and she turned round slowly.

The world began to spin for Lana as she stared into the familiar blue eyes of the woman she'd thought she would never see again.

"Hello, Iolana."

"Hello, Mother."

CHAPTER THIRTEEN

LANA'S PULSE WAS still thundering between her ears as she shut the door to her office. She had showed her mother in, because she really didn't want to be discussing anything with her estranged mother with the door open to a hallway of the hospital, where anyone could be listening. She didn't need any more rumors flying about.

Her mother's impromptu arrival today was the last thing that she needed.

Didn't she have enough to deal with? She didn't need a woman who had checked out of her life, given up her children, forced Lana into early adulthood, to suddenly appear.

And as she eyed up the woman who'd left her all the things she wanted to say to her remained locked away. There was so much she wanted to ask her, to tell her how she really felt about her abandonment.

Why did you leave Jack and me? Are you inherently selfish? How could you break Dad's heart?

Why didn't you love me?

Why wasn't I good enough?

Only, like always, she lost her voice.

"I suppose I should explain why I'm here."

"Does it matter?" Lana asked, crossing her arms; she

found it hard to look her in the eyes. Jack had her eyes and it was eerie now to think about it.

"You're so like your father."

And that angered Lana. How would she know? She knew nothing about her.

"Why did you come back?" Lana asked.

"I wanted to talk to you."

"Then talk, because I really don't have much time. I have patients to see."

"How long will you give me?" her mother asked.

"Ten minutes." And that was ten minutes too long.

"I don't think that's an adequate amount of time to properly talk to you."

"Take it or leave it."

"Can we meet later for coffee perhaps?" her mother asked.

Lana was tempted, only because some part of her wanted to know the answers to all those questions that had plagued her, her whole life. Those questions which had crippled her self-esteem and made her doubt herself far too many times, but that part of her was small. The other part of her didn't want to get to know the woman who had abandoned her and Jack. The woman who'd broken her father's heart.

"No, I don't think so." Lana opened the door to her office.

Her mother sighed and moved toward the door. "Okay. I see then."

Lana shut the door behind her mother, her hands shaking.

Get a grip on yourself.

And she glanced at the clock on her wall and realized that it was after three and that Andrew was being taken down to the operating room and she wasn't there.

She checked herself in the mirror and made sure that she'd calmed down. Lana was relieved when she opened the door to her office and saw that her mother was nowhere to be seen. She'd taken her advice.

Lana made her way to the OR floor and took her place in a packed gallery. One of the residents offered to give up his seat in the front so she could sit in the front row, but Lana wouldn't let him get up.

"You need to watch this, Fergus. More than I do."

Lana preferred to stand anyways.

Her heart was hammering as she saw Andrew under general anesthesia. Those beautiful blue eyes taped shut, a tube down his throat and her father making the incisions to drop the instruments into the shoulder.

Oh, God.

A rush of emotion washed over her and she closed her eyes to pray. She prayed this worked, because she was worried that if it didn't he'd blame her and she didn't want that.

"Did you know that Dr. Tremblay applied to the ISC?" one resident said to another.

"What is the ISC?"

"The International Surfing Commonwealth. If he gets in there he'll be leaving to go to California. It's a high profile job and he'd be working with some of the best athletes in the country. That's why he's finally getting his shoulder fixed properly. He won't get the job if he can't do surgery. They want surgeons and the surgeon who invented the Tremblay method would be an asset."

Lana's heart sank. She didn't know why it surprised her.

Of course Andrew would've applied to the International Surfing Commonwealth. He'd mentioned that as one of his goals, one of his reasons for staying in the

United States and getting his green card. Only she hadn't known that he'd actually gone and applied for the job. It was just the confirmation of the fact that their time together really was limited and that she would be alone with these babies.

She would be all they had.

And she would have to be enough.

When Andrew woke up from his surgery he was in some pain, but pain that he was used to, so it didn't faze him too much. Then he recalled that he'd had surgery on his shoulder and his eyes popped open, but since he didn't have his contacts in or his glasses on the room was fuzzy.

"Here," Lana said from the haze, slipping his glasses on. He was relieved to see her smiling face, which surprised him.

"Thanks," he whispered, his throat bothering him from the general anesthesia tube.

"No problem."

"How did it go?"

"It went smoothly. Dad removed the adhesions and as soon as the nurses in the recovery room feel that you can go home I'll take you there and make sure you're comfortable."

"You don't have to do that," he said. "I can take care of myself."

"Of course I do. I can't let you recover on your own."

"I should be taking care of you."

"Andrew, I'm only five weeks along. It's okay. Let me do this for you. Later, when I'm as big as a house and probably very grumpy, you can make it up to me."

He sighed, because it hurt to laugh. He didn't want her staying because he didn't want to put her out, but he was relieved she was there. He was relieved that he didn't have to do this alone.

It took him a couple of hours to shake the effects of the anesthesia, but soon the world became clearer and Lana never left his side. Finally her father came in and he was smiling.

"You did excellently. You need to rest that arm for at least ten days and then you can start to work it again— gently at first, though."

"Thank you, Dr. Haole," he said.

"I think you can take him home now, Lana." He nodded and then squeezed Lana's shoulder.

"Well, let's get the IV out of you and get you home where you can rest."

"That sounds good." And it did. It had surprised him when she'd said *home*. He didn't have a home, or hadn't had a home in so long, that it felt weird when she referred to the place he was temporarily living as home, but he wasn't going to argue that fact.

He needed some rest.

The nurse removed his IV and helped him get dressed. And then an orderly brought a wheelchair. He was going to argue about being wheeled out, but Lana fixed him with a gaze that brooked no argument. So Andrew let the orderly wheel him out to Lana's car, which was waiting in the front loop outside the hospital.

The orderly helped him into the car and Andrew dozed during the short drive home. When Lana parked at her house Jack was waiting and he helped Andrew inside to the bedroom upstairs, where he was tucked into bed.

"Thanks, Jack," Andrew said.

"No problem, Coach. Get some rest."

"Thanks, Jack." Lana kissed her brother on the cheek.

"Are you going to be okay, Lana, or do you want me to stay?" Jack asked.

"I think I can take care of Andrew. Go home. I'll talk to you later."

"Okay, 'night."

Lana turned back to Andrew and pulled out a thermometer.

"What are you doing with that?" he asked suspiciously.

"I was just going to ask you to roll over and drop your drawers." There was a twinkle of humor in her eyes as she stuck the thermometer in his ear. "I'm taking your temperature to watch for a post-operative fever, you dolt."

"God, you're a pain." He winced as it chimed in his ear. "Well?"

"No fever. Which is good." She set the thermometer down. "Anything you need?"

"No." Lana got up to leave but he reached out with his good arm and held her back. "Don't go." It surprised him, but he didn't want to be alone. He was tired of being alone.

She sat back down. "Are you okay?"

"I just want you to sit here for a while. Last time I had a surgery I was alone when I recovered. There was no one caring for me and… It was scary. So just sit with me until I drift off."

"Okay," she whispered softly.

"You can lie next to me."

"Okay." She rounded the bed and cuddled up next to him. "So why were you alone last time? Didn't your family help you?"

"No," he said. "I haven't spoken to my parents since I was in the accident."

"Why?"

And maybe it was the painkillers, or because he was

tired of holding it all in and needed to talk to someone about it. "Because my father is a drunk and my mother was just a pawn for him. They blamed me for my sister's death, you see."

"They blamed you?" she asked, confused.

"She was in the car with me when we hit the moose. I know it wasn't really my fault, but they blamed me. Or Dad did and Mom just went along with him. They disowned me and I haven't been home in a very long time. I took the blame, because I am to blame. Maybe my reactions weren't fast enough. Maybe I could have steered a different way. Maybe I should have been concentrating more."

"I'm sorry," she said. "I'm sorry you had to go through that last surgery alone. I'm sorry you lost your sister, but I don't think you're to blame, Andrew. It was a tragic accident. You don't have to be alone this time either. I'm here for you."

"I appreciate it."

"Speaking of parents, I had an unexpected visitor today."

"Oh, yes?" he asked, intrigued. "Who?"

"My mother."

Now he was surprised. "What did she want?"

"I don't know. I didn't really talk to her. It was a shock to see her."

He was going to ask more questions, but he was getting tired again. The painkillers were taking effect. "Does Jack know?"

"No, but I will tell him. He has the right to know and make up his own mind. He was very young when she left; he doesn't remember her."

"That's good," he mumbled and then he slouched over and laid his head on Lana's shoulder. The scent of her shampoo and the warmth from her body lulled him off to sleep. And, for the first time in a long time, he felt as if he was safe.

As if he was home.

"Would you stop fussing over me? I'm fine."

Lana crossed her arms. Andrew had been off for the ten days since his successful arthroscopic procedure. While she'd been at work she'd made sure that Jack came and looked after him. About day three was when Andrew started resisting help and wanted to get back to doing everyday things.

And not once did he complain about his shoulder.

There was tenderness as it healed, but the pained expressions from the constant ache he'd felt wasn't there. At least as far as she could tell, observing him.

"Today is your last day off; you get assessed and then tomorrow you can go back to work and start your rehabilitation. Until then, you should take it easy."

Andrew shot her a look of derision. "My incisions have healed well. They weren't even stitched up. The incisions were minor."

She rolled her eyes. One thing she'd never believed was that old saying that stated that doctors made the worst patients, but in Andrew's case it was true.

"Sit down and eat your breakfast." She set down a plate of fruit and scrambled eggs in front of him.

He cocked an eyebrow and looked at it in disbelief. "You cooked this?"

"Yeah, sure. I know how to scramble an egg."

"Since when? When you made me breakfast a couple of days ago the toast was black and I swear I ate eggshell."

Lana rolled her eyes. "Fine, I ordered in."

"Whew, then I can eat it," he teased.

She picked up a tea towel and tossed it at his head. "I'm so done looking after you!"

"Sit down and eat," he said. "You need to eat more than I do."

Lana took a seat at the table and took a bite of fruit. She was glad the Diclectin was helping her keep her food down and her morning sickness was now subsiding as she approached week seven of her pregnancy.

"How is your arm feeling today?" she asked.

"It's good," he said in slight disbelief as he flexed his fist. "Stiff, but good. I'd take the stiffness and the healing pain over the electric shock of an impinged nerve any day."

"I bet." She pushed the scrambled eggs around on her plate. "Have you called your parents?"

His eyes widened. "Uh, didn't I tell you about my parents? They disowned me."

"I thought you would tell them about the babies."

"And did you tell your mother about the babies?" he countered.

"Good point." She took a sip of the orange juice, though what she really wanted was coffee. "I did, however, talk to Jack about it. He hadn't been checking his messages. Apparently she called him before she went to the hospital to try and find us."

"How did that go?"

"Surprisingly well. He wants to meet with her and I told him that he could contact her."

"Do you know what she wants?"

"No, and I don't need to know." She glanced at the clock on the wall. "You need to finish up. We have an appointment to get you cleared for surgery."

"Right." He didn't seem to be enthused about it.

"It'll be great. You'll get cleared, I'm sure."

"You seem so sure." He smiled at her. "I like your enthusiasm. It's a refreshing change from the Dr. Iolana Haole, Ice Queen."

She frowned. "Ha-ha. I'm still an ice queen."

"Is that a fact?"

"My residents still fear me." She picked up her plate and put it in the dishwasher. "Are you done? Come on, let's go."

"Fine." He got up and scraped his plate into the garbage disposal and then put it into the dishwasher. He was standing so close to her and for one minute she reveled in the feeling of domestic bliss. Which scared her. She didn't want that. She didn't want to trap him if he was offered an ISC position, the way she'd been trapped when her mother left.

She moved away and grabbed her purse. "Come on, you don't want to be late for my father. If you think that I'm an ice queen then you haven't had to deal with the tyrant too much."

"That's because he likes me."

Lana rolled her eyes and opened the door. Andrew was still chuckling to himself as he climbed into her car and they took the short drive to the hospital.

When they entered the hospital, the staff who knew that Andrew had undergone the surgery welcomed him back. He seemed uncomfortable with the well wishes and she knew that he was nervous about what the assessment would say.

Without thinking, she took his hand but he didn't try to pull it away. Instead he squeezed her hand.

"If the assessment goes well and they clear me for work I think I'll spend the rest of the day in the skills lab," he said.

"That sounds like a good plan," she said.

"I'm not returning to surgery until I'm fully confident that my hand doesn't shake."

"I get that, but really there's only so much a skills lab can prepare you for. You won't really know your abilities until you get back into the OR and work on a patient."

"I'm not risking a patient's life," he snapped.

"I didn't say that, Andrew."

He scrubbed his hand over his face. "Of course. I'm sorry, I'm just nervous about this."

"I get it." She opened the door to her father's office. "It'll be okay. You got this."

A strange expression crossed his face when she said that. Words that he'd said to her time and time again. He let go of her hand then and headed into her father's office.

Lana sighed and followed.

She wished she could do more to help him. She wished she could help heal the emotional rift between his parents and him.

You're one to talk.

The thought caught her off guard and she shook it out of her head.

The door opened and Andrew looked up from where he'd been working on his skills for a few hours, ever since he was given the all-clear to go back into surgical rotation.

He'd been working and his arm was behaving. There was pain, but it was good pain. Now he understood the difference.

Still he was not satisfied.

I can't go back into an operating room.

"You've been in here a while," Lana said and in her hand she was holding a bag of takeout food, which smelled delicious. "Hungry?"

"Yes. Starving."

She shut the door and brought the food over to a table that wasn't cluttered. "How is it going?"

"It's going." He reached into the bag and pulled out a box of Chinese food.

"Don't push yourself too hard. You're still healing."

"Yes, Doctor," he teased. "I promise I've been good."

"Good."

He dug into the food. "Thank you for bringing me dinner."

"Well, I wanted to go home, but I didn't want to abandon you at the hospital so I brought you food as a bribe to get you to leave."

"I can take a cab. It's fine. You need your rest."

She shrugged her shoulders. "I've gotten used to you being around and sleeping beside you."

Fire flooded through his veins. In his worry over his arm and whether he'd be able to operate again he'd forgotten that they'd been sharing a bed. It had been nice, but it had to end. He didn't want to lead her on. To hurt her.

But you have kids together. That can't be erased.

And the memory of how they'd conceived their twins came flooding back to him. Every night she'd been by his side, yet he had blocked out the fact that for the last ten days Lana had been sleeping next to him.

Usually curled up right beside him.

That first night when he'd come home after surgery he hadn't wanted her to leave him. He'd wanted her to stay until he fell asleep and she had, but he'd woken up beside her. Every night they went to bed together, her arm over his chest as he slept on his back.

It had been the best ten days of sleep he'd ever had, but he hadn't put much thought into it until now, because it had always felt right. It was scary.

"Well, it's been nice, but I think we should probably go back to the way things were."

"You're right," she said quietly and he knew then that he'd hurt her. It hurt him too.

She finished her dinner. "Will you be at the obstetrician appointment tomorrow?"

"I'll try to be. What time is it?"

"Seven. Dr. Green is staying late to accommodate the both of us."

"I'll try to be there, but I do have rounds. I may not go into the OR yet, but I do have my regular patients to look after." Then he swallowed the lump that was forming in his throat. "Thank you for taking care of my patients, by the way. I... You've done so much for me."

"Well," she said softly, not looking at him. "That's what friends are for."

Hearing her refer to them as friends stung. Why did he think that they were something more?

They didn't say anything else to each other as they finished their dinner, cleaned up the skills lab and then drove home together. Once they got home Lana said a quick goodnight and headed back down to her bedroom downstairs and Andrew headed upstairs.

The house was silent, emptier somehow.

This is for the best.

He got out of his clothes and had a quick, cold shower, trying to chase away thoughts of her and cool down the fire which burned him. Of course, since this was a different kind of fire, the cold shower was doing absolutely nothing to help him.

He turned off the faucet and opened the windows. The wind was coming off the ocean and the palm trees were moving quickly. There was a storm blowing in. He could hear the distant rumblings and, as he stood there, he could see the flash of lightning.

Footfall behind him caused him to turn around. Lana was standing in the doorway in her nightgown, her hair loose and spilling over her shoulders. She was mesmerizing and all he wanted to do was take her in his arms again.

Just once more.

"Lana?"

"I couldn't sleep. I know that it's better this way, sleeping separately, but can I sleep beside you tonight?"

Andrew didn't answer her. Instead he closed the gap between the two of them, cupping her face in his hands and kissing her the way he'd wanted to since their wedding night. If his shoulder wasn't newly repaired he would've picked her up in his arms and carried her to bed, but the bed wasn't far and she seemed to have the same idea as him because she led him over to it. He pressed her against the mattress, this time not worrying about the need for protection.

All he had to think about was how good she felt in his arms.

Mine.

He braced his weight on his good shoulder, his other arm moving between her legs, causing a groan to bubble up in her throat. One that drove him wild with need. His blood thundering through his body, like the thunder rolling outside.

Andrew couldn't get enough of her. He burned for her. She was his drug and he needed her and it terrified him how much he wanted her. How much he craved her and how he'd missed her presence.

"Andrew," she whispered in the darkness. "Please."

He kissed her as he entered her tight heat.

Oh, God.

She moved with him and he knew that he was a lost man. Lana controlled his heart and mind—he needed her. He tried to formulate the words that he needed to say to her, the words that he wanted to say to her, but he couldn't say the words.

Instead he kissed her as their bodies joined together, moving together as one, and when she finally came around him, her fingers digging into his back, all he did was hold her closer to him as he came and kept the words to himself.

I love you.

CHAPTER FOURTEEN

WHEN LANA WOKE up it was because the sun was stream-
ing hot on her face and the sheets were tangled around
her legs. She rubbed her eyes as they adjusted to the sunlight and she reached out for Andrew, but his side of the
bed was empty.

She sat up. "Andrew?"

There was no answer.

She got up and put on the nightgown that had been
eventually discarded during their night of lovemaking.
When she went out into the living room there was a note
on the coffee table which was addressed to her.

*Gone to the hospital. Making rounds. Didn't want
to wake you up.*

Lana smiled as she folded the letter back up and got
ready for the day. She had a shower and mulled over
everything that had happened last night between them.
When he'd first suggested they return to normal she'd
agreed with him, though it stung.

Then she'd tossed and turned in her bed, missing his
company.

She hated that she needed him to sleep. It was something she'd never needed before. She'd sworn when she

moved out of her father's house and started to build a life for herself that she wouldn't rely on anyone else.

And then David had accused Andrew of using her, just like he'd used her.

As she was toweling herself off after her shower she could see perfect waves over the ocean. And as she stepped outside on the balcony the wind was blowing offshore and there were so many people out on boards, enjoying the pipelines.

Instead of putting on her clothes, she pulled on her board suit and braided her damp hair. She picked up her board and headed down to the beach. Her pulse was racing with anticipation. Lana rarely surfed, but when she did it always helped her see things clearly.

Her father hated that she loved it just as much as Jack did, but she did love it.

As she stood there Jack scrambled out of the water, shaking his head from the surf. He saw her standing there and jogged over.

"How is it?" she asked.

"Choice," Jack said, panting.

"You ready for the championships in two weeks?"

He nodded. "Oh, yeah—you'll be there, right?"

"I'll be there."

"Good. I don't expect Dad will be there, huh?" Jack asked hopefully, but their dad never came to the surfing events, which were important to Jack.

"Doubtful."

"Have you talked to Sheila yet?"

"Who?" she asked, confused.

"Our mother." Jack's brow furrowed. "You should really talk to her."

Lana ignored him. She didn't want to discuss the person who'd abandoned them. "Are you too tired or are you going to come and surf with your sister for a bit?"

Jack rolled his eyes. "You're going surfing in your condition?"

"I'm not that far along. I'm fine. If I don't get it in now I won't be able to."

"Okay, you have a point. Yeah, let's go. I don't want you to pearl yourself out there. Andrew would kick my butt if anything happened to you."

Lana snorted. "Yeah."

Jack stopped and smiled at her tenderly. "Yeah, he would, Lana. I don't know why you doubt yourself so much. You are worth it, but you don't see it and I don't get it."

Lana's heart swelled at her younger brother's tenderness and her emotions got the better of her. "Come on, before the wind changes direction and we lose the waves."

She waded out into the surf. The water was cold but it felt so good. She climbed onto her board and paddled out beside Jack. Her arms were noodling faster than they usually did, and the current was stronger than she was used to, but she swallowed her fear. She was going to conquer the pipeline today. Something she'd never been able to do.

As they continued to paddle she caught sight of the wave brewing. The wave that she'd tame today. She worked her arms hard and just as it began to crest she climbed on her board, catching the wave and popping up. She rode it, cycling herself in the pipeline, following the flow and motion of the water. She kept her balance and rode it, her soul screaming with joy, releasing every bit of tension and fear that she'd been carrying for so long. As she rode the pipeline, the turquoise water roaring in her ears and sparkling in the sunlight, she felt free for the first time in a long time.

As if nothing was going to stop her.

In that moment, while she conquered her fear of the big wave, she knew that she could conquer anything.

Even the thing she was scared of the most.

The pipeline shrank and she maneuvered her way out of it, crouching down and riding it until she was safe, out of harm's way. She dropped into the water, going under and breaking through the surface. A baptism of spirit and soul. Lana clung to her board and watched Jack riding another large pipeline. Only he didn't ride it so cautiously as she had done.

He was doing new school maneuvers that he would need to do in order to impress the judges at the International Surfing Championship in two weeks.

Jack was so free.

He didn't have any hang-ups and she envied him that. She was envious of the life he led. He could go anywhere or do anything.

She had to stay here. Even more so now that she was expecting twins.

Here she had stability, a job and a home. She couldn't give that up to see the world. To practice medicine far away from Oahu.

With the twins, that dream had sailed.

Staying in Oahu was her only choice.

It's not. You're just afraid to try.

"What do you think, sis?" Jack asked, paddling up to her.

"It's great. You've got this, Jack."

Jack grinned proudly. "Do you want to catch another one?"

"No. I do have a job to do." She climbed on her board and paddled back to the shore. After climbing out of the buoyancy of the water, it felt as if she weighed a thousand pounds. Her body was completely exhausted.

She needed another shower before she headed to the hospital to make her rounds. When she tried to grab her board Jack took it from her.

"I got this, sis. You look tired. Go get ready for work. I'll take care of your board for you."

"Thank you, Keaka," she gently teased him. He rolled his eyes but she kissed his cheek and headed back into the house, putting the ocean out of her mind.

Conquering that pipeline gave her a sense of accomplishment she hadn't felt in some time, but that would be something she would have to keep to herself.

Just a secret memory she could cling to when she needed to remind herself that she was doing the right thing, the safe thing, by staying in Oahu and eventually taking over her father's position.

She had more than herself to think of now.

"Dr. Tremblay speaking," Andrew said, answering the phone in his office.

No one spoke on the other end, but he could hear breathing and some background noise.

"Hello?" he asked, confused.

"Why did you call?"

The voice sent a shot of dread through him. He hadn't heard that voice in so long, except in his nightmares.

"Dad?" Andrew asked. "How did you get this number?"

"Why the hell did you call?" his father demanded once more; he was slurring.

Well, some things hadn't changed.

"I didn't call. You called me."

"Don't give me that crap. I know that you called her."

"Who?" Andrew asked with dread, hoping that his father wouldn't bring up his late sister. He didn't want to talk about Meghan, or the guilt he felt about that situation.

"Your mother. You called her. Why?"

"I never called Mom. Go drink another one." He slammed down the phone and it rang again. He ignored it, but it continued to ring over and over again.

"Hello," he said in a cautious tone, knowing full well who would be on the other end. His father began to cuss a blue streak at him.

"How dare you? Who do you think you are, hanging up on me? You killed your sister! How dare you call your mother?"

"I didn't call Mom." And then in the background he heard crying, his mother begging her husband to stop, and Andrew's heart broke. "Mom?"

"Don't you be talking to her!" his father screamed. "I saw you called from your fancy new home in Oahu. Told your mother you got married, eh, and that you're having a baby with your wife. I hope you don't ki—"

Andrew lost his cool. "Don't you even dare, old man. Don't you even dare imply that. I didn't kill Meghan. Our car hit a moose. She wasn't wearing a seat belt. It wasn't my fault. Being from the north, you, above all people, should know that! I couldn't save her. She was my sister, and it kills me to know that I couldn't help. That I had to leave her life in another surgeon's hands. Even if I could, by law, have operated on her she still would've died. I don't know why you care so much, though, when you were just as much of an asshole to her as you were to me. The only difference is she took it. She tried to keep the peace, to make you happy, to protect Mom, and you didn't care one bit because you were and are just a monster."

Andrew slammed down the phone again.

His hands were shaking—he was livid. He hadn't called his mother. She'd been weak and stuck by his father's side when he'd been disowned. She'd cut ties with him too, so why would he call her?

When they'd disowned him, he'd sworn that he would have nothing to do with them again. So the question remained—who'd called them? Was it the senior Dr. Haole? Was it the hospital?

The hospital wouldn't tell your mother that you got married and were expecting twins.

"Hey," Lana said as she entered the office and shut the door. She stopped in her tracks when their eyes met. "Whoa, what happened?"

"Did you call my parents, by any chance?"

She bit her lip. "I know you told me not to, but you'd had surgery and…they had a right to know."

"God dammit, Iolana." He slammed his fist against the desk. "They had no right to know. They disowned me. I told you that. I didn't want them knowing anything about my life. They don't deserve to know."

"They're your parents," she snapped. "They should know."

"Oh? And have you told your mother what's happening? No, that's right, you dismissed her without hearing what she had to say."

Her eyes narrowed and her face was like thunder. "That's different."

"How?" Andrew demanded hotly. "How is it different?"

"My mother left when I was a child."

"And my parents left me when I was an adult. It's the same damn thing."

"Stop yelling at me. I was trying to help."

Andrew scrubbed a hand over his face. "Well, you screwed things up royally."

"And you're so perfect? So blameless?"

He leaned over the desk. "Are you insinuating that I'm at fault for my sister's death?"

"No, but you might as well be because of the way you carry it. You blame yourself. You believe them."

Andrew saw red, because she was right. She'd hit close to home.

Even though he wasn't responsible, he bore the burden. Every time he enjoyed an aspect of his life. Anytime he was close to being happy, he reminded himself of all that Meghan didn't ever get to experience. He'd been such a doofus most of his life and Meghan had always been so good. She didn't deserve to die.

He did. And he didn't deserve happiness.

"You need to leave, Lana," he said quietly. "You just have to go."

"I'm not going until we work this out."

"What is there to work out, Lana? This is a fake marriage. It'll be over in a year. I applied to a position in California before we were married and once my green card comes in I'm leaving Oahu. You'll never leave Oahu because who will take care of you then? Sorry I knocked you up, but you'll manage with your dad's help. If you can't take care of yourself, he can take care of you, which is what you let him do. You let him control you. You may strut around here like some kind of queen, but inside you're just a lost, lonely girl."

The slap stung his face.

And she didn't say another word to him. Just turned on her heel and walked out of his office. He held his hand up to where she'd struck him.

It burned. It hurt him right down to his core. The moment he'd said the words he regretted them, but it was for the best.

The words needed to be said.

There was no future for them because he didn't deserve one. At least his kids would be well taken care of.

They would be better off without him. He wasn't going to ruin Lana's life like he did Meghan's.

CHAPTER FIFTEEN

Two weeks later

LANA PICKED HER way through the crowd that had gathered in Waikiki for the International Surfing Championship. The wind was blowing offshore, which was making it perfect to catch waves. There were a lot of people from the International Surfing Commonwealth here. The ISC was where Andrew had applied to work. As soon as he got what he wanted, as soon as that green card came in, he was going to divorce her and head to California. She knew that.

But that's what you agreed to.

She couldn't think about Andrew. She hadn't seen him in two weeks and though she wanted to believe it didn't bother her, it did. There was a hole in her life. She was lonely, but he'd left her. So she was here for her brother, Jack. Not for Andrew, who had, as expected, crushed her heart so completely. She hated that she'd been right. That if she let herself fall in love with him he would break her heart.

And that was exactly what he'd done, but she supposed she'd had it coming to her.

She'd let her guard down and lost her heart. It was her fault. No one else was to blame but herself.

Now she had to make sure that her children were protected from Andrew, who apparently wanted nothing to do with them as he hadn't even shown up at the obstetrician appointment. That had hurt her.

What did you expect?

She had just been trying to help, to make the peace by stretching out an olive branch to Andrew's estranged parents.

Funny you can't extend the same olive branch to your own mother.

Lana found a shady spot, high in the stands, where she could see all of the action. She pulled out her binoculars and watched the competitors. On one of the boats that patrolled the water for injured surfers she caught sight of Andrew and her stomach clenched.

He was grinning and wearing an ISC red shirt. It suited him and he looked happy out there. And a bad niggling thought crept into her mind that he was probably happier without her.

Because when she'd got home that night two weeks ago, he'd already moved out.

"Next up is local surfer Keaka Jack Haole Jr., from the beautiful Waikiki. Give it up for ISC contender Keaka!" The announcement blasted over the crowd.

Lana cheered her brother, even though he wouldn't be able to hear her. She turned her binoculars over to the waves and caught sight of her brother and his bright neon-green surfboard. He caught a pipeline but wasn't in the hollow; he was riding it high as he did his tricks, much to the delight of the crowd.

He's going to win this.

And, just as he was about to perform a Shove-It, which was a tricky maneuver, his board flipped and he was tossed into the rocks.

Lana let out a cry and the boat with Andrew on board raced toward the rocks. She didn't waste time as she climbed down off the bleachers and started running for the beach.

Oh, God. Oh, God.

"I'm sorry, miss, you can't go past this point." A security guard barred her entrance to the beach.

"I'm a doctor and Keaka Haole is my brother."

The security guard let her past and she waited on the shore desperately.

It felt like an eternity that she waited.

She heard the distant sound of an ambulance making its way down the beach and then she saw the boat coming back from where Jack had been tossed. Lana waded out in the water after the boat stopped in the shallows. She could see Andrew had Jack strapped to a back board. There was blood everywhere and, just from a quick assessment, her brother was pretty mangled.

"Oh, God," she whispered as she ran forward.

"Lana, you need to step back," Andrew said gently. "It's bad."

Lana ignored him and helped carry the back board through the water. This was her brother, who she'd raised. He was all she had, the only man who had ever really seen her. She couldn't lose her only ally in this world.

"Lana, I got this," Andrew snapped.

"He's my brother. I don't care how bad it is. I'm not leaving his side," she snapped back. "I'm here, Jack. I'm here."

The paramedics took over and Andrew began to bark orders as they did the ABCs on Jack and started a central line. Jack was unconscious but breathing, but his trachea had been damaged, so they were inserting a tube.

Lana felt powerless as she knelt next to her brother in the sand, her hands covered in his blood.

The only man who really understood her. Who loved her. She couldn't lose him. She would be lost without her brother.

"It's okay, Jack. I'm here. I'm here."

The paramedics got him stabilized and strapped down onto a gurney to take him to the hospital. They loaded him into the back and Andrew followed, but when Lana tried to climb in the paramedic stopped her.

"Sorry, miss. Only family."

"It's okay, she's his sister and she's a surgeon," Andrew said.

The paramedic nodded and helped Lana up, shutting the door and then climbing into the front, while another paramedic in the back continued to monitor Jack.

"Thank you," Lana said quickly, not looking at Andrew, because she couldn't look at the man who'd broken her heart.

"You're welcome." Then he raked a hand through his hair. "Lana, there's… Look, I…"

"No, I don't want to talk about it, Andrew." She shook her head. "Not now. My brother is clinging to life and that's all that matters."

Andrew nodded.

She kept her focus on Jack during the ride to the hospital. Which felt like an eternity.

Once the ambulance door opened she jumped out and ran into the trauma department.

"Someone page my father to Trauma, stat!" she shouted.

Dr. Page, one of the residents, ran off to a phone and Lana turned back to the paramedics wheeling Jack in. Andrew was helping them.

"Page a trauma surgeon," Andrew shouted. He was barking orders as they wheeled Jack into a trauma pod. A crash cart was pushed into the room and Andrew was putting on a gown. All Lana could do was stand back and watch in horror as the paramedics handed Jack over to Andrew and the trauma surgeon, Dr. Rodman, who had come rushing into the pod.

"Iolana, what's going on?" her father said as he came rushing toward the pod. Then his eyes widened in shock. "You're covered in blood!"

"It's not me," Lana said and she held her father back. "It's Jack. A wave tossed him and it's bad, Dad. It's really bad."

Her father raked a hand through his hair. "I told him not do it. I told him it was dangerous."

"Yeah, but he loves it, Dad! He did something he's passionate about, just like you. You two are so alike."

Her father snorted. "We are not alike, Lana."

"You are both exactly alike. You're stubborn, unbending and you both nag me until you get what you want!"

Her father's eyes widened as the words came out of her mouth.

"I raised Jack so I know that he's like you. He just did what he felt passionately about. Just because he didn't follow your path doesn't mean that his path wasn't right."

"His path led him to this, Iolana. He might die!" her father shouted.

"And he dies loving what he was doing. I was too busy trying to keep the peace between you two, to take care of Jack when you were working doing what you loved, I sacrificed most of my life to give you both what you wanted."

"You love surgery..."

"I do, but I wanted to leave Oahu. Dad, you left us."

She was tired of holding it all in. Tired of pretending. She wasn't just angry at her mother; she was angry at him too for controlling her life.

"I didn't leave you," her father said darkly. "Your mother left."

"She left physically, but you weren't there either, Dad. I raised Jack. I didn't have a childhood."

Her father's head hung. "I couldn't be home."

"Why? We needed you and you weren't there," she said.

"It was too hard. I loved your mother and she left us. Home was a reminder of my broken heart."

Tears welled in her eyes. "I loved her too, but we needed you, Dad. And I'm sorry we're such a disappointment to you. Such a burden"

"You're not. You weren't. I'm sorry."

She nodded and then swallowed her fear to tell him more. She was tired of lying. "Jack had me marry Andrew for a green card."

"What?" her father demanded. "Iolana…"

She held up her hand. "At first, but I fell in love with Andrew. I want these babies. Don't be mad at Andrew or Jack. It was my decision, it was my mistake and I'm owning it, but I have to take charge of my own life, Dad, and you need to be more supportive of Jack. I can't be the peacekeeper between the two of you anymore. I'm done. It's time I get to live my own life. I can't follow in your shadow any longer."

Her father was taken aback by her outburst and so was she, to be honest. "Iolana?"

Then she broke down in tears and her father pulled her close, holding her and comforting her the way he had never done. The last time she'd embraced her father it was when he'd been crying because her mother had left and she had held him while he cried. Now he was holding her, because she was terrified.

A code blue was called and she could hear Andrew shouting over the fray as Dr. Rodman shocked her brother as he coded.

"Oh, God, I can't lose my son! I can't." Her father broke down. "Please, God, no."

Lana held onto her father tighter and then, as Jack's heart stabilized, she knew exactly who she had to call, but she was afraid to do it.

Andrew came out of the trauma pod. His face was grim.

"What's going on?" her father demanded.

"He's stabilized, but it's not good. They're taking him down to do a CT scan right now. Dr. Rodman is an excellent trauma surgeon and he'll be able to tell us the extent of the damage."

Her father nodded. "I'm going to go down with him."

"Okay, but Dr. Haole, remember that Dr. Rodman is the surgeon. Not you. You can't interfere."

"I know," her father said quietly and he left Lana and Andrew standing in the hall as he followed Jack's gurney down for an emergency CT scan.

She turned to leave, but Andrew grabbed her arm and dragged her into a private room. He discarded the trauma gown and washed his hands.

"Why did you bring me in here?" she demanded. "I should be with Jack and my father."

"They're fine. It's you I'm worried about. You and the babies."

"Could've fooled me," she snapped.

"I know I didn't go to that obstetrician appointment. I'm sorry. I was angry and scared."

"And now?" she asked, crossing her arms.

"I don't know. Worried. I'm worried about my friend."

"Yes, Jack has been a good friend to you. Got you hooked up with his sister so you could land your cushy job with the ISC."

"Lana, you know that's always been my dream."

"So you were offered a job?" she asked.

"No, not yet, but if I am I'm going to take it and if you weren't so scared you could come with me."

"Why would I go with you?"

"You wouldn't. I know you wouldn't."

Before she could answer, Dr. Page, the orthopedic resident, stuck his head in the room. "Sorry to interrupt, Dr. Tremblay, but Dr. Haole is requesting you come down to the CT scan. They have results and they need you down there, stat."

Andrew nodded. "I'll be right there. Thank you, Dr. Page."

Dr. Page left and Andrew turned back to her. "This isn't over. We need to talk."

Lana didn't say anything else. Andrew left the room and the room began to spin as the adrenaline of what'd happened began to wear off.

There was a phone on the wall and she knew what she had to do. She left the trauma department and made her way up to her office. It was a Saturday so her assistant Kelley wasn't there.

Which was good. She had to pull herself together to tackle what she was going to do. There was a card on her desk. One that had been left when her mother had come to see her a month ago.

With trembling hands she picked up the phone and dialed the number.

"Hello?" It was the voice she recalled from when she was a girl. Before her mother left, the gentle voice that had sung her Hawaiian lullabies to calm the night terrors. The voice that had haunted her for years, until it faded into the recesses of her memory after she'd left. Now it was all rushing back and she had to keep her voice calm.

"It's Iolana," she managed to say.

"Iolana, I'm so glad you called me!" Her voice was genuine. She was happy and now Iolana had to break the news to her.

"I have bad news," she choked back.

"What is it?"

"It's Keaka... I mean it's Jack. He's been in an accident. It's not looking good. You should prepare yourself."

There was a strangled cry on the other end. "Oh, my God. I'm coming. Hold on. I'll be there soon."

"I'll meet you at the ER doors." Lana disconnected the call. Her hand still shaking, she buried her face in her hands and wept.

Things were going to change.

Life was too short.

"His pelvis and his hip are fractured. His femur is also broken, all on the left side. It's like his body was crushed on one side only. There is a fracture of some of the right ribs, but those aren't as serious as the pelvis, hip and femur," Andrew said, pointing to the images that were on the computer. "The pelvis is crushed on this side and he has extensive internal bleeding."

Dr. Rodman nodded. "I need to get him into the OR and control the bleeding."

"Agreed, and once the bleeding is stabilized his bones need to be repaired. As long as he can tolerate it. We'll see how he does after you stop the bleeding."

Dr. Rodman left the CT room and went to speak to Dr. Haole. Jack needed to go straight into surgery.

Andrew just stared up at the screen and had the other two orthopedic surgeons paged. One was in the OR doing a hip replacement and the other was away at a conference.

Dr. Haole couldn't perform the surgery because he was Jack's father and Lana couldn't perform this surgery either.

He broke out in a cold sweat.

"It's bad?" Lana asked as she came into the CT room.

Andrew nodded. "I'm sorry. You can see the extent of his injuries. When he hit the rocks, it crushed the left side of his body."

Lana nodded, but kept her calm. "He'll need extensive work."

"Right, and one surgeon is in the operating room and the other is at a conference, which just leaves…"

"You," she said as a matter of fact. "You've been cleared for surgery. You're one of the best orthopedic surgeons, Andrew. Dad can't do it. I can't. There's only you. My other two orthopedic surgeons are fine, they're good, but I want the best working on my brother. It has to be you."

"I can't, Lana…" Which was pathetic. He had to, but he was terrified in that moment. It had been four years since he'd picked up a scalpel and operated on a patient. His first patient couldn't be his friend, the brother of the woman he loved.

"You have to," she snapped. "I want the best for my brother. Save his life."

"What if I can't? It's been four years, Lana. And if he dies… I know I've screwed up, but if he dies I can't lose you."

Lana didn't say anything for a moment. Then she grabbed him by his shoulders. "You've got this. I'm not your parents. You won't lose me, unless you walk away from this."

Andrew pulled her into his arms and kissed her. Terrified about what he was about to do, not fully believing that his hand wouldn't shake, that Lana wouldn't walk away if Jack didn't survive. But she was right—if he walked away Jack would die and he would lose her.

He couldn't lose her.

And their two weeks apart, when he'd left, had been brutal. He'd missed her and he realized how lonely his life had become. He wanted Lana, but he was worried that he'd blown it. Now he had a way to make it all right.

And he would make sure that after all was said and done he'd win her over.

And he would never leave again.

CHAPTER SIXTEEN

LANA WAITED FOR her mother, her insides turning as she paced. Jack was in the operating room with the trauma surgeon and Andrew was in the skills lab with his resident, Dr. Page, trying to come up with a game plan on how to save her brother.

Jack.

He was still alive, she could feel it, but if she lost her brother she didn't know what she'd do. And then she had an inkling of what Andrew must've felt when his sister died in the accident. Jack had always been someone she could rely on when they were growing up.

He butted heads with her father constantly, but Jack was always there for her. He gave her the hugs she'd craved from her parents, the unquestioning love, and, though he drove her nuts, she couldn't imagine her life without him.

Just like she couldn't imagine her life without Andrew.

Love had crept up on her so fast and stealthily. It was something she wasn't expecting, but it was there nonetheless and Jack's accident made her realize that she couldn't be the moderator in her family's life any longer.

There would be hurt, pain, but also happiness. She couldn't live her life anymore to keep the peace. She had to live her life for herself.

She had to do what made her happy. She had to not

act like a strong woman, but be one. Be the one she knew was in there. So when Andrew left for California, if he wanted her to, she would go with him and their kids.

Lana was tired of living the life her father deemed appropriate. It was now time to live the life she wanted and take it.

The doors to the emergency room slid open and her mother came in, this time not in a business suit but yoga pants, running shoes and a hoodie. Her silver hair brushed back and those blue eyes filled with pain and worry.

"Iolana," her mother whispered as she came forward, as if to hug her, but then thought better of it and stood back.

"Mom," Lana said and then pulled the woman she'd been mourning since she was ten and held tight to her. Like she should've done when she'd come in that first time a month ago. Her mother broke down in sobs as she clutched her tight. As if she didn't want to let her go.

"Iolana... Oh, God."

"It's okay, Mom. It's okay." They broke apart and Lana took her mother's hand and led her to her father's office, where he was waiting.

As soon as she opened the door, her father spun around and saw the tears. "Not Jack. No."

"No, Dad. It's not Jack. Not directly." Lana turned to her mother and pushed her into the room.

Her father's expression softened and then hardened. "Sheila."

"Keaka," her mother said in the same tone. There was no love lost there.

"What're you doing here?" her father demanded.

"Iolana called me. I'm here because our son is in the operating room."

Her dad shot Lana a look, which would usually have her contrite, but instead she crossed her arms and stared him down.

"She did, did she? I don't know why you bothered to come here now, after all these years. Your son won't care that you're here."

"Yes, Dad, he will," Lana snapped. "Jack has been talking to Mom for over a month. He's made amends."

"You knew about this?" Her dad bellowed.

"Don't bully her," her mother said, stepping between them. "You were always a blow hard."

"You left. You gave up your rights to these kids."

"I left because we didn't love each other. I left because I was suffering from severe postpartum depression. It took me many years to heal myself and, if you recall, I've tried to come back but you've turned me away."

Now her dad looked contrite.

"Jack wants her here, Dad. So do I." Lana turned to her mother. "I want to make amends too."

Her mother smiled and took her hand. "I want that too, Iolana. More than anything."

Lana nodded and turned to her father. "I love you, Dad, but as I said I'm tired of being the peacekeeper between you and Jack. I'm tired of having my life dictated to me."

"I only did those things because it would be better for you," her father said. "You had a talent for surgery. You needed to be here so I could pass on my gift."

She took her father's hand. "And I thank you for that gift, Dad, but it's time to let me go. It's time to let me live my life. Even if it means that I don't make the choices you would want. I'm not going to be a stay-at-home mother. I'm going to continue performing surgery. I want my kids to see a strong woman and I love surgery, but I don't want to be Chief of Surgery when you retire. I want to work for the International Surfing Commonwealth. I want to do research, maybe even teach medicine. The options are endless, but I have to leave Hawaii to do that."

"What are you saying?" he asked suspiciously.

"Andrew has applied for a job in California and if he gets it I'm going to go with him."

"Do you know if that's what he wants?" her father asked. "You may love him but, as you said, you married him to get him a green card. He may not want you to come."

She sighed. "That's a risk I'll have to take, but I know that I can't live under your wings. I have to step out of your shadow. You have to let me go. And you have to stop fighting with Jack because he decided to live the life he wants and not the life you designed for him. And you have to bury the hatchet with Mom. I want both of you in my children's lives and I know Jack wants you both in his life. He will have a tough road to hoe. Lots of physical therapy after his surgery. He's doesn't need your condemnation for his lifestyle choices. He needs your support. He'll need it from you both!"

Her father didn't say anything.

"Now, I'm going to check on Jack and leave you two to talk it through. You need to put your past hurts aside and move on. For Jack. For me."

"Very well, Iolana." Her father kissed her on the top of the head and her mother nodded, but eyed her father warily.

Lana left her father's office, shutting the door and telling his administrative assistant not to let anyone disturb him.

Sophie came running up then, out of breath. "Lana, I just heard about Jack. How is Keaka handling it?"

"Well, I think." Lana took her stepmother aside. "Sophie, I want you to know I love you. I've always thought of you as a mother."

Sophie gasped. "Oh, no. What's happening?"

"My mother is in there and is making peace with Dad. For Jack's sake."

Sophie sighed in relief. "I'm so glad."

"You don't seem surprised."

"I'm not. I've known Sheila for three years. She works on the Waikiki arts council and I worked with her for a fund-raiser. How do you think she got the information about you and Jack?"

Lana chuckled. "So you knew?"

"Of course. This has been a long time coming and I'm glad." Then she pushed an errant strand of hair off Lana's face. "I love you too. I never had kids of my own, but I think of you and Jack like mine."

They hugged and Lana held her tight, because even though Sophie had been a wonderful maternal figure through her later teen years, Lana had never embraced her before and it was highly overdue. Especially since Sophie had been instrumental in bringing her and her mother back together. For healing the pain that Lana had been feeling since her mother had walked away. If she hadn't been so blind to it in the first place, it might've saved some pain in the past.

"I'll leave them to work it out and head to the cafeteria for some coffee after I leave a message for your father. Where are you off to?" Sophie asked.

"The gallery. I'm going to watch Jack's surgery."

"Is that wise?" Sophie asked.

"Yeah, Jack needs to know I'm there. And so does Andrew."

Sophie nodded. "Text me if there are any changes."

"I will." She kissed Sophie's cheek and then left.

She needed to be in that gallery. She needed to be there if something happened to Jack. Not that her presence would help, but she wanted to be there nonetheless.

She wanted him to know that she was there for him. And she wanted Andrew to know that she supported him, whatever happened in that OR. She wanted Andrew to know that she was there for him and she always would be.

There would be no more running away. She was in this for the long haul.

"You could've saved her! You killed her!"

Andrew rolled his shoulders out of habit from years of pain, now it was to loosen them up. He wasn't quite a month post-op from his surgery, but his hand had stayed stable in the skills lab until Dr. Rodman paged him. There was still work to be done, but they would work together. Dr. Rodman would address the injuries to the organs in the abdomen and thoracic area and Andrew would work on the pelvis, hip and femur.

Jack's left arm had been severely fractured too, but that could wait.

There would be several surgeries over the next little while.

It would be a long road to hoe, but what was most devastating was that Jack probably would never surf again. Maybe now Jack would get his head out of his butt and go to school to become a kinesiologist, like he said he wanted to do after he retired from surfing.

And Andrew was going to support his friend, who was now his family. As long as he didn't screw up this surgery. As long as Jack survived, because he just couldn't believe that Lana would ever be able to look at him again without thinking that he couldn't save her little brother.

And it made him think about his children that Lana was carrying, his twin babies.

There was no other option. He would succeed.

Please let him live.

Andrew took a deep breath and headed into the OR. No words were needed; he knew what had to happen. He knew where he was going to start first. He was going to repair the pelvis, where most of the internal bleeding had been coming from. Once the pelvis was stable, then he would move onto the hip and femur, as long as Jack was able to stand it.

The arm could be fixed later if needed. And the ribs would knit themselves back together. A nurse held out a surgical gown, which Andrew slipped into. And then into the gloves. His pulse began to race and he rolled his shoulder again.

He glanced up into the gallery. Lana was there, watching, and this time, instead of him giving her a nod of encouragement, she did.

Andrew took his spot and took a calming breath. "Hold that retractor tight, I will need a lot of room to maneuver the pelvis. Is the hardware ready?"

"Yes, Dr. Tremblay," Dr. Page said. "I brought an assortment for all the fractures. I also have an external fixture ready."

"Good man." Andrew picked up a surgical drill. "Let's go. We have to get Jack back up on his feet."

And as he went to work he felt as if his sister was right there. One of the injuries she'd sustained was a pelvic fracture when the moose crashed through the windshield and landed on her. Her pelvis had been shattered and she'd lost a lot of blood, but ultimately it was the head injury that did her in.

Jack's head hadn't sustained an injury. There were no bleeds in his brain.

Which was a miracle, but blood loss, a clot or being under too long could be detrimental to him.

I got this, Jack. You're not going anywhere.

He tuned the world out and instead he heard his sister whispering that he was going to succeed, that she loved him and that he was a good surgeon.

It wasn't Andrew's fault that she'd died. Just like it wasn't Lana's fault that Jack was injured. Meghan had been an adult and had chosen not to buckle up that night. No one was at fault and Andrew deserved to have happiness.

He deserved to have Lana.

"You do," Meghan's voice said in his head. Like a blessing from beyond. His own guardian angel watching out for him. It calmed him.

Even if he'd messed it up royally, he was going to earn Lana's love back. He couldn't lose her. He needed her. He needed their kids. And he would do anything to be with her, even if it meant giving up the job with the International Surfing Commonwealth in San Diego because Lana wanted to stay in Hawaii with her family.

He didn't care. He just wanted to be with her. Whatever it took.

He was tired of living alone. Tired of thinking that he didn't deserve happiness.

He wanted a family.

He wanted Lana.

Lana went to check on her brother. He was still in a medicated coma, but he'd survived and the bleeding had stopped. Tomorrow Andrew was going to go in and fix the fractures in Jack's left arm and shoulder, which had dislocated.

The pelvis and hip had been repaired and was being

held together with an external fixator. The femur had been repaired with some heavy-duty hardware.

But the point was, he was going to live.

Jack was very lucky to be alive.

Andrew was standing at the foot of the bed, filling out Jack's chart while Dr. Page waited diligently for instructions. Dr. Page was the resident on call for Jack tonight and she couldn't have picked a better resident herself.

Andrew handed over the chart and then left the room. His eyes widened in surprise when he saw her.

"Lana, I thought you went home! It's the middle of the night."

"I had a nap in my office and some food. Don't worry. I'm taking care of myself."

Andrew nodded. He was going to say something, but then her parents came down the hall. Her father didn't say anything; he just patted Andrew on the back and nodded. Her father, Sophie and Lana's mother all filtered into the room.

Lana stood at the doorway, watching, as her father broke down in tears and took Jack's hand. Sophie and Lana's mother held hands and Lana sighed happily. Then she turned to Andrew.

"Thank you," she said.

"For what?" he asked.

"For saving Jack's life. I know that was hard for you."

"It was, I won't lie, but… I couldn't let him die."

"You didn't let your sister die, Andrew."

He took her hand then and pulled her into an empty on call room and locked the door. He crossed his arms and she could tell he was struggling.

"I couldn't let him die, because I didn't want to lose you." He stared at her intently. "I couldn't lose you. I know I screwed up when I walked out…"

She cupped his face. "You wouldn't have lost me. I know it was out of your hands. You weren't at fault for your sister's death and I wouldn't have blamed you if Jack had died."

"I love you, Iolana," he said quickly. "It's been hard for me to say, but I love you more than anything and the thought of losing you forever, the thought of you walking away from me like my parents did, of not seeing your face every day—it was more than I could bear."

Tears streamed down her face. "I love you too, Andrew. I'm sorry for calling your mother. I just wanted to make amends. I thought if you could make peace with your estranged family then you could move forward."

Andrew took her in his arms and kissed her, making her weak in the knees. "Lana, they may not want me, but it doesn't matter. All I want is you. You showed me what I was missing, what I didn't think that I deserved. I'm a better man because of you and I won't lose you again."

"I love you, Andrew. I never believed in love. I didn't think I wanted this, but I do and when you're offered a job with the ISC I'll go to San Diego with you." She chuckled softly. "I mean *we'll* come with you."

"No, I was going to turn down the ISC job. You belong here in Hawaii."

"No, I don't. I was afraid to leave because I was afraid to step out of my father's shadow. There's so much beyond Hawaii. There's so much more life to live and if I can be with you I would follow you to the ends of the earth."

"Ditto," he teased and then kissed her again. "So you want to move to California after my green card gets in and I can move legally?"

She nodded. "Let's go. Let's live our life. One that we decide."

He grinned. "It's a deal. What does your father think?"

"It doesn't matter what he thinks. All that matters is that we're together. The four of us."

"You're right. That's all that matters. I love you, Iolana." And then he reached down and touched her stomach. "I love all three of you. And I will make it up to you."

"Make up what to me?" she questioned.

"As soon as possible we're going to renew our wedding vows, because this time I really mean it. The last time we got married, we did it to keep me in the country, but this time I want it to mean something. When I marry you again, it'll be because I can't imagine my life without you."

"Andrew, we don't need to get married again. Once was enough, but just knowing how you feel now is enough for me. There's no way I'm stuffing myself back into that dress."

A smile crept across his face. "Okay, no wedding renewal, but how about a repeat of the wedding night?"

She laughed and wrapped her arms around his neck. "Now that I can handle, Dr. Tremblay. Gladly."

After he kissed her again to give her a preview of what she could expect, they went hand in hand to visit Jack and be with their family.

And to break the news that they would be leaving after the babies were born, so they could start their life together.

For real this time.

EPILOGUE

One year later, San Diego

ANDREW RAN ACROSS the road, under the bridge. The palm trees were swaying and he hoped that the wind whipping down from the mountains wouldn't delay the flight that was coming in.

Lana was on her cell phone and waiting outside.

Even though it was windy, it was a nice day and in the double stroller were two babies who were almost six months old and just starting to be aware of their surroundings. Two little girls who were almost identical except Meghan had brown eyes and Jackie had blue. Right now they were staring up at the sky, at the palm fronds and the roar of the planes as they came in for landing over the city.

Lana ended the call. "Did you get the car parked okay?"

"Yeah. Why did we have to come so early again?"

"To get a good spot," she said.

"But I can just drive in the loop and do a pick-up."

Lana narrowed her eyes. "I am not greeting your mother by myself, so since you can't park in the loop you can get a good parking spot out there."

Andrew knelt down to his smiling happy babies. "Your mother is crazy!"

"Ha-ha," she said.

"Who was on the phone?" he asked as he took the helm of the large double stroller.

"Jack."

"Oh? And did he get into the school of his choice?"

"He did, so there's some good news and bad news."

Andrew's stomach clenched. "What?"

"He got into his first choice of school to become a kinesiologist."

"Right?" Andrew asked cautiously.

"It's here in San Diego and he's going to move in with us."

Andrew started laughing. "Are you serious? Where are we going to put him at the beach house?"

"There's the little bunkie out back by the hot tub and the pool. It has a bathroom. He can live there."

"He just wants to use our hot tub again. Just like he did when we lived in Waikiki. I say we move back now that he's coming here."

Lana laughed. "Dad would love that, but where would we work? Dad retired and is travelling the world with Sophie. Mom is busy with the art council and Dr. Rodman is Chief."

"Dr. Rodman would hire us both back in a minute."

She rolled her eyes but laughed. "You just got promoted at the ISC and I just started teaching medical students at the University of California. We're happy here—do you really want to move back to Hawaii?"

He grinned and then kissed her on the lips. "Sometimes, because I think of those few nights we spent on the Big Island for our second honeymoon."

Lana wrapped her arms around his waist and pulled

him closer. "You know, maybe it's time for the girls to have a brother?"

"I'm willing to try for that, but I think we have more than we can handle with these two. But I'm really game for trying."

And he forgot that he was at the airport as he pressed Lana up against the wall, trapping her there as he thought about their second honeymoon and their private hide-away. A howl from one of the girls brought him back to reality.

"The flight's probably landed. Let's go," he said reluctantly. He pushed the stroller into the arrivals lounge at San Diego Airport and waited near the luggage carousel, his eyes trained on the escalator for the arriving passengers to make their way down.

He was nervous and as if she sensed that Lana took his hand and gave it a squeeze.

"You got this."

"I know, it took a lot of guts for her to come here." Then he glanced at the board and saw that the flight from Toronto had landed. "I still can't believe that she left him. I can't believe that she called me."

"She was powerless, you know that, and she wants to bridge the gap. She's obviously realized that by staying with your father she lost out on so much."

Andrew nodded, but he was nervous all the same.

When his mother had called it had shocked him. She had left his father soon after his father had called him and ranted at him. She'd gone to a women's shelter to try and piece back together her life. Three months ago his father had been killed in an accident; it had been his fault and thankfully no one else had been hurt.

Andrew had hated leaving Lana to go to Canada, but he'd needed to go and bury his father, to bury his past.

His green card had come in and he was able to go back to Canada.

That was where he and his mother had reconnected, but there was still a lot of healing to do. Finally, his mother was able to come to San Diego for a long visit and to see her grandchildren, which was why she'd left his father.

She wanted to be a grandmother more than anything. She was tired of living in the past—one full of bitterness, abuse and sorrow.

Andrew's mother wanted her family back.

And he wanted his mother back.

A bunch of people started to come down the escalators and he let go of Lana's hand to take a step forward, scanning the crowd.

Maybe she didn't come.

And then he saw her. Saw the long silver hair, the weary face, but she smiled and waved when she spotted him and his heart soared.

She got off the escalator, pulling a carry-on behind her.

"Mom, I'm glad you made it."

His mother reached up and pulled him into a hug. When he'd been up for his father's funeral, his mother had been stand-offish and in shock. He understood that. She'd never been an affectionate woman so he was taken aback by the hug now, but he loved it all the same.

"Andrew, I've missed you," she whispered.

"I'm so glad you've come, Mom. I've missed you too." He broke off the embrace and looked down at his mother. The blue eyes—the same that his late sister had, that he had and his daughter Jackie had. He turned. "This is Lana, my wife."

His mother didn't say much but embraced Lana, kissing her, and then knelt down, crying, as she looked at the babies.

"They're so beautiful," she whispered as she took a chubby fist into her hand. "Just as I imagined them. Which one is which?"

"The best way to tell them apart is Meghan has brown eyes," Lana said. "And Jackie has blue."

"So they do. Oh, now I see the difference in them." She stood. "Thank you for having me come here. I've... I've wanted to come for some time, but it's been hard."

"I know, Mom, and we're glad to have you here too. Do you have any more luggage?"

"No, just a carry-on. I wasn't left with much in the way of personal belongings." She blushed, embarrassed.

"That doesn't matter, Mom. You're welcome to stay as long as you want."

"Well, Customs in Canada said to buy a return ticket home, an open-ended one, as long as I return in six months."

"We would love to have you for as long as you want to stay, Annie," Lana said.

"Thank you, dear. Six months is a start. I don't fancy getting a green card the way you did, Andrew," she teased. "I'm glad you did it that way, though. You have a beautiful family."

Lana smiled up at Andrew and he put his arms around his mother and his wife, as he looked down at his girls. One who was cooing and one who was drifting off to sleep in the stroller. The hole that had been aching in his heart for years, another pain that he'd gotten used to over time, was finally healed.

Now his heart was bursting with joy.

"I do have a beautiful family. I have all I ever wanted."

And he walked out of that airport complete.

* * * * *

MILLS & BOON®

MEDICAL ROMANCE™

THE ULTIMATE IN ROMANTIC MEDICAL DRAMA

A sneak peek at next month's titles...

In stores from 27th July 2017:

- **Tempted by the Bridesmaid** *and*
  Claiming His Pregnant Princess – Annie O'Neil

- **A Miracle for the Baby Doctor** – Meredith Webber
  and **Stolen Kisses with Her Boss** – Susan Carlisle

- **Encounter with a Commanding Officer** –
  Charlotte Hawkes
  and **Rebel Doc on Her Doorstep** – Lucy Ryder

Just can't wait?
Buy our books online before they hit the shops!
www.millsandboon.co.uk

Also available as eBooks.

Join Britain's BIGGEST Romance Book Club

50% OFF your first parcel

- **EXCLUSIVE offers** every month

- **FREE delivery direct** to your door

- **NEVER MISS a title**

- **EARN Bonus Book points**

Call Customer Services
0844 844 1358 *

or visit
nillsandboon.co.uk/subscriptions